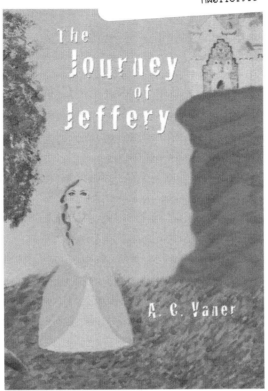

Edited by Joanne King

The Journey of Jeffery

First printing © 2016

ISBN-13:
978-1530643639

ISBN-10:
1530643635

Edited by Joanne King. Cover illustration by Sara Pawluk. Cover engineering by Mehtap Kızılırmak

Printed in the United States

Dedicated with love to:

Sara, Claire, Lisa, & my mother, Nimet.

For joining me on this journey, keeping faith during my darkest hours, and for all of your love and magic that has truly influenced me as a human being.

Thank you.

Disclaimer

This novel is written purely out of love and its characters and content are intended to be read and comprehended on fictional terms. The author, publisher and credited contributors will not be held responsible for those who decide to misinterpret the novel or take it literally thus creating damage upon themselves or others be it mentally, physically, socially or otherwise. The author, publisher and credited contributors will also not attest, support or be subject to any sort of accusations, propagandas and theories concerning any sort of agendas and will consider such actions defaming. This book is not to be used as evidence for or against any spiritual or religious congregation; it is also not to be used to challenge those of religious faith and those who do not adhere to a religious faith (including the undecided). This novel is not to be used as a tool to mock, disrespect, prove or disprove established religious, political, artistic, economic, legal and/or medical ideologies. If this book is taught in academic institutes, it is only to be taught for educational purposes and is not to be used for imposing personal gain and perspective upon students. All responsibilities for violations of this disclaimer and jurisdictional and/or federal laws are to be accepted by the sole individual(s) involved and by nobody else regardless of their sanity, ideologies, lifestyle, occupation, mental health and personal/religious views. Claiming to not have read this disclaimer does not exempt anyone from anything mentioned in it thus the author, publisher and credited contributors will still not be held responsible for, or support, such actions.

"The past influences the present to create the future."

Chapter One

Twizzle-Dropped the Room and Out Came the Fogbusts

At the first feel of cold air touching the skin, one usually knows whether it is a gentle breeze or a chill from really cold weather. However, it is somewhat rare for someone to stand tall and feel a windy tickle on their arm—not the kind of tickle that happens from the feeling of running fingers, but the tickling of cold air dancing graciously on the skin like a figure skater. That was the kind of windy tickle that Jeffery felt on his arm. It was a cold, little blow and also very spontaneous, like the flash of a comet.

Jeffery grabbed his arm and looked at it curiously with his hazel eyes. He let go of himself then held out his hand to see what that tickle was. As expected, it happened to be mere cold air. While feeling neither disappointed, pleased, nor satisfied, Jeffery became more aware of where he was standing. At first, he thought himself in a forest of some sort; there were leaves everywhere in varied shades of green. The sight of the surreal bushes made Jeffery feel mildly dizzy. He felt his head and eyes get thicker, more swollen, and he felt a need to regurgitate. Jeffery felt his nausea worsening so he looked in the other direction but felt no different. Only the distance to the leaves seemed closer. Jeffery considered reaching out to touch them.

Trying to bear his nausea, he looked up to gaze at what seemed like the sky. There was a flat, dark surface painted with stars. Unlike the rest of the area, the sky did not look all that natural. In fact, it looked like a painting.

It seemed as though someone had painted a picture of the sky and placed it on the sky, which, to Jeffery, seemed quite peculiar. Even though he was over six feet tall, he could not reach it. Trying to remain calm despite his nausea, he instead decided to be brave and explore a little.

Jeffery was shirtless, wore dark blue jeans and black ankle boots. His skin was pale and wan due to the lack of sunlight. In fact, how could one expect him to have a tint of tan in an area so green and cluttered with leaves? His soft, brown hair was gently combed to the side, which gave him a rather classy and handsome appearance.

Jeffery looked closer at the painted ceiling. He reached out his arm in pursuit of feeling it but noticed that it was too high. He then wandered around to see whether he could get between the bushes. After walking close to one, Jeffery placed his hand on it, but the surface was flat! This startled him for a second. Jeffery used both hands to feel against the flat surface and continued exploring it as he walked along the length of it. It was impossible! There was no forest, nor were there any bushes; the whole thing was just drawn across all the walls. Jeffery looked at the floor beneath his feet and noticed that it was just a drawing as well. He began to touch every bit of the floor and the walls with increasing curiosity. From afar, it looked like a real forest and all the greens seemed to be moving, but really, this was just one whole room where every surface was just as flat as the one before. Jeffery stood in amazement.

"And who would want to come up with a place like this?" he asked aloud. He sat down on the floor with his back against the wall, and looked around. His chest and armpits were mildly sweating. Jeffery breathed deeply and tried to make sense of the place. "Someone must really enjoy making others wonder," he added with his deep voice, "and a bit sick."

Jeffery stared closer at the floor and saw that it wasn't too different from the rest of the room—a seemingly live forest that wasn't real except for a flat surface under his feet. Jeffery focused on the floor more carefully and saw that the little bits of lighter green spots on the leaves were moving. After focusing even more, he felt the whole room moving, so, naturally, his eyes and head throbbed harder. While lost in thought, he focused more on one part of the floor. Jeffery then leaped and slammed his hand on it in hope of stopping the movement. The slam was unpleasantly loud and stung his palm. After noticing his failure, Jeffery just leaned back against the wall in dismay and continued to wonder. He looked back up at the ceiling and confirmed that it was obviously not the sky, but instead, an amateur painting trying to mimic the sky. Splashes of dark green and black were its dominant colors and some white stars were scattered across it. Jeffery also noticed that the stars varied in size. Some were pointy and round, while some were less circular. Even though it was obvious that this painting was quite juvenile in comparison with the walls and floor, for Jeffery it was far less nauseating. He kept his head relaxed against the wall and continued to stare at the ceiling. This eased his nausea, as the quickest glance at the wall or floor was utterly uncomfortable for his eyes and mind.

At the same time, Jeffery wondered what it would be like to live in a forest, or perhaps even a jungle. He thought about witnessing strange creatures, fluctuating weather, and maybe even some strangely shaped fruits. Jeffery sighed, lost in thought.

"I guess it might be possible," he thought out loud. He put his head in his palm and sighed again.

"Well, anything can be possible," suddenly boomed a male voice seemingly out of nowhere. Jeffery opened his eyes wide and silently questioned whether it was possibly the voice of another man. "One doesn't just enter a lifetime expecting things pre-ordained, no?" Jeffery's chest tightened and he felt his hormones boiling in his gut as his adrenaline rushed.

"Who's there?" he questioned fearfully as he glanced in different directions.

"Just me," answered the male voice. Jeffery looked left, then right, and then continued glancing at different parts of the room. "Down here," said the voice, "close to your right leg." Jeffery looked down as instructed and, to his amazement, he discovered a ladybug about a foot away. It was red with a black head, shiny, and about the diameter of a quarter and nearly three inches high. It seemed quite thick and fleshy for its size.

"Huh?" said Jeffery.

"Yeah, that's me," said the male voice. It felt very strange to Jeffery looking at the ladybug and hearing that male voice coming out of him.

"What... *who* are you?" asked Jeffery.

"Just me," replied the ladybug. "No one bothered to give me a name in this lifetime. Who are you?"

"Well, I'm Jeffery," replied Jeffery hesitantly. "I've never seen a ladybug so big before."

"Well, size isn't all there is to a creature now, is it?" said the ladybug, walking closer to Jeffery. Jeffery started to relax as he found the talking ladybug to be somewhat soothing. He watched him carefully and with great curiosity.

"Well, no," said Jeffery, "I just think it is a bit abnormal."

"Sometimes the abnormal have more to offer," stated the ladybug in a gentle tone as he rested very close to Jeffery.

"No kidding," agreed Jeffery with a scoff. Without caution, he picked up his new friend and rested him on his knee.

"You should ask others before touching them or picking them up," suggested the ladybug.

"You're so sarcastic," laughed Jeffery. "Really, what can I call you?"

"I don't know if that's too important. As I said, they never called me anything in this lifetime," answered the ladybug. Jeffery looked at him closely and discovered nine spots that were arranged in an orderly three by three pattern that looked like a rectangle at first glance. Each spot was black except for the one in the middle, which was forest green.

"How did you get here?" questioned Jeffery.

"Oh, I've always been up and about," replied the ladybug. "I've kind of been around here all my life."

"*Kind of?*" asked Jeffery.

"You are a really curious man," said the ladybug.

"Well, can you tell me what's with this place?" asked Jeffery.

"What about it?" inquired the ladybug.

"Well, it looks like a forest but it isn't. It's just a room, really," answered Jeffery, "like, a few walls and a ceiling."

"Oh," started the ladybug, "that's just an optical illusion. What you see is just wallpaper."

"It's killing my eyes," said Jeffery.

"It can be a nuisance to larger-sized organisms," agreed the ladybug. This caused Jeffery to frown. He looked closely at the ladybug. Sure, he was big for his kind, but he was still, in a sense, a talking little bug. The idea of this seemed amusing, curious, and also touching to Jeffery. It was like discovering a little friend who seemed to possess wisdom and extensive knowledge.

"And how long have you been here?" asked the ladybug.

"I," started Jeffery then hesitated, "have sort of always been here."

"Sounds like a lifetime of optical illusions," replied the ladybug.

"Thank you," said Jeffery sounding slightly uncertain. "This is ridiculous. You must have a name or something that I can call you by."

"You're too kind," insisted the ladybug, following with a flip. "Life is like a wild rainforest. And if you are too kind, you can get shamelessly sacked for it."

"Well, how about I name you... " Jeffery paused in hesitation, "George?"

The ladybug looked right at him. "Well, I'm not that remarkable," he protested.

"Well, you get what I mean," said Jeffery. "Everybody needs a name." They looked at each other and smiled.

"Well, George it is," said the ladybug. "You're too kind. You just had to name me something." This sentence went right to Jeffery's heart. How could no one ever have thought to name such a cute little fellow?

"Alright, George it is," agreed Jeffery. George happily did another flip. "How did you obtain that green spot?"

"I was just born with it," answered George. "I forget that I have it sometimes."

"Really?" asked Jeffery.

"Well, you don't always have the chance to look at your back's reflection now, do you?" asked George in response.

"No," said Jeffery. "But I can only wonder."

The bonding between Jeffery and George came at a peaceful ease. It wasn't every day that Jeffery had the chance to meet a talking ladybug, so giving him a name was somewhat special to him. He now had a little friend that he could talk to about his dissatisfaction with the ominous wallpaper. And not only that, but the idea of having another talking organism gave him a sense of peace and left him feeling restful about the fact that he didn't have to sit with his head and back against the wall in solitude and stare at the childishly painted ceiling.

On the other hand, even though Jeffery was pleased about being engaged in dialogue with George, he still wished there was a way to see beyond the wallpaper. Jeffery wished that George was big enough to cover a part of it so that he could just look at him and not see anything else. Of course, that would make George the biggest ladybug ever recorded in history.

"You see, Jeffery, things are often unpleasant, and kind of irritating," said George. "Although sometimes things can be gross and sticky, as those who live and breathe, we mustn't let things like that prevent us from moving ahead." To Jeffery that didn't seem to make any sense; there really was no way to move *ahead* in the room.

"Well, I cannot seem to see much ahead here, other than the fake bushes that look like they are real and are making me feel kind of sick," he answered, still feeling queasy.

"The world must look smaller to your eyes than it does to mine," said George, following his words with a small flip. Jeffery smiled courteously.

"Much smaller and denser," he reinforced, "probably two thousand times smaller."

"Wow, I've always wondered what that would be like," said George with a short laugh. "But that would make hiding a lot harder."

"Hiding from what?" asked Jeffery.

"Well, you know," said George, "if this was a real forest, or even a jungle, there'd be plenty of predators out there. The bigger and more visible one is, the quicker he'll get eaten by a frog or something. Of course a frog can't eat someone as big as you, but you never really know what's out there."

Jeffery put his head back against the wall and looked at the ceiling. He knew that this was right. Maybe in a sense he was actually fortunate to be sheltered in the room with George, away from wild predators. Jeffery tried to take a closer look at the ceiling by staring more deeply at the black and green

7

background with the different stars. He noticed that the dark green parts were not in fact the same shade. Focusing gave him a small rush of uncertainty.

"Well, there surely aren't just wild predators out there. I mean, there must be something worth exploring or experiencing, don't you think?" he reasoned.

"Well, sure," replied George after a long sigh. "But you see, oftentimes, exploration and experiences don't happen that easily or with good outcomes. Oftentimes, people go out there to explore and all they are really left with is just... " George sighed for a moment.

"With just what?" Jeffery questioned.

"Just... utter disappointment and a sense of solitude," answered George softly.

Jeffery couldn't help but stare gently at George, who possessed so much knowledge for someone so small. He sounded like he had experienced a journey somewhere far away from here and lived to tell the tale. Jeffery was also captivated by how much he was learning from George. In fact, he wondered about George personally and some of the things that he was discussing.

"I take it that you're a philosopher of life," suggested Jeffery kindly.

"Oh, I am no philosopher or anyone important," said George. "I was taught to stay humble, mainly because of my size. I was always told that I was not necessarily born in the right body so I just go with the waves. I can't say that there is much that I find flexible, but I do at least try to help others on their journey."

"What do you know about my journey and destiny?" asked Jeffery with genuine curiosity.

"More than you think," winked George before doing another flip. "I can't say that I am destined to tell you your life before you experience it on your own, though. You see, Jeffery, what is the point of burning something

8

for someone who's got more fuel than you?" In response, Jeffery smiled while secretly astounded at what his ears were hearing.

"Are you saying that I have a journey beyond these walls?" he asked, sounding interested.

"Most certainly!" confirmed George. "I just can't tell you!" Jeffery laughed and watched George do a couple more flips.

"I wonder if being born with that green spot is the reason you learned so much," said Jeffery.

"Life is more than being born with a spot. It is more about how the spot lives," answered George. "You ought to remember that being born with a certain and unique trait mustn't be the scapegoat for all your mysteries."

"You think so?" asked Jeffery.

"Definitely!" replied George. "There is a reason that *we* exist and talk, and not the actual spots and marks on us."

"You smart cookie, you," teased Jeffery. Without caution, he flicked at George with his middle finger and thumb, sending him careening halfway across the room as though he had been jounced off a bouncy limb. As George soared, he let out a scream of fear and agony that echoed in the room. Within seconds, George landed on the floor with a very loud splat. That's when Jeffery saw the burst of slimy green explode through the air. His eyes widened.

"Um, George?" asked Jeffery. "Are you alright there?" After receiving no answer, Jeffery focused on where George landed. He felt as though the green leaves were moving even faster, even though they were not. "What happened?"

Jeffery got up and quickly went to the spot where George had landed. There was a thick puddle of lime-green liquid that looked really sticky. Right in the middle were two broken wings. Jeffery imagined piecing them together and realized that the crack down the middle would click the two like puzzle pieces forming the exact same spot pattern on George's back. Jeffery gazed at them in complete dismay as his jaws dropped.

"No way," he whispered silently. He poked his finger into the thick, lime-green puddle and held it up. The smell was a little acidic. Jeffery looked around the floor and between the drawn leaves to see whether any other parts of George had scattered. Not far from the landing spot was a cracked ladybug's head that looked as though it had been mercilessly decapitated. The sight of George's empty eyes made Jeffery gasp and a shriek escaped through his open mouth. "It can't be!" he shouted. He picked up George's lifeless head and held it close. Jeffery thought about how just a moment ago, it had contained the life of a small and harmless ladybug that made him feel so warm that he had insisted on naming him. Within seconds, Jeffery's eyes were filled with tears and his heart pounded hard.

Jeffery's tears ran down his cheeks like salty streams and landed in tiny puddles on the floor. This added to the optical illusion of the leaves by making them look as though they had been rained on. The sight of that caused Jeffery's head to throb more. He couldn't believe that he had murdered George; he had only wanted to make a friendly joke. Even though George was quite big for a ladybug, Jeffery realized that he was no giant, and weighed less than an ounce. Jeffery realized that his friendly joke had turned George to juice, which felt like a stab in his heart.

"Goodbye, George. I am sorry my friend, I wish you'd forgive me," cried Jeffery. He put down George's head and went back to where he had been sitting. He rubbed his hand down his arm then sighed. He realized that the result of the accident was total solitude. It felt like a totally abysmal end where nothing was destined to happen. Jeffery shivered.

His stomach ached, not only from the fact that George had died, but also, the sight of his carcass—his cracked wings, his damaged head, and the puddle of thick, lime-green liquid that contained all of his internals. Jeffery

10

felt a slight need to regurgitate so he lay down and curled his legs behind his knees, then his knees into his stomach. While lying there, the optical illusion of the forest leaves moving looked faster than ever so he closed his eyes.

"I'm sorry, George," Jeffery whispered. "I'm sorry," he repeated. "I am so sorry." He cried again but with his eyes closed. Jeffery felt the room spinning around him. As it spun faster and faster, he thought this was just a stronger mental reaction to the optical illusion. Then, before long, something felt different. Jeffery felt the movement of the room slow down a lot, then for a split second he heard footsteps, so he opened his eyes. Everything was the same, but the sound of the footsteps gradually got louder. Jeffery stood right up and looked in all directions of the room. He heard the footsteps get closer then suddenly disappear. Jeffery looked to his left. He did not take notice of any changes, he just felt rather uneasy. After wandering around the room for a few seconds, he heard the footsteps again so he halted.

"I know there is someone in there," called a strong male voice. The voice sounded as though it were coming from another room so Jeffery quickly and nervously glanced at all the walls.

"I don't think so, you fool, you just want to waste my time," said a woman's voice from the same direction.

"Trust me, Fruit, there is someone in there," said the male voice. "I heard those weeps and I know that's where they came from."

"And if there isn't anyone?" asked the female voice, sounding closer.

"Then it wouldn't hurt to find out so," answered the male voice, also sounding closer.

"You just want to waste my time, Apple," said the female voice, sounding displeased.

"Oh, shut up, Fruit!" said the male voice. "Someone *is* in there and we ought to discover who!"

Jeffery quickly sat back against the wall. His eyes were shifting and glancing at almost every inch of the room. His gut was shaking, as were his legs. He felt a bit sweaty in his forehead area and his breathing turned into panting.

"Who's here?" he whispered cautiously. He felt like grabbing a handle or something to provide him some security but all he found was the flat surface of the deceptive wall behind him.

"It's probably just an old rat giving birth to a bunch of pups," suggested the female voice.

"Oh, shut up, you old hag," scolded the male voice, followed by a slapping sound.

"Oh!" yelled the female voice.

"These guys sound mad," said Jeffery quietly while in shock and trying to not make any movements, "and oddly disturbed."

The floor began to sway left and right, throwing Jeffery off balance. Trying to focus on the ceiling, he was alarmed to notice it slowly descending. The walls started sliding to the left, causing the room to tighten. The shift accelerated in a spiral, speeding up as the walls came in.

"What's happening?" questioned Jeffery. "What is happening in here? Who's there?"

"You hear that, Fruit? I told you there's someone or something crippled in there."

"What's happening?" shouted Jeffery. The room continued spinning faster and faster, then suddenly, an eruption of glittering green smoke blinded Jeffery. Thus, he lost control of himself and felt his body fall forward. Jeffery didn't land on anything, though. Instead, he felt as though he was falling eternally.

"Must you always create so much smoke just to lighten up the room?" yelled the female voice as she coughed. Jeffery blacked right out. It was unclear whether he had a concussion or not, but he couldn't feel his body, open his eyes, or sense anything about himself and his surroundings.

After a span of time, Jeffery slowly began to feel his body again. His eyes were closed and he felt as if he was lying down. The floor felt a lot thicker than before and was rather soft and comfortable. Jeffery also felt something thick in texture poking his nose which gave him a slight bit of reassurance that he was alive.

"Why, who could that be?" asked the female voice, sounding much closer than before.

"I told you that someone was in here!" said the male voice.

"I should have believed you," replied the female voice.

"Because you're such an idiot!" scolded the male voice.

Jeffery opened his eyes. About four or five paces away, he saw three heavy shoes that formed the three points of a triangle. They were black and were done up with green laces. Jeffery's heart started to pound heavily.

"He's alive," said the woman's voice. Jeffery sat up and looked around. He couldn't believe his eyes. Right in front of him was a broad figure, standing huge at nine feet tall. It wore a soft green top tucked into aqua-green pants with white cotton fluff around a waist that was decorated with small silver stars made of glossy paper. The pants had three legs, all connected into the black heavy shoes. The figure also had two massive arms. The sight didn't end there! At the top of the figure were two heads, each atop a short neck. The one on the left was very round and bore the face of a man with a thick beard that matched his copper-red eyebrows. His eyes were hazel and his nose was thick and round like a potato, which made his balding, white head look even more plump.

The right head had the face of a woman, with the same copper-red eyebrows but much sharper, angular features. Her hair was very curly and rested below her jawline. Her lips were royal green, very similar to the carpet, but covered in sparkles and glitter.

Jeffery's jaw dropped in disbelief at what stood before him! The ceiling was still the same and the painting hadn't altered. Only one thing was added: a lime-green chandelier that provided a lot of soft, white light. The walls were also in the same place but gone was the wallpaper of the optical illusion. Now, accompanying the comfortable look and feel of the carpet, the walls were painted a white-green pattern of vertical stripes that were perfectly even in width. The room was unfurnished and on the wall was a wooden clock. Next to it was a circular aqua-green ornament with a hole in the middle. Jeffery also noticed that the room didn't contain a window or a door.

"What happened?" asked Jeffery. "Who are you?" Both heads of the large figure looked at him in a surprised manner. "What's happened in here?"

"Jeffery?" asked the woman's head.

"It can't be," added the man's.

"And I thought it was a rat!" said the woman's.

"We've been expecting you for quite some time," said the man's head. Jeffery felt like he couldn't speak and lost his words. His mouth was open but he was unable to express himself. The sudden shift in the room was too quick for him to handle and processing the sight of the two-headed figure wasn't any easier.

"He looks scared," said the woman's head after noticing Jeffery's facial expression.

"We are the Fogbusts," introduced the man's head. "I am Apple, and she is Fruit."

"And he's quite bossy," added Fruit.

"Shut up," scolded Apple as he coldly glared at her.

"What's happened?" asked Jeffery, sounding as if he was running out of air.

"We've been expecting your arrival for quite some time," said Apple. "Help him up," he then ordered Fruit. The Fogbusts moved closer to Jeffery and reached out their thick arms to help him stand up.

"And you've been sent at last," said Fruit gladly.

"You see there, Jeffery, every eternity starts with a beginning," explained Apple. "You're destined to begin your eternal endeavor quite soon. It is our responsibility to make sure that you are prepared so that when you are out there in a hostile world full of creepy ones, you'll be prepared to face them the right way."

"What do you mean?" asked Jeffery.

"Oh, Apple," said Fruit, "not everyone out there is berserk and wants to eat him."

"You can't be too kind," insisted Apple. "It's a rough journey."

"Well, it is," agreed Fruit quietly.

"Who sent me here? What does all this mean?" asked Jeffery.

"You've been sent here by God," replied Fruit.

"God?" asked Jeffery.

"Yes," said Apple. "And God specifically has asked us to look after you until you're ready."

"I don't understand. Who's God?" asked Jeffery. "Am I going to meet them?"

"Curious young man, aren't you?" said Fruit.

"Well, sure, you'd be too," argued Jeffery.

"A young man mustn't ask too many questions," said Apple. "You just need to learn."

Jeffery looked at the Fogbusts. There was so much information being thrown at him all at once that his head felt heavier. As a result, he felt the throbs slowly coming back. Jeffery looked down, turned around, then walked and stood against the wall. He sat down on the thick, royal-green carpet, rested his head against the wall and looked up at the ceiling. Jeffery managed to get a closer look at the details of it—the different shapes of the stars and the way they were patterned. Each star seemed to contain something individual and unknown. Jeffery thought for a second about what sort of obscurities lay in the heart of each star.

"I know you like this drawing," said Fruit.

"Perplexing, isn't it?" winked Apple.

"I do," said Jeffery, "I really do. Yes, it is beautiful and bizarre in its own unexplainable way."

"Unexplainable, eh?" asked Fruit.

"Absolutely," said Jeffery after looking at her and smiling.

"Gentleman," suggested Fruit sarcastically after looking towards Apple. Apple smiled reluctantly.

"You mustn't be too kind," he told Jeffery firmly.

"Well, what he really means is don't let others take advantage of you," elucidated Fruit. "A bit of kindness doesn't hurt," she added.

"What is it like to have three legs?" asked Jeffery.

"Normal," replied Apple.

"Normal?" asked Jeffery.

"Yes, very normal," insisted Apple. "We are all made in our own unique way and there's nothing we can do about it—not that it matters anyways."

After hearing this, Jeffery remembered what George had told him: *Life is more than being born with a spot. It is more about how the spot lives.* Jeffery was certainly able to apply this to the Fogbusts. They had three legs and two heads in one giant figure, but they sure had knowledge that he lacked and seemed as though they were well maintained. The thought of

16

George made Jeffery's eyes sparkle and got him to look at the carpet. There was no presence of George's carcass or internal liquid.

"Are you all right?" asked Fruit. Jeffery began to cry gently.

"Are those tears I see?" asked Apple. "They won't benefit you much."

"Apple, come on," said Fruit. "What's wrong, Jeffery?"

Jeffery sighed and continued tearing. He looked at his knees and remembered the flips that George used to do and how they were so simple. Jeffery mourned the loss of this innocence and was saddened by the fact that it came and left so soon.

"Before you two arrived, this room was different," Jeffery started. "It looked like a forest that was real but it wasn't. It gave me a strange feeling."

"Yes, that means the lights were off," explained Fruit.

"That's how it looks before we turn on the lights," told Apple.

"Well, it was kind of dark. It did not feel the best," said Jeffery. "And while all alone, I saw this ladybug that was a little bigger than normal. He was kind, and knowledgeable."

"And then?" asked Apple.

"Well," said Jeffery after looking down. "I killed him. I swear I didn't mean to! I just wanted to flick him as a joke, which I did, then it sent him flying across the room and he was gone."

"Just like that?" asked Apple.

"How interesting," said Fruit.

"He landed on the floor and his body just burst into a thick liquid," told Jeffery, "lime-green." The Fogbusts exchanged looks.

"Have you heard of such?" asked Apple.

"No, never," replied Fruit.

"He just appeared out of nowhere," said Jeffery. "I named him George."

"George?" repeated Fruit.

"Yes," said Jeffery. "He was very friendly and because of my misdoing he died. I'll never see him again. I killed him, and unfortunately, I'll never get to apologize to him." Jeffery sobbed again. He knew that his tears were useless, but he couldn't help feeling sorrow and guilt.

"That sounds very unfortunate," said Fruit.

"Very much so," agreed Apple. Fruit looked at him sharply for a second then looked back at Jeffery. "We all make mistakes, then we learn, Jeffery. I really hope that you now know not to flick things again."

"Most definitely," said Jeffery, wiping his tears.

"I can imagine," said Fruit.

"Don't dwell too much," Apple advised. "It'll only hinder you."

"Absolutely," said Fruit. "I mean, I know that you can't give him his life back but at least you'll always have a fond memory of this little George."

The Fogbusts began wandering around the room casually. Fruit appeared to be feeling annoyed judging by her frowning facial expression, but Apple seemed very casual. They walked up to the clock and glanced at the time. The way they moved and walked with their plump body and three legs interested Jeffery. He observed them and merely wondered. Not only did he wonder about their physical form but also about their relationship. It seemed awkward to him seeing a man and a woman in one body constantly arguing and bickering about pesky things.

"You think God would like him to go on now?" Fruit asked Apple. Apple gave her a look of uncertainty. In fact, he looked at her as though he didn't even have an answer. He didn't smile or frown, but kept his gaze focused on her as Jeffery took notice again of the name *God*. Hearing the name repeated spiked his curiosity.

"Who exactly is God?" he asked politely. "Is it a man or a woman?"

"He's a man," replied Apple. After taking a couple of breaths, the Fogbusts walked close to Jeffery and faced him.

"He's never heard of him," Fruit said to Apple.

"I know, I see that," Apple replied sternly.

"What do you know about him?" asked Jeffery. "Is he your friend?"

"He sort of is," said Apple as they put their hands together in front of their belly. "We can't see him but we hear him. He mentioned that he'd be sending you here."

"What else did he mention?" asked Jeffery.

"To teach you," answered Fruit. "To supply you with whatever knowledge you need."

"I wonder," started Jeffery, "if you can't see him, then how do you hear him?"

"We just do," told Apple. "Whenever he's got something to say, he just comes over and says it."

"And how long have you known of him?" asked Jeffery.

"Most of our life," replied Fruit in a sweet tone. "He has helped us a lot."

"Sounds like a good friend to have," said Jeffery as he tried to make sense of it. "You can't see him, but he comes over for visits, and he's also sent me over?" He then looked down and sighed. "You think he may have sent George along?"

"Quite possibly, yes," agreed Apple. "He probably knew you needed his company hence he sent him to you."

"Although," started Fruit, "we don't always refer to him as *God* directly. We just call him Allie."

"Yes, Allie suits his character I must say," added Apple.

"Interesting," said Jeffery with a pause. "Allie," he recited as he thought deeply. "Will I ever get to meet Allie? Or even hear him?"

19

"Maybe," said Fruit. "If he needs to talk to you, you'll hear him alright."

"But I'll never know what he looks like," said Jeffery. The Fogbusts raised their shoulders then looked at each other.

"Possibly not," agreed Apple.

"He sounds intriguing though," said Jeffery. "I wonder if he can bring George back to life?"

"Usually when someone dies, they just go," said Fruit. "But if you're lucky, you may get to communicate that to him yourself."

"Possibly so," said Apple after receiving a glare from Fruit.

"I am willing to bet that he is good-looking also," Fruit added sarcastically.

"What do you mean?" asked Apple sounding frustrated.

"Oh, you know," replied Fruit, "I just get curious."

"I am curious," said Jeffery. Fruit looked at him and smiled.

"Now I ought to have a word with you," said Apple. "Good-looking, eh? You're aware that this is the man who answers our prayers?"

"Oh, don't get furious," defended Fruit, "a little bit of curiosity does not hurt." Jeffery took notice of Apple's facial expression. It seemed tense, as though he were trying to lift a bucket twice his weight.

"I don't think so," stated Apple. He paused for a second, then continued speaking. "Curiosity left you with a dead baby rabbit in your pocket for a week!"

"Hey," said Fruit, "it's not always your business what captures my interest!"

"You bet it is. I wouldn't be married to you otherwise," yelled Apple.

"Oh, don't be ridiculous," said Fruit.

"I mean it, woman!" reinforced Apple. "You know very well that that's exactly what Allie wanted for us!"

"And that is why we are here, you old fool," said Fruit.

"Who are you calling an old fool there, Fruit?" shouted Apple as his face turned red.

"Your plump bald head, that's who," retorted Fruit.

"Watch your mouth there!" yelled Apple. After saying that, he slapped her hard on her face.

"Ouch!" screamed Fruit after receiving it. "You quit being a beast, you!"

"Then learn to shut your mouth, especially when your man asks you to!" shouted Apple. "It is the will of God!"

Jeffery's eyes widened. He felt sweaty and his blood pressure rose out of fear. He did not want the Fogbusts getting too out of control so he wondered whether he should interrupt their conversation, but then thought about whether or not he should even say anything at all. Jeffery kept shifting his eyes between the two of them then realized that he had to be clever.

"When did Allie say you two must be together?" he questioned gently.

"When he lost his mind and said that I must be with *him* as if I am his lung or something," answered Fruit. Apple gave her a violent look, almost ready to hit her again.

"Get over here," he growled. The two of them walked to the other side of the room.

"Can I ask," started Jeffery as he hesitated, "um, what has all this got to do with me?"

"Nothing really," answered Apple. The Fogbusts walked back towards him. "God doesn't always give you what you want," he said, "but you must accept it and live *with* it if not *for* it."

21

"Yes," reinforced Fruit. "And never be too judging of him either." Apple looked her straight in the eye and Jeffery right away knew that he wanted to point out her hypocrisy.

"Just cherish the special things," he then told Jeffery, causing him to remember George once again. Not only did he think of him personally, but also of his green spot. Jeffery thought it was pretty special and that it gave George character. Jeffery wondered how the Fogbusts would have reacted to the sight of George talking and flipping. This triggered more tears for Jeffery.

"Now what's the matter?" asked Apple.

"Sorry about our rudeness," said Fruit.

"You mean *your* rudeness," said Apple.

"No, it's not you!" yelled Jeffery which caused them to instantly look at him. "I'm just thinking about George, that's all."

"Now that, Jeffery," started Apple, "is what we are talking about. When Allie gives you something, cherish it—sweet or bitter, dark or light, shiny or revolting, just cherish it." Jeffery looked at Apple's hazel eyes then turned to Fruit's green ones. They resembled George's green spot so much that Jeffery hallucinated, seeing them come together as one and forming it. He quickly shook his head and tried to stay focused.

"What a night for you," said Fruit.

"What a night for all of us," said Apple rigidly, while looking at her.

"Don't start," said Fruit.

"Oh, please, you two!" cried Jeffery as he stood up. "Is this arguing necessary?"

"You're right, how rude of us," said Fruit.

"I think you need a talk with Lake Morgan," suggested Apple.

"Lake Morgan?" asked Jeffery.

"Yes," replied Apple.

"You really think having a word with Lake Morgan is going to be the best for him?" asked Fruit.

"I think so, yes," answered Apple. "I think Lake Morgan would have a good talk with him."

"Who is that?" asked Jeffery.

"Oh, just someone we know," replied Fruit. "He is very knowledgeable."

"You think he can help me?" asked Jeffery. "How about Allie?"

"Allie is around all the time," explained Apple.

"He's around all the time," reinforced Fruit.

"You can have a word with him," said Apple. "In fact, you *must* have a word with him!"

"Is he coming here?" asked Jeffery.

"No, we'll send you there," replied Fruit.

"But first, I must ask," started Apple as he focused his look on Jeffery, "you haven't accidently killed anyone else or done something you haven't told us about other than flicking George, no?" Apple's serious expression turned into a slightly threatening frown. Jeffery looked at his bald head then ran his eyes down to meet Apple's. Fruit focused her gaze on Jeffery's face after she noticed the intensity of the moment between the two.

"No, never," answered Jeffery in a nervous manner while sounding quick.

"I see," said Apple.

"Lake Morgan wouldn't be too thrilled," said Fruit.

"You must know him really well," said Jeffery.

"Oh, we do," answered Apple.

"In fact, we really do," added Fruit.

In his head, Jeffery reflected upon God and Lake Morgan. He tried to figure out how the Fogbusts knew of such connections and also wondered about how they looked. Jeffery also wondered whether God and Lake Morgan were as gentle as George, or were they fierce and talked with a grunt. He also thought carefully about their names, *Allie* and *Lake Morgan*. Without feeling shy, Jeffery proceeded to question the Fogbusts further.

"Does Lake Morgan know of Allie?" asked Jeffery.

"You really are too curious," said Apple. "Well, why don't we just send him now?" he recommended to Fruit. "I think that'd be best and would save us all some time."

"Well," said Fruit, hesitating. Her lack of response turned into a moment of silence as both of the Fogbusts thought. Jeffery had a gut feeling that Lake Morgan was about to enter and that they were going to pretend it was a coincidence. He felt his stomach rumble a couple of times but noticed that they hadn't heard it. The last thing he needed was to feel embarrassed in front of them.

"Is there anything else you wish to know?" asked Apple.

"Well, how far is Lake Morgan from here?" asked Jeffery.

"You'll be there soon enough," replied Apple. "Come on." The Fogbusts were about to turn but their movement was interrupted by Fruit.

"But Apple, don't you think he might be hungry?" she asked worriedly. "We should feed him before sending him off." Apple looked at her sharply. "We need to have a heart; the young man's got a long journey ahead of him," continued Fruit.

"Fine," said Apple. The Fogbusts turned to look at Jeffery which caused him another uncomfortable feeling in his gut.

"A bit of food would be nice," smiled Jeffery, sounding vulnerable.

"See, he's hungry," said Fruit.

"Ok, let's get him some food," agreed Apple. The Fogbusts looked up and closed their eyes. As they inhaled deeply through their noses, a light green fog swirled around them, twisting into discernible shapes. An emerald-green table and chair appeared in mid-air, landing right in front of Jeffery, quickly followed by the thud of a wooden plate loaded with fruit. Next to it, appeared a silky, royal-green table napkin folded in an intricate design. Finally, a glass of red wine landed on the table and then the fog faded out.

Jeffery took a seat at the table and looked at the plate of fruit. Along the edges he saw the dark green rinds of a juicy watermelon, couching small bunches of green grapes so translucent they appeared to be glowing from within. Closer to the center were cubes of Derby cheese, with their bright green veins of sage, separating the grapes from a cluster of olives brined in lime oil, which gave them an almost fluorescent hue.

"That looks good," cheered Jeffery. "Thank you!"

"You're welcome," smiled Fruit kindly.

"Enjoy," said Apple in a callous manner. The Fogbusts turned around and continued to wander. Jeffery took a cheese cube and put it in his mouth. It was soft, very fresh, and light. He then sipped on some wine, nibbled on the olives and grapes, and a few more cheese cubes. The fruits were very juicy and the wine was dark and dry.

Jeffery looked at the slices of watermelon. Of all the foods, these looked the juiciest and darkest. He grabbed a slice and ate it, amazed at the taste. Jeffery realized that it didn't taste like an average watermelon. Instead, it tasted somewhat like a blend of blueberries, green apple and kiwi. Before long, he began eating his second slice and accompanied it with a couple of savory cheese cubes. Of the entire experience Jeffery had in the room, he felt that eating that meal was the most comforting and delicious. In fact, Jeffery forgot a bit about George, the Fogbusts, and the room's transformation. He drank more wine then looked up at the ceiling and noticed that the artwork of the green-black sky really added a special feel to his dining experience. Jeffery took the table napkin and wiped his hands and mouth. Its silky material felt very smooth on his skin, like the lips of a beautiful lover's kiss.

25

Jeffery nibbled more on the grapes and olives then went on to finish his meal and wine. After wiping his hands and mouth again, he stood up and walked to the Fogbusts.

"Thank you," he said kindly.

"Oh, you're welcome," replied Fruit.

"That was very delicious," expressed Jeffery.

"The cheese is imported," said Apple.

"And so are the olives," squeaked Fruit.

"I really enjoyed it," said Jeffery.

"I take it that you are full?" asked Fruit.

"Oh, I am," answered Jeffery. "All that food and wine was incredible!"

"Very good," said Apple. The Fogbusts looked up into the air again and closed their eyes. After breathing through their noses once more, the green fog appeared again. This time, the table and everything got sucked into it and then it gradually disappeared.

"Well, it's time to send you to Lake Morgan," instructed Apple.

"Alright," said Jeffery.

"You think he's ready?" questioned Fruit as the Fogbusts walked towards the clock.

"Absolutely," said Apple. "We have looked after him long enough."

"I think we should provide him with some caution first," suggested Fruit. The Fogbusts took down the aqua-green circle ornament with the hole in it and walked back to Jeffery.

"Well, he's going to face things sooner or later," argued Apple.

"Well, yes, but Allie said to watch over and guide those whom we care for," reminded Fruit.

"What's that?" questioned Jeffery.

"This is… " started Apple.

26

"Before you start," interrupted Fruit, "I am serious. We need to provide him with some guidance."

"Alright!" yelled Apple in utter frustration. "What do you have to say?" Fruit turned to face Jeffery. Jeffery stood there facing them with his arms down by his sides.

"You see, Jeffery, life is filled with unexpected things," began Fruit. "It really is."

"What sort of unexpected things?" questioned Jeffery.

"Well, Lake Morgan will go through that with you in more detail, but really, Jeffery, you must understand," said Fruit, "it is like a jungle out there. And when you're on your own, do not be afraid. Just live and experience what you need and those around you will guide you to the right place."

"And don't ask too many questions," added Apple.

"And that, too," reinforced Fruit while sounding frustrated after quickly glancing at Apple. "And Jeffery, whatever happens, always remember to stay strong and navigate your way. You are born a man, and it is the destiny of every man to be brave."

"Alright," said Jeffery. "I will be brave and I will stand up to whatever is out there."

"Don't just say it, live it," said Apple bluntly. "If someone takes advantage of your kindness and decides to use you for it, you'll be left with nothing, not even pulp from leftover orange juice."

"And that's why Allie brought you to us, to warn you of this," explained Fruit.

"And remember, once you fledge, there is no coming back here," warned Apple.

"You mean I'll never see you again?" asked Jeffery.

"Nope," answered Apple.

"Apple, would you quit being so harsh on him?" ordered Fruit.

"What's he got here?" asked Apple.

"Well, thank you for feeding me," said Jeffery.

"Don't be ridiculous, it is our duty," insisted Fruit. "And we will see you again."

"Perhaps in dreams somewhere," said Apple boldly. "And don't kill any more ladybugs."

Fruit gave Apple an unsatisfied and disappointed look. Jeffery looked back and forth between the two then looked back at the aqua-green ornament in their hands.

"Well, thank you," he repeated gently. "And what is that?"

"This is the crocksvenbulb," said Apple. "It is what you'll need to take with you."

"Don't lose it," squealed Fruit. "He'll understand you better with it."

"And where did you get it?" asked Jeffery.

"Well, we sort of always had it," answered Apple.

"Not quite," argued Fruit. "The crocksvenbulb is very useful. It was actually given to us a long time ago by Lake Morgan so that we'd find our path."

"Are you really going to tell him our life story?" asked Apple.

"Well, sure, just for the sake of guiding him," answered Fruit as she lost her patience. "We were curious at one point and along our journey we met Lake Morgan, who is very informative I must say, and he let us have it so that we'd stay grounded within our philosophy." Fruit looked closely at Jeffery then softened her voice. "That is why we are giving it to you. You'll need to have it when you see him."

Jeffery reached out and accepted the crocksvenbulb. He looked at it, holding it with both hands. It felt a little cold in some spots and a little warm in others.

Jeffery then looked up to them and noticed Fruit crying. Her tears were slowly running down her cheeks like melodic notes playing from a violin. He stepped closer trying to give them a hug but the Fogbusts pushed him back.

"No time for hugs and goodbyes," said Apple. "It is time you were on your way."

"Apple, this isn't fair," sobbed Fruit. The Fogbusts walked to the center of the room. "It isn't fair! Let me say goodbye!" shouted Fruit.

"You've had your chance," said Apple. Even though Fruit had her own head, Jeffery noticed the Fogbust body was controlled entirely by Apple, as though she were a foreign soul. He was certain that Apple at times enjoyed taking advantage of this.

Jeffery breathed, then looked at the crocksvenbulb. As he held it, he felt a rush of energy flow through him. He wondered if the Fogbusts felt the same current each time they held the crocksvenbulb, and if there was something about it that they hadn't mentioned.

"Alright, Jeffery," started Fruit sadly, "it is time." Jeffery looked at the Fogbusts one last time—their nine-foot-tall round figure with the three legs and two heads. Apple looked sternly back at him while Fruit continued tearing.

"Just look at the crocksvenbulb and focus," instructed Apple. Jeffery looked at the crocksvenbulb as directed, and as he focused on it, he noticed that it weighed quite a bit for a reasonably flat object. Its back side looked the same and had a small silver metal object used for hanging. Jeffery wondered many things about the crocksvenbulb and its connections to Lake Morgan. After asking himself several questions in his head, he looked back up but saw that the Fogbusts were not in their place. Jeffery looked around the room and they were nowhere to be seen. Instead of getting startled, Jeffery wandered around the room gently calling their names. He didn't hear any replies or footsteps.

"Are you telling me that you two just vanished?" he asked casually. "How'll I get to Lake Morgan?" Jeffery continued walking across the room slowly while closely holding the crocksvenbulb. He cautiously looked left and right, trying carefully to hear or find a trace of the Fogbusts. Jeffery stopped near the center of the room and crossed his eyes. He was annoyed at the fact that the Fogbusts had spontaneously disappeared, and probably under the demand of Apple. "If you two could be just a little bit more insightful," he said out loud, in hope of a response. The silence continued as he wandered the room, uncertain of what to expect.

Jeffery observed the thick, royal-green carpet under his boots and admired it. He sat down and rubbed his hands through it. He liked the feeling of the fluffy texture. For a second, he even wondered what it would be like to have a quilt made of its material.

While sitting, Jeffery crossed his legs then looked at the striped wall in front of him and noticed an interesting alteration. Near the bottom of the wall, there was a laminate image of the Fogbusts that was about eighteen inches long. It looked exactly like them with one exception—in the middle area around their belly, there was a drawing of the crocksvenbulb, only it was very dark green.

"Say what?" said Jeffery as he rubbed his eyes and looked at the image again. He got up and went closer to it. He rubbed his hands on its smooth surface and then looked back at the crocksvenbulb. Jeffery hesitated. "How am I supposed to get to Lake Morgan?" he asked quietly. Jeffery sat down next to the image and rubbed his hands on it some more. "Strange," he huffed quietly.

Jeffery looked around and again huffed, expressing his boredom. But before long, he heard something strange. It sounded sort of like a hardboiled egg rolling on a counter but really slowly. The sound gradually got louder so Jeffery looked at the ceiling and saw that it was in its place along with the chandelier. He looked back down and saw some shift taking place in the center of the carpet and discovered that that was where the sound was coming from, which gradually got louder.

Jeffery stood up and walked to the center. A flat green square had appeared and was growing. As it grew, it covered the area of carpet space on which it was growing. Jeffery stepped back as it stretched towards him and looked at it while feeling puzzled. After expanding to about five feet on each side, the square stopped growing and a thin dividing line ran vertically through its center. After the line reached the other end, the square opened horizontally like two doors sliding, and left a square-shaped gap. Jeffery walked closer and found a staircase within it, leading downwards. The stairs looked solid but were glowing as if inlaid with green lightbulbs.

"What is this?" Jeffery questioned out loud. There was no response. Jeffery continued walking around the gap while peeking at the staircase, trying to figure out where it led. Jeffery felt his heart sinking into his gut so he sat down next to the edge of the gap.

"Go on, go down the stairs," spoke Apple's voice.

"Huh?" said Jeffery as he looked around. "Apple? Where are you guys?"

"Just go down the stairs and quit wasting time," said Apple's voice.

"Well, alright," answered Jeffery hesitantly. "Where does this lead to?"

"Just go," yelled Apple's voice. Jeffery looked at the stairs again and sighed. He stood up then took one step on the first stair and took his foot back off.

"I don't think I can do this," moaned Jeffery.

"Hurry up," said Apple's voice, "just go down."

31

"You'll be alright," reassured Fruit's voice, sounding much more caring. This made Jeffery smile briefly as her voice gave him a sense of inner peace.

"Ok, then," said Jeffery. He put his foot back on the first stair and started going down. He continued going down into a dark room that contained nothing except the glowing staircase. The green light mixed with the darkness of the empty room intimidated Jeffery but he continued walking down. As he did so, he noticed that the stairs went in a spiral form. Jeffery continued walking down until he reached the floor. He looked back up and noticed that he was at least sixteen feet away from the gap, possibly more.

"Are you down there?" yelled Apple's voice from the top of the gap.

"I am!" yelled Jeffery. "Can you hear me?" Then in seconds, the staircase rolled up quickly like a measuring tape and the gap closed from both ends like a sliding door. The whole space was pitch black and Jeffery couldn't see an inch in front of him. His heartbeats raced very fast and his blood pressure quickly rose to his head.

"What happened?" he yelled. "Apple! Fruit!" Within seconds, Jeffery fainted.

Chapter Two

Masculine Glory on Walls of Wealth

When Jeffery regained consciousness, he discovered that his mouth was wide open and that he had a little headache. He slowly opened his eyes and scratched his head while on his stomach with his cheek against the floor. He breathed and tried to become more alert. His body felt a lot heavier and so did his head. Jeffery closed his eyes again and fell into a short sleep.

After a little while, he woke up feeling less heavy but just as hazy. He heard some music playing that sounded very angelic. There was a rhythm to this music and the volume was on the lower side, which was relaxing. After waking up more, Jeffery sat up to see where he had fallen into.

The carpet under him was cyan, and next to him, in the center of the room, was a rug that was a darker blue with patterns of white and turquoise flowers. At the center of the rug was a silver and glass coffee table with dark blue accents. Jeffery looked up to see the ceiling, which was actually quite high. It was light blue, like the walls, with several things that seemed enchanted and luxurious mounted in various places. He stood up and browsed around the room. There was a blue leather living room set that consisted of a sofa and two love seats and next to one of the love seats was a darker blue ottoman covered in some kind of fur. On the other side, behind the living room set, stood a tall podium made of high-quality plastic. It was mainly dark, the color of dusk, and the rim at the top was turquoise. Just below the rim were the initials *LM* in turquoise, with golden lining around each letter.

Next to the podium, on the right, was a large harp made of turquoise and lapis lazuli. The strings of the harp were white, made of horsehair, and behind it was a comfortable blue chair with patterns of crescent moons where a nearly naked woman sat playing. The only two items she wore were a silky royal-blue bra and a necklace of black pearls. Her wavy and shiny blue hair hung below her shoulders and swayed as she played. Jeffery widened his eyes at her presence. He did not think that this music was actually being played live as he listened to it.

The harpist glanced at him with her blue eyes. She quickly shifted her gaze back to the harp and continued playing. She did this a couple of times, leaving Jeffery to wonder what he should say.

"Um, hello there," he started. She didn't answer. "I don't mean to be rude, but I am supposed to meet Lake Morgan. Do you know of him?" The harpist continued to play and gave him a few glances and smiles. "Do you not hear me?" Jeffery asked. After receiving no response, Jeffery wandered around the room. He couldn't seem to absorb the amount of luxury in that space all at once. He decided to take a seat on the sofa and looked around. One of the objects mounted on the wall was a silver picture frame with shiny, brilliant-cut sapphires and opals that held the picture of a mermaid. The frame was about four feet in circumference and its sides swirled in different directions like swift vines dancing off a tree. The mermaid looked a lot like the lady playing the harp, but instead of being naked from the waist down, she had a shiny blue tail that matched her hair. She was sitting on a large rock somewhere outdoors and on her lap was a light, grayish-blue daisy. Jeffery looked back at the harpist and saw her smile at him as she played.

"You're still not going to talk to me?" he asked jokingly. She did not answer. "I wonder, has something gone wrong with your hearing?" Jeffery

34

looked back at the picture. He found it very beautiful that he imagined taking the daisy and placing it on the harpist's head. He also imagined having a conversation with her and listening to her friendly tone. In his mind, Jeffery questioned her ability to hear him. Would she, in fact, be interested in telling him what brought her to this location?

Before falling into a mental sea of wonders, Jeffery looked to another part of the wall and found a picture of another mermaid in a solid black frame. It was about a third the size of the previous one. The outdoor background in the picture was very similar, but this mermaid was completely topless. Her tail was a bit lighter and her facial expression more gaunt. Jeffery observed closely and noticed how she sat upright, which allowed her waist-length blonde hair to cover most of her torso. Jeffery then turned around and saw hanging on the wall behind him an ornament of a bird. The bird seemed to stare right back into his eyes. It was mostly sky blue in color and its eyes and beak were white with a bluish tone. The wings and tail were a little bit darker than the rest of its body and were patterned with an intricate design made of beige fabric.

Jeffery looked closely at the bird and smiled. Something about the bird seemed far more comforting than the idyllic portraits of the mermaids. Next to it was an ornament of a butterfly. It was a little bit wider than the bird with patterns of clear and dark-blue crystals accentuated by strong black lines.

"So spectacular!" said Jeffery. "And how artistic!" He then looked at the wall behind the podium and the harp and tried to look at the individual things hanging there. A large silver television screen was mounted above a long, horizontal, dark-blue speaker that was also affixed to the wall. On each side of the speaker were identical ornaments, two small turtles made of white gold and blue amber. In the center of each turtle shell was a single fossilized black bug with big eyes and legs. Jeffery dropped his jaw as he admired the elegant craftsmanship of the two ornaments.

"Somebody must really like to decorate," he said out loud after turning to the harpist. She only continued to play while glancing at him. "They probably like using you as a part of their décor," Jeffery added with a short laugh. On the floor by her chair, he noticed a small statue of a horse with its two front legs in the air and its head held up high. The statue was sea green at the base and the horse was white with blue eyes, mane and tail. Jeffery shifted his eyes between the horse statue and the lady. Briefly caught in a daydream, he imagined the horse galloping proudly to the gentle hymn of her music.

Having looked around the whole room, Jeffery tilted his head upward and noticed three very large chandeliers hanging from the ceiling. The one in the middle was slightly bigger than the others and was made of black diamonds and clear crystals. At the very top of the chandelier was a heart made of blue diamond. The other two were made of mostly sapphire and a little bit of alexandrite that was a mix of green and peach tones. On each side of them were hanging decorative ornaments of spiders that were made of white gold.

"It must have taken a very long time to create this," said Jeffery, sounding amazed. He shifted his gaze back to the wall in front of him. Hanging there was an exquisite star made of turquoise with the initials *LM* etched onto each of its points. Jeffery took a closer look at the star. It was fairly big to his eyes, and from its bottom right corner hung an ornamental silver and navy tea kettle. "*LM*," Jeffery read aloud. "What could that possibly stand for?" Jeffery continued to browse the walls. He then stood up and walked slowly to where the podium and harp were located. "Could that possibly be Lake Morgan's initials?" he asked the harpist as she played a new melodic tune. As expected, she did not reply. "Gosh, you're useless,"

36

said Jeffery, sounding cross. Then, along the bottom of the wall behind the podium, Jeffery took notice of something entirely unexpected. There was an ornament of the sun with a smiling face made of white gold with blue outlines on each sun ray. Right under that ornament were six dark-gray nails, hammered in a horizontal line. Hanging on them unevenly from the central hole, on the first three and last two were ornaments that looked exactly like the crocksvenbulb. The difference was, none of them were aqua. They were each an individual shade of blue. The first two were turquoise, one a little bit lighter than the other, and the third one was cyan and it almost disappeared into the color of the wall. The ones hanging from the last two nails were much darker, closer to navy blue. The last one was the darkest of them all.

"The crocksvenbulb?" asked Jeffery. "These look exactly like the crocksvenbulb!" He checked his pockets and noticed that it wasn't there. He quickly ran back close to the rug and coffee table and started looking for it. "It's got to be here somewhere," he said, searching the floor. After a few seconds of panic, he found it on the floor where he had woken up. Jeffery quickly snatched it up and walked back to the area by the podium. He held out the crocksvenbulb with both his hands and compared it to the other ones. It was the exact same size and made of the same kind of ceramic. Jeffery flipped it over and looked at the silver hanging hardware. It seemed the Fogbusts had installed it themselves.

"Amazing," said Jeffery. Crouching down on his knees, he put the crocksvenbulb on the fourth nail and let it gently bounce like the other ones. Jeffery stood up and smiled, feeling a sense of accomplishment. He looked at all the crocksvenbulbs dangling gently from their nails. Turning to the harpist, he began to take note of the melody she was playing. It was very sweet and melancholic. She kept on glancing at him and smiling every now and then, which added to the feel of the music. "You seem kind but at the

37

same time useless," said Jeffery. He turned and walked to the love seat closer to the podium and sat quietly, listening to the harp.

Jeffery remembered the Fogbusts telling him that he needed to talk to Lake Morgan and that's why they had sent him here. Besides the initials *LM* on some objects in the room, Jeffery couldn't seem to grasp how he was going to find Lake Morgan or what benefits meeting him would bring. Jeffery began to nod his head slowly to the sound of the harp and tried to clear his mind. He looked at the wall with the portraits of mermaids and his eyes rested on a blue shelf, mounted to the wall and its edges gilded. Situated atop the shelf, he noticed a small, hand-sized figurine of a navy-blue harp with light-blue strings. The idea of listening to the sound of a real harp while looking at a miniature one seemed to have some sort of subliminal meaning to Jeffery but he couldn't figure out exactly what.

The harpist continued to play effortlessly and endlessly, causing the music to sound somewhat ethereal. Jeffery even wondered for a second whether she ever got tired or hungry. Feeling a little frustrated with her lack of communication, Jeffery questioned her importance to the place. Sure, she was playing beautifully, and to some she may look attractive, but what was really the point of all that if she couldn't speak? He decided to not take notice of her. Jeffery started to feel heavier so he got more comfortable on the couch. Feeling more relaxed and hazy, his eyes closed gently as he fell into a deep sleep. His mouth was open a little where his lips met. Then in the deepest stage of sleep, Jeffery began to dream.

* * *

Jeffery dreamed he was standing on top of a white cloud very high up in the sky. Beneath him were several other clouds of various sizes, all in different shades of blue. Jeffery looked around but could not see anything else except for those clouds. The temperature was warm and he could feel his body balance gracefully on top of that cloud. Suddenly, a few small, blue songbirds came flying by and landed on his cloud as they sang like angels. They were quite round with tiny black feet and beaks. Jeffery reached into his pocket and pulled out some seeds, which he offered them. The birds started eating happily and this made Jeffery smile. As he stood back up, Jeffery noticed it was getting a bit windy and put his hands back in his pockets. The current began to pick up. His arms began to shiver and the birds flew away leaving some seeds behind. Jeffery crossed his arms in an attempt to keep warm and walked to the edge. Right beneath it he saw a turquoise cloud of a similar size float by with an oval-shaped mirror, about a foot long, resting at its center. Swirling around the mirror were indigo flames forming artistic shapes. Jeffery looked directly into the mirror and saw dark-blue shadows approaching but couldn't see his own reflection. He stared into the center of the mirror and saw the shapes getting even darker. He felt powerfully drawn to the mirror and these shadows. Though he did not remember tilting, Jeffery found himself falling into the mirror, where the dark shadows enrobed him in what felt like an abysmal eternity. Jeffery kept falling and could feel his body falling faster and faster until finally he heard a splash and realized he had landed in warm water. Even then, he kept falling deeper. He adjusted his head trying to see the surface but noticed that he was far from it. All he could see was the dark indigo water around him and a bright blue beam piercing the water overhead.

* * *

Jeffery woke up with a gasp. Thinking he was all wet, he began rubbing his hands all over himself but was surprised to find that he was already dry. As he looked around the room, he noticed that nothing had changed. Even the lady was still sitting in her place, playing the harp. Jeffery got up and began to look at the walls again, nervously trying to find anything resembling his dream. Feeling frustrated and annoyed, he walked right up to her with all his fury.

"Really, all you do is play all day and not make one peeping sound?" he said angrily while attempting to hit the harp. Instead of knocking it over, his hand went right through it as if it weren't even there. This left him in a state of shock. Jeffery attempted another hit but his hand went right through it again. Jeffery looked at the harpist and saw her look up at him and smile for a second, then she continued to play. "Are you not even touchable?" he asked in amazement. He reached out both his arms attempting to push her but his arms went right through her. "Amazing!" he exclaimed. After pulling his arms out, Jeffery walked back towards the living room, wrapped in thought. He couldn't get over what he had just experienced.

"So it's like you're there but you don't even exist," said Jeffery, ranting. "Just unbelievable. I mean, how were you even born?" he added, opening out both his arms. Jeffery dropped them back down to his sides and began walking around. Confusion began to preoccupy his mind. Where was this Lake Morgan supposed to be? Had the Fogbusts accidently sent him to the wrong place? Jeffery rubbed his hands through his hair then down the back of his head. "I am supposed to meet with Lake Morgan. Have you even heard of him?" he asked the harpist again. After not getting a response, Jeffery kicked the carpet. He began to walk around faster and faster, beginning to feel anguished. He decided to sit on the love seat, facing directly across from the podium and harpist. Jeffery kept bouncing his eyes back and forth between the two while her soft hands played on.

His eyes rested on her exposed white thighs, causing him to wonder more about her origin. As he thought more about this, he began to hear a noise, like some sort of machine had started up in another room. Jeffery began to look around. The noise was coming from the direction of the podium, so he focused his gaze on that. The sound began to get louder but the harpist continued playing as though nothing out of place was going on.

40

She kept playing calmly, her fingers running through the strings as though she were gently picking flowers.

The noise level increased even more, and then blasted into a great electric boom which caused the podium to shake. It shook really hard, before a soft blue light began streaming out of it in a pulsing flash. Jeffery sat back, holding on to the love seat as the room lit up hypnotically. His eyes squinted with each flashing beam of blue, as he struggled to keep them open.

After a few seconds, the commotion came to a sudden halt and the room went back to normal. Jeffery put his hands down and continued to stare at the podium. He glanced at the harp and the lady but saw no difference there. Then, from the top of the podium, a figure arose and floated above it. It was a big, white masquerade mask with two black lines for eyes and a short black line acting as a nose. It had firm black lips with a mustache made of a black line, like a twig snapped in half. Resting around the edge of the mask was a mane of blue smoke that swirled in all directions—round and round, slowly one way, quickly the other. The figure focused its attention on Jeffery and Jeffery stared back while the harpist histrionically played on.

"Lake Morgan?" asked Jeffery.

"Yes," replied the figure, "and you must be Jeffery."

"I am," said Jeffery.

"I have been expecting to meet with you," said Lake Morgan.

"I as well," said Jeffery. The two of them looked at each other. Lake Morgan's face, being a solid mask, didn't express any emotion. Jeffery felt as though some sort of competition was about to arise but he decided to be polite.

"Well, I was sent here by the Fogbusts to obtain some sort of knowledge from you," explained Jeffery.

"Yes, I am well aware," said Lake Morgan.

"Have you spoken to them?" asked Jeffery.

"I have," replied Lake Morgan. "Let's get started, shall we?"

"Sure," said Jeffery.

"Well, take a seat," said Lake Morgan. Jeffery sat back down on the love seat and got comfortable. Lake Morgan glided gracefully, moving like a stingray swimming through clear waters, and slid noiselessly onto the love seat across from Jeffery. As he flew, the bluish wisps fluttered gently around him like a cape, but with elegance and cool air. Jeffery noticed the harpist look their way and smile as she played her instrument. Her tune and the flight of Lake Morgan combined to create a very peculiar scene that was quite theatrical.

"Who is she?" asked Jeffery. "She plays really well but it's like she doesn't exist."

"Yes, I know," said Lake Morgan. "She's one of my harp players and she is instructed to do nothing but play."

"One can't even touch her!" protested Jeffery. "I tried touching her earlier and my hands went right through her!"

"I know," said Lake Morgan. "That's how I want her to be."

"You were actually able to make her like that?" asked Jeffery.

"Of course," said Lake Morgan. "A man can do anything he wants if he has wealth and power."

"So you mean—" started Jeffery, hesitating before continuing, "that you made her specifically to play the harp for you?"

"Yes," admitted Lake Morgan, "simply for my own entertainment."

"And she likes it that way?" asked Jeffery.

"You really think I care?" asked Lake Morgan calmly, trying to sound dignified.

"Well, you at least must have some sort of idea," argued Jeffery.

"How so?" asked Lake Morgan.

"You never thought about it?" asked Jeffery.

"Never," said Lake Morgan. "And there is no need to worry about that."

Jeffery frowned for a second, and then glanced at the harpist, attempting to see the woman within. "There's got to be a reason," he insisted.

"Maybe there is one," said Lake Morgan. "But why sweat over her? She is here just to play me the harp, that's all."

"You just... " started Jeffery.

"Jeffery, a man mustn't be too concerned about those beneath him," said Lake Morgan sternly. "That is why you are sent here, to learn so." Jeffery fell silent. Lake Morgan rose from the love seat and flew over to the harpist. "Let me ask you," he started, "what is the point of giving value to those who don't claim it themselves?"

Jeffery's eyes widened with shock at Lake Morgan's callous comment. Nonetheless, he remained seated. He looked at the harpist and briefly observed her gentle hands playing, her luminous hair and eyes gleaming, and her smooth body without a single blemish. How could one not value such a lady, entirely devoted to playing her harp? After all, she had no other purpose.

"Do you at least appreciate her?" asked Jeffery, focusing his eyes on Lake Morgan. Lake Morgan fell into a silence as the harpist continued playing gently. After a moment, Jeffery couldn't help but ask, "Or do you not?"

"I see exactly why Apple insisted on sending you here," said Lake Morgan. He then flew back to the love seat across from Jeffery and looked at him from across the table.

"What do you know about the Fogbusts?" asked Jeffery. "And why does that even matter? I asked you, do you at least appreciate her or not?"

"Enough," said Lake Morgan. "You're beginning to get on my nerves."

"As if you're not doing the same to me?" argued Jeffery. The two of them paused and looked at each other.

"Are you a man?" asked Lake Morgan. "Are you a member of the male sex?"

"What's that got to do with my question?" said Jeffery.

"Everything," said Lake Morgan. "You have been sent here to me to learn your place. As a man, you need to not worry about pesky things. You need to concern yourself more with how you will rise to power. Power is everything to a man."

"Power?" asked Jeffery.

"Your masculinity," replied Lake Morgan. "You have really tender thoughts. You're a man as long as you are able to have what you want and what you think you deserve. That is what matters."

Jeffery felt those words enter his ear and circulate through his body causing his blood to rage in disapproval. "What do you mean?" he questioned further in frustration. "Why is this even important?"

"It's what you were sent here for," said Lake Morgan, without changing his tone.

"The Fogbusts said that I am here to learn some sort of life lesson from you," said Jeffery.

"And this is it. I need to coach you on your masculinity. Apple thinks you are too tender and sweet-minded. Those are not the proper qualities of a man," explained Lake Morgan.

Jeffery then thought of George and Fruit. He missed their kind words and gentle approach but he knew that they might be considered helpless in the eyes of Lake Morgan.

"Well, what have you got to say?" asked Jeffery calmly, after a pause. Lake Morgan continued staring at him. He then flew to the wall behind the sofa and floated near a long sword made of white gold which also had the initials *LM* etched into it.

"Being a man is all about being free. Free to control what you want, even who you want," said Lake Morgan. "Take a look around this room. You can see that my success over the years has brought me all this luxury and comfort. *Why,* you might ask? Because I think like a *man.*"

Jeffery looked again around the room at all the hanging ornaments and figurines, and then glanced at the harpist. "And what's the significance of all this?" he asked, looking back at Lake Morgan.

"Well, you clearly can see how much I have," replied Lake Morgan.

"I see that," said Jeffery, "but I also see that you don't have a body. You're just made of fuming gas and a mask."

Lake Morgan tilted to his side. "And what's that supposed to mean?" he asked, sounding casual and undisturbed.

"Well, you just fly around listening to that harp and blast in from lights out of nowhere. Where exactly is this masculinity of yours?" questioned Jeffery.

"A man isn't about the way he looks," answered Lake Morgan. "It's about how much he has and is able to do." This made Jeffery's left eyebrow arch up inquisitively.

"What *can* you do?" asked Jeffery. Lake Morgan flew back to the love seat he was situated on and floated while facing Jeffery.

"Can I offer you a drink?" he asked sternly.

"Alright," said Jeffery hesitantly. Lake Morgan sent out a flashing beam of light-blue light from his forehead and aimed it at the end of the coffee table. The shot lasted a few seconds then disappeared, allowing a small puddle of smoke to form then evaporate, leaving behind a glass of blue martini. Next to the martini lay a small pile of blue powder and beside it, some kind of stick, stained with an indigo dye.

"What's that?" asked Jeffery.

"Martini," answered Lake Morgan.

"And that?" asked Jeffery, pointing at the pile of blue powder.

"That's just cider," explained Lake Morgan. "I like to enjoy it on the side while having my drinks." Jeffery picked up the glass and started sipping the martini. It was very sweet and tasted like a blend of fruits with a rich dose of vanilla.

"It tastes good," said Jeffery.

"Just drink it, don't talk about it," ordered Lake Morgan. "You're a man."

Jeffery drank quietly and looked around the room. He felt as though he didn't have much to say, partly because he didn't feel at ease with Lake Morgan. Jeffery drank a bit more of the martini and felt a drip run down his lips and land on his bare chest. He looked down and wiped it off with his hand, then put the drink down.

"Got anything else to say?" Jeffery asked. Lake Morgan just looked at him. "I asked you, have you got anything else to say?"

"You have lots to learn," said Lake Morgan after pausing his stare. He looked to his left then scoffed. Jeffery crossed his eyes in response to Lake Morgan's attitude. He picked up the stick and started poking at the cider. It was finely ground but contained a few crystals. Jeffery was also able to make out tiny flecks of dark blue and silver sparkles.

"Do you eat this?" he asked curiously.

"No," said Lake Morgan, "you inhale it through your nose." Jeffery was puzzled. He examined the hollow stick in his hand, noticing it had two small holes on each end. After poking at the powdery cider a few more times, Jeffery looked back at Lake Morgan.

"You mean I actually stick this in my nostrils?" asked Jeffery.

"Yes, you do," answered Lake Morgan. "Try to go a bit slow and after a few snorts it should kick in."

"What is this stuff?" asked Jeffery, sounding as uncertain as he felt.

"I told you," said Lake Morgan, "it is cider—powdered cider." Jeffery bent in a bit and started slowly bending his head over the cider. He tried to smell it but couldn't smell anything. He placed the indigo stick in it and brought his head down closer. He gently inserted one end of the stick into his right nostril. It poked him a bit but Jeffery adjusted it to his comfort. Taking in a deep breath, he snorted hard and felt the cider run up his nostrils and into his nose like desert sand. Jeffery took another snort then started doing the same with his left nostril.

All Jeffery then could smell was hot apple cider. He began to feel smoke coming out of his ears, which also smelled like apple cider. His eyes turned a bit red and he felt his whole head getting heavier. Jeffery felt somewhat relaxed but didn't have much control over his body, so he sat back facing Lake Morgan and watched the gray-blue smoke come out of his ears and gradually disappear into the air. Lake Morgan focused his gaze on Jeffery but showed almost no emotion, just casual observation from his mask-face while his blue plumes gently wafted in the air around him.

"Feeling better?" asked Lake Morgan, giving Jeffery a sly look.

"Not really," replied Jeffery, his heart pounding faster.

"That's what it feels like to be a man," said Lake Morgan. As if on cue, the harpist began playing another melody that contributed to the eccentric state of mind Jeffery had entered. His jaw slowly dropped and his eyes rolled back in his head. He was still conscious and aware of his surroundings, but he felt paralyzed. Lake Morgan flew up to the ceiling and started flying around and between the chandeliers, looking down at Jeffery.

"What's happening to me?" questioned Jeffery, intoxicated.

"You're watching me," answered Lake Morgan sounding as if he were teasing a child. "I am up *high*." Jeffery passed out; he felt as if everything had disappeared. Lake Morgan lowered himself and started flying around Jeffery. He began to dance to the harmony of the harp as though he were celebrating some joyous holiday. He danced his way upward towards the ceiling, then flew around the room.

A long span of time went by and Jeffery woke up feeling as though he had taken another short nap. He looked around the room, stretched, and rubbed his eyes. He took notice of Lake Morgan dancing and flying around the room to the melody of the harp. Jeffery then looked at the lady but she continued playing without taking her eyes off the harp. Her turquoise nails looked like little pearls rolling across the strings as she played. Lake Morgan flew behind Jeffery then back to the love seat and floated down, returning to his seat.

"Feeling good?" asked Lake Morgan with a manly tone.

Jeffery did not respond. Instead, he glanced around the room then down at his boots. He really didn't want to talk to Lake Morgan anymore and had started feeling pain in his left shoulder. The harpist slowed her tune and returned to the one she had been playing initially.

"What can you tell me about the Fogbusts?" asked Jeffery, exchanging looks with Lake Morgan.

"Well, I've known them for quite some time," replied Lake Morgan.

"They said that you have helped them, and at one point even gave them the crocksvenbulb to guide them on their way, or something," said Jeffery. Lake Morgan laughed.

"They said that to you?" he asked shamelessly. Jeffery nodded in response. "Yeah, they have a long history together. They still believe that their marriage is the will of God or something. They're lunatics—that's why they sent you to me. They expect I am going to get you to man up."

"And how is that significant?" asked Jeffery.

"Your feelings are too tender," said Lake Morgan. "And I don't know if I can even help the way they expected."

"I don't think it's necessary," said Jeffery. "I am who I am."

"You won't benefit yourself that way," responded Lake Morgan. "Take a look at all the possessions around you. Do you really think that I would have all of this if I were as tender as you? That's not what a man is destined for."

"I'm not sure I need all your possessions," said Jeffery.

"A man is all about power," said Lake Morgan assertively.

"And what about the crocksvenbulb?" asked Jeffery. "It seemed to mean something to them. They had it hanging on their wall."

"Well, I coached them for a while in their marriage," started Lake Morgan, "so I gave it to them as a gift. They said that they were expecting you from their god and would give you the crocksvenbulb so that when I coach you, you'd never forget my lessons." Jeffery frowned at this with confusion. He really didn't think that Lake Morgan had provided him with useful *lessons*. Jeffery felt patronized and frowned upon by Lake Morgan and he also disapproved of his need for objects to represent his wealth.

"Well, I put it back next to the other crocksvenbulbs," said Jeffery. "I thought that it belonged there."

"It did, initially," said Lake Morgan. "But they liked it and they said that it almost matched their pants so I let them keep it. After all, it isn't that difficult for me to get anything I want." Jeffery looked back at all the walls and all the hanging objects. "You can be a very wealthy man," explained Lake Morgan. "You need to accept the fact that every man's worth is based on his wealth and power. It is the only way he earns respect."

"Is that all the Fogbusts sent me here to hear?" asked Jeffery.

"Precisely," replied Lake Morgan, causing Jeffery to scoff.

"Sounds like something Apple would say," muttered Jeffery.

"Same letter, different envelope," said Lake Morgan, smirking at his own cleverness.

"I'm sure that must have been Apple's idea, not Fruit's," stated Jeffery.

"It doesn't matter," answered Lake Morgan. "A man is here to learn, not worry about the sentiments of women."

"And anything else?" asked Jeffery, trying to sound confident.

Lake Morgan gave him a calm look. "Would you like to go for a walk?" he asked invitingly.

"A walk?" asked Jeffery. "Where?"

"Come with me," instructed Lake Morgan, flying over to the podium. Jeffery stood up to follow Lake Morgan, who was by now hovering behind and slightly above the podium. Seeing where he was expected to go, Jeffery walked around the living room set and approached him.

"I wonder where you're taking us?" questioned Jeffery.

"Somewhere perfectly relaxing for a man," replied Lake Morgan. Jeffery wondered whether it would be as relaxing for him.

"Well, alright," he breathed softly.

Lake Morgan looked at the wall in front of the living room set and opened his mouth wide. He breathed out dark blue air that followed the length of the wall, touching all the ornaments in that area before it slowly disappeared. Jeffery looked and wondered what he was about to witness. He heard the sound of a crack start at the top of the wall. Gently, the wall separated from the ceiling and began sliding vertically, disappearing underground. All the ornaments and shelves remained undisturbed throughout the somewhat slow process. When the wall was almost halfway down, Jeffery saw a bright beam of medium blue light reveal itself. After the wall had completely disappeared into the floor, behind the beam of light

Jeffery saw another wall, slightly darker than the beam of light, and about three times his height. The beam itself was in the shape of a star with several small points that seemed to move as the beam glowed. Lake Morgan flew towards it then looked at Jeffery. Jeffery took this as an invitation and quickly walked to the beam. Lake Morgan entered it from the top and disappeared in an instant. Jeffery first put his hand in it and noticed that his hand was going right through it. He turned his head back and looked at the harpist and thought about her for a brief moment. After feeling a sense of empathy, Jeffery turned his head back and entered the beam. Once inside, he felt his feet standing on solid ground and that the floor was much harder under his boots. He also noticed that his torso was reflecting blue light from the beam and that he couldn't see anything but the beam's lighting around him.

"We're almost there," Jeffery heard Lake Morgan say. Jeffery looked around but saw no sign of him. All he felt was the light from the beam bouncing off his body and that his head was shifting as if he were entering another time zone. "Almost," repeated Lake Morgan.

"Must be a very bright place," said Jeffery.

"You'll see," said Lake Morgan.

"It's almost like traveling into a bolt of lightning," said Jeffery. Then shortly after, the beam completely disappeared to reveal a rather distinct and extravagantly glorious place. Jeffery found himself standing on a floor that stretched out far ahead of him. It was made of marble, white in color with many shades of blue. On both sides of the floor there were gaps so wide that if someone were to walk over them, they would fall into an abyss of darkness. Across the gaps were two very large walls made of aquamarine that stood proud and looked indestructible. Jeffery looked back and saw a wall behind him made of solid limestone encrusted with jewels—sapphires neatly arranged forming the initials *LM* in large letters. Turning back around,

51

Jeffery walked forward a few paces and heard his footsteps pound against the hard marble floor. The two gaps on either side of the floor made it feel like a walkway. Up ahead, Jeffery noticed that the floor seemed to lead to another limestone wall but it was far away, giving the walkway the feel of a bridge. As he stood looking at it, he felt Lake Morgan rub against his right shoulder then gently float up. Jeffery looked up to face him then continued looking around the place.

"I had this all built within a week," started Lake Morgan, sounding proud. "I… "

"And how was that possible?" interrupted Jeffery.

"Well, as a man, why believe in a god when you can actually become one?" argued Lake Morgan. "With enough power, a man can have everything ready and done for him in no time!"

Jeffery looked down. The two of them started walking slowly down the marble floor. The air felt cool and was very breathable.

"How did you end up having all of this?" asked Jeffery.

"Some of it I inherited from my father, but most of it I created with my strength and power," explained Lake Morgan.

"You have a father?" asked Jeffery.

"He died," answered Lake Morgan. "Now I hope I will have my own son someday. Having a son is very important for a man."

"Why is that?" asked Jeffery.

"It just is," answered Lake Morgan. "It is part of your manhood, living on, and it also allows for inheritance." Jeffery looked at Lake Morgan talking and saw that he was not making eye contact with him. He began to feel a slight attraction to Lake Morgan even though he was upset by his bigotry.

"You never considered allowing someone to share your will?" he asked, trying not to sound lustful. Lake Morgan laughed as if he had just heard the stupidest joke ever.

"Not a chance!" replied Lake Morgan, then laughed some more. Jeffery looked at the aquamarine wall to his left, trying to hide his shyness and hoping that Lake Morgan wouldn't notice. "There is no need to let anyone half your worth share your prosperity," Lake Morgan added. Jeffery crossed his eyes. He felt as though Lake Morgan was able to read his thoughts and therefore directed his words clearly at him.

"I bet Apple may have liked to have some of it," suggested Jeffery nervously while trying to change the subject. Lake Morgan let out another laugh.

"The Fogbusts," started Lake Morgan with a sigh. "I hope their god is well enough for them." This brought Jeffery a flashback to some of his conversation with the Fogbusts. He remembered them making a reference to a god named Allie and how he had wondered if he would ever meet him. He also remembered their appearance, them being really tall and round with three legs and two heads sharing the same body. Jeffery also began thinking of Fruit's voice and how gentle it was, especially when referring to Allie.

"Well, if you're there, Allie, I wish you could show him his imperfection," Jeffery whispered to himself.

"What was that?" asked Lake Morgan.

"Oh, nothing," said Jeffery.

"I thought you said something," said Lake Morgan.

"No, nothing," said Jeffery.

"A man must not be ashamed of his thoughts," said Lake Morgan. "Unless it is something shameful, a man must always be proud of his thoughts and not fear saying them." Jeffery felt trapped and even a little bit embarrassed. He didn't want to admit that he had thought of Allie, knowing that Lake Morgan would start preaching something else at him.

"I was just wondering how this place would look if these walls were also made of marble and decorated with pink pearls," said Jeffery.

"Pink?" asked Lake Morgan, sounding unsatisfied. "No, that's not a man's first choice. Would you like it?"

"Not really," said Jeffery untruthfully. "I think it'd be odd; that's why I thought about it." Jeffery cleared his throat.

"Very well," said Lake Morgan after finally looking at him briefly. The two of them continued to walk.

"Is blue your favorite color?" asked Jeffery.

"It is," said Lake Morgan. "It's a man's choice. Blue is also the color of elegance and class."

"Interesting," said Jeffery. "And why is that?"

"It just is," responded Lake Morgan, sounding blunt.

"What do you think of green?" asked Jeffery. "The Fogbusts' room was green and they were dressed all in green."

"Green is nice," replied Lake Morgan, "but color isn't something that one is supposed to dwell on. You see, Jeffery, a man's choice in color isn't about how much he likes it, but more about how he uses it. I like blue, for instance, but you see how many things I own and how valuable they are."

"True," said Jeffery, uncertain but trying to sound congenial.

"Why, no!" said Lake Morgan disappointedly. Jeffery turned to his right and noticed Lake Morgan flying fast over the gap on his side. Lake Morgan flew to the aquamarine wall and lowered himself. Jeffery walked to the edge and stood looking at Lake Morgan.

"Is everything ok?" asked Jeffery loudly.

"No, there is a scratch on the wall," said Lake Morgan. "That will detract from its value."

"Oh," said Jeffery. He hesitated for a second and thought about what he had whispered to himself earlier.

"Good thing I can fix it," said Lake Morgan. This sent a rush of energy-flow through Jeffery's veins, causing his eyes to widen. He couldn't believe what he had just heard. Lake Morgan opened his mouth and blew some light-blue smoke on the wall, and the scratch faded away.

"Better now?" asked Jeffery. Lake Morgan kept looking at the wall. He blew a bigger gust of smoke at the damaged part of it and watched the blemish disappear completely. After looking over his work, Lake Morgan gave a nod of certainty and flew back.

"A man must not allow things to go unfixed or fall below his standards," explained Lake Morgan. Jeffery nodded gently.

"Shouldn't that be applied to everyone?" asked Jeffery calmly.

"Sure," said Lake Morgan, "but believe me, only a real man can live up to this standard."

The two of them resumed walking. Jeffery sighed but continued observing the elegance of the place. He was wrapped in thought about what had just happened. How was it possible that he hoped that Allie would show Lake Morgan his imperfection and within minutes Lake Morgan had discovered the scratch? Then again, Jeffery didn't think that it was a huge deal to Lake Morgan, who had been able to fix it within seconds with a couple of breaths. This also made Jeffery wonder whether Lake Morgan had even lived through enough experiences to give him the legitimacy to teach any sort of lessons. Finally, Jeffery also began questioning whether the Fogbusts' choice of sending him to Lake Morgan was even a wise one.

Jeffery looked down and observed the coloring of the marble tiles once more. He really admired the splashes of white and different blues which gave the floor a warm and calming feel. Jeffery saw that Lake Morgan had an elegant taste in designs, but wished he had a less callous and strict heart.

Jeffery then noticed that some tiles had little bits of powdered gold and platinum permanently scattered on them; he smiled with deep admiration.

"Yes, it gets more valuable from here," said Lake Morgan, taking notice with pride.

"Really?" asked Jeffery. "What more do you own?"

"Way more than you think or will ever see," replied Lake Morgan. "A whole lot more." Jeffery wondered—did he even want to see more? But the thought was disrupted when his eye glimpsed a shadow roaming across the aquamarine wall to his left. Jeffery took a second look but saw nothing.

"I have spent years making the most of myself," said Lake Morgan. "My father was a *real* man and he taught me well."

"I see," said Jeffery. Then he noticed the shadow again, moving a bit faster this time. "They say that the pear falls close to its roots."

"Exactly," agreed Lake Morgan. "I come from a bloodline of very honorable men." After noticing the shadow a third time, Jeffery stopped and faced the wall. This halt got Lake Morgan to turn and face Jeffery. "Is everything alright?" he asked with his deep voice.

"I keep seeing some shadow," answered Jeffery. "I can't seem to tell what it is. Oh wait, there it is!" Jeffery pointed at the wall and saw the shadow coming closer and next to it was a lighter shadow.

"Want to watch them closely?" offered Lake Morgan with a sly smile.

"What are they?" asked Jeffery curiously.

"Just watch," instructed Lake Morgan. Jeffery looked carefully and began to see the shadows getting closer. Then before long, he noticed sharks swimming in his direction then turning around.

"Sharks?" questioned Jeffery.

"Keep watching," said Lake Morgan. Jeffery then realized that behind the aquamarine wall was actually water; the whole wall was actually a large aquarium parallel to the marble walkway!

"Amazing!" exclaimed Jeffery. He noticed that there were small fish swimming behind the wall as well. One of the sharks got really close and ate one of them then turned around, swimming with its tail facing him. "This is incredible, how did you come up with this?"

"A fine man only affords the finest," replied Lake Morgan.

"Magnificent!" exclaimed Jeffery. He turned around and walked to the other side of the walkway and noticed a similar shape on the other wall.

"They get closer to the wall when they're feeding," clarified Lake Morgan. "Most of the smaller fish are located there."

"This is just incredible," said Jeffery. "Unbelievable. I am curious, why sharks?"

"They're a symbol for power and competition," replied Lake Morgan. "They represent that not even the most aggressive competitor can defeat me, or own better." Jeffery watched the sharks closer. To him, Lake Morgan's words were very bitter, yet seductive.

"The best for the very best," said Jeffery, trying to sound polite by adding a smile. Lake Morgan took notice of this but did not reply. He just continued strolling, leaving Jeffery with no choice but to follow. As he walked, Jeffery observed the walls on both sides and enjoyed the sight of the sharks and fish swimming. He also began to think about his feelings towards Lake Morgan. Jeffery despised his callousness and lack of emotions towards anything other than his masculinity. But he also admired Lake Morgan's physical appearance—that of being a mask figure surrounded by swirls that allowed him to fly rather than walk. Jeffery imagined Lake Morgan blowing out love from his mouth and bottling it like a fragrance. It would be the finest love potion, mixed with the ingredients of lust and wealth. On the other hand,

Jeffery didn't deny that the ingredients of bigotry and arrogance would make their way into this potion.

As the two of them drew closer to the other end of the walkway, Jeffery began to slow down. He noted that the limestone door before him was identical to the one at the start of the walkway. He turned around and looked at the place one more time. The sharks were slowly disappearing; the aquamarine and marble seemed more lustrous than ever.

"Having a good view?" asked Lake Morgan. Startled out of his reverie, Jeffery turned around and faced him.

"Are you able to read my mind?" he asked curiously.

"Are you ready to see what's past this door?" Lake Morgan questioned after a brief scoff.

"Most likely," said Jeffery, sounding hesitant. "What's in there?"

"Remember when I told you that the Fogbusts liked the crocksvenbulb and I let them keep it?" asked Lake Morgan.

"Yes," said Jeffery with a small nod.

"Well, that wasn't entirely true," announced Lake Morgan.

"What do you mean?" asked Jeffery.

"It's a long story," said Lake Morgan. "But my point is, whenever I give someone a possession, it always makes its way back to me." Jeffery thought for a second. He remembered when the Fogbusts gave him the crocksvenbulb, then later on he hung it on the nail next to the other ones.

"And?" asked Jeffery, expecting Lake Morgan to say more.

"You," started Lake Morgan, "perhaps that's something you will discover by yourself later." He then turned to face the limestone wall and gently blew some warm, blue air on it. The wall gradually reflected the color and turned translucent. Lake Morgan flew right through it then looked at Jeffery, indicating that he do the same. Jeffery stepped in through the wall then turned back to get one last view of the walkway and aquamarine walls, only this time they were all reflecting the blue color of the translucent wall. Jeffery stared in awe at the place, as though he were looking out a window. But before long, the view disappeared and Jeffery was greeted with a solid navy blue wall made of brick. Jeffery turned around to explore. The whole room was made of navy blue brick and at the corner was a tall lamp with a silver and dark blue shade providing some gentle blue light. In the center of the space was a car, metallic blue in color, which looked very modern. It seemed like a dream car that was designed and constructed in the very distant future. It had four doors, four wheels and a very curvy shape. Immediately across from the front of the car was a big garage door that was also blue and metallic. Above it was Lake Morgan, floating around as usual.

"This looks incredible," stated Jeffery as he stepped closer to get a better look at the car.

"Don't touch it!" ordered Lake Morgan with a scold. Jeffery stepped back and looked at him. Lake Morgan flew down and came face to face with Jeffery. "Are you a real man?" he asked coldly. Jeffery looked innocently into Lake Morgan's eyes. Their flat lack of dimensions made Jeffery feel a sense of unknowingness.

"Sure," replied Jeffery calmly.

"I am not totally convinced," said Lake Morgan. He flew back up into the air. "This isn't actually my car; I kept it for a friend who later on died."

"I am sorry," said Jeffery.

"It was his own fault," said Lake Morgan. "He was an idiot." Jeffery was shocked and widened his eyes. "But now, I will give you a taste of it. Cars are very important for a man," Lake Morgan continued after turning to face Jeffery.

"How so?" asked Jeffery.

"They represent structure and strength," answered Lake Morgan, "and above all, *control*." Jeffery looked at the car. It seemed to have a solid chassis and also looked very luxurious. It had silver wheels with black tires that were made of rubber.

"I see," said Jeffery.

"And before I let you try driving it," said Lake Morgan, "I want you to have something until it finds its way back to me."

"Have what?" asked Jeffery, feeling a small shake in his gut.

"This," said Lake Morgan, looking straight at him. Lake Morgan opened his mouth and blew out a small piece of navy blue cloud that fell out and landed on Jeffery's chest. Jeffery felt its soft bottom press against his skin then the cloud faded out, leaving behind wisps of lingering bits. Once its bits had dissipated, they revealed a small version of the crocksvenbulb that hung like a pendant from a silver necklace around Jeffery's neck. Jeffery held the pendant and looked at it carefully. It was dark blue but its ceramic material was the same as the larger crocksvenbulb.

"Thank you," said Jeffery politely.

"Don't," said Lake Morgan. "Just keep it on. Your manhood will develop with it as it'll always remind you to stay in place." Jeffery looked at Lake Morgan once more, then sighed.

"Then it will come back to you, somehow," he said softly. Lake Morgan just looked at Jeffery for a moment and said nothing. Jeffery looked at the car and began to wander about. Lake Morgan flew down to the right side of the car. He willed himself into the car, passing through the metal door, and floated above the passenger seat. At that same moment, the left door opened. Jeffery saw Lake Morgan looking back at him through the rear window of the car. He walked to the driver's seat, got in, and closed the door. The second the door was closed, the car jumped to life as the dashboard and interior illuminated. Jeffery saw blue and white lights flashing in front of him, reflecting against the garage door.

"Keep your feet on the gas and brake," said Lake Morgan. "Here comes the experience of a lifetime for you." Jeffery did as instructed and grabbed hold of the steering wheel. The engine roared with energy, like a horse pounding the ground, eager to explode down a raceway.

"Are we going out that way?" asked Jeffery, pointing at the garage door.

"You bet we are," said Lake Morgan, sounding serious. As he turned to look at the garage door, Jeffery felt a slight vibration in the room. The garage door opened slowly upwards and revealed a tunnel. The walls were black with blue lights that ran in circular patterns up one wall, up and around the ceiling, then down the other wall.

"Wow!" exclaimed Jeffery, his skin electrified with goose bumps.

"Well, what are you waiting for?" yelled Lake Morgan. "Drive!" Jeffery pushed the gas pedal and began to drive towards the tunnel. Before long, he drove into it and began to pick up speed. "Faster, feel the speed!" cheered Lake Morgan.

"Where are we going?" asked Jeffery.

"Just keep driving," scolded Lake Morgan. Jeffery gradually increased his speed and as he drove on, he noticed that the tunnel wasn't a straight path like the walkway; it turned left and right, making the path seem like a one-way road.

"Do you think we're going too fast?" asked Jeffery.

"Shut up and drive faster," ordered Lake Morgan. Jeffery began to drive faster but began to feel a rush going through his head.

"This is a bit scary," said Jeffery.

"Come on," said Lake Morgan, "a man enjoys the rush of speed, especially when he's in control of it." Jeffery drove even faster. The blue lights began to look like stripes as he drove. Up ahead, Jeffery saw what looked like a punching bag in the shape of a clown hanging from the ceiling of the tunnel. The clown was round, had very curly hair and his clothes were striped blue and white.

"Uh oh," said Jeffery worriedly. But before he had time to hesitate, he drove right into the punching bag, sending it flying ahead across the tunnel. The bump shook Jeffery and caused Lake Morgan to laugh briefly. Jeffery drove over the punching bag, causing the wheels to let out an irritating sound that made him shriek.

"Come on, you should be enjoying this!" said Lake Morgan. "This is the core of masculinity right here." Jeffery couldn't seem to grasp Lake Morgan's way of thinking, especially while driving so fast in that tunnel. Driving on, Jeffery saw a woman playing a black electric guitar ahead in the distance. She was undressed, wearing only a pair of thigh-high boots of patent leather so shiny that it reflected the lights in the tunnel. Her hair was curly and light blue, in contrast to her dark blue top hat. Jeffery took notice of the initials *LM*, embossed on her hat in glittering thread, but before he could look again, he hit her, knocking her down along with the guitar, and drove right over her.

"Oh God!" yelled Jeffery. "That was an accident!"

"Doesn't matter," said Lake Morgan madly, "just keep driving the stupid vehicle." Jeffery wanted to stop but noticed that he didn't seem to have control over the car.

"What's happening?" asked Jeffery in a panic.

"Listen, Jeffery," started Lake Morgan sternly, "wherever you go, never forget that you are a man. And a real man never dwells on benefits other than his own. You knock down clowns, or you knock down whores, what matters most is that you create for yourself and seek *power*." Jeffery felt infuriated. He felt a strong rush of adrenaline and wanted to stop the car.

"How can I stop this?" he yelled.

"A man never stops," replied Lake Morgan. "Manhood is meant to be lived on."

"No, seriously!" yelled Jeffery. "This needs to stop!" Jeffery felt the car driving faster after he said this, so he grabbed onto the crocksvenbulb around his neck.

"So long," said Lake Morgan. Jeffery turned to face him.

"What do you mean?" asked Jeffery. Before he had finished his sentence, Lake Morgan had floated up and out through the roof of the car. Jeffery looked back and saw him floating up near the top of the tunnel, quickly shrinking in size as the car kept driving. Within seconds, the sight of Lake Morgan disappeared. Jeffery turned back around and grabbed the steering wheel. He tried stepping on the brakes a few times but only felt the car getting faster. Jeffery encountered another woman who was scantily dressed in a ripped, blue bikini. She was jumping in the air and waving her hands, which revealed the initials *LM* in large print tattooed on her stomach.

"Hi!" she said enthusiastically at Jeffery's approach.

"No! No! Move over!" yelled Jeffery. In seconds, the car hit her and barely slowed before it started accelerating again. Jeffery felt her flesh get crushed and thud against the car as it drove on, which sickened him. Soon afterwards, Jeffery saw Lake Morgan in front of the car.

"Enjoying a little psychedelic ride?" Lake Morgan asked, with the same teasing tone one might use when tickling a child. The car drove right through him. Jeffery sat still, in fear of looking in the rearview mirror. He did not want to see another sight of Lake Morgan, especially the way he willed himself in and out of places like a ghost.

"Oh God," said Jeffery. He felt a tightening sickness in his stomach so he turned to the passenger seat next to him and vomited. He threw up all of his bottled emotions, endlessly bursting out and splattering across the seat.

After sitting back up with tears in his eyes, Jeffery saw that the tunnel was coming to an end. A patch of indigo on the wall up ahead looked like an exit. "Oh no," said Jeffery. He tried to stop the car by stomping on the brakes, but again, only felt the car go faster. "Can't I have control over this insane agility?" he yelled. He sat back and looked at the exit ahead. Within seconds, the car drove right through it and went flying into an open sky. Jeffery held his head with both hands and let out a loud and anguished scream. Once the scream had used up all his breath, he looked back and saw that the tunnel had disappeared. High up in the sky hung a full moon so clear it appeared violet, illuminating for Jeffery a landscape of dark water and forest that seemed thousands of miles across. "Just no," sobbed Jeffery, feeling extremely nauseated. Closing his eyes, he felt the car tilt forward, thus he felt his weight being pulled down ahead. Jeffery opened his eyes and noticed that the car was lining up to take a long, slow dive into the water. Jeffery screamed even louder. The car dove and continued falling, nose down, toward the water. The sensation felt very similar to the dream Jeffery had had prior to meeting Lake Morgan. His heart raced faster than ever as the unstoppable force of gravity pulled him close.

Jeffery fell through an eternity, or so it seemed, until the car plunged into the water, causing a large and loud splash. The splash echoed in Jeffery's ears and the sudden stop of the car against liquid caused his body to bounce, bumping his head. After crashing through the surface, the car continued falling into the water, frightening Jeffery as he imagined an eternal drowning.

Chapter Three

Flying Among Unicorn Grace

Jeffery quickly opened the car door and forcefully pushed it, trying to battle the weight of the water. As the water began to seep into the car, he started to panic. He pushed and pushed and eventually pushed his hardest and got the door to gradually give way. This allowed more water into the car, soaking all of its interior, and Jeffery. He made his way out of the car and swam towards the surface, realizing that the car was sinking deeper. Jeffery continued swimming up, shivering due to the cold temperature of the water. Below him, he noticed a huge, dark orca that hadn't yet noticed him. Feeling startled, Jeffery tried to swim faster even though his arms were aching. The orca turned and seemed to disappear. Jeffery wondered whether it had eccentric abilities like Lake Morgan and might be watching him closely from a hiding spot. Trying to push all his thoughts and fears away, Jeffery continued swimming until the violet light of the moon grew brighter, indicating that he was getting close to the surface.

As Jeffery made his way up, a fish swam right up to his face, its eyes glowing pink in the dim moonlight. Jeffery looked at the fish and watched it quickly dart away. Realizing that he was almost out of air, he managed to swim faster until he finally reached the surface. The moment Jeffery popped out of the water, he threw his head back and took in an enormous breath. He continued gasping for air as he began treading near the surface, with most of his body still in the water. He noticed that there was land across from him, across from behind, and all around. The land behind was all forest while the land in front was a beach with a forest that was set back from it. Jeffery looked up and took notice of the violet moon. It was huge and the sky was indigo. After taking in a few more breaths, Jeffery decided to swim ahead to the beach in front of him. Suddenly remembering the orca, he swam as fast as he could, disregarding the pain and cold that threatened his body. Pushing beyond his own limits, he swam until he reached the shore and slowly crawled onto the beach. He took off his boots and tossed them aside then lay flat on his stomach and let his left cheek drop onto the sand. At the sight of the full moon, Jeffery exhaled and relaxed. His breathing slowed gradually until a wave of gratitude washed over him.

"I'm alive," said Jeffery slowly. "I'm alive," he whispered again and repeated until he closed his eyes and fell asleep.

* * *

The following morning, Jeffery opened his eyes and noticed that he hadn't moved since falling asleep. He felt something hard gently poking at his arm. Jeffery sat up and looked around. It was broad daylight and the sun was shining its warm, purple light across the beach. The water was a lighter purple and gleamed in response to the sun's reflection. The trees of the forests were dark purple and the sand on the beach was violet. Some sections of the forests were a pale gray and contained tiny dots of violet and maroon sparkles that danced to the hymn of the breezing air.

Jeffery searched to see what was poking him and was surprised to see a purple lobster, about a foot long. The lobster had a gentle smile on its face and watched him with curiosity. Jeffery raised his left eyebrow and observed the lobster. Its head and claws were very smooth and somewhat glossy. All of its legs were thin and not quite as dark as its top half.

"Hello there," said Jeffery with a smile. He reached out his hand in front of the lobster and allowed it to rub its cool claw against his palm. "You seem gentle," said Jeffery, petting the lobster. The lobster really enjoyed this companionship and seemed to relax. "I promise I won't flick you," Jeffery added, thinking back to George. "You're a bit too big anyways. I think you'll be ok."

Jeffery felt a sudden but slow breeze as a large shadow briefly covered the beach then disappeared. Turning around and craning his head to look at the sky, Jeffery saw a large black dragon flying proudly overhead. It had a long tail with purple scales and its front legs and jaws were very big and muscular, like the rest of its body. Its wingspan was extremely wide and the undersides of its wings were veined in purple and had thick, leathery edges that were patterned with purple scales matching the ones on its tail. The dragon flew casually across the sky then over the trees without taking notice of Jeffery.

"That was huge!" exclaimed Jeffery. He looked around for the lobster, picked it up carefully and put it on his lap. Jeffery found that petting the lobster helped ease his worries. Not long after, the dragon flew back in the direction from which it had originally appeared. Behind it flew two unicorns with white angel wings. Their bodies were a pale violet and their manes and tails were deep purple. Their hooves were jet black and their horns were a mix of silver and light purple. They flew gently and gracefully as though they had all the time in the world and as if immortality powered their wings and fueled their souls with joy. Above the forest on the facing island, another smaller dragon appeared and started flying in their direction. Jeffery stared at the sky in amazement. He adored the sight of these animals and their ability to fly despite their huge size. The lobster cuddled itself into Jeffery's lap, a sure sign it wanted more petting. Gently, Jeffery began rubbing his hands on it as though it were his favorite pet. "The power of animals is oftentimes greater than the power of anything else," said Jeffery.

The lobster hopped out of Jeffery's lap and began to play in the violet sand. Jeffery took a handful of the sand and poured it gently on the lobster's back. The lobster enjoyed this and started doing a happy little dance, which made Jeffery laugh. He took another handful and repeated this so the lobster shook it all off in an amusing manner and raised its claw asking for a high five. Jeffery gently clapped it with his hand and smiled.

"You're a cute little one, aren't you?" said Jeffery sweetly, feeling entertained. The lobster nodded and smiled back, causing Jeffery to laugh again. The lobster started bouncing lightly then looked at Jeffery. "You want me to jump?" asked Jeffery. "Alright." Jeffery stood up and began to jump in the air, amused that the lobster was eager to jump along. Clearly, this was just as amusing to the lobster. Suddenly, the lobster stopped jumping, ran between and around Jeffery's legs then took a turn into the water. It swam in for a bit then swam back out and ran back to Jeffery. Jeffery sat down and started petting it again. "You're wet," he said teasingly. The lobster jumped back into Jeffery's lap and curled up. Jeffery continued petting it then began to hum to it. He was sure the lobster was relaxing in response to his gentle rubbing. The lobster even rubbed its claws on Jeffery's knees, signaling its appreciation.

Jeffery looked at the shore and the island across the water. He focused on the dark purple foliage and thought about the dragons and unicorns. He asked the lobster whether it knew anything about them but the lobster just smiled. Jeffery looked up at the sky and saw a couple of clouds slowly float by. Both were purple and small; only one was slightly darker and denser than the other. A sudden movement in the water caught Jeffery's attention. It did not seem violent or weather-related, rather, it was a small swirl, yet mysterious. Before Jeffery could guess what this shift was, an enormous black orca leaped out of the water, soared right up into the air and landed with a splash so large it forced a lot of water onto the beach. The orca repeated this a second time, soaring upward, and flaunting every inch of its body. Jeffery noticed that its tail was purple and had lots of glitter that shined in the sunlight. After it landed back in the water, it created an even bigger and louder splash.

"Amazing," said Jeffery, astonished at the sight. Not a moment later, another unicorn flew by and plunged forward until it disappeared beyond the horizon. "Did you see that?" Jeffery asked the lobster. "That was fantastic!" Jeffery felt a vibration in the sand, like a tiny earthquake. He looked to his right and saw a dragon. It was roughly the size of the one he had seen earlier, but this one was walking along the shore. The dragon wagged its tail gently then flew off into the sky and over the forest of the neighboring island. Jeffery looked back down at the lobster. It did not seem fazed by the presence of the dragons, the unicorns or the orca. It was relaxed and really seemed to enjoy Jeffery's company and affection. Before long, the lobster began to let out a gentle squeak, low in volume and melodic in harmony. Its eyes were wide open but its body didn't move.

"Are you alright?" asked Jeffery.

"*Squeak squeak*," replied the lobster. Jeffery felt the clouds move and the sun pointed directly at them. Its bright purple light shined hot on Jeffery like a spotlight, causing his back and chest to get hot and sweaty. The lobster continued to squeak and before long, another unicorn flew across the sky. This unicorn was a bit bigger than the previous ones. It was a very dark and rich purple, almost black, and its hooves and wings were the same shade of purple as the sky. Like its eyes, its mane was a dusty lavender but its tail was short and white. Jeffery noticed its horn was quite long. It looked like purple porcelain dotted with violet specks.

"Look at that one!" said Jeffery, pointing at the unicorn. The lobster continued to squeak and rub its claws gently on Jeffery's knees, indicating that it wanted more petting. "You kind of remind me of a friend I had once, you know," Jeffery said to the lobster. "He was a good little fellow." The lobster squeaked back. "Yes, I know," said Jeffery. "Animal love is special."

Jeffery glanced at the lobster one more time and noticed that it had fallen asleep, so he put his hands by his sides in the sand and let the lobster enjoy its nap.

Jeffery remembered the crocksvenbulb around his neck. He thought more about what he had experienced the previous day and how that memory was, in a sense, held within the crocksvenbulb. He stared at the shore and at the facing forest and remembered the car's tragic and dreadful crash. The heat of the warm sun made Jeffery close his eyes and relive the incident in a flashback. When he opened his eyes again, he noticed another large black dragon fly across the sky. This dragon turned its head as it flew and looked at Jeffery then continued flying until it disappeared. After that, Jeffery saw another unicorn fly slowly across the sky. This one was medium in size and seemed young. Its horn was short and beige while its body was violet and its tail, mane and feet were a lot darker. Jeffery looked carefully at its eyes and noticed that they were pink with a purple outline. Something about the unicorn's young and innocent look sent a rush of thoughts into Jeffery's mind, especially the sight of its small light-purple wings. He looked back at the lobster that was sleeping in his lap.

"It seems like in the animal kingdom you don't have to worry much about who does what and resembles what," Jeffery said calmly. "And I can tell you're much happier this way." Jeffery continued watching the lobster in deep sleep. It snored gently and innocently like a newborn baby who didn't know much in the world. "It doesn't matter," said Jeffery, sounding certain. "What matters is what I think. And I think I have survived."

Jeffery looked up again at the sky to embrace his confidence. He took off the crocksvenbulb necklace and threw it into the water. It made a small splash and sank. He didn't care that it might be challenging for him to find it again. What mattered most was that it was no longer around his neck and that those set conditions didn't apply to him any longer—gone with the

70

ripples. The lobster opened its eyes and quickly hopped off Jeffery's lap. It ran, tilting on its side, along the beach. Jeffery asked it where it was going but all he received in response was a squeak. Jeffery got up and quickly followed the lobster.

"Where are you going, little one?" Jeffery questioned again, amused by the lobster's cute and bouncy walk. The lobster continued a bit further then came to a halt and started digging in the sand with both claws.

"What's in there?" asked Jeffery.

"*Squeak*," squeaked the lobster.

"Yeah?" said Jeffery as he watched the lobster dig. Within seconds, the lobster went head-on into the sand and disappeared. Jeffery raised both his eyebrows, shocked at what he had seen. It had happened so spontaneously it led Jeffery to question whether the lobster even had such ability. "Strange," said Jeffery with a frown. Jeffery sat next to the hole that the lobster had dug. It wasn't a hole *per se*, just a gap in the sand. Jeffery scooped up sand with both hands and covered it, feeling as if he wasn't going to see the lobster again.

Jeffery really enjoyed the feeling of the warm sand on his hands. He looked at the water, its surface so clear and ever so shiny. It looked invitingly warm and clean. He couldn't tell whether the orca was planning to rise up again because there was no further movement. After covering the hole and evening out the sand, Jeffery stood up and admired the view. Two black dragons flew by, side by side, with their mouths open wide. After they had flown away, Jeffery looked back at the water and decided to accept the invitation. He walked back to where he had slept the night, took off his jeans and threw them over his boots. He waded in and swam naked along the sun-heated surface of the water. Its warmth soothed him and washed his skin clean. He dove underwater for a bit and popped back up, feeling refreshed and satisfied.

Jeffery floated on his back, looking up. A unicorn flew across the shore towards the area of the beach where he had been sitting. The front half of this unicorn was purple and the back half was white. Its tail was lavender and its mane a few shades lighter while both its eyes and hooves were black. Its wings were a creamy white with purple and silver lining. Jeffery caught a quick glance of its horn, which was quite long and darker than the front half of its body. The sight of this unicorn flying across where Jeffery had been and then disappearing beyond into the forest was magnificent. Jeffery took deep breaths, stretched out his arms in wide strokes, then relaxed in the water. He felt free and not judged. He dove underwater and swam a bit deeper. Down there, he saw several fish that were roughly the size of his head. Some of them were white but most of them varied in many different shades of purple, and all had lustrous pink eyes that glowed.

"Unbelievable!" exclaimed Jeffery, which allowed some water to get into his mouth. He quickly swam back up and began to pant. "That was unimaginable!" he exclaimed happily. Jeffery then swam back underwater and took another look at the exhilarating fish that to him, seemed to define all of the world's wonders. He returned to the surface and began swimming back towards the beach. His body had started hurting so he halted and floated which allowed him to enjoy the warmth of the sun and water. Jeffery began to feel vibrations coming from the water on the right side of him. Before he could look to see what it was, the orca jumped right out of the water and soared into the sky in a slight curve. Jeffery stared at the sight in amazement. The orca curved right over him then plunged down back into the water to his left. This made a large splash, causing a wave that flipped Jeffery over and sent him falling deep underwater. He swam back up and opened his eyes.

"That was beautiful!" he said loudly. Jeffery swam around some more and made his way back to shore. He stood on the beach then faced the water again. He was feeling very relieved and very grateful for what he had just experienced. After taking another look at the serene environment around him, Jeffery put his jeans back on, then his boots. He sat back down on the beach and saw another dragon fly out from behind the forest across, towards him. The dragon was high in the sky and flew up past Jeffery, causing him to turn around. It flew past the horizon of the other forest and disappeared. Jeffery looked back down. Unexpectedly, the lobster popped out of the sand and jumped right onto his lap. This startled Jeffery briefly but after noticing the lobster, he smiled.

"There you are!" said Jeffery. "I was hoping to see you again." The lobster let out a couple of squeaks then jumped off Jeffery's lap and continued to play in the sand. Jeffery took some sand and poured it on the lobster again, which got it to dance and smile.

"You should have seen what I saw," said Jeffery. "I swam in the water for a bit and saw beautiful fish under there. The temperature was warm. The feeling of the sun on my skin was nice; it's unforgettable what I saw. I even saw the orca leap out and dive back in over me." The lobster smiled and started dancing. Jeffery lay down on his back and stared at the sky. He closed his eyes and relaxed by breathing and remembering what he had experienced. The lobster leaped onto Jeffery's chest, causing him to open his eyes and find the lobster's face staring into his own. Jeffery laughed and petted the lobster, then closed his eyes again. The lobster closed Jeffery's nostrils with its claws making Jeffery shriek and sit up.

"You're hilarious," said Jeffery.

"*Squeak squeak*," said the lobster. It did a little dance then went running back in the direction from which it had come.

"And now where are you going?" asked Jeffery. The lobster just ran while doing a little waddle and didn't look back or squeak. "Interesting," said Jeffery. "You really want me to get up and follow you again?" Jeffery continued sitting and observed the surrounding environment once more.

Before long, an albino unicorn came flying over and landed on the beach next to him. It was entirely white except for its eyes and horn, which were lustrous and purple like a few of the feathers on its white wings. The unicorn galloped gently then stood next to him. Jeffery stood up and petted the unicorn. It smelled like lavender and its coat was clean and shiny. Jeffery felt the unicorn's wings and noticed that they were very fluffy and full of feathers. He looked back to see whether the lobster was present but it had taken off. Jeffery told himself that maybe he'd see it again and decided to pet the unicorn some more. The unicorn bent down and gave out a little huff, causing Jeffery some confusion.

"What do you want, there?" he asked kindly. The unicorn grunted. Jeffery took it as a sign that the unicorn wanted him to ride it. "You must be joking," said Jeffery. The winged horse huffed and grunted again so Jeffery climbed onto its back. The unicorn stood proudly and began flapping its wings. "I hope you don't go too fast," said Jeffery. The unicorn then turned towards the direction in which the lobster had gone and started galloping. Jeffery began to bounce as it galloped so he held on as tight as he could to keep himself secured without suffocating the horse. It galloped then eventually plunged forward for takeoff. After it flew off, it took a slight turn to the right and began flying over the purple water. Before long, Jeffery was once again up in the sky, only this time it felt safe and enjoyable. Jeffery felt a breeze run down his body and the gentle slipstream moving his soft hair. The unicorn flew gracefully and charmingly across the sky, letting Jeffery see how big the purple water was and giving him a view of several purple islands with violet sandy beaches. The unicorn flew even higher and Jeffery saw a few more black dragons fly by. He didn't fear them. In fact, Jeffery found them quite fascinating and felt honored to be flying up in the sky with them.

Jeffery held the unicorn's neck and began to gently rub it. The unicorn enjoyed this affection and began to fly smoother and more gracefully. Jeffery felt very thankful of the unicorn's cautious approach; he needed the company of someone who was kind, graceful and far from condescending. As they flew, the unicorn did a turn in the shape of a large horseshoe and began flying back. Jeffery noticed that far below, on one of the islands, there was a young lady standing who was preoccupied with some sort of task. Jeffery pointed her out to the unicorn and asked whether it could fly down there. The unicorn raised its head gently, indicating a proud nod, then soared downwards, flapping its wings and keeping them spread wide so that it could land gracefully. The air blew in Jeffery's face, giving him a small tickle which made him laugh.

As the unicorn got nearer, the young lady took notice of their approach. Jeffery saw that there were many purple lobsters around her that looked exactly like the one he had encountered earlier. After she moved to create landing space, the unicorn elegantly landed and galloped gently on the violet sand. Before coming to a halt, it turned to face the shore, giving her a side view of itself and Jeffery. Jeffery looked at her and at all the purple lobsters. They were really playful as they interacted with one another through cuddles, laughter and flips. Some of them had even stopped to look at Jeffery and the unicorn. Jeffery began counting all of them in his head but after he counted the thirtieth one, he was interrupted by the young lady.

"That was a beautiful landing," she said kindly, with a unique and angelic accent.

"Thank you," said Jeffery, "and hello!"

"Hello, and welcome," greeted the young lady happily. They both smiled. Jeffery got off the unicorn then walked up to its head.

"Thank you, that was the most beautiful thing ever," said Jeffery as he rubbed the unicorn, causing it to smile. After adoring its gemstone-like eyes again, Jeffery kissed the unicorn on its side and gave it a friendly pat. The unicorn then galloped forward and flew off into the purple sky. It flew and flapped its virtuous wings then slowly shrank in the distance. The young lady stood closer to Jeffery while watching this graceful and heavenly sight. Their eyes were fixed on the unicorn while it took their breath away. The unicorn eventually disappeared beyond the horizon never to be seen again.

"That was just beautiful," said the young lady.

"It was an unforgettable and magnificent experience," said Jeffery. "I got to see this place from up high. Everything was purple. It was just glorious and breathtaking."

"Oh, yes," said the young lady, "it absolutely is."

"You've flown before?" asked Jeffery.

"Many times," replied the young lady. "Unicorns are gorgeous."

"They are, and they come in so many colors!" said Jeffery.

"They do," said the young lady. "But the albino one shows up once every thousand years or so."

"Really?" asked Jeffery.

"Yep, and the one who rides it is very lucky and well watched by someone divine," said the young lady. "And I am pleased to have witnessed this. I am Sabina. What's your name?"

"Jeffery," he replied. He reached out his hands and kindly shook Sabina's. They were very soft, like freshly bloomed roses, and welcoming like spring air on an equinox morning. Jeffery looked at Sabina and observed her appearance. She was wearing a purple maxi summer dress and dark sandals that were the color of plums. Her hair was very curly and dark brown. It seemed very long and was tied back, revealing some of the ends that were streaked with different shades of purple. Finally, Jeffery looked at her eyes. They were brown and her gaze was very gentle.

"Where do you come from?" she asked with her charming accent. Jeffery sighed.

"Long story," he said, sounding uninterested.

"Well, you must have some sort of background if you were lucky enough to fly the albino unicorn," said Sabina. "It's written in The Book of Legends."

"The Book of Legends?" asked Jeffery.

"Yes," said Sabina. "I have a copy of it at home." Jeffery felt his stress level rise.

"Let's worry about that later," he said. Jeffery then looked at the lobsters and began to walk closer to them. They all looked identical and seemed to possess the same personality. Jeffery sat down on the sand and waved at them. Two lobsters came up to his knees and started loitering. A few others began to play around him.

"Pleasant creatures, aren't they?" said Sabina, walking ahead.

"Most certainly," said Jeffery. "They are so playful. I saw one earlier today and it was quite the character."

"Yes, Twookies are lovely," said Sabina. "I've always loved Twooky lobsters." One lobster held her dress in its claw and began to smile. "You like my dress?" she asked it.

"How many of them are there?" asked Jeffery.

"A lot," answered Sabina. "They live all over the islands and they are all very cheerful."

"They sure are," laughed Jeffery as he handled a few.

"And they love being touched," said Sabina. While spending time with Sabina and the lobsters, Jeffery noticed a dark shadow cover the beach. He looked up and saw that it was a large dragon. It flew away slowly, seeming a bit heavier than the average dragon.

"I like those," said Jeffery.

"Me too," said Sabina, after putting down a lobster. "They're unique in their own way. They're very big but very gentle at the same time."

"They are," agreed Jeffery. "I saw a few of them while flying on the unicorn earlier. We flew right by them and they almost didn't notice."

"Typical," said Sabina. "Sometimes I sit here or visit another island and one lands right by me and just chills, really."

"Yeah, that's fascinating," said Jeffery.

"Have you seen similar where you come from?" asked Sabina.

"No," answered Jeffery with a short sigh. "Where I come from, I was advised that I could be eaten by something that huge!" The two of them laughed.

"Sometimes we are sheltered," said Sabina. "It's normal."

"Yeah," said Jeffery, "except for these fellows. They enjoy the random company of others." Jeffery tickled one of the lobsters and it ran away to Sabina.

"They really do," nodded Sabina, tickling the lobster. The lobster chuckled then ran into the crowd with the other lobsters. Sabina sat down and looked at Jeffery. "You seem to have thick skin," she said calmly.

"I suppose that I do," suggested Jeffery, rubbing his arm. Sabina smiled. "I do like the breeze out here."

"Yes, it's nice," said Sabina, turning to look at the water and then glancing around. "It's really nice; I enjoy it." Jeffery briefly thought of the rooms at the Fogbusts' and Lake Morgan's. He was so much more thankful to be at this beach with Sabina that his body shook while he brushed off the memories.

"Are you alright?" asked Sabina, noticing this.

"Yeah," said Jeffery, looking at her and smiling. "I am fine." Sabina ran her eyes down him then continued cuddling the lobsters. One of them jumped onto her shoulder and rested casually. Jeffery watched Sabina pet it gently then put it back on the sand. He then noticed three unicorns that were all different shades of purple fly by as a group. They flew by so fast that Jeffery couldn't observe any details other than their long purple-silver horns.

"I guess it doesn't matter where you came from or when," said Sabina. "What matters is that you are here." Jeffery saw her smile gently and allowed the words to sink in.

"Thank you," he replied. "It sure is beautiful here."

"I am still amazed at what I saw," stated Sabina.

"Is this a known legend around here?" asked Jeffery. "About the albino?"

"Yes," said Sabina. "Only once every millennium or so it gets spotted. When we go home later, I will show you The Book of Legends."

"And how old is this book?" asked Jeffery.

"Ancient," replied Sabina, exaggerating her tone. "It's been reprinted several times with legends going in and out of it."

"Sounds remarkable," said Jeffery.

"It totally is," agreed Sabina. "We just don't know which legends in it are true and which ones aren't." Another dragon showed up on the beach and walked close to where Jeffery was sitting. It looked out and began to watch over the water.

"No legends about these guys?" asked Jeffery.

"Maybe," replied Sabina after turning to view the dragon. "I am not sure. I admire their scales."

"They're pretty," said Jeffery calmly. Jeffery began to observe the dragon closely. It flapped its wings slowly as it watched other dragons and unicorns fly by. After it wagged its tail a few times, it looked at Jeffery and smiled.

"Seems to like you," said Sabina.

"Maybe," said Jeffery with a short laugh. "It may have seen me in the sky earlier."

"Oh, quite possibly!" said Sabina. The dragon then turned its head back towards the shore and flew off.

"Well, I hope it enjoys the rest of its day," said Jeffery.

"It probably will," said Sabina with a laugh.

"Amazing how all creatures here are harmless," said Jeffery.

"Do you come from a place where others can be harmful?" asked Sabina.

"A little bit," said Jeffery. "They follow really strict and unnecessary rules."

"I see," said Sabina with a short nod. "Over here, we all live in harmony and don't impose rules on anyone or take advantage of others. And, we don't allow others to do that to us. The saying goes: *Don't let others use you as the flower to their fragrance.*" Jeffery smiled and allowed the soft accent of Sabina's words to echo in his ears.

"That's beautiful," said Jeffery. Sabina smiled in response. Jeffery turned to face the water and saw a now familiar movement. "Have you seen this?" he asked Sabina after pointing at the movement.

"Oh, yes!" said Sabina with a smile. "The Twooky Orca is lovely!"

"What are *Twookies*?" asked Jeffery, taking notice of the word a second time.

"Twooky. This land, all of the islands—it's called Twooky," replied Sabina. "They're from here so they're Twookies."

"That's cute," said Jeffery with a short laugh.

"But there is only one orca," said Sabina. "I hope it lives forever." Jeffery turned back to look at the movement. "I think it's ready to leap," whispered Sabina. Jeffery kept staring at the rippling water that seemed ready to explode. The orca soared right out of it and directly into the sky with a giant splash, exposing its unique purple tail.

"Wow!" yelled Jeffery in amazement. The orca bent over then went soaring back down into the water and created another large splash.

"Fabulous!" said Sabina. "I love that sight!"

"It's magnificent," said Jeffery. "I was swimming earlier by another island and it leaped over me. It was splendid and quite epic."

"Oh, that must have been," said Sabina. Jeffery looked at her eyes and saw she was looking back at him. The two smiled at each other then Sabina looked back down at the lobsters shyly. Jeffery turned to look at the ripples created by the orca's splash. He fell into a reverie, as a unicorn flew gracefully over. It was only a few feet tall, and appeared to be quite young. Its coat was light purple and its mane and tail were white, like its hooves. Jeffery noticed that its wings were rather short and very dark, and that its horn was also a shade of purple.

"That one is adorable," said Sabina. "I think it was just born a few weeks ago." Jeffery then noticed movement in the water again.

"Uh oh," he said. "I hope it doesn't get accidently hit by the orca."

"Probably not," said Sabina. "They're usually good dodgers, even when they are young."

"I hope so," said Jeffery, sounding a bit worried.

"Believe me," said Sabina. As the movement began to build up again, the unicorn slowly flew away.

"Well, that's good that it's gone," said Jeffery.

"Indeed," agreed Sabina with a short laugh. "But believe me, it would have been fine."

"I am glad to hear," said Jeffery, sounding comforted. He looked again at the movement in the water and noticed it was closer than before. The movement intensified and Jeffery felt a vibration along the beach. He looked

81

at the lobsters and saw that they didn't seem to take notice, unlike Sabina, who had a frown upon her face.

"What's happening?" asked Jeffery.

"I think that… " started Sabina, then paused. Jeffery saw her look at him then smirk. The orca splashed out of the water again and soared very high into the sky. Jeffery and Sabina looked at it in admiration, but also had a worried look drawn across their faces. After the orca completed its leap and began its descent, it looked as though it might land right on the beach. As the orca fell closer, Jeffery panicked and moved away, causing all the lobsters to flee. Jeffery saw that Sabina was tranquil but that she moved away as well. The orca landed with a loud thud on the beach, causing the sand to be thrown up all around. Jeffery gasped in astonishment. The lobsters all stood still, watching curiously, their eyes barely blinking.

"Yes, that can sometimes happen," Jeffery heard Sabina say from the other side of the orca. Jeffery shivered at the sight of the enormous orca lying flat on its side, almost motionless. Sabina came around and stood next to Jeffery. "Yes, I've dealt with this before," she said with a sigh.

"How?" asked Jeffery.

"We just push it back into the water," said Sabina casually.

"We push it back?" Jeffery asked in disbelief.

"Yes," said Sabina. "Let's start now before it begins to dry out."

"Is there a certain way to do it?" asked Jeffery.

"Um, yeah, just follow me," said Sabina. Jeffery followed Sabina as she led him to the head of the orca where it was pointing away from the water. Jeffery watched Sabina put her soft hands on its head and pet it gently while saying calming words. "Now you push," she instructed. Jeffery put his hands on the orca's head as well. It was quite wet and felt somewhat oily.

"Alright," said Jeffery. He pushed the orca with Sabina and felt its heavy weight.

"And *pu-ush!*" said Sabina, her accent emphasizing the vowel in her second word. Jeffery continued pushing. "And *pu-ush*," repeated Sabina. The orca moved a little bit.

"I think we're going to need to push harder," said Jeffery.

"We're trying," said Sabina. "It usually takes a while to get it back in."

"I can tell!" said Jeffery with a short laugh. "Oh, look!" Jeffery pointed to the lobsters. They were helping, attempting to push the orca from the bottom.

"Aw... " said Sabina. "They are very helpful." Jeffery noticed that the lobsters' effort was making a difference and that the orca was gradually moving down into the water, tail first.

"It'll be back in the water in no time," cheered Jeffery, sounding determined.

"Yes," said Sabina. "We need to keep pushing." The orca started letting out sounds that indicated it wasn't too comfortable.

"I can tell it isn't enjoying this," said Jeffery as he continued to push.

"No," said Sabina. "It's too heavy and I think the sand is burning its skin a bit." Jeffery made a sad face, expressing his sympathy towards the large animal being so vulnerable and helpless.

"We'll manage," said Jeffery. He continued pushing with Sabina and the lobsters as the orca moaned louder.

"I think it is running out of time," said Sabina. "Push harder, please."

"Ok," replied Jeffery.

"Just try your best," said Sabina, "it's almost in there." Before long, Jeffery was in the water with Sabina along with most of the orca. He continued pushing with Sabina and the lobsters until the orca was finally able to turn around and swim away. Jeffery walked back up to the beach and sat down to wring out his jeans. Sabina came and sat next to him, wringing out the bottom of her dress.

"Well, I'm glad it's off and swimming away safely," said Jeffery.

"Sooner or later, it'll leap out again," predicted Sabina.

"And hopefully not land on the beach," replied Jeffery, making both of them laugh.

"It is good to be loving," said Sabina with a smile.

"It is," he agreed. "It feels good and important." He looked at her and smiled. His smile seemed almost synchronized with hers. "Where I come from, I was taught that a man mustn't worry too much about helping others, but instead, find the power within him and rise." Sabina looked at him, unsurprised.

"I understand," she said gently, "but you see, a man's charisma and inner strength are never visible when he is following others' way of thinking. Instead, it shines when he confronts these norms and has the confidence and courage to rise above them regardless of challenges that paranoid others throw his way. Only such men can really feel and embrace the core of masculinity and live to experience the highest potential of the male sex." Jeffery felt Sabina's words penetrate his being. Like a bolt of electricity, they quickly circulated throughout his entire body and halted his mind with a miraculous epiphany.

"I think you're right," Jeffery said quietly. "If only others would see that."

"Well, you can teach them," said Sabina.

"It isn't that, it's a deeper thing," said Jeffery.

"What?" Sabina asked curiously. Jeffery took a deep breath and sighed. Sabina ran her hands down his bare shoulder, with a wanting to help look in her eyes that were filled with passion. Sabina leaned in closer but the moment was interrupted by a shaking in the ground and the sound of galloping. Jeffery saw Sabina look back and he noticed two unicorns galloping towards them. They galloped until they approached where Jeffery was sitting with Sabina.

"Hello," said Jeffery happily.

"Unicorns sure seem to be attracted to you," said Sabina with a short smile, glancing at him. The two unicorns made very friendly faces. They were almost the same shade of purple with manes and tails that were a few shades lighter, like their hooves. Their eyes were purple, like shiny sets of amethysts dug out from the most northerly cave. They were also the same size; the only two things that differentiated them were their horns and wings. One had black wings with some royal-purple feathers and its horn was shiny and very dark purple, almost black. The other had purple wings, slightly darker than the body of the first horse, and its horn was shiny and silver, sprinkled with purple and lavender glitter.

"It seems so," said Jeffery, observing the unicorns.

"I think they are gorgeous," said Sabina.

"They absolutely are," said Jeffery openheartedly.

"I can't imagine Twooky without them," said Sabina, "I just can't."

"Me neither," said Jeffery. The lobsters began to loiter happily around the unicorns and made welcoming faces at them. The unicorns bent over and made grunting sounds at Jeffery and Sabina.

"It seems we are going for a ride," said Sabina happily, turning to Jeffery.

"I'm good with that," said Jeffery excitedly. He stood up and leaped onto the unicorn with the purple wings. Sabina followed and got on the second one. Jeffery exchanged a smile with Sabina and before either of them said anything, the unicorns began galloping. Jeffery held on tightly and felt the palms of his hands and the soles of his feet grow numb.

"We're almost up," said Sabina. In a matter of seconds, the two unicorns began flapping their wings gently and flew off, soaring into the air. Jeffery felt the wind blowing in his face. He turned back to see where Sabina was and noticed that she was behind him to his right.

"Holding on back there?" he asked.

"Yes!" said Sabina happily. As the unicorn adjusted its balance, Jeffery looked at all the purple islands and water from his bird's eye view.

"Magnificent," he said, as he admired their elegance. Jeffery then noticed that Sabina's unicorn was flying next to his, only farther to the left.

"I see you really like riding the unicorns," said Sabina lovingly.

"I really do," said Jeffery. "They are full of grace and the view from up here is just gorgeous!" The two unicorns then diverged from one another to allow four dragons, varying in size, to pass by. Jeffery looked at their tails, teeth, and bumpy, black skin. He admired their sense of strength but also their sensible caution. After the dragons passed by, the two unicorns drew closer and flew side by side again.

"That was interesting," said Sabina with a short laugh that left a smirk on her face.

"Indeed!" said Jeffery. "They're so big!" The unicorn he was riding plunged downwards as though it were going to land. It then took a slight turn to the left and Jeffery noticed that its flight was synchronized with Sabina's unicorn, which was forty feet above him.

"They're putting on a show!" called Sabina enthusiastically.

"What's that?" yelled Jeffery.

"I said, they're putting on a show!" repeated Sabina. Jeffery noticed that both sets of wings were synchronized in flaps and speed. Jeffery felt his unicorn soar back up and fly in front of Sabina's. Then, he looked down and saw that the unicorns were switching places. After they re-synchronized at a forty-foot distance, Jeffery looked over and saw that Sabina was looking up at him and waving. He waved back with a smile. The view of her on the unicorn and the water and islands below her was fascinating. After a few minutes of flying, Sabina's unicorn flew back up then in front of Jeffery. His unicorn dodged to the left and sped up to fly next to Sabina's.

"Just glorious what these two can do," said Jeffery.

"It really is," agreed Sabina. Then her unicorn veered to the right and Jeffery's split off, turning to the left. The two unicorns began flying in opposite directions in a large circle, allowing Sabina and Jeffery to pass by each other every so often. On the second pass, they exchanged high fives and as they came closer again, Sabina blew him a kiss, which made him laugh.

"This is so theatrical," said Jeffery.

"It is," said Sabina before another pass. "It is impressive." When the two unicorns were directly across from each other, they turned and flew towards one another face to face. Jeffery saw Sabina getting closer in front of him and wondered whether he should indicate a turn to the unicorn. To his surprise, the two unicorns flew to face one another and rose gently, positioning their bodies as though rearing up on their hind legs, and causing Jeffery to hold on tighter. While gently flapping and floating in the sky, the two unicorns kissed one another romantically for a long moment.

"Look at that!" said Jeffery.

"That is just beautiful!" said Sabina. Jeffery felt his unicorn moving and noticed they were straightening out their bodies while gently flapping and kissing. He was right in front of Sabina when the two unicorns began floating slowly in a circle, still kissing.

"Just look at that," said Jeffery. "It's majestic." He noticed that Sabina was crying in admiration of the beautiful and angelic sight, and her tears were reflecting the purple light of the sky. The artistic sight of this left a look of admiration on Jeffery's face.

"I can't believe it," said Sabina, crying gently. After kissing for another moment, the unicorns turned to Jeffery's left and continued flying side by side back in the direction from which they had flown.

"That was unforgettable," said Jeffery.

"It was beautiful," said Sabina, wiping away her last tear. "Love is remarkable."

"It is," said Jeffery, a little nervously.

"And wherever you come from," started Sabina, "others need to learn that kindness is not weakness. Weakness is not being able to be kind." Jeffery sighed.

"I concur," he said quietly. He turned to Sabina and took notice of her looking at him calmly, in a sense, expressing her sympathy. "But some just don't learn."

"Their loss," said Sabina. "It really is."

After landing back on the beach, Jeffery got off the unicorn and petted it in appreciation. He saw Sabina do the same, then the unicorns flew away. Jeffery sat down on the sand and began to rub his hands through its warm and powdery texture. He leaned back halfway and rested his body on his elbow and looked towards Sabina who seemed preoccupied with the lobsters. Some of them had disappeared during their absence. Jeffery questioned Sabina's activity with the lobsters as the remaining ones seemed much calmer.

"I am picking out a couple for dinner," said Sabina.

"You eat them?" asked Jeffery.

"Oh, yes," said Sabina, "they're delicious. I cook them really well and one is usually enough for one person."

"Interesting," said Jeffery. "And how do you pick which one is for dinner?"

"I try to pick the ones that stay out," said Sabina. "That's because they're not going back in for breeding. They breed almost every day."

"I see," said Jeffery. Sabina then settled two lobsters on her shoulders and advised them to stay seated.

"Well, shall we go?" she asked.

"Where to?" asked Jeffery.

"To my cottage," replied Sabina. "I am going to make us dinner."

"Alright," said Jeffery. "I think that will be lovely."

"For sure," said Sabina. "After that, I will show you The Book of Legends."

"Great," said Jeffery happily. He stood up and followed Sabina, walking in the direction opposite the sunset while they both played with the lobsters.

That evening, after walking past the beach and into a purple forest of exquisite-looking trees and shrubs, Jeffery arrived with Sabina at her cottage, which was located in the center of a glade, surrounded by some flat purple grass. The cottage was circular in shape, like a gazebo, and predominantly deep purple with lighter purple and violet trim. It was also very high. Sabina guided him to the door and unlocked it with a long purple key that she kept in her dress. She gently welcomed him in. Upon entering, Jeffery noticed that one side of the cottage was a living space with couches and tables that were predominantly purple, and on the other side was the kitchen which was big, and varied in shades of purple. In the center was a staircase covered in thick, white carpet that led to the upstairs level of the cottage. Jeffery walked up and took a seat at the table in the kitchen as he watched Sabina take the lobsters right to the sink. She teased them playfully a bit then pulled out a large lavender pot and set it on the stove.

"It's important to make them feel appreciated," said Sabina. "They really feel it." Jeffery looked at the lobsters smiling and bouncing in the sink.

"Yeah, they are something," he said gently. Sabina cut up some vegetables and herbs then put them in the pot and added water to boil.

"That is why it is important to pick out the ones that are out longer," explained Sabina. "They don't want to breed anymore and so would rather be consumed."

"Interesting," said Jeffery.

"Yes," said Sabina. "They make a really delicious soup at that point." She opened a cupboard and took out a glass container, similar to the shape of a bottle, which held some sort of dry spice. She took out a pinch and sprinkled it over the lobsters. As the spice landed, it made a tinkling sound and released some purple vapor. "And this is a relaxer," explained Sabina. "It helps keep them relaxed before being cooked. It puts them to sleep in a sense."

"I see," said Jeffery. He watched the lobsters relax, then gradually fall asleep. Sabina stirred the pot for a few minutes then picked up the lobsters one by one and added them to the pot before covering it. She lowered the temperature of the stove then walked back to the counter. She pulled out a couple of glasses and a bottle, brought them to Jeffery at the table and sat next to him.

"This is called the lovers' drink," said Sabina. "I brew it fresh." She opened the bottle and poured a glass for Jeffery.

"Thank you," said Jeffery after accepting the drink. He smelled it closely and enjoyed its scent of fruitiness. After Sabina poured herself a glass, she said a toast, and let them drink. Jeffery savored the drink in his mouth. Its taste and texture combined were very smooth and refreshing. "I like it," said Jeffery after putting his half-consumed glass back on the table. Sabina poured him more, then gave him a wink. "You must really like this lovers' drink."

"I do," said Sabina. "It is enjoyable."

"How do you make it?" asked Jeffery.

"I never share the recipe," answered Sabina. "It is a family tradition to not share it until you're ready to. And I haven't been ready to share it as of yet."

"Interesting," said Jeffery. He gulped more of the lovers' drink and enjoyed the smell of the boiling lobsters. Something about the aroma gave him a strange feeling in his gut, but at the same time, pleasured his sense of smell. "I think they're going to taste great," he said after glancing at the stove.

"Oh, yes, you will like it," said Sabina. "You really will."

"It smells juicy and filling," said Jeffery.

"Oh, yes," said Sabina, "and especially with the lovers' drink."

"Which tastes amazing," added Jeffery.

"Yes, thank you," said Sabina. "I may share the recipe with you later," she added with a lascivious tone. Jeffery smiled nervously and watched Sabina get up with her drink to go stir the pot. As she removed the lid, a burst of purple steam came out, filling the kitchen with a delicious smell. Sabina stirred for a while then covered the pot again, and returned to her spot while drinking the lovers' drink. Jeffery continued to drink until he finished his glass. Sabina reached out to the bottle and refilled it for him.

"I am good actually," said Jeffery. "I don't—"

"I insist," interrupted Sabina. "Drink, and don't be shy." The two of them laughed and Jeffery continued drinking as he took a closer look at the lovers' drink; it was light purple and had a gleaming shine, like wine.

"So where is The Book of Legends?" asked Jeffery.

"I'll show you later," replied Sabina. "Dinner is almost ready."

"Ok," said Jeffery, "I am really curious."

"Yes, it's an interesting book," said Sabina. After taking a few more sips, she went to a cupboard and brought out two big purple plates and bowls and put them next to the stove. She took out some cutlery and set it on the table. Jeffery watched Sabina go back to the stove and serve the lobsters onto the plates, then pour the soup into the bowls. He got up and helped her carry them to the table.

"This looks delicious!" said Jeffery excitedly. "I am going to enjoy it, thank you."

"You're welcome," said Sabina. "Enjoy, and don't be shy." Jeffery started with the soup, tasting the beets, as well as the various other vegetables and herbs. He then started to eat the lobster as though there were no tomorrow.

"This is great," said Jeffery. "I never thought that they'd taste so good, those lobsters."

"Yes, they're scrumptious," said Sabina with a laugh. "Keep eating." Jeffery felt shy but continued eating as he wasn't able to resist the taste.

"It would be nice to eat this on the beach," said Jeffery.

"It would," said Sabina with another laugh, "except that the sight of cooked lobsters might scare away the other lobsters." Jeffery then looked at his plate and saw that he had consumed most of his lobster. There was not much remaining besides its inedible parts. The lobster now looked really dull. Jeffery turned to Sabina, who was looking at him while she was drinking.

"Well, thank you," he said, with slight hesitation.

"You're welcome," answered Sabina. "Would you like more to drink?"

"No, thank you," said Jeffery, "I am good." Sabina smiled at him so he kindly smiled back.

"Now will you show me The Book of Legends?" asked Jeffery, taking in a deep breath with a hand on his bare stomach.

"Sure," said Sabina. She collected the plates, put them in the sink and began washing.

"Need help with anything?" offered Jeffery.

"No, don't worry," said Sabina, "but thank you."

"Anytime," said Jeffery. He walked to the living room and sat on the couch. Rather, he fell into the couch as it was very soft and somewhat bouncy. He enjoyed that feeling along with the material of the couch. He looked by the window, which was small, and saw hanging there a medium-sized portrait of Sabina that contained the text *love is not only a word,* in lowercase letters. The words sank into Jeffery's mind and got him wrapped in thought. He turned to Sabina who was doing some chores in the kitchen, then, before she could take notice of his glance, he looked back at the window. Jeffery remembered when he was flying the unicorn the second time with her and how it had kissed hers as they floated up high. Jeffery also remembered her tears and her admiration towards the atmospheric sight. It was one of the most beautiful sights Jeffery had ever seen.

"I am done," said Sabina. "Now I'll go upstairs to get the book."

"Sounds good," replied Jeffery.

"Do you want anything?" asked Sabina.

"No, thanks," answered Jeffery, "just excited to see the book."

"Ok, sounds good," said Sabina. She jogged up the stairs, creating a small echo with her footsteps. After the sound of Sabina's footsteps disappeared, Jeffery leaned back and remembered the delicious soup and lobster meal, the warm steam, and tender chewiness. Before getting wrapped in another thought, Jeffery heard Sabina's footsteps returning so he sat up and adjusted his posture. Sabina walked close to him with nothing in her hands.

"I didn't find it so I am just going to check in the other room, alright?" she said, sounding a little worried.

"Yeah, no problem," said Jeffery.

"Ok, hopefully I won't be long," said Sabina. Jeffery watched her go back up the stairs and disappear. While waiting, he decided to stand up and look out the window. The sun was setting and their surroundings were dark, but nonetheless, still very purple. The sky was darkening and so were the shadows in the forest. Jeffery looked down and saw that the grass was very flat yet very fresh and moist. As he looked, he smelled the cool atmosphere that was so fresh and restful. He looked at the sky to see if he'd catch sight of any flying unicorns or dragons, but there weren't any. Jeffery assumed that they probably all went home somewhere for the evening. He walked back to the couch and sat down, hoping for Sabina to show up any minute.

As he sat there, wrapped in thought, he looked at the main door of the cottage and saw an unusual ornament hanging on the wall right next to it. Jeffery gazed at it. It looked identical to the crocksvenbulbs, only though it was purple. He relived several flashbacks from his time with Lake Morgan. His stomach began to feel uncomfortable. Jeffery looked around the place in search of anything else that seemed peculiar, but didn't spot anything.

Sabina stormed back downstairs and sat next to Jeffery, looking disappointed. She seemed very cross and lost in deep concentration. Jeffery asked her what was wrong but she didn't reply.

"Where is the book?" he gently questioned.

"I couldn't find it," replied Sabina, sounding frustrated. "It's a very important book but I couldn't find it."

"Well, just relax," said Jeffery.

"I think the legend goes something like this… " started Sabina. Jeffery watched her pause to think briefly before resuming. "The albino unicorn only flies in every thousand years or so. If one gets a chance to ride it, that person must be very holy or something."

"And?" asked Jeffery.

"And is being watched by some sort of divine figure. Also, whomever that may be, will likely also catch sight of an albino fairycorn, who'll hand them… " Sabina paused again.

"Hand them what?" asked Jeffery.

"I forgot what it is called," replied Sabina. "The fairycorn will hand them something that they'll need to stab themselves with and it'll take them somewhere." Jeffery opened his eyes wide.

"That sounds scary!" he exclaimed. "Also, what is a fairycorn?"

"Just little figures you find in the forest," explained Sabina. "They're usually in different shades of purple and maroon. This particular one is albino."

"That's scary," said Jeffery.

"It is," said Sabina, "but also, that person is very blessed." Jeffery looked at Sabina and watched her stare at him deeply.

"Well, if you ever find The Book of Legends, I would love to read it," he said casually.

"Yes, of course," said Sabina as she moved closer to Jeffery.

"What is that?" he asked, pointing at the ornament by the door.

"That's called a crocksvenbulb," answered Sabina, after glancing at it. "The Book of Legends talks about it as well. They come from some high figure and are meant to be our principles for guidance."

"Really?" asked Jeffery curiously.

"Yes, and also, I think they're meant to go back up to some higher power," added Sabina. Jeffery stared at the crocksvenbulb. He narrowed his eyes in resentment and felt the urge to crush it.

"And where'd you get it?" he asked, trying to sound normal.

"Some relative," answered Sabina. "I can't even remember. I just have it. Why do you ask?"

95

"I had one like it," Jeffery muttered in shame. "It was a different color though." Jeffery looked down at the floor and Sabina gently ran her eyes over him. She moved even closer and began rubbing his arm.

"Well, there are many different rules and principles," she whispered softly. "That doesn't mean you must stick to them all." As Sabina continued rubbing him, Jeffery began to feel a sense of discomfort. Sabina's rubs turned from friendly to sensual, explicitly indicating her desire for him. After turning to face her, Sabina lightly pressed her lips on his and kissed him. Jeffery received her kiss but sat still. It felt soft, like her sensual rubs, and also smelled like the fresh bloom of an exotic flower. When Sabina stopped kissing him, she sat back and ran her eyes down his chest.

"There is something I need to say," said Jeffery, looking down.

"What's that?" asked Sabina.

"You see," started Jeffery, "I don't feel the same. I understand you seem to like me but it isn't mutual. I mean, I don't feel too different from you."

"What do you mean?" asked Sabina.

"I can't explain it," said Jeffery. "I am not what you see. I am someone else in this shape." Sabina looked at him in a loving way.

"I know," she whispered softly. "I knew it all along." Jeffery turned to face her and saw that she had stood up and walked to the window.

"When I first saw you land on that unicorn," she started while looking back, "I knew there was something different about you—something divine! And really, you still haven't told me where you come from, but wherever that is and whatever they've shown you, they are probably wrong." Jeffery looked up to Sabina and focused on her soft lips. "I mean it," she said firmly. "Even though I cannot love you romantically, I still love you as Jeffery. And I wish that you'd forget everything you were taught before and keep moving along. Jeffery, find yourself, find who *you* are, and unleash you!" Jeffery began to cry and looked down at himself.

"What I am afraid of," Jeffery muttered while crying, "is what is the point of having hands when there is nothing that you can control?" He slowly looked back up to Sabina. She sat back next to him and held him close. Jeffery hugged her in return, embracing her security. He hadn't felt this feeling since George was alive.

"Never be afraid," said Sabina. "In fact, I am certain that the legend is true."

"What do you mean?" asked Jeffery, sitting back.

"About the albino fairycorn," stated Sabina. "One second." Sabina got up and ran back upstairs. Jeffery looked out the window and thought about Sabina's words. They were indeed empowering, but he wasn't sure if he had fully expressed himself to her. He turned his gaze to the crocksvenbulb and wondered what sort of morals Sabina had been taught on her journey. Jeffery also wondered whether she had endured similar situations with abrupt others, such as Lake Morgan, that may have caused her to be such an angelic person.

He turned back to the window and took notice of a small wooden side table that stood in the corner. On it stood a metallic purple frame which displayed the picture of an old woman. She was dressed in an elegant, violet suit and wore a matching hat that revealed some locks of her gray hair. Looking at it closely, Jeffery noticed that she was wearing a brooch of the crocksvenbulb that was the same color as Sabina's. Jeffery glanced back and forth between the crocksvenbulb on the wall and the one in the picture, only increasing his curiosity. Sabina returned downstairs with two nets in her hands, each about half the length of her arm. Her face was dry but it seemed as though she had washed it to get rid of her tears.

"Let's go into the forest!" she said excitedly. "We'll catch some fairycorns and then maybe you might find the albino one."

"Alright," said Jeffery, "then what do we do with the ones we catch?"

"We just release them," replied Sabina.

"Sounds like fun," said Jeffery.

"Yes, and don't forget to be gentle with them," instructed Sabina.

"Yeah, for sure," said Jeffery as he got up to accept a net.

"They're quite delicate," explained Sabina.

"I bet they are," said Jeffery, taking a net. He followed Sabina to the door while examining the net. It seemed deep and harmless. On the way out, Jeffery looked at Sabina's crocksvenbulb one more time. Before thoughts and flashbacks began to enter his mind again, Jeffery quickly exited and closed the door behind him. He followed Sabina across the grass and into the forest. Jeffery noticed that Sabina was storming along so he tried to keep up with her. The sky had gotten darker and Jeffery was certain that he didn't want to get lost in the woods alone.

"Now, it shouldn't be hard to spot them," said Sabina while looking around the purple trees and shrubs. "They glow all the time."

"Do they?" asked Jeffery.

"Yep," answered Sabina. "I remember hearing a long time ago that others used to make juice out of them. I can only wonder how horrible that must have tasted."

"That sounds horrid," replied Jeffery with a casual look. He began looking around for glowing dots to see whether there were any fairycorns.

"Follow me," instructed Sabina. Jeffery followed her as she walked deeper into the forest. "I think they might be there. I see a cluster of glowing dots."

"And how big are they?" inquired Jeffery.

"Not really big," replied Sabina. "They're really small, about the size of your palm." Jeffery continued following her to a tree that had some purple light around it on one of its branches. After he got closer, he caught sight of the fairycorns. They were tiny little ladies in scanty dresses that glowed in various shades of purple. They had small unicorn horns on their foreheads, some were purple and some were silver. Some of their eyes were in various shades of purple and some were black. As Sabina had said, they were about the size of Jeffery's palm and had small wings that matched their dresses, which also glowed. Their heads were bald and some had short violet braids hanging from the back.

"Well, there they are!" said Jeffery.

"Yep!" said Sabina as she swung her net. She landed it on the branch with a fast *thwack* that sent the fairycorns flying all over the place. They looked like glowing dots in the air, some of them maroon. Jeffery noticed that Sabina had caught two in her net, both in purple dresses and one of them with a braid on her head.

"They look beautiful," said Jeffery.

"They really do," replied Sabina as she held the open end of the net with her other hand.

"I hope you're not going to juice us," protested the fairycorn without the braid. Jeffery couldn't help but laugh at her cute and small voice.

"No, we'd never hurt you," said Sabina. "We're just playing with you." Jeffery then received a wink from Sabina. She let go of the net and let the two fairycorns fly.

"Wheeeeee!" they both cheered, which made Jeffery and Sabina laugh.

"Go on and catch some," Sabina told Jeffery.

"Ok!" said Jeffery. He jogged ahead then waved his net and slammed it against a tree. The fairycorns flew everywhere, making their funny noises, then Jeffery noticed that he hadn't caught any. He tried again against another tree but the result was the same.

"Try to be a bit faster," demonstrated Sabina as she swung her net. Jeffery watched her catch a fairycorn in front of her by landing the net on her belly. Jeffery walked closer to Sabina to get a better look at that fairycorn. Her dress and wings were maroon and her horn was silver and smooth like her bald head.

"Hello there," greeted Jeffery while waving at her.

"Hi!" replied the fairycorn. Sabina then moved the net away from her and the fairycorn flew off.

"You like them?" she asked tenderly.

"Oh, I do," said Jeffery happily. He went up in front of a cluster of fairycorns and replicated what Sabina had just shown him. After landing the net on his bare stomach, he looked down and saw that he had caught three purple fairycorns. Jeffery greeted them and the fairycorns laughed.

"Keep at it!" yelled Sabina. Jeffery released the fairycorns and continued catching and releasing other ones with her. "I am trying to catch some from that cluster. They fly faster for some reason," explained Sabina, pointing at a group of fairycorns.

"Let's try," replied Jeffery. "Let's wait until they are closer to a tree."

"Yes, alright," said Sabina. Jeffery slowed down and followed the cluster with curiosity. He noticed that their lights were actually a bit brighter for some reason, which caused him to avoid looking at them directly. Sabina followed him and the two paused to see where exactly these fairycorns were going. As they came close to a tree, Sabina instructed Jeffery to stay still until the cluster flew back his way. Jeffery figured out the plan after glancing back at the cluster of fairycorns, and giggled. He watched Sabina observe them closely and shifted his gaze between them. Sabina leaped ahead like a frog and waved her net, which sent the cluster of fairycorns flying towards Jeffery. He then leaped and swung his net and loudly slammed it against a tree. The fairycorns made a strange sound then dispersed among the other fairycorns. Their lights made a beautiful pattern that left Jeffery gazing while holding the net against the tree.

"Oh, my," Jeffery heard Sabina say as she approached him. "This is amazing!" Jeffery turned to the net and saw the reason for Sabina's surprise. In the net was a fairycorn with a pair of white wings, who happened to be a bit smaller than the rest, wearing a white dress. Her light was very bright and white and she was silent.

"Look at that!" said Jeffery.

"The legend is real!" cheered Sabina.

"Now she's supposed to give me something?" asked Jeffery.

"I am not sure. I think so," replied Sabina. Jeffery continued looking at the fairycorn, who looked back at him almost motionlessly. Her eyes gently blinked, revealing her soft, white eyelashes that were full of finesse, like the wings of a blissful dove.

"I've got an idea," said Jeffery.

"What?" questioned Sabina as she watched Jeffery slowly insert his hand into the net while holding it against the tree. "What are you doing?" Jeffery grabbed the fairycorn tightly then quickly pulled her out and dropped the net. He turned around and held her out in front of Sabina.

"You said they juice them?" he asked her confidently.

"I heard," replied Sabina, with an astonished look.

"Well, maybe that's how you get what they should give you," suggested Jeffery. He looked at the albino fairycorn one last time then quickly threw her in his mouth and chewed. Sabina gasped and put both her hands on her mouth, trying to cover her giggles. Jeffery chewed faster and savored the albino fairycorn. Her texture was very soft, like pudding, and was full of juice that tasted like fresh coconut milk. After Jeffery swallowed, he looked at Sabina and smiled.

"Now she is in me forever," he said happily, opening his arms wide. Jeffery then felt himself getting shorter, and his legs were slowly evaporating into deep purple smoke. He looked down and saw that his belly button was bleeding black ink that streamed down his jeans.

"Uh oh," said Sabina. Jeffery looked at her and continued bleeding and evaporating. Black steam came out of his waist and worked its way up his spine.

"Help!" shouted Jeffery as he shrank and continued disappearing.

"Jeffery!" yelled Sabina with tears in her eyes. Finally, Jeffery's entire body evaporated and his head landed on the ground. After looking at Sabina for the last time, his head exploded and black ink shot everywhere then evaporated into deep purple smoke before hitting the soil in front of Sabina, who dropped down on her knees and began to sob.

Chapter Four

Lines from Mermen and Prophecies of Light

Jeffery opened his eyes and felt his body fading in with black smoke. He felt a little bit off balance and closed his eyes again. He looked around and saw that he was breathing under golden yellow water. Checking himself, he discovered that something had changed besides his breathing, from his waist down. His jeans were gone and so were his legs. His lower body was closed together in a big yellow fish tail, ending a bit longer than where his feet would have been. On the tips of his tail was a golden pattern of small suns and crabs. Startled by this discovery, Jeffery darted through the water and realized that this was his permanent figure. Jeffery tried swimming upwards but noticed that breathing became harder as he got close to the surface; this made him turn around and swim deeper instead.

He plunged, swimming downwards as fast as he could and then made a loop. He saw a lot of fish swim past him that were all yellow with black eyes and varied in size. Jeffery turned back around then swam downwards again. He continued swimming until he reached the bottom. The water was fresh and not salty. The sand was neon yellow and was full of crabs and corals in shades of yellow and beige. Jeffery turned to his right and swam straight ahead. He took notice of a large cave that had a few etchings of suns and crabs that looked just like the pattern on his tail. Feeling intrigued and curious, he plunged forward and swam into the cave. There were a few crabs loitering on the ground and the walls looked very smooth. Jeffery swam until he reached the other end of the cave and discovered a door. It was canary yellow and had a handle that was shaped like the head of a man, with long hair and a big beard. He noticed that it was made of shark bones and was hollowed in the eyes. He turned the knob and opened the door slowly, noticing that it was quite heavy and solid. Jeffery made his way in then shut the door behind him.

He swam into a room that looked somewhat exquisite in its own unique way but was also fairly casual. There was yellow flooring that matched the walls and a few golden bars around. Close to one of them, he noticed a golden stage that was a bit high and also had the same yellow floor. On it was a golden microphone on a tall stand. Its wires were yellow and were plugged into an outlet at the corner of the stage. As Jeffery swam in, he noticed the place was filled with mermen that had the same fish tail as him. Some were loitering casually with beer in their hands and some were sitting at the various bars. Jeffery swam around and observed the room. He noticed that the walls had pictures in golden frames of various mermen and male sex symbols. Some of the male sex symbols were alone and some were intertwined with others. Jeffery looked around at the various mermen and noticed that they were all happy. Some were telling jokes and laughing and others were just loitering while enjoying their beer. Jeffery swam up to the bar by the stage and took a seat on one of the plastic yellow stools.

"Can I get you a beer?" asked a merman after sitting on the stool next to Jeffery.

"Sure," said Jeffery. The merman ordered a couple of beers from the merman bartender and handed one to Jeffery. Jeffery thanked him and gulped down half his beer. It was sweet and mixed with mangos which felt very smooth and tasted great.

"Been here before?" asked the merman.

104

"First time," said Jeffery after shaking his head. Jeffery introduced himself to the merman and said that he had found the place while swimming casually.

"I see," said the merman. "Well, I am Rick."

"Pleasure," said Jeffery as they shook hands.

"I am glad you're here," said Rick. "Tonight is poetry night and there are some really awesome readers here."

"Really?" asked Jeffery.

"Totally," replied Rick with a nod, before gulping his beer. "You'll see, actually, in just a few minutes. You arrived at the right time, my friend."

"Good," said Jeffery, drinking more of his beer. Over his beer mug, Jeffery noticed a few more mermen enter from the canary yellow door. They were greeted by a few other mermen who were all very cheerful. Jeffery turned to look at Rick and took notice of his unique appearance. He was about the same size and shape as Jeffery but with slightly more pointy lips. His hair was blond and his eyes were blue. Jeffery saw that Rick had also taken notice of the recent arrivals and was looking at them.

"They seem excited," said Rick.

"Totally," agreed Jeffery. "Do you come here often?" he questioned Rick.

"I do," replied Rick. "I meet mermen here all the time."

"Interesting," said Jeffery. "I am here just to explore a bit," he added with slight cautiousness.

"I see," said Rick. "Do you see that merman over there?"

"Yes," replied Jeffery, turning to the merman Rick had referred to.

"He writes really well," explained Rick. "I have seen him read his poems before and he is actually really talented." Jeffery looked at the merman again. His skin was black and his body was very muscular. His head was bald and on the side he had a green tattoo of a crab. He was also tattooed

105

on his right upper arm. The merman looked somewhat intimidating at first glance but Jeffery noticed that many mermen were comfortable and happy talking to him.

"What does he write about?" questioned Jeffery.

"All sorts of things," answered Rick. "His poems deal with life, strength, and other things. He is also very inclusive. He likes to make sure that everyone is happy."

"Sounds like a gentleman," stated Jeffery.

"Absolutely," said Rick, "I think you'll enjoy listening to him." Not long after, another blond-haired merman with blue eyes came and sat next to Jeffery on his other side.

"You two having a good time?" he asked kindly.

"Absolutely," said Rick. Jeffery nodded.

"I'm Andy," said the merman, extending his hand.

"I am Jeffery," said Jeffery as he shook Andy's hand.

"And I am Rick," greeted Rick while leaning sideways to reach Andy's hand.

"Are any of you reading tonight?" asked Andy. Jeffery shook his head.

"Not tonight," said Rick.

"I see," replied Andy.

"And yourself?" asked Jeffery.

"Nope," said Andy. "But maybe next time," he added with a giggle then swam away.

"What was that all about?" asked Jeffery.

"Mermen," said Rick as he gulped his beer. "Just having a good time and talking to others."

"I see," said Jeffery with a short smirk. "I think he may have had too much beer." He laughed with Rick as they clinked their mugs and finished off their beer. Rick ordered another round and handed one over to Jeffery.

"Enjoy," he said happily.

"Yeah, you too," said Jeffery.

"That's why a lot of mermen come here," said Rick. "They just have beer, laugh, talk to one another, and some even find dates here."

"That's nice," said Jeffery, observing what Rick pointed out. "Do other creatures besides mermen come here?"

"Nope," replied Rick. "It is open to everyone but it is always mermen. It is kind of made for us to be with one another during our free time and stuff."

"Interesting," said Jeffery. "I like it. It is very cozy."

"It is," said Rick. "It is a very friendly atmosphere and all mermen are usually very happy." Jeffery gulped more beer and saw the lights dim before his eyes. All the mermen fell silent and looked towards the stage. Jeffery looked at the stage as well and saw an older, bald merman with some gray hair on both sides of his head and a large belly. His body was a little bit hairy, similar to his mustache and goatee, and he wore a golden ring on one of his fingers that shone under the yellow-white spotlight over him. Jeffery quickly noticed that the older merman wore a thick chain necklace that carried a pendant of a yellow crocksvenbulb! Jeffery looked around the place to see whether he could see another one, but couldn't because of the dimmed lighting.

"How are you-all gentlemen doing tonight?" the older merman asked calmly. The mermen cheered with excitement in reply. "That's great," he added with a smile. "I see that you are all very excited. We have a really good lineup of poets ready to read to you-all tonight. They've all worked hard on their poems and are very proud to present on this very stage. First up, we have Ross. He is excited to recite two of his poems for us, so please, give a round of applause to Ross!" The whole crowd cheered and clapped as Ross entered the stage. Jeffery saw that he was the same man that Rick had pointed out earlier. Jeffery looked up and down at his tattoos and then noticed that Ross was wearing a ring similar to the one that the older merman wore. He also noticed a thick golden chain around Ross's neck with the same crocksvenbulb.

"I'm glad he is going first," said Rick. Jeffery smiled then looked back at Ross. Jeffery was intrigued by the fact that he was quite tall and really muscular.

"How's everyone doing tonight?" asked Ross. The crowd hollered in greeting and enthusiasm. "Great to hear!" cheered Ross. "Well, I have two poems for you tonight. One of them is a short love poem and the other is a personal one about a dark time in my life. I have memorized them for you and I am very thankful to be here with you all." Ross adjusted the microphone and himself and then looked back at the audience. Jeffery felt his heartbeats getting faster, so he drank more of his beer. Ross then recited his first poem wholeheartedly:

I found a rose one night last summer
I refused to pluck it because I thought that its thorns were too sharp
But now, as I look back
I realize that it was a very luscious rose."

Ross looked down and everyone clapped. Jeffery was impressed by the poem so he clapped as well.

"I told you he's good," said Rick.

"Totally," agreed Jeffery. "I bet that this rose he's referring to is another merman."

"Most likely," said Rick. After the hollering and cheering faded out, Jeffery looked back at the stage and saw that Ross was ready to recite his second poem. He looked much less calm and more encouraged. He now had a stern look on his face and deepened his voice as he recited:

"On this battlefield I stand

Ready to conquer

And not afraid to die

On this battlefield I stand

Gods watch over me

Ready to make my move

On this battlefield I stand

A golden sword in my hand

A steel shield in the other

On this battlefield I stand

I face my enemy

Whose eye's ablaze

On this battlefield I stand

Adrenalin drops from my head

Flowing anger through my veins

On this battlefield I stand

Victorious and full of pride

With an intimidating lust for blood

On this battlefield I stand

Your head will be my pride

And your blood will be my wine

On this battlefield I stand

The slayer of life

The only warrior who will survive."

Ross then bowed his head and flexed his muscular arms. The entire place clapped even louder and cheered with the deepest of admiration.

Jeffery could not believe his ears so he turned to Rick with a look of astonishment.

"I told you," repeated Rick, "this guy is something."

"He really is," agreed Jeffery.

"He's actually won trophies before," explained Rick.

"I am not surprised," said Jeffery. "And how many gods are there?" he very quietly wondered to himself while briefly thinking about Allie. The older merman went back onstage and shook Ross's hand. After Ross swam away, the older merman began to speak.

"Well, now, that was quite something, eh?" he complimented contentedly. "Now our next merman is a sporadic guest; we only get to see him once every now and then. Tonight, he brings us a poem that he says is really personal to him, so please show your support for George!" Everyone clapped again and Jeffery saw another merman enter. His appearance was actually similar to Jeffery's and he did not wear a crocksvenbulb. Jeffery listened carefully.

"Hello everyone, nice to see you," greeted George. After the crowd cheered again, George gently recited his poem, trying to avoid making any eye contact:

"I see you and I dream of you
You held me close and never let go
Your eyes were the same color as mine
And your hands were firm and loving
You laughed at my flips and loved my words
Wherever you may be today
I dream of you continuously
And maybe someday we will unite up on a hill
Up on a hill at a charming castle."

George became tearful and everyone clapped. Jeffery clapped along then thought deeply. He remembered George the ladybug, and how some lines from George's poem applied to him by creating a strong sense of nostalgia. Jeffery watched George swim off the stage and before long, he disappeared and Jeffery forgot his appearance.

"Ready for the second reader?" asked Rick.

"The second one?" asked Jeffery.

"Yeah, there are a few readers tonight," replied Rick.

"I know," confirmed Jeffery, "but George was the second one. Do you mean the third?"

"George? Who's George?" asked Rick.

"As always, Ross is a fantastic reader," began the older merman cheerfully from the stage. "Are you-all ready for our second reader of the night?" All the mermen cheered in demand.

"Strange," said Jeffery.

"What happened? Who is George?" questioned Rick, crossing his eyes.

"I thought there was another merman who just read after Ross. He was also introduced, read a sweet poem, then finished and swam offstage," expounded Jeffery, confused.

"Nope," said Rick. "That's peculiar. Do you need some fresh air?"

"That would be good," said Jeffery.

"Follow me," instructed Rick. Jeffery followed Rick and swam to the other end of the place. There was another canary yellow door that had a topaz knob made of coral. There seemed to be some letters carefully etched in it, but Rick quickly opened the door and Jeffery followed him. Rick took Jeffery close in his arms and shot upwards. Jeffery felt Rick swim very fast so he turned to look at the bottom of his tail and saw that it was spinning like a vortex at a rapid speed, creating many bubbles. "Be prepared," he warned.

"For what?" asked Jeffery.

"We're going out of the water," answered Rick. Jeffery looked up and saw a golden-yellow jelly form that was almost the same color as the water. It split in two, then one piece went on his head like a helmet and the other did the same on Rick's.

"Almost there," cautioned Rick. Jeffery kept staring at the approaching surface and allowed Rick to continue taking full control. Jeffery then plunged through the surface and went soaring up into the sky while held by Rick. After exiting the water, the two jellies transformed into a jelly boat, allowing them to land safely. Jeffery breathed heavily as the boat lowered itself and landed next to a golden-yellow pond beside long and healthy dandelions with bronze stems. The jelly boat melted, allowing Jeffery and Rick to gently land on the yellow grass.

"That was wild," said Jeffery.

"Just relax until our legs come back," said Rick.

"Our legs?" asked Jeffery. He opened his eyes and saw the bright yellow sky. It was clear except for one cloud in the shape of a large dot that was lined with golden sparkles. Jeffery sat up and looked at the grass and the pond. Everything was yellow, like his fish tail. "Where are we?"

"Don't worry, relax," reassured Rick, "just relax." Jeffery saw a couple of small, plump yellow birds fly by and land on the grass between him and Rick. They were half the size of his head and had thick feet and beaks that were white and smooth. Their eyes were quite flat, which made their faces seem large. They chirped softly and ate some of the grass.

"Look at those," said Jeffery.

"They're cute, eh?" replied Rick.

"They really are," said Jeffery. He reached out to pet one but they both flew off, causing Rick to laugh briefly.

"It isn't time yet," said Rick.

"Time for what?" asked Jeffery.

"When you manage to pet a bird, it means that there is something coming for you," elucidated Rick. "But if the bird flies off, it means that there is something but it isn't time."

"I see," said Jeffery.

"And who is this George?" asked Rick. Before Jeffery could reply, he felt something happening to his tail. He saw it fading away back to his legs, boots and jeans. Jeffery then turned to Rick and saw that he was barefoot and in yellow shorts with a matching yellow tank top.

"Well, George was someone that I knew very well," answered Jeffery, softly.

"How well?" asked Rick.

"Well enough to name him," replied Jeffery. "I just saw someone who had his name, George, and he recited a poem."

"Yes, and there was no George down there," replied Rick. "In fact, I don't ever recall meeting a George." Jeffery turned and faced him.

"What could that mean?" he asked as his eyes reddened.

"Well, it isn't time for it," insisted Rick. Jeffery then saw the two birds fly past and watched them as they disappeared. "Just not time, but soon." Jeffery tried to smile.

"He had a good heart," told Jeffery, "but I want to leave it at that."

"Fair enough," replied Rick. "We all get our hearts broken every now and then."

"Please, I said enough," said Jeffery firmly.

"Alright," said Rick.

"And what is this place. Where are we now?" asked Jeffery, looking around.

"We're just out of the water," clarified Rick. "There are several ponds around here that take us back into various parts of it."

"Do the other mermen come up here?" asked Jeffery.

"Not too often," replied Rick.

"Why?" inquired Jeffery.

"Well, not many of them like it up here," said Rick.

"Really?" asked Jeffery.

"Really," Rick reassured him.

"Then why are we up here?" asked Jeffery.

"Well, you needed to space out," answered Rick. "You clearly aren't from around here."

"I am not," admitted Jeffery.

"Where do you come from?" asked Rick.

"Please, that's a long story," said Jeffery with a sigh.

"That's ok, just relax," said Rick. "I have someone I want to introduce to you after."

"Who?" asked Jeffery.

"I'll tell you later. For now, just lie down and take a rest," said Rick. "You are awfully stressed." Jeffery threw himself back and closed his eyes. When he opened them again, he saw Rick lying down next to him with his hand on his stomach. Looking away, Jeffery saw the two birds fly back and land in the grass close by. He closed his eyes again and wondered. After a while, Jeffery stood up, then went and sat close to the pond. While looking at it, a baby yellow crab came out and then ran away, disappearing in the grass. Jeffery wafted his hand through the water, causing some ripples to form that let out a gentle echoing sound. Rick came over and sat next to him. Jeffery was hesitant to talk so he said nothing and stared at the pond.

"From the minute I met you," started Rick, "I knew there was something interesting about you."

"Like what?" asked Jeffery, turning to face Rick.

"I don't know exactly," replied Rick, "I really don't. Truthfully, you seem like you are on some sort of adventure."

"I don't know that I'd call this an adventure," said Jeffery.

"Well, you know... life," said Rick. "You just seem to be managing your way, like all of us."

"Well, I am trying," replied Jeffery. He turned back to look at the pond and saw his reflection. While looking at it, Rick moved closer to him and started speaking.

"I brought you up here for a reason," said Rick.

"What?" asked Jeffery, looking up to face Rick.

"My father lives here, by the sea, on the other side of the moor," explained Rick softly. "He is really gifted. We don't usually go to see him unless there is something urgent, and I think you need to see him."

"Why is that?" asked Jeffery kindly.

"He can give you some clarity," answered Rick. "Here, I will guide you to him." Jeffery stood up and walked behind Rick. The land was rather flat with a few trees here and there. In front, along the horizon, Jeffery saw a large body of water that seemed far away. It was also yellow, but far more lustrous than the rest of the landscape. Something about it seemed very curious to Jeffery, but his train of thought was interrupted by Rick who pointed in that direction and explained that his father lived close to there. Jeffery began to think about what he'd experienced up until this point and what was next to come. He also thought about the mermen and wondered whether he should tell Rick how he really felt. Jeffery felt his mind getting cluttered with questions so he decided to look away and tried to breathe them out. He looked at the clear, yellow sky, then around at all the surroundings in search of something restful.

While walking, Rick tripped and fell sideways so Jeffery bent over and caught him. He grabbed him by his arm and side, and then held him until he had adjusted his balance.

"That was close," said Jeffery.

"Yeah, but thank you," said Rick with a small limp. "The grass is so thick."

"It is quite thick, yes," agreed Jeffery. "Does that mean anything?" he asked as they walked.

"I don't know," said Rick, "I hope not."

"How old is your father?" asked Jeffery.

"Old," replied Rick, "late sixties."

"I see," said Jeffery. "How long has he been gifted?"

"Since before I was born," said Rick. "I remember when I was a child he'd always predict things and say things that I found amusing. And little did I know that they would happen within a matter of time."

"What is he like?" asked Jeffery curiously.

"He's a nice guy," answered Rick, "really gentle and helpful. He's very honest."

"That's good," said Jeffery. "Do you two get along?"

"We really do," answered Rick, "we just don't see each other all the time."

"Why?" asked Jeffery.

"He likes being alone a lot," explained Rick. "It helps him focus on his readings and stuff. That is why we only go see him when we really need to." As Jeffery walked, he noticed that they had gotten a lot closer to the sea. To his left he saw a cottage, similar to the one Sabina lived in, but it was painted yellow and it was a little bit smaller. There was a window on one side and a small, canary-yellow door with topaz linings in the center.

"Well, time sure went by fast," said Jeffery.

"Don't tell him that," instructed Rick. "He has lots to say about that subject."

"Really?" asked Jeffery.

"Really," replied Rick.

"Does he go down to that place where all the mermen were?" asked Jeffery after hesitating.

"No," answered Rick, "that's not really his thing."

"Why not?" asked Jeffery.

"He tends to enjoy his space more," said Rick. "That's why he has this little house. It is his sanctum, where he can do his readings and stuff."

"Fair enough," said Jeffery. "I sort of like that, actually."

"Really?" asked Rick. "I think you two will get along. He has had some rather unique experiences throughout his lifetime." Rick then stepped ahead of Jeffery and knocked at the door. After a moment of silence, he knocked again.

"You think he's home?" asked Jeffery.

"Oh, yes," said Rick with a nod, "he always is." The door opened and Jeffery found himself and Rick being greeted by an older man. He did not look sixties-old, more like late thirties or early forties. He had a very round head with really short, dark hair and a dark beard that was nicely kept. After entering, Jeffery took a closer look at Rick's father's appearance. He wore a tight yellow suit with a black shirt under it and black shoes that were pointy at the tips.

"Well, have a seat," said Rick's father. "My name is Alp, and what can I do for you today?" Jeffery took a look around the room and saw that the house was small inside and on a single level. It was somewhat circular and the floor was made of yellow-orange hardwood. The kitchen walls were a soft yellow with nothing on them, while the living space walls were dandelion yellow and decorated with a few ornaments. Next to the window was a classic golden birdcage that hung from the ceiling with its door open. Inside it were three small yellow birds with bright golden eyes that quietly sat in a fluffy nest. They chirped softly and gently preened one another with their small and slightly round beaks.

"Well, Dad," started Rick, "I met Jeffery earlier, at the poetry place. You know, when it's day here, it's night there, so yeah, I met him and he claimed to have seen a poet named George and there was no such merman. I brought him up here for a little break and I think that you should do a reading for him." Jeffery looked back at the window and noticed right above it hung a yellow crocksvenbulb. He wanted to act as though everything was fine so he looked back at Alp. He noticed that Alp wore a crocksvenbulb as a pendant on a gold chain that was slightly peeking from behind his shirt.

"Very well," said Alp, looking directly at Jeffery. Alp took a seat at the dark golden-yellow table between him and Rick and continued looking at Jeffery directly. Jeffery looked back at Alp and saw that he looked very distinct from Rick. "You are very confused about something."

"I am?" asked Jeffery.

"You are, don't act like you're not," said Alp. "You are really confused and you had this conversation with a woman, not very long ago."

"Yes," said Jeffery nervously. He glanced at the crocksvenbulb then back at Alp.

"And she was in love with you," stated Alp clearly.

"I guess," said Jeffery.

"I know," said Alp. "You can't hide things from me that easily." Jeffery felt a small nudge in his gut that caused him to swallow. Alp then asked Rick to bring Jeffery a glass of water. Rick filled up a tall wineglass that was decorated with a yellow crab at its base, and delivered it to Jeffery. Jeffery sipped on it nervously and looked at Alp.

"What else do you see?" asked Jeffery.

"I see a lot," replied Alp. "And the name George represents more than just a poet to you." Jeffery looked down and tried not to cry. "But it doesn't matter what I see in your past. What matters more is your future."

"Do you see a lot happening for him?" asked Rick.

"I wouldn't say a lot," answered Alp, "but it is very significant." Alp shifted his gaze back to Jeffery. "I know there is a lot of pressure on you to be a certain way, but that won't last long."

"Please," said Jeffery, "is there anything I need to do to get there?"

"Just live," replied Alp. "It will happen sooner or later. But you see… " Alp paused and turned to Rick. "Rick, do you mind going back? I need some time alone with Jeffery."

"Alright," replied Rick, turning to Jeffery. Rick got up and walked to the door. After opening it he turned and looked at Jeffery for a moment. Jeffery looked back at him and wondered what Rick might have wanted to say. At that moment, Rick walked out and closed the door. Alp got up and locked it, then sat back down with his gaze on Jeffery.

"It will be alright," said Alp calmly. "The journey is already halfway through."

"Really?" asked Jeffery.

"Really," Alp reassured. "You will have an opportunity down the road to come face to face with something really precious. And it will be a milestone for you."

"Is that right?" asked Jeffery.

"Mark my words," said Alp clearly. "It will be a great experience, and almost colorless."

"And as for George?" asked Jeffery.

"I see some incident in the past and it involves a splash," explained Alp, closing his eyes. "It was very painful."

"Yes, it was," agreed Jeffery.

119

"Yes," said Alp, "but move on."

"What do you mean?" questioned Jeffery.

"It is in the *past*," reinforced Alp. "There is nothing you can do about it. The up-there have something else planned for you and it is related more to your self-discovery, which is connected to your confusion."

"You mean, there is no way to solve the past, is there?" asked Jeffery softly.

"It doesn't matter," said Alp. "That is not your destiny. Your destiny is to discover yourself and I see the letter *C* involved in your future."

"The letter *C*?" asked Jeffery.

"Yep," replied Alp. "It is something that you will have forever. You will also cherish it with all your heart. There will be pride and there will be glamor."

"That's great," said Jeffery with a gentle smile.

"Believe me, I am never wrong," said Alp. Jeffery watched Alp closely as he reached into his pocket and pulled out a deck of cards. Alp shuffled them well then asked Jeffery to pick the first number that came to his mind. Jeffery closed his eyes and thought for a few seconds.

"One," he said the moment he opened his eyes. Alp shuffled the cards again, drew one, and then put it face down in front of Jeffery. Jeffery reached out to flip it over but Alp interrupted him and asked him not to move. Alp closed his eyes again and put his right hand on the card as Jeffery observed its obscure patterns.

"This is beautiful and divine," he said gratefully. "There is a lot of light and a huge gift coming to you." Alp then opened his eyes and sat back. "I have never seen such energy in my life. You will come face to face with the divine."

"What do you mean?" asked Jeffery.

"You are a unique being," replied Alp. "And the inner strength you will discover someday will be unleashed with the power of something higher." He then reached over and flipped the card, revealing a beautiful painting of a woman resting in a heavenly sky. "You may even be back here on this particular land," said Alp, "but this one is a maybe."

"It looks beautiful," said Jeffery.

"Yes, that's where you'll be," said Alp. The birds began to sing softly and Jeffery saw more sunlight enter the house and brighten it up. "I also keep seeing boulders that look very hard and daunting. That tells me there will be lies and suffering in your future, but keep in mind that the number one represents unity and being at peace with yourself. It oftentimes also represents a solid and divine figure."

"That is gorgeous. It's what I want," said Jeffery. "But do you have any advice on the hardship that's coming up?" Alp smiled at him and gave him a positive look of certainty. "Remember, Jeffery, that courage, inner strength, positive attitude and smart thinking have enough power to alter fate." Jeffery thanked Alp and held onto his glass tightly. "Not saying there aren't any bumps down your path, but as many of the mermen say: one can't create the rainbow without rain."

"Well, thank you again," said Jeffery. "If you don't mind me asking, does Rick have similar abilities?"

"He does but he doesn't want to explore them," replied Alp. "He is too busy exploring with the mermen."

"I see," said Jeffery. "You two don't look alike."

"I know," said Alp. "But two spirits don't need to look alike to be ultimately connected."

"I guess that is true," agreed Jeffery.

"It is true," stated Alp. "I have had so many experiences with divine figures and things outside of this reality—I have been around long enough to know."

"I see that," said Jeffery. "You seem to know my inner self really well."

"Yes, and I actually adore that character," said Alp.

"Thank you," said Jeffery.

"Very caring and passionate," added Alp.

"How did you learn this beautiful ability?" asked Jeffery.

"That is a long story," said Alp. "It really is more my journey than it is anyone else's." Jeffery glanced at the crocksvenbulb then back at Alp, who then stood up and walked to the birdcage. He smiled at the birds and let them peck on his fingers, then he walked to the window and looked back at Jeffery. As Jeffery drank more water, something completely unforeseen happened. A small whirl of energy started at Alp's feet, creating a sound like wind. Jeffery watched it closely as yellow and white light descended onto Alp and transformed him into a wizard-like figure. Alp was now taller and very old-looking. He had a lank white beard that was down to his Adam's apple and wore a long yellow cloak that covered all of him. His head was bald and his nose was a bit long and arched. Jeffery was stunned by what he had witnessed.

"Wow, what did you do?" asked Jeffery in admiration.

"I am an old soul," replied Alp, "and I don't always appear in one way."

"Just astounding!" exclaimed Jeffery.

"You see," started Alp, "the up-there are telling me that it is best that you now continue on your journey. There is a lot ahead of you. Just remember that the divine light is at the end of this journey and you must go on."

"I will," said Jeffery, sounding brave.

"Come on," instructed Alp as he proceeded to the door. Jeffery followed as they both exited together and walked back in the direction from which he and Rick had come. After walking for some time, Alp stood and observed the yellow grass. He bent over and picked up a small yellow crab and looked at it.

"They seem to be everywhere here," said Jeffery.

"Indeed," agreed Alp, "they are very harmless and very gentle." Jeffery took the crab and allowed it to wander around his palm. "A lot like George, eh?"

"Yes, except that George talked," answered Jeffery. Alp laughed subtly then turned to face the sea, which was now quite a distance away.

"Remember, Jeffery, that each end is the start of a new beginning. And if it ends in slime, it starts a cycle," said Alp.

"What do you mean?" asked Jeffery.

"Don't worry too much, you'll see," replied Alp, laughing. "Just look at the sea and focus." Jeffery looked at the sea and saw that the horizon was tan in color and seemed to divide the sky from the water in a jolting manner. It looked very arbitrary but also very necessary.

"It's beautiful," said Jeffery trying to start another subject after releasing the crab.

"Are you ready to launch your way across it?" asked Alp.

"Maybe," answered Jeffery, "it depends on what's beyond there."

"Well, just keep looking at it," said Alp. "Your destiny will take you where you belong." Alp took a few steps ahead then turned and looked at Jeffery. Jeffery took another look at Alp and at his old appearance, still amazed at the transformation he had seen earlier. He looked back at the sea and felt a brush of cool air paint across his forehead. As he looked around, he saw that he was being lifted up from the ground. After reaching a height of about forty feet, Jeffery saw a ball form around him that was yellow and made of jelly.

"Look! Another jelly!" he yelled excitedly. Looking down, he noticed that Alp couldn't hear him. The jelly began to slowly move ahead as Alp waved goodbye. Jeffery waved back and floated around in the jelly bubble. As it flew ahead, it flew higher up and made a turn. After going around in a circle, it went forward quickly and traveled over the sea, leaving Alp behind. Jeffery felt frightened about where he was being sent off to but then he remembered some of Alp's words and tried to keep calm, encompassed in his newly learned wisdom. He looked up at the clear sky and saw birds flying back and forth. One bird even flew over the jelly and landed on it but flew off after a few seconds. Jeffery floated downwards and sat down.

He looked ahead and saw that the sea across was endless. Turning around, he saw that the land behind him had completely disappeared. Jeffery sighed and began to think about where he was being sent off to next. He reflected upon Alp's reading and thought of the card. The image of the woman resting made him feel sleepy so he lay on his side. Jeffery kept his eyes open and watched the waves of the sea come and go with the birds. After a brief nap, he woke up and felt the jelly descending. It dropped down until it was about twenty feet above the sea then flew back up again. Jeffery scratched his head and began looking around. He didn't see any change but he noticed that the smell of the air was slightly different and more polluted.

As time passed, Jeffery began to get bored. He bounced from side to side in the jelly and even tried to eat some of it but noticed that it couldn't be damaged. Jeffery sat back down at the bottom of the jelly bubble and observed the sea again. The smell became a little bit more pungent which caused him to plug his nose. Jeffery felt the jelly fly faster and after another slight turn, he saw some land at the end of the sea. It was expansive with large trees. As the jelly got closer, Jeffery noticed that the land was much darker in color and the smell worsened. The jelly flew faster towards the land then crashed right into its soil, traveling right through it. It traveled through a tunnel that looked like it was made of really dry soil. After reaching the end of the tunnel, it disappeared and left Jeffery standing on his feet, curious of what to expect.

Chapter Five

A System So High and Stubborn

Jeffery saw a large hole at the end of the copper soil-tunnel so he walked right to the threshold. While leaning on his side, he saw a large pyramid across from him that was made of hard stone, copper in color with a long path that circulated upwards around it almost like a spiral. On that path, Jeffery saw many tiny figures walking single file up towards the peak of the pyramid, which had a small window that was releasing ghastly smoke, slightly lighter than the color of the pyramid. Around the pyramid were several of these tiny figures digging and lots of spare shovels were scattered across the ground. Jeffery took a close look at the small figures that were hard at work and saw that they were shaped like eggs and were about three feet tall. They had tiny arms and tiny legs with really flat hands and feet that were a couple of shades darker than the rest of their bodies. Some of them were a dark copper, almost like a blend of red and brown, and some were light copper with a tint of orange. While Jeffery watched, he saw that after the figures would dig out something, they'd drop their shovels then run and make their way up the path. Jeffery found the sight interesting but his gut felt a bit strange about the situation of these figures. It seemed like something irrational that was normalized and presented as an option with no other choice. He also tried taking a closer look at the window they were going into at the pyramid's peak but saw that none of them were exiting again. Jeffery shifted his focus to the ones that were digging and noticed that the top first

126

quarter part of their bodies were hollow and therefore seemed a little translucent.

Watching his step, Jeffery crossed the threshold and ventured onto the soil field. He walked towards the pyramid and took a closer look at the preoccupied figures that were digging. One dropped its shovel and ran off to the pyramid so Jeffery decided to look at where it was digging. Jeffery saw a gap that was very deep causing the copper color of the soil to shine. Jeffery wondered what the figure might have found. He saw another one drop its shovel and run so he decided to walk over to its area. Before taking a closer look, Jeffery heard a man's voice yelling towards him. He turned around and saw a midget approaching.

"And where do you think you're going?" scolded the midget. Jeffery felt his boots sinking into the soft soil as sweat ran down his palms.

"I am just observing, sir," he said sounding slightly intimidated.

"Observing what?" asked the midget while looking up at Jeffery, noticing his perceived-to-be eccentric appearance. The midget was three feet tall and wore a copper top hat that was one foot high and a small suit jacket that was also copper-colored and accompanied by a matching vest. His pants were striped with vertical lines alternating between copper and pale white. The midget also wore platform boots that were made of polyvinyl chloride that added inches to his height and perfectly matched the color of his outfit. On the side of each platform was a dollar sign, one made of yellow gold and the other of rose gold. His face was that of an old man with a really big and curved nose that matched well with his wrinkles and thick, auburn eyebrows. His beard was white with bits of auburn and copper, and his eyes were hazel and very forbidding.

"Just at all this," answered Jeffery nervously.

"Nobody observes here," ordered the midget, "you either are put to work or you get sent out!"

"Pardon me?" said Jeffery.

"Come on, just grab the shovel," said the midget. "Dig right here, and whatever you find, take it up to the pyramid and I will show you what to do with it."

"Well, alright," said Jeffery. After bending over and grabbing the shovel that was left by one of the figures, Jeffery dug into the ground but continued to secretly observe.

"And everybody around here calls me Ribs," said the midget as he walked away.

"Ribs," Jeffery repeated to himself quietly. He looked at the midget who was walking away, then looked back at the ground. "Your rib probably fits in my ear just well," he added as he plunged forward and began to dig. After digging a small hole, Jeffery felt his shovel hitting something a little bit hard. He moved over some of the soil and saw something metallic. Jeffery continued to unearth it until he discovered a trophy of a big fly made of bronze. Jeffery dropped the shovel and picked up the trophy. The fly was round and had wings, two big eyes and a mediocre look on its face. Jeffery walked to the pyramid and saw several of the figures following him with objects in their hands. He allowed them to pass by him so that he could replicate their actions accordingly. They all ran behind the pyramid, which caused Jeffery to realize that the path around started there. While getting in line, Jeffery saw Ribs standing nearby with a thick cigar in his mouth, exhaling very thick, copper-colored smoke, similar to the smoke that was being released from the window at the top of the pyramid.

"There you are! What have you found?" asked Ribs.

"Some trophy of a fly," replied Jeffery while looking down at Ribs.

"Yeah, ok," said Ribs, "I'll walk with you."

"So, what is this place exactly?" asked Jeffery.

"This is my workforce," replied Ribs, "I own it."

"And who are they?" asked Jeffery while pointing at all the figures around them.

"People," said Ribs, "they're called people, now hurry up." Jeffery followed Ribs as they went onto the path and began walking single file. The peoples' walks and movements weren't synchronized, as they were all carrying various things, but Jeffery was able to see that they all had the same target in mind: delivering to the top. He also observed the path that he and Ribs were walking on. It was flat, very sandy and quite wide.

"These people are surely small in size," said Jeffery. Ribs looked up at him with a rather despising look.

"And where did *you* come from?" he asked disgustedly. "I have never seen figures more than a few feet tall."

"That's a long story," said Jeffery as he thought of the Fogbusts. While walking, he felt his leg muscles and quads hurt but he didn't complain as he knew that reaching the top was quite some ways away.

"Not interesting," said Ribs bluntly. "But wherever you came from, make sure that you work hard. I treat my workforce with care."

"Alright," said Jeffery sounding a bit uncertain. "Where did all these people come from?"

"They have always been here," replied Ribs. "They needed something to do in exchange for some currency so I put this together. I give them currency and I profit."

"Really?" asked Jeffery. Ribs did not reply. He just kept walking then moved next to Jeffery while all the people remained in single file. This made Jeffery feel a little bit awkward but at the same time, curious as to what sort of adventure this was leading to. He looked up and tried to see what was above the pyramid, but all he could see was a ceiling of copper dirt with a small hole not far from the point of the pyramid that allowed a little bit of light to enter.

"Walk a little faster, would you?" yelled Ribs at the people ahead. The people panicked a bit then began walking faster while trying very hard not to drop the things they were carrying. Jeffery saw that Ribs began to walk faster so he picked up his pace as well and started panting lightly. Before long, Jeffery felt the path turn and move uphill, and he noticed it was getting sandier. Some of the people had sand kicked back at them causing them to cough, but all they did was continue to walk. Because of his height, the sand only reached Jeffery's ankles. He wondered how it must feel for the people to have sand kicked back at their faceless selves. Nonetheless, Jeffery sympathised with them.

"Sometimes they walk a bit too slow," Ribs told Jeffery.

"Right," replied Jeffery, "and what is currency?"

"It's something you exchange labor for," answered Ribs. "Usually it is in coin form, but it can be paper bills at times, you know, just something meretricious that they think is valuable."

"I see," said Jeffery.

"And don't worry, you'll get some of it as well," said Ribs.

"Alright," said Jeffery. He then asked himself how much he would benefit from this currency thing, and why it was so important to these people. He decided not to ask any further questions as he was panting heavier while carrying the trophy. He was also curious to see what was inside that window. Jeffery looked to the side and saw that he had made a loop around the pyramid, giving him a view of where he'd dug earlier and saw that there were lots of people digging and running to the pyramid.

"What is your name?" asked Ribs.

"Jeffery," replied Jeffery.

"Interesting," said Ribs, "some people have names but I don't always bother to remember them."

"There are quite a lot of them," said Jeffery.

130

"There are," agreed Ribs while looking down. "They cost me a lot of currency." Jeffery sighed. While walking, one of the people, a dark copper one, came running and pushed Jeffery aside and raced ahead, causing Jeffery to accidently bump into Ribs, which tipped his balance. "You see what I mean? They are just always eager to get to the top to deposit what they've found, but they don't know that it'll never benefit them in any way—just a little extra currency, if that." Jeffery glanced at the people behind him and in front of him. "They don't hear very well," added Ribs after taking notice of this.

"Interesting," said Jeffery while feeling puzzled.

"They're so worthless but what can I do?" said Ribs.

"Don't say anything," said a male's voice. Jeffery looked around but didn't see anyone. "I mean it, keep your calm."

"We're almost there," announced Ribs after noticing that Jeffery had looked back. "We are almost at the top." Jeffery turned and looked to his side and noticed that, indeed, they were more than halfway up the pyramid. The view of the ground and people digging looked much smaller. He questioned where that male voice had come from. In his mind, he imagined a bright white light shining before his eyes, but this thought was quickly interrupted by Ribs scolding at the people in front to walk faster.

"I thought you said we were almost there?" questioned Jeffery.

"We are, but I have other things to do," answered Ribs. Jeffery looked to his side again and saw that they were walking on the path that was facing the other side. It didn't look much different from the other one. There were several people digging and running to and from the pyramid with energy and enthusiasm.

"So what happens at the top?" asked Jeffery.

"That's where you deposit what you found," replied Ribs.

"Deposit it?" asked Jeffery, looking at the fly trophy sharply.

131

"Yeah, you will see," said Ribs. "It is simple, then you come back down and find some more stuff."

"Alright," replied Jeffery. Before long, he reached the window of the pyramid with Ribs and was greeted by a big gust of thick copper smoke. "That is some really polluted smoke," Jeffery added while coughing.

"Yeah, you must feel it more from up there," said Ribs, looking up at Jeffery. Jeffery bent his head down and stepped in alongside Ribs. After entering, he saw a large cauldron that was made of copper, standing in the corner of the small room and that it was generating all of the copper-colored smoke; it was a bit corroded from the bottom thus some light-green scratches were visible. Next to it was a dark and wide hole that all the people were jumping into after dropping in their items.

"This is scary," Jeffery whispered to himself, trying not to be heard. He looked to the wall next to him and saw a crocksvenbulb hanging and that it was camouflaged into the color of the pyramid. Around it were several dollar signs that circled in a pattern and were made of copper. They were much shinier than the crocksvenbulb and right under them was an etched statement that read *In God We Trust*. Jeffery right away thought of Allie and lost his grip over the trophy but caught it before it was too late. Before he had time to think, all the people in front of him had deposited their items and were long gone into the hole.

"Well, hurry up! What are you waiting for?" yelled Ribs. Jeffery quickly threw the trophy into the cauldron, which then released a bigger gust of smoke, then went on and jumped into the hole with his eyes closed. As Jeffery fell, he felt the wind run through his hair and saw a flash of white light pass by.

"Just hang on," said the male voice again. Jeffery felt goose bumps grow on his body and before long, he had fallen onto some soil. He opened his eyes and saw that he was back on the site, and several people fell after him. As soon as they fell, they got up and quickly ran around the pyramid to continue digging. Jeffery looked up and saw that on the pyramid, about a third of the way up from ground level, there was a big, rusted and grotesque-looking pipe sticking out that more people were falling from. Jeffery stared at it curiously.

"Well, you got the drill, there?" asked Ribs rigidly while standing next to Jeffery and looking down. Jeffery took notice of Ribs's presence and nodded. "Well, hurry up and go dig some more. Pretty soon we'll be switching to the next task." Jeffery stood up and slowly walked around the pyramid and looked to find a shovel. He tried digesting everything that he had just witnessed but couldn't seem to make sense out of anything. He thought about the cauldron, the crocksvenbulb, the pipe, the dollar signs, and even the smoke. Jeffery asked himself what all this could mean. While walking, he found a shovel on the ground next to a dug area so he picked it up and continued digging through the soil. As he dug, he noticed a shiny copper-colored metal shimmer as if it were some luminous reflection.

"Just dirt," Jeffery told himself as he tried to ignore it. He continued digging until he found a heart pendant that was about the size of his palm. Jeffery dropped the shovel and picked up the pendant. It wasn't made of actual copper, but some sort of metal that seemed to mimic it quite well. Jeffery looked on the back and found some engraved writing. "My parents, Margret and John," Jeffery read aloud. "My three siblings and my wife, Cassidy," he finished. Jeffery held the pendant tightly and felt that there was some sort of meaning to it. He turned around and walked back towards the pyramid to deposit it.

After entering the window at the top of the pyramid again, Jeffery took a closer look at the crocksvenbulb, circle of dollar signs, and the etched writing. Before it was his turn to deposit the pendant, he stepped out of the line and faced the crocksvenbulb for a moment. He noticed that there were twelve dollar signs in total. Jeffery glanced back and saw that the people weren't looking at him. They were waiting eagerly to make their deposits and hopped into the hole as soon as they did so. Jeffery turned back and looked at the dollar sign that was directly above the crocksvenbulb, at the top center of the circle. In very small print, at the bottom part of it, Jeffery saw the name *Leanne* engraved clearly. He repeated the name to himself and started thinking about the dollar signs individually while going clockwise around the circle. The next two dollar signs had nothing engraved in them, but the third one, which was directly to the right of the crocksvenbulb, had the name *Ingrid*. The following two were also not engraved but the third one, which was directly under the crocksvenbulb, contained the name *Edith*. Jeffery followed this pattern and saw that the dollar sign that was directly to the left of the crocksvenbulb had the name *Solomon*, as the remaining two had nothing.

"Leanne Ingrid-Edith Solomon," Jeffery said to himself trying to put the names together. "Or could it be, Leanne Ingrid Edith-Solomon?" After looking at the dollar signs and the crocksvenbulb, Jeffery reread the etched statement, recited the four names, and then raced right to the cauldron. He threw the heart pendant into it and quickly jumped into the hole with his eyes open. As he fell, Jeffery noticed that the inside of the hole was black and rusted, but also wide. Before long, he fell flying out of the pipe and landed back down on the soil as before. Jeffery got up and carried on walking, ready to find another shovel. As he walked, he took notice of two of the lighter copper-colored people walking and whispering while seeming unhappy.

"I don't know if there is anything after. We just do all this work, get very little currency, and continue," one of them, a female, said to the other.

"That's the system," replied the other one, also a female. "They think they are doing us a favor by giving us a duty, but really, it is draining us to benefit them."

"It is immoral, I say," said the one who had spoken first. "Destitution, prostitution, all caused by your pompous constitution, that is now taking us into prosecution," she added while contemptuously looking at the top of the pyramid. The other one held and shushed her, warning of severe consequences.

"Settle down now, you don't want to get in trouble," said a dark copper-colored person as he walked past them in the opposite direction. His voice was obviously male. This made Jeffery notice that the darker copper-colored ones were males and the lighter ones were females. After reciting her words to himself, Jeffery began to feel some frustration rising inside him. He felt the injustice that she felt and realized that there really wasn't much that he could do.

"How does this whole thing really work?" questioned Jeffery in disgust. He stomped then walked away until he reached the nearest shovel. He began digging a new hole and went at it with full force. Jeffery set a foot on the shovel and flipped it while digging, which tossed some soil in the air and landed on one of the people walking by. Jeffery noticed that he was a male one, and he continued walking fast as if nothing had happened, eager to get to the pyramid. Jeffery was so mesmerized that he paused his digging. He wanted to at least apologize to the fellow but he didn't even care for one. Jeffery then looked around and took a closer look at how all the people were busy engaged in this system that took so much out of them with almost nothing in return. Jeffery continued to dig, with a sad look on his face. He kept Alp's reading in mind, but at the same time, he felt that he was lost in the cruel system's cycle as well.

After digging a bit deeper, Jeffery looked to see if Ribs was around but he caught no sight of him. Even though he was shorter than the people and dressed in similar coloring, his eccentric top hat would be recognizable in a crowd of a thousand, yet Jeffery still didn't see it.

"Wherever he is, and whatever he's doing," said Jeffery quietly, in disgust. He kept digging until he felt his shovel hit something hard. He started digging around it trying to unearth it as quickly as possible. After doing so, Jeffery picked up his newfound object and saw that it was a crown made of rose gold. He was tempted to wear it but also feared he would get into trouble for doing so. After looking around, Jeffery put it on and looked at the pyramid. As he looked at it, he remembered the oracle card from Alp's reading. He glared at the window in despise then took off the crown and headed towards it. While on his way, Jeffery heard his name being called so he turned back and saw Ribs heading towards him. Jeffery felt tempted to kick him, but instead, he internalized his anger.

"What have you got there?" asked Ribs.

"I found a crown," replied Jeffery bluntly.

"A crown, eh?" said Ribs. Jeffery remained silent and looked at the midget in a patronizing and unsatisfied manner. "Well, once you deposit it, make sure you meet me behind the pyramid. I got another task for you, alright?"

"Sure," said Jeffery. He then turned around and walked towards the pyramid. While walking, he held the crown in both hands and began looking at it. He felt as if he wanted to keep it and cherish it, but he knew that that wouldn't be possible. Its fate was to get tossed into the cauldron, off to no-one-knows where, and to never be seen again. Jeffery looked back and saw that Ribs was running and accidently crashed into one of the people, causing both of them to fall.

"Look out, you!" yelled Ribs disrespectfully.

"I am sorry," said the person, who happened to be a male. After apologising, he stood up and ran off hurryingly to find a shovel.

"You idiots!" shouted Ribs.

"It was your own fault, you moron," said Jeffery under his breath while turning around. As he walked, he looked at the crown again and discovered that there was an image of a small ladybug standing on a leaf, observing a forest across a lake. Jeffery was stunned at how well it was carved and by its symbolic feel. "It really is a jungle out here, my friend," he said with tears in his eyes.

When Jeffery reached the pyramid, he walked around the path and arrived at the window after a few minutes. He took another look at the crocksvenbulb and the circle of dollar signs. After reciting the names *Leanne, Ingrid, Edith,* and *Solomon* a few times, he deposited the crown into the cauldron and watched it fall into the gust of copper smoke. While dropping it, Jeffery felt his body shake and his head and eyes began to spin suddenly. Before jumping into the hole, the people behind him started quickly depositing their items, causing him to go faster. He jumped into the hole and before long he landed on his stomach on the soil right next to Ribs.

"Deposited that crown, alright?" asked Ribs.

"Yeah," answered Jeffery while looking up at the midget.

"Good, I knew you would," said Ribs. Jeffery stood up and brushed some of the soil off himself. "Now let's go, follow me," instructed Ribs. Jeffery followed Ribs as he walked them away. While walking, there was a long pause that made Jeffery feel uncomfortable. He saw that Ribs seemed unmoved and was walking to the destination feeling prepared, causing Jeffery to feel even more uncomfortable. He was curious about what the next task might be, but he was not sure if he should ask. As they walked further away from the pyramid, Jeffery noticed that the place was getting darker and felt more like a cave. The copper-colored soil remained, but more caves made of some soft, copper-colored stone seemed to appear. Jeffery couldn't help but wonder more about what he was to expect and felt like he didn't want to follow Ribs any longer. Although Jeffery was certain of how he felt, he intuitively knew of no other options.

Ribs made a turn to the left, indicating to Jeffery to follow. The pyramid was no longer behind. Ribs had led him onto another path, taking them out of the area. Jeffery saw a chubby, copper-colored mouse with a bony face and thick whiskers pop out of the soil. It did not look both ways, but instead, ran across the path and disappeared beneath one of the shadowy caves. Jeffery looked down at Ribs and saw a sly smile on his face, his eyes satisfied as if he thought Jeffery was too tall to see it. This made Jeffery a little anxious, but he didn't say anything, and instead, continued to walk silently alongside Ribs. He then looked up at the ceiling and saw that there were a few cracks through the dirt that allowed barely any light, making the place mysterious and unfathomable.

After walking for a little while longer, Jeffery was told by Ribs to enter a door that was on the corner of the path. After entering, Jeffery held the door back and looked down to make sure that Ribs had entered as well. After that, Jeffery followed Ribs down a set of broken stairs and around to a small room that had a door. Ribs opened the door then exited and Jeffery followed. He saw that they were back on the copper-colored soil with several people—only this time, it was a different place with a different set of people. Jeffery looked around curiously at what the people were doing. There were a few cranes and trucks that were being operated by the people who seemed to be involved in some sort of construction of a building.

"What is going on?" asked Jeffery.

"They're building," answered Ribs. "This is a new tower that is supposed to be almost as tall as the pyramid you saw earlier."

"Oh, ok," said Jeffery with a frown and his eyes crossed. Ribs looked up at him with a sudden shock.

"You know, there," started Ribs, "I am not really liking your attitude much and if you are going to work for me, I'm going to expect you to be a little bit more happy than this, alright?" Jeffery looked down at Ribs and thought of how he should respond. "Now follow me," instructed Ribs, not allowing Jeffery to speak. The two of them walked to a smaller division of the construction site where there were four people working. Two of them were piling up rubble with shovels, and the other two were going back and forth in a truck bringing rubble and dumping it in front of them. Jeffery noticed that where they were working was a little bit far from where the tower was being built.

"Ok, so this group right here," started Ribs while pointing at them, "has not been working as hard. They have been a bit slow."

"How do you mean?" asked Jeffery.

"They took a while to pick up on things, and as a result, for some reason, they aren't as fast at their tasks," replied Ribs. "The two in the truck are supposed to bring all the rubble and debris that is caused by the construction and dump it here. And these two are supposed to pile it up neatly so that at the end of the day, we just burn it to ashes." Jeffery looked at the two people piling and noticed that they were struggling with the weight of the shovels and the rubble. "You see what I mean? I just need you to stand here and supervise them and make sure they don't go any slower. Now, please, I do care about my workers, so don't be too harsh on them." Before Jeffery could open his mouth to speak, Ribs ran away and became preoccupied with something.

"This guy is a lunatic!" exclaimed Jeffery with utter frustration. Before long, the truck arrived, and the two workers in it got out and unloaded all the rubble. The other two, who weren't finished piling the previous load, right away began to shovel the newly delivered rubble and piled it up with the previous one. The two people got back in the truck and drove off. Jeffery

139

looked up towards the *ceiling* and found a giant rock, very round in shape, that was copper-colored and made of the same stone as the pyramid, tied with rusted copper chains to the side between the ceiling and the wall of the cave. While looking at it, Jeffery experienced a strange vibe in his gut and felt as if he didn't want that rock to be there. He didn't even want to look at it, but he couldn't help but stare at it while shivering. He wandered around and kept watching the people work and observed the construction site. Not long after, Ribs passed by.

"Just making sure that all is going well," he said casually.

"Yeah, alright," replied Jeffery. "Allow me to ask, what is that thing up there?" Ribs looked up at the rock then adjusted himself.

"I keep some of my belongings up there," he whispered. "Only *I* have access to that area; it is out of bounds for everyone else."

"I see," said Jeffery thoughtfully as he looked back at it.

"Yes, now I will be back later," said Ribs. "As I said, watch them carefully, I'm warning you."

"Sure you are," scoffed Jeffery after Ribs ran off and disappeared. He took a deep breath and watched the people work. His arms began to feel sore due to the digging and depositing he had done earlier. This caused him to wonder how these people, who were about a quarter of his size, were able to provide such intense labor. Jeffery looked with sad eyes and a throbbing heart at the two who were piling rubble in front of him. One was male, and the other was a female. Even though their colors were different, their movements were almost synchronized, as if they were birthed by the same mechanical creator—adhering to a work ethic that forbade thoughtful processing. "I'd help you guys but I don't know how Ribs would react," whispered Jeffery, softly. He watched them hard at work, continuing as if they didn't even notice his very existence.

Jeffery heard a sound that was quite strange to him. He arched his eyebrow and looked around curiously. While keeping his assigned area in view, Jeffery walked away a bit and tracked where the sound was coming from. He heard it screeching in his direction from one of the people, a male. Jeffery saw that the person was buried halfway into the soil along with both his arms, and that he was forcefully making this strange sound as a call for help. Without hesitating, Jeffery quickly ran to him and began pulling him up. The person was struggling and made every attempt to squeeze himself out, worrying of dreadfully losing his life against kismet.

"I'll get you out," said Jeffery as he kept pulling him. He looked around and saw that several people were around but all of them were too busy to be helpful. "None of you can give me a hand?" he called. None of them replied. Jeffery saw a female person walking past with a scythe in her hand so he went and grabbed it from her yelling, "Give me that," and kicked her hard with his heel. The kick sent her careening and she landed trembling on the soil. She quickly got to her feet, blew her arm lightly, and went to search for a new tool. "That pompous snob," yelled Jeffery as he used the scythe as a shovel, trying to remove some of the soil. The person gradually calmed down, seeing that aid was in progress. Jeffery then threw down the scythe and started digging aggressively with his bare hands. Before long, most of the person was exposed so Jeffery pulled him upwards, until he got a firm grip on him, and managed to pop him right out. Jeffery placed the person down on his feet and brushed some of the soil off his small, egg-shaped body.

"Thank you," squeaked the person, his voice sounding as if it were coming from behind a scarf. He then ran off hurriedly to a crowd of workers who were trying to drag a huge and heavy box, and started helping them.

"Wow," said Jeffery, "just wow." Feeling mind-blown, Jeffery didn't know whether to laugh or clench his fists. "They didn't even recognise you

141

and now you're running to help them out?" he questioned. Jeffery returned to his assigned area, exasperated by the situation. After he arrived, he saw that the two people were about halfway through piling their load, and that the other two had just arrived with another one. They exited their truck, unloaded all the rubble, then hopped back into the truck and drove off. Jeffery watched the two dig and pile, while in total dismay. He wondered if he should offer them aid but didn't know if they even deserved it.

While standing there, Jeffery heard another sound and felt some sort of shake. This sound was different and more seismic, as well as a warning of something destructive. Jeffery looked around to see if any of the people had taken notice but all of them seemed busy with their tasks. Jeffery then felt a small shake in the ground so he looked up and saw that the giant boulder that was tied close to the ceiling was moving. Jeffery watched it closely and stood frozen with his hands loose—trying really hard not to envisage what was to come. Before long, the rock broke out of some of the chains and hung downwards for a moment. It remained motionless, then suddenly it swung right across the open area and smashed through the tower like a wrecking ball. After that, it hit several people and continued swinging until it smashed into the wall across then pulled back and dangled casually. All the people panicked and ran around in terror while looking for places to hide. Jeffery ran to the door that he and Ribs had entered from earlier and turned back to observe the ordeal. The boulder broke free of the last chain and landed with a loud thud then rolled towards the wall that it had previously smashed into.

Jeffery dropped to his knees and started shaking. Everyone was in a giant panic and didn't know what to do. His breathing got heavier and his body felt overwhelmingly fatigued. He looked around to see if he could find water anywhere but saw no sign of a fountain or any other source of water. Looking to his left, Jeffery saw Ribs walking calmly towards him. Jeffery

142

looked him right in the eye and felt a strong rush of energy run through his body, like an ocean with giant waves, washing away his sanity.

"You can't say that they handled this pretty well, or can you?" started Ribs. Jeffery just looked at him, sweating. Ribs walked up to him and looked down at him, his eyes absorbing every movement of Jeffery's fatigued and sweaty body. "I can't say that you did either," he added with a wink.

"What do you mean?" asked Jeffery.

"I see that you have never taught anyone a well-deserved lesson, have you?" answered Ribs with a wink. Jeffery began to shiver again and his bottom lip split from the middle, and began bleeding.

"I want water!" he panted.

"Alright, follow me," replied Ribs. He opened a nearby door and allowed Jeffery in. Ribs led him up the staircase and around into a room that was dark and contained a wooden shelf with some water bottles on it. Jeffery grabbed one and quickly opened it. He drank it very fast then grabbed another one. Ribs instructed Jeffery to follow him back downstairs and onto the work field. Jeffery followed him back down the stairs slowly, then out the door. While drinking, Jeffery looked around and saw that the people were organizing the work area and restarting the construction. He also saw that there was a lifeless pile of some of the people stacked blatantly in a small corner.

"Are those the ones who died?" Jeffery asked.

"Yep," replied Ribs, "it got them right in the face." He laughed briefly causing Jeffery to feel infuriated.

"Didn't you say that you are the only one who has access to that area?" he inquired sharply.

"Yep," replied Ribs with a short laugh.

"Then how did this happen?" asked Jeffery in a very demanding tone.

"It just did," replied Ribs. He then looked up at Jeffery. "I am going to show you something, and you can't tell anyone, otherwise I will have to kill you."

"What do you mean?" asked Jeffery in disgust.

"Come and I will show you," instructed Ribs excitedly, "this way!" Jeffery followed him as they walked across the construction site, past where the building was being demolished, and into one of the caves. Inside, there was a staircase made of rose gold that led downwards. While going down, Jeffery saw that he was being led to a flat surface that was quite small, and that a matching staircase was located across. Jeffery continued following Ribs up the staircase until they reached a big, round door that was made of copper and had the head of an eagle hanging near the top, and a delicate pattern around the knob.

"What's in there?" asked Jeffery while cautiously looking around.

"You shall see," answered Ribs. He jumped up, turned the knob and pushed the door open. Jeffery assisted him by opening the door further. He then saw a small walkway made of white and copper-colored tiles that formed a pattern by the way they were placed. The walkway made a turn at the end of the hall, which had walls that were painted dark brown, with a reddish tone. Ribs started walking so Jeffery followed him and walked along the walkway feeling more worried by the second. After turning, Jeffery saw another copper door, and heard some noises coming from behind it. He quickly opened the door and saw that it opened outwardly, exposing to a very fast-paced setting. There were several machines that looked like they were placed in the setting of a kitchen amongst counters and sinks. Everything was made of copper and some things were even green from corrosion. Jeffery followed Ribs in and looked around. There were some people doing several

144

different things at once and they were all very fast at their tasks; they were so fast that Jeffery thought they were wired to some pace-controlling device.

"What is happening?" asked Jeffery with a frown.

"This is one of my production and services area," explained Ribs.

"How many of them have you got?" asked Jeffery.

"A lot," replied Ribs, "a whole industry."

"How much does one need?" said Jeffery under his breath.

"Look, you," said Ribs after stepping up and stopping one of the people, "I need you to start picking up the pace because taking care of orders is the only thing you're good at. I need someone who is going to make me currency, and if you can't do that, you are of no use to me." The person stood there quietly and looked at Ribs. His color indicated that he was male. "Now go on!"

"What was that about?" asked Jeffery.

"Just a slacker," said Ribs. "I have had him for only a few weeks and he doesn't seem to get anything." Jeffery turned and observed the person and saw how fast he was running back and forth.

"I see," said Jeffery while trying not to sound dramatic.

"They all have different tasks in this area," explained Ribs, "but I expect them to take on more than just their assigned task. I have orders coming into this section quite often, and I need to ship them out fast. Why else do I pay them currency?"

"Well, it seems like they are doing well to me," stated Jeffery.

"Nah, I want them to work faster," said Ribs. "And don't worry, you'll catch on with them." Jeffery widened his eyes in shock. He did not want to be involved in any of these tasks! "I will pay you the same as I pay them, three bills."

"Three bills?" asked Jeffery.

"Yep, that's minimum," said Ribs. "But believe me, I would pay less and demand more if I could." Jeffery held his breath. "Now follow me, this way." Jeffery followed Ribs to the other side of the kitchen. There he saw a window that looked out to the construction site. Jeffery was appalled by how fast the people had managed to reorganize it.

"I want to get out of here," said Jeffery softly to himself.

"Now look here," instructed Ribs. Jeffery turned and saw five people standing next to him and Ribs. They were all ready to start some sort of task. Ribs quickly explained to Jeffery that they were in training and were now about to write a test to determine their worthiness.

"Their worth—" started Jeffery.

"All of you this way, you too, Jeffery," instructed Ribs as he pointed at a nearby room. Jeffery followed them into it and realized that the setting of the room was very similar to the kitchen. It had the same tiled floors, copper appliances, and pale, red-brown walls. Jeffery saw that all the people went and stood next to a big machine that had a slider on the other end. They stood next to it calmly, and Ribs began handing out papers to all of them.

"I don't get this," said Jeffery.

"You will," said Ribs. "I will get you to go last. Just observe for now." Ribs then walked over to the people and told them to start. They all pulled down round copper helmets that were attached to the machine on a black rubber holder that bounced gently, and wore them over their heads. Ribs went to the side and pushed a big round button that turned on the machine that then started to make a mechanical sound. Shiny copper pens then dropped from the side of the helmets and the people caught them fast before they could fall to the floor. They began to look at the papers that Ribs gave them and wrote things on them.

"I still don't get it," said Jeffery. Ribs shushed him and told him to watch. The people were writing on the paper while holding it with nothing

146

underneath. To Jeffery, this seemed difficult. He continued observing until one of them, a female, took her helmet off. After doing so, the machine released a medium-sized jar that was clear and lidless. She inserted her paper in it then sent it back into the machine. This caused the machine to create another noise that was a little bit louder but slightly amusing. She walked to the other side of the slider where Ribs was standing. While waiting, Jeffery saw that the machine released the jar again, which came standing on the slider as it was being delivered to the other side, only this time the jar was sealed and contained some jelly that was three-quarters full. The jelly was the same color as she was, and had bits of minced fruit in it. After it was delivered to the other side, Ribs jumped up and took the jar and started observing it.

"Not full, but not bad, can you promise to pick up the pace a bit?" said Ribs. The person nodded. "Well, congratulations, you have made it." The person took a step aside and waited patiently. Jeffery turned to look at the people who were writing their tests and saw that three of them, two females and a male, had completed it and repeated the same cycle. Jeffery waited to see what their jars were going to look like, and under his breath he wished them luck. Before long, three jars came sliding down in the order they were inserted. The females' jars were full, and their jam looked fresh, while the male's was three-quarters full and contained bits of minced fruit. Ribs put his hands around the two female people and gave them a very warm compliment. "You there," he said as he turned to the male person, "promise me that you'll do well, alright?" The person nodded and looked down. Jeffery then saw them all turn to the remaining person, a male, and saw that he was still writing the test. Ribs looked at Jeffery and scoffed, indicating his impatience. Jeffery ignored it and wished the person luck, trying his very best to ignore Ribs's facial expressions. When the person completed his test, he took off his helmet and waited for the empty jar. After putting his paper in it and re-entering it, he walked up to where Ribs was standing with a long face. Jeffery stared at the machine and glanced at Ribs every so often and then noticed that the machine was taking longer to process.

"Oh please, I hope this doesn't go wrong," muttered Jeffery under his breath. He started praying silently and then heard the same male voice he had heard earlier while walking up the pyramid.

"Just watch," it said clearly, "watch carefully." His voice was so clear that Jeffery looked around and couldn't believe that no one else heard it. "I am here, just relax and watch." Jeffery looked at the machine and heard it go a little bit quiet. A jar then came out on the slider and started making its way to the other end. It contained only a spoonful of jam with a little bit of liquid at the very bottom, making the jam look almost like an island. The other people started smirking subtly while trying to hold their laughter. Ribs looked at the jar then looked at the person.

"I know what I will do with you," he said threateningly with his eyes narrowed. "The rest of you, back in there, you know what to do, and you, stay with me." Jeffery watched the first four leave the room then looked at Ribs expecting instructions, but instead, saw him glaring at the remaining person, who stood motionless. "I am going to give you one more chance, and if that doesn't work, I am letting you go, is that clear?" The person nodded shyly. Ribs waved his head to the right, indicating to the person to follow, and then looked at Jeffery. Jeffery followed them out and listened as Ribs instructed the person to take out some pastries from one of the ovens. The two of them walked to one and the person opened the oven gently. Ribs quickly slammed it shut while the person's left hand was still in there causing him to yell loudly and open the oven door with his other hand. Jeffery's eyes widened and he clenched his fist. He wanted to intervene but was interrupted by a female person who stormed by carrying a large copper pot in her hands that contained a lot of scoops and knives.

"What a jerk," said Jeffery under his breath while looking at Ribs.

"I got you there, didn't I?" said Ribs sarcastically. "You see, I have got a saying: *If you don't burn, you don't learn*." The words echoed in Jeffery's ears for a moment. He looked at the person and saw that he was dunking his hand in cold water, trying to relieve the burn. Ribs walked up to Jeffery with a smile on his face and asked him to follow. Jeffery walked behind him with a very disgusted look on his face. He looked down at Ribs and felt tempted to kick him, but clenched his fists instead. After following Ribs to another copper door, Jeffery entered a room that looked completely different from anything he had seen yet. The walls, ceiling and floor were made of the same copper-colored stone as the pyramid, and the architecture of the room itself was very round. It was also small, and furnished with a soft couch, and a small desk that had some papers scattered across it and around a laptop. At the very end of the room, close to the desk, Jeffery saw a big, round black gate and behind it was a bit more of the stone wall, ceiling and floor. To the side there was a small window. Jeffery wandered inside towards the middle of the room and noticed another crocksvenbulb with the dollar signs around it on the wall. It replicated the one he had seen inside the pyramid, only there weren't any quotes. Jeffery turned to the other wall and saw the same thing.

"Don't get too comfortable," said Ribs as he took a seat at the desk, contentedly. Jeffery looked at the dollar signs carefully and read the same names that he had read while in the pyramid.

"Who is Leanne Ingrid Edith-Solomon?" asked Jeffery, raising his eyebrow. Ribs just looked at him. "I even saw this when I was in the pyramid, you know, the crocksvenbulb. Except that there was a quote etched under it but I can't remember what it read." Ribs just kept looking at him. "Seriously, are you going to answer me or not?"

"You know the crocksvenbulb?" asked Ribs.

"Yes, I do know the crocksvenbulb, now tell me who is Leanne Ingrid Edith-Solomon," said Jeffery sharply. Ribs just looked at him, completely unfazed.

"I haven't been enjoying your attitude as much," he said with a calm tone. "You are forgetting that I am the one in charge here."

"And you seem to not know how to be in charge," yelled Jeffery. "You abuse others for the sake of creating your stupid workforce that you aren't even benefiting much from anyways!"

"Has anyone complained to you?" asked Ribs.

"Do I need to hear a complaint to say that this is unethical? I mean, look at the way you slammed the oven door on that poor person's hand. What had he done wrong?"

"It is what it is," defended Ribs. "He did not do well on his test and I just don't see him being kitchen material."

"Doesn't give you the right to assault him," argued Jeffery. "And who is Leanne Ingrid Edith-Solomon?"

"Leanne Ingrid Edith-Solomon is from a legend," answered Ribs, reluctantly. "I can't remember much of it myself, but she was supposed to have founded this place and this system and we keep her in memory for encouragement and moving forward."

"And by *we* you actually mean *yourself*," stated Jeffery.

"Perhaps," replied Ribs with a short smile that revealed a crowned tooth.

"No, not *perhaps*—are you really trying to tell me that any of the people actually know of this?" Ribs shook his head then looked down.

"What exactly are you here for?" asked Ribs.

Jeffery fell silent, searching for the right answer. In fact, in his head, he admitted that there was no answer. He also questioned whether Ribs would believe him about Alp and the mermen. Jeffery just continued looking at Ribs, silent and unsure.

"Well, perhaps you may need to try something else," suggested Ribs calmly while playing with his hands. Jeffery looked at his nose and imagined snapping it right off with his bare hand.

"Like what?" asked Jeffery, raising his voice.

"Come here," instructed Ribs. He turned his chair and faced the laptop. "Can you enter some data for me, perhaps?"

"What kind of data?" asked Jeffery while looking down at the papers.

"This is how many baked goods were purchased," explained Ribs. "One of the people recorded this, and I like to keep a record of the inventories on my computer here. Why don't you enter it?" Jeffery looked at one of the papers and read all the items, amounts, and other sorts of information that were scribbled on it.

"Alright," he said calmly.

"Just right there," said Ribs as he pointed at a spreadsheet on the laptop screen.

"Ok," said Jeffery as he continued reading. After feeling comfortable in doing the task, he moved the cursor and selected a box on the spreadsheet.

"No, not that one!" yelled Ribs, slapping Jeffery's hand hard. "That one! See? Look at the paper!" Jeffery crumpled the paper and threw it in the air.

"I have had it!" he yelled at the top of his lungs, creating an echo that caused Ribs to plug his ears. "You are a freak!" he cursed after Ribs unplugged his ears. "You have no right to hit me or to assault me, is that clear?"

"I am just showing you," explained Ribs. "It is just how I am."

"You must change that!" yelled Jeffery. "I will not tolerate you treating me like this anymore. I have had it with you and your stupidity, you foolish-looking piece of dirt!"

"Watch your mouth," warned Ribs with a higher tone. "I own this place, and I am paying you, so you'd better respect me."

"I will never respect you until you respect others and yourself," scolded Jeffery. "I can take those reports, and shred them into a thousand pieces." Jeffery stomped up to the desk and pushed Ribs and the chair to the floor. He ripped many of the papers and threw the bits at Ribs as he lay across the ground with his eyes closed. Jeffery, panting, felt a sense of relief. After calming down a bit, he looked at Ribs and questioned if he had killed him. He picked up the chair and sat on it then began to cry. His blood pressure had gone up so high that he could feel the top of his head throbbing.

A while passed as Jeffery continued trying to catch his breath. After feeling comfortable with his breathing again, he got up and walked to the black gate. He located the handle and then opened it. After entering, he turned to his right to look out the window and discovered that there was a small copper door located right under it. It had a copper crocksvenbulb in the middle that was also surrounded by twelve dollar signs. Jeffery didn't look at it closely. Instead, he looked out the window and saw the site of where the building was being constructed. The people were still re-organizing and seemed a lot more worried as they worked. Outside the window was a bit of stone and some copper chains, which indicated that the giant boulder had been tied there before.

"Who else could it have been?" asked Jeffery in disgust while thinking of the incident and how many people it had killed.

"Jeffery!" yelled Ribs. Jeffery looked and saw that Ribs had woken up and was looking for him. "What are you doing back there?"

"I am looking out your window, freak," replied Jeffery. "Now I know who sent that wicked rock swinging out and killing everybody. Who else but you has access to this place?"

"Now you have done it," shouted Ribs. "Get over here, now!"

"Why? You want to kill me too, freak?" yelled Jeffery as he stomped towards Ribs.

"I can kill you anytime and anywhere I want, you just watch me—" threatened Ribs. Before he could finish his sentence, Jeffery kicked him hard in the face. Ribs landed on his head and started bleeding heavily. Jeffery walked up to Ribs and looked down at him.

"You disgust me, you miserable, heartless monster," he cried as Ribs continued to bleed. Jeffery turned around and walked back to the window. He looked around at the construction site then felt his stomach begin to hurt. He turned around then went and sat on the chair. Jeffery held his stomach and looked down at the stone floor. He felt exhausted and as if all his energy was used up. Jeffery looked back up and ran his eyes across the room. He looked at Ribs who was now drenched in blood, and then faced the other direction.

"It is time to carry on," said the male voice. Jeffery stood up and looked around. "Don't panic, I am watching over you."

"Who are you?" asked Jeffery, shaking.

"Relax," said the voice after gently shushing. "Just carry on." Jeffery quickly got an image in his mind of the small copper door beneath the window. He focused on that thought, then turned and looked in that direction. "That's it, go on," added the male voice.

"Ok," said Jeffery, "I will carry on." He walked back to that area and looked at the door. He opened it then crawled in, and realized that he had crawled into a narrow tunnel. It was made of copper-colored soil, which was reminiscent of the tunnel he had traveled through in the jelly. After crawling for some time, Jeffery discovered a hole at the end so he crawled out of it and fell down. He landed on some soil that was just a few feet below. While trying to maintain control of his shaking body, he stood up and brushed the dirt off himself. As he did this, he suddenly heard a strange yet familiar sound. Jeffery glanced around and confirmed the direction it was coming from. After careful consideration, he walked towards it.

Jeffery walked up a short hill and noticed that the sound was getting louder. The place looked very familiar and seemed like a larger tunnel. After walking for some time and taking a turn along the path, he saw that he had reached the same spot by the threshold that he had previously flown into. In front of him was the worksite with the really big pyramid standing in the middle. Jeffery walked closer and looked at all the people who were working hard. They were just as breathless and hasty as before. The pyramid stood before them large and proud as the thick, polluted smoke continued pouring heavily from the window.

Jeffery kept staring at it and questioned out loud, "How is it possible that this pyramid is standing strong and indestructible?" To him, this seemed like a rather difficult question with a miraculous answer that might never be found.

Jeffery saw a female person with a shovel in her hand running to a small hole that was close to him. She started digging vigorously, causing herself to pant. She dug quickly as if there were no tomorrow. Then she threw the shovel aside and started digging with her bare hands in a robotic manner. Jeffery continued watching her, curious to see what she was going to find. He waited patiently, and as he observed, he saw that she didn't take notice of him at all. She got down on her knees, and dug slower, as it seemed that she had discovered something. Jeffery saw that she had found a bouquet of fresh flowers, all varied in types and colors. After taking it and brushing all the soil off of it, she ran hurriedly towards the pyramid, disappearing into the crowd of people.

"Stubborn and indestructible," said Jeffery with a sigh, looking up at the pyramid. While lost in deep thought, he felt a sharp kick to his right calf. "Ouch!" he yelled, jumping and turning around.

"You really thought that you could kill me?" yelled Ribs.

"You?" shouted Jeffery, feeling shocked. He noticed that Ribs didn't have his hat on, and he was covered in blood.

"You will never destroy my workforce! It has been standing here since before you entered it!" shouted Ribs, intensely anguished. Jeffery quickly ran and grabbed the shovel that the person had left earlier. He turned to face Ribs and held it out in a sign of defence. "What do you think you're doing?" asked Ribs aggressively as he came marching over the threshold.

"What do you think I am doing?" shouted Jeffery in response. "I am trying to keep myself away from you!" He plunged forward and hit Ribs in the face with the tip of the shovel, knocking him over on his back and causing his nose to pop in a fountain of blood. Jeffery pushed the shovel down on Ribs's neck, stomped his right foot on his gut and looked at him in the eye.

"No matter how hard you fight me, I will never die," yelled Ribs in agony. "People will work for me forever."

"You think so?" asked Jeffery.

"You watch as I let you go," said Ribs miserably. He pulled out a small, copper pistol from his pocket, revealing a camouflaged crocksvenbulb on its side. He aimed at Jeffery's heart and pulled the trigger shouting, "You're fired!" The pistol released a big bolt of fire that hit Jeffery in the chest, causing him to feel a hot shock, which then spread around his upper body. Jeffery shook rapidly and dropped the shovel. He felt burning and an electric shock that dissolved into his skin and right into his bones, shaking them, and searing through his heart. Jeffery screamed, unable to bear the excruciating ordeal.

"I am protecting you," said the male voice calmly. Jeffery looked at the pyramid then at Ribs's glaring eyes, screaming in agony. Not long after, the fire spread throughout his body and burned him to ashes.

Chapter Six

Part I

On Contraption Hope

Jeffery slowly opened his eyes then closed them again. He heard a faint sound that he couldn't recognize, but he felt too heavy to move and figure out what it was. He closed his eyes again and tried waking up slowly, but realized that he didn't have much control over his body. As he lay there, he heard another sound that was somewhat mechanical, gliding away. The sound suddenly became more prominent, then gradually faded. Jeffery didn't pay much attention to it, and eventually the sound disappeared. He began opening his eyes more, and thereafter, he heard the mechanical gliding sound come closer. Jeffery slowly began to move his head. Looking around, he could see that he was in a bed in a dim room where the walls, ceiling, and floor were made of some sort of strong, lustrous metal and was entirely dark gray. Jeffery felt more in control over his body so he moved around and tried to get a better view of the room. He noticed that the bedspread was a very pale gray, and its softness added to the comfort of the bed. Becoming more alert, he heard the gliding sound to his left and turned to see where it was coming from.

It turned out to be a very unique figure wandering around that part of the room. Its base was almost flat, not quite rectangular, not quite round, and had some sort of motor at the bottom that gave it its gliding ability. The rest of its body looked like a curved spine that was over three feet long with its curve near the top where its flat head pointed out like a cobra looking down. Its bottom was connected to one end of the base, yet it seemed very balanced. The figure was dark gray and made of metal, and, as it turned to face Jeffery, it revealed two small glowing red dots around its head that happened to be its eyes.

"Hello there," said Jeffery.

"Why, hi!" greeted the figure with a female voice, sounding ecstatic. "Patient 451, how's it going?"

"Um, alright," answered Jeffery, feeling a little bit of pain at the back of his head. "Who are you?"

"I am Caster," said the figure. "I look after patients when necessary."

"I see," said Jeffery.

"Want some water or anything?" offered Caster.

"No, thank you," replied Jeffery. "I just want to know how I got here."

"I will get the guidemen to explain all that to you," replied Caster.

"The guidemen?" asked Jeffery.

"Yeah," replied Caster, "just a minute." Caster let out a strange sound that Jeffery supposed was her calling the guidemen. He looked to his right and saw that there was a dividing light-gray wall that stood on a thick, metallic base with wheels. For a second, Jeffery thought that there was another patient behind the wall. He looked back towards Caster and saw three figures fade in from the air. They were tall men, made of dark-gray steel and they were very muscular. Their faces had eyes, a mouth, and a nose, but they didn't move or blink. Instead, their features were etched on their faces and their eyes were flat with no lashes, brows, or eyeballs—like mannequins. Their hair was the same, etched on top of their heads and combed neatly to the back, except one of them, who was standing to the far right, had his combed to the side. Aside from the etching of his hair, they all looked identical. They wore light-gray t-shirts that were tight around their muscular bodies, and dark-gray sweatpants that were a little bit loose. They also wore running shoes that were gray and white and a silver chain-bracelet on their left wrists. The three of them took a few steps towards Jeffery's bed and stopped to look at him. Caster glided over with a smile on her robotic snake-like face. Jeffery looked at all of them and wondered about what brought him to this unusual setting.

"Alright, Jeffery," started Caster, "meet the guidemen. They are here to answer your questions and provide you with the support you need." Caster then turned to the guidemen and introduced Jeffery to them.

"Pleasure to meet you there, Jeffery," said the one in the middle. "I am Fred."

"I am Nate," said the one to the left of Fred.

"And I am Joseph," said the one to the right of Fred, with a small nod that emphasized the difference of how his hair was carved.

"And what would you like to know?" asked Nate.

"Well," began Jeffery after hesitating and looking at all of them, "I'd like to know how I got here. You see, I was shot, and—"

"You were fired," interrupted Fred. "It happens—it's normal."

"It certainly is," added Joseph.

"And when you get fired, you end up here," explained Fred.

"And how did I end up here?" asked Jeffery.

"That is something more for Dr. Peters to discuss with you," replied Fred.

"Do you want to see him?" asked Nate.

"It'd be useful," added Caster gently.

"Sure," replied Jeffery, sounding confused.

"Well, let us go and let him know, and he'll call you when he's ready, ok?" suggested Fred.

"And hopefully he won't be too long," added Joseph with a mellow tone.

"Well, alright," said Jeffery. The guidemen and Caster turned around and headed in the opposite direction while exchanging some small talk. Jeffery got out of bed and walked around the dividing wall. There was a small gray couch, made of leather, which was located next to the divider, and next to it on the other side was a pale gray nightstand. On it stood a silver alarm clock that happened to be very wide and rectangular in shape. Right across from him, Jeffery saw a big window with pale gray drapes opened to the side. The view was of a black sky with several white and silver stars, like glowing diamonds. Jeffery walked to the window and looked outside. He noticed that there was nothing else besides the black sky and stars, which seemed to be moving. He turned back to his right, then looked at the couch and noticed that right above it was a gray crocksvenbulb hanging on a thick nail. Jeffery turned back to the window and felt as if a small panic attack was about to happen.

"So, Dr. Peters will see you in a bit," said Caster as she glided by. "There are over four thousand patients here, you know."

"I see," replied Jeffery. "Could you please tell me where are we exactly?"

"Don't panic, hon," said Caster softly. "Relax. Everything is going to be alright."

"Ok, but could you please tell me where are we?" begged Jeffery.

"I can't," replied Caster after gently shushing him. "Just relax. Dr. Peters will explain everything to you, and believe me when I say *everything*."

"I feel like I am losing my mind," explained Jeffery. "One minute I get shot by this atrocious little beast and now I am flying in the sky out in—"

"Jeffery!" called Caster sternly. "Relax," she added with a gentle shush.

"You're right, I am sorry," said Jeffery. "Panicking won't get me anywhere, at least not right now."

"Here, just go sit down and I will get you some water," said Caster. Jeffery went and sat on the couch and watched Caster glide away. After she disappeared around the dividing wall, he turned around and looked up at the crocksvenbulb. Jeffery then looked at the clock that read *05:68:699:05:34*, and wondered what the numbers meant. After that, he looked at the blank metal wall in front of him and then looked back at the crocksvenbulb. There wasn't anything written or drawn around it; it just hung casually and undisturbed. Jeffery looked down at his boots and noticed that they were a bit rusted and dirty from everything that he had gone through. As he stared at them quietly, Caster glided back in. Jeffery saw that there was a glass of water floating next to her and next to it was a medium-sized gray feather that had a small white stripe near the top and a white outline around the quill. He looked at the feather closely and felt a tightening around his chest as if he needed to let go of something.

"There you go," said Caster. Jeffery stood up and grabbed both the glass and the feather then sat back down. "See, it is nice to relax," ensured Caster as Jeffery drank.

"Well, for the time being," replied Jeffery as he looked at the feather. "This is pretty."

"It is," agreed Caster. "I like them. I find them to be relaxing, hence I got you one."

"Well, thank you," said Jeffery.

"You bet," replied Caster. "And just between us," she started, "I really like how you beat up Ribs. I think that it is about time someone taught him a lesson," she whispered. Jeffery's eyes widened and he looked Caster right in the eyes. "We have had lots of patients sent here because of him. He is such an ass, I say. I just wonder why is it that those who get fired by him

161

are the ones who need to be separated and no one asks why he isn't ever separated."

"Well—" started Jeffery.

"No need to reply," interrupted Caster, raising her tone. "Just keep that between us."

"Alright," said Jeffery, finishing his water.

"Want another one?" asked Caster.

"Sure," answered Jeffery with a smirk. Caster smirked back and glided away. As she glided, the glass floated out of Jeffery's hand and followed her. Jeffery sat back against the couch and continued fiddling with the feather. It was really soft and its quill was quite solid and smooth. He leaned in and smelled it as he closed his eyes. Jeffery felt almost at peace, but not completely there. His head felt like a bubble floating above him, unable to process much. Jeffery pointed the feather down then stared out the window, almost motionless. The stars were quite bright and they varied in size. For a moment, Jeffery remembered the painting on the ceiling in the room at the Fogbusts' and made a mental comparison of the two views. Feeling the lack of familiarity towards both, he just sat quietly.

Caster returned with another glass of water floating next to her, so Jeffery got up and took it. While drinking, he walked up to the window and continued looking out while glancing at the crocksvenbulb every so often. The water was colder than the first one. Jeffery enjoyed this so he took a huge gulp that gave him a brain freeze.

"You know," began Caster, "of all the patients I have monitored, I feel that you are the most special."

"You think so?" asked Jeffery as he continued looking at the stars.

"Absolutely," replied Caster. Jeffery took notice of her reflection in the window and saw that she was looking at the crocksvenbulb. "You are very brave. You believed in what you thought and actually fought for it. I wish *I* was able to do that at some point in my life." Jeffery did not respond. He continued looking out the window and briefly at Caster's reflection. She turned away from the crocksvenbulb and started gliding around. Jeffery finished drinking his water then took notice of a unique constellation formed by several stars. It was almost like the letter *C*, but slanted, and the top curve seemed slightly longer than the bottom one. Jeffery smiled at it and saw that Caster took notice of this.

"That's the constellation of life," she said as she glided over next to his left. "Of all the patients I've met, I think only three others were able to fully see it."

"It's beautiful," said Jeffery. "I really like it." He noticed that he had put the feather down on the window ledge, so he picked it up and held it upwards, slightly slanting it as if he were placing it across the constellation.

"It will happen," said Caster. "You will be free." Jeffery turned to face her and smiled, thinking that she was able to read his mind. "You must remember, Jeffery, that it isn't all about your achievement, it's about your mind." Jeffery felt Caster's words penetrate right through him and then felt a gust of energy exit him.

"Sounds a bit like Ribs," explained Jeffery. "He seemed to have all the achievements but his mind was really not in a healthy state."

"Exactly," agreed Caster. "And that's why so many end up here, from his unhealthy environment."

"Right," said Jeffery. "I felt it right from the start that he was a sneaky and cruel man. I am most positive that he made that wrecking ball-like rock kill all those people on purpose."

"What do you mean?" asked Caster, her eyes widening.

"Oh, long story," said Jeffery as he turned back to face the window with a hand over his head. "It was so traumatic."

"I understand," said Caster with a sigh. "He has done a lot of harm. Anyways I shouldn't be talking to you about any of this." She then glided away and Jeffery went back to looking out the window in dismay at the horrible memories. He looked back at the constellation of life and started to reassure himself. Jeffery saw Caster in the reflection as she glided back and looked at him caringly. He continued looking at the stars and thought about his meeting with Dr. Peters. While wrapped in thought, Jeffery saw a large comet soar by. It was very bright and white with some yellow flares at its end. It streaked right across then disappeared beyond sight. Jeffery heard Caster generate an electronic sound like a rhythmic song that was quite catchy. He turned to look at her and saw that she was processing something in her head. She turned to him and began to speak.

"I just heard back from the guidemen," she explained, "and Dr. Peters is pretty booked up for now. They recommend that you get some rest and he will talk to you later, when he can."

"Alright," said Jeffery. "I hope he hasn't got too many other patients to see."

"Well, you know, your turn will come. I am going to get some medication for you, ok?" said Caster.

"Sure," said Jeffery.

"Come on, let's get you back into bed," instructed Caster. Jeffery followed her around the dividing wall and hopped back into bed. He noticed that next to it was a sink and some bottled items around the counter. Caster came to his side along with a floating glass. The glass contained some sparkling, clear liquid with a small, light-gray fluffy cloud floating right above it. Jeffery took the glass and observed the unique appearance of the drink.

"What's this?" asked Jeffery.

"It's a sedative," replied Caster. "Just drink it and relax." Jeffery looked at the liquid one more time then drank it. As he drank, the cloud floated above the glass, close to his mouth, then worked its way down into the liquid as he consumed it. After drinking most of it, the cloud landed into the liquid and dissolved. After drinking it completely, Jeffery watched the glass float back up into the air and disappear.

"Great, it's off to get washed, and now you need to sleep," said Caster.

"Alright," said Jeffery sounding calm. He rested his head back and listened to Caster glide away. Before long, the lights were dimmed, and he felt his head become heavy. He shut his eyes and let go of his tension.

* * *

Jeffery woke up to the sound of Caster's gliding, and stretched until he was able to sit up. He looked towards Caster and saw that she was busy processing something in her head so he got up and walked to the window. The view was the same, except that the stars were rearranged. He looked at the crocksvenbulb and saw that it hadn't moved. Jeffery glanced at the clock and saw that it read *06:72:699:05:99*. He didn't think too much about it, but turned back to the window and continued to stare. Caster glided towards him with a plate with a donut on it floating next to her, along with a glass of water.

"You sure slept well," Caster stated happily in a friendly tone.

"I did," replied Jeffery. He sat on the couch, took the plate and ate the donut.

"I was talking to the guidemen," started Caster, "and they should be here soon to take you down to Dr. Peters."

"Oh yeah?" asked Jeffery.

165

"Yep," replied Caster. "Now remember, there isn't anything to worry about, and make sure that you are frank and open with him because he will explain everything that you wish to know, alright?"

"Sounds good," replied Jeffery. "Have you met him yourself?"

"Hundreds of times. We work together," answered Caster.

"Well, I guess that was obvious," said Jeffery.

"Don't worry too much about me," said Caster. "You need to speak to him about you, what happened with Ribs, and all that stuff. That's the reason you were brought here."

"Right," said Jeffery.

"Would you like another donut?" asked Caster.

"I am good, thanks," said Jeffery. He put the plate on the nightstand then walked back to the window.

"You sure like the view of those stars," observed Caster.

"I do," replied Jeffery. He looked at one particular star that started flashing. Its light shone very bright, like an eyelid that couldn't stop blinking.

"You wait until you see what it's like at Dr. Peters's," said Caster. "It is huge and the view is nice."

"Wow," said Jeffery.

"You'll see it. I just wonder where those guidemen are," said Caster. Jeffery turned and faced Caster and saw that she seemed annoyed.

"Helping another patient?" he asked.

"Well, of course, I am just wondering why it is taking so much time," replied Caster.

Jeffery turned back and faced the window. As he looked at the stars and all the galactic lights, he felt some sort of movement behind him. He quickly turned around and saw that it was the guidemen fading in. They all seemed to be smiling, even though Caster was frowning.

"Forgive us," said Nate, "we just—"

166

"Yeah I get it, just take him to Dr. Peters before he's late for the visit," instructed Caster.

"Are you ready?" asked Fred as he looked at Jeffery.

Jeffery looked at all of them and didn't say anything. He didn't know what to expect so he just opened his mouth slightly.

"Well, are you?" asked Joseph.

"Sure," replied Jeffery.

"Alright, shoo!" said Caster. "Get on with it."

"Come on, Jeffery," said Fred. Jeffery walked closer to the guidemen then turned and faced Caster. He felt the guidemen hold him gently as his vision blurred. Vey soon after, he saw the room fade away and some other room fade in. He felt very wobbly and nearly fell, but the guidemen held him close.

"What is this?" asked Jeffery while struggling not to fall.

"Don't worry," replied Fred, "we are almost there." Jeffery tried standing still until the room completely faded in. Once it had, he felt some sort of click that indicated that he and the guidemen had arrived.

"He should be in here soon," said Joseph.

"I expected that he'd be here right away," stated Fred. Jeffery walked a few paces ahead of the guidemen and looked around the large room. The floor and walls looked very solid and were dark blue-gray. In almost every part of the room there was a pair of escalators operating, one going up and the other going down. Jeffery tried to count them but lost track after his train of thought was interrupted by Fred asking the other two guidemen to be patient. Jeffery looked up ahead and saw a staircase located across and not very far away, that was fairly long, made of metal and painted black. At the top of the staircase was a camouflaged door. Jeffery heard some sounds coming from behind it, but couldn't identify them. He turned to face the guidemen, curious to see if they had taken notice.

"Really, Fred, we can just take him up. I can go first and knock," suggested Joseph.

"I said, no," answered Fred. "Dr. Peters specifically asked us to meet him here so all we can do is wait."

"Where do all these escalators lead to?" asked Jeffery.

"Different parts of the place," replied Fred.

"What place, exactly?" asked Jeffery.

"Dr. Peters will tell you," replied Nate. Jeffery looked at Fred and saw that he was nodding while looking at him. Jeffery then turned around and started wandering around the new location. It did not feel relaxing to him as it was very plain and didn't have much other than the escalators.

"And there he is," said Joseph, indicating to the top of the staircase. Jeffery turned and looked in that direction and saw a man standing with the door open behind him. The man had straight, short brown hair, and wore a silver coat and metallic sunglasses with dark, translucent shades.

"Patient 451?" he asked casually.

"Yep," answered Fred.

"Well, come on up," instructed Dr. Peters. Jeffery saw him re-enter the room while leaving the door open. The guidemen walked to the staircase so Jeffery followed them until they reached the door. They let him enter then followed behind, shutting the door.

Jeffery looked around the new room and was astonished by its appearance. The floor was made of linoleum and was a blend of various shades of gray and neutrals, unlike the wall that was a soft shade of light gray. The room was about triple the size of the one he woke up in and the window at the front was huge, just as Caster had said. Upon the walls, various things were hanging, including pictures and digital equipment. To the right-hand side was a couch, which looked the same as the one in the room where Caster was, and across from it was a chair on wheels that was made of the same material, only a little darker. The guidemen walked right to the center of the room so Jeffery followed, slowly, looking all around. He noticed that Dr. Peters was giving the guidemen some sort of instructions so he decided to meander about. Eventually, Jeffery made his way to the couch and sat down.

Before sitting, he noticed that there were two crocksvenbulbs nailed to the wall above the couch, and a picture in a silver frame of a three-leveled spacecraft that was hanging towards the left of the couch. The spacecraft looked really big and rich in architecture. It was light gray and had many windows and various exits.

Jeffery shifted his gaze then saw that the guidemen faded out and Dr. Peters was making his way to the chair. Jeffery took a closer look at his appearance and saw that under the silver coat he wore a light-gray suit, a dark-gray shirt and a silver tie with thin, dark-gray stripes. After Dr. Peters sat on the chair, he introduced himself.

"Hello, I'm Dr. Peters. Patient 451, you must be Jeffery," he said with his slightly squeaking voice.

"I am," replied Jeffery.

"Excellent, I have been wanting to meet with you," said Dr. Peters.

"And I really want to know where I am and how'd I get here," said Jeffery.

"Yes, for sure, I will tell you all of that," assured Dr. Peters. Jeffery looked at Dr. Peters's lanky body and felt a bit hopeless. He expressed this with a frown and didn't move. "Look at the picture next to you there," instructed Dr. Peters. Jeffery glanced at the picture of the spacecraft then looked back at Dr. Peters, expecting a further explanation. "That is *Contraption Hope*, it's where you are now."

"And how did I get here?" asked Jeffery.

169

"It's automatic," replied Dr. Peters, "once you get fired, you automatically get sent here after taking that shot." Jeffery looked out the window at the black sky and the white stars. He turned back towards Dr. Peters and focused his gaze on him.

"And why is that?" asked Jeffery sternly.

"Well, after going through what you've gone through, there have got to be some things that you need to talk about," replied Dr. Peters. "That's why it is called *Contraption Hope*, to give you hope. And, that is also why there are plenty of escalators downstairs, to remind patients that life is always up and down, and that the choices we make drive our directions."

"And what happens next?" asked Jeffery.

"Before wondering about that, let's face where you are now," said Dr. Peters. He bent forward and looked closely at Jeffery. "You're just lost in your own maze trying to explain all of this. That's not easy."

"I know it's not, it's difficult," said Jeffery with a huff as he raised his voice.

"Easy, there," said Dr. Peters as he sat back. "I am agreeing with you here. Now let's talk about it." Jeffery looked at Dr. Peters and sighed. "We'll start wherever you want," added Dr. Peters gently.

"It started when Alp sent me over and across the sea," started Jeffery. "I don't remember too much of it but I remember that I met Ribs, who right away put me to work. He was a monster."

"Everyone seems to say that," said Dr. Peters with a quick smile.

"Because he is!" protested Jeffery. "He purposely slammed the oven door on the hand of one of the people! He is very sneaky, and I am certain that he was the one who released that rock that killed so many people."

"Well, you see," started Dr. Peters, "I doubt that Ribs would kill anyone on purpose."

"He is the only one who has access to the room behind where the rock is located. Who else could it have been?" argued Jeffery.

"It could have been anyone," suggested Dr. Peters.

"I don't think so," said Jeffery assertively. "He is a monster who has no respect for anyone."

"Ok, please," said Dr. Peters, "we are not here to contradict anyone, that's why it's called *Contraption Hope*. Tell me about how you are feeling."

"Miserable," replied Jeffery. "My body still aches because of what happened. I mean, I dealt with this pathetic midget having full control over everyone, and then he shot me, and then I woke up on some contraption. Tell me, how would *you* feel if that were you?"

"Well, not the best," said Dr. Peters, "but this is about you. You also need to realize that you are here until you are properly rehabilitated, then you will be going back to the workforce."

"Why?" protested Jeffery. "I don't want to go back. I don't want to have anything to do with that place."

"I am afraid that isn't a choice," replied Dr. Peters calmly. "It is what happens here and that's how things work." Jeffery clenched his fist and looked out the window. He was out of words so he just stared out into the galaxy in dismay.

"And Alp said that I would come face to face with the divine," Jeffery murmured softly.

"Oh, what does he know?" scoffed Dr. Peters. Jeffery faced Dr. Peters, while his body was shaking and his eyes sparkling.

"Alp wouldn't lie," said Jeffery quietly.

"And the Fogbusts and Lake Morgan would?" asked Dr. Peters.

"How do you know about them?" asked Jeffery, sounding surprised.

"It is our job on *Contraption Hope* to know as much as possible about every patient, Jeffery," answered Dr. Peters. "I know a lot about you

171

already. I am afraid, though, that our session is ending, and the guidemen will be here soon to take you back."

"And that's it?" asked Jeffery.

"No, I will see you again later, but before you go, I have something for you."

"What?" asked Jeffery.

"Follow me," instructed Dr. Peters. Jeffery stood up and followed him across the room. Jeffery was led to a small shelving cabinet that was built into the wall. Dr. Peters pulled out a book and handed it to Jeffery. "This is the journal of a patient I once had. I think you should read as much of it as you can. You might be able to connect with her." Jeffery flipped through the medium-sized journal and saw that most of the pages were blank. He closed it and looked at the cover. It was dark gray, hardcover, and had no title. Its spine had some scratches, which indicated that it was read and handled more than it was actually written in.

"Alright," said Jeffery.

"Yeah, read some tonight," said Dr. Peters. "Now come on." Jeffery was led outside the room and down the staircase, back to where he had faded in with the guidemen. The escalators were moving a lot faster than they were before. Jeffery saw Dr. Peters take a very close look at him and that the blue-gray tone of the room was reflected in his sunglasses. Jeffery looked back at him casually expecting to hear something. "Remember, Jeffery, Ribs owns that workforce. He needs everyone to work hard, so sometimes he will be strict just so that he can bring perfection out of everyone's guts. It doesn't mean that he is cruel." The guidemen faded in and walked towards Jeffery.

"Sorry we are a bit late," said Fred.

"No worries," replied Dr. Peters. "Now, take Jeffery to his room and make sure that he is safe and sound."

"Of course," answered Fred. The guidemen stood around Jeffery and held him.

"And remember, Jeffery, read the journal," said Dr. Peters.

"Ok," said Jeffery. He turned and looked at one pair of the escalators and saw that they started to go faster. About a second later, the room began to fade out and the previous room began to fade in gradually. After Jeffery saw that he had completely arrived, he went to the nightstand and placed the journal on it.

"So, you're back," he heard Caster say to the guidemen.

"He needs to rest," said Nate.

"Yeah, put him to sleep, and also, Dr. Peters gave him a journal that he needs to read. You know, the journal of patient 514," said Fred.

"Oh, yes," said Caster, "alright." Jeffery saw the guidemen look at him, then they faded out. He sat on the couch and watched Caster glide towards him. "Well, Jeffery, it's time to put you to sleep."

"Can I read some of it now?" asked Jeffery.

"I am afraid not," answered Caster. "You really need your rest, but later on, for sure. I actually have some things to tell you about it."

"You do?" asked Jeffery.

"Yes," replied Caster. "Now come on, let's put you to rest. Jeffery took off his boots then got into bed. He lay there until Caster glided by with another floating glass with the cloud on top. He sat up, drank it, and lay back down.

"I promise I will tell you everything," whispered Caster after gliding close by. Jeffery looked right into her eyes then closed his.

* * *

Jeffery opened his eyes and was greeted by the sight of the solid, gray metal ceiling. He looked to his left and saw that there was a glass of water with ice in it atop the counter. He yawned and took a couple of stretches then went to the sink and drank the water. After noticing that Caster wasn't in the room, he went straight to the couch, sat down and picked up the journal. He looked again at its solid cover and back side. While holding it, he felt a rush of energy circulate through him. It gave him a sense that there was a lot that he needed to know. Before opening the book, Jeffery looked out the window and stared at the stars for a moment. Then he glanced at the crocksvenbulb above and turned to the book. He opened it and started reading the first page, his gut tensing up.

Time only knows how long I've been inside this contraption with all of the black leather seating. And only time knows how long I've been sitting by this window and how I ended up here. My body does not feel sore. It's very pristine here. I am high above with the stars and the galaxy. I am wrapped in thoughts that keep me calm and warm, like a blanket that's as flat as the black sky.

Space is scarce inside this contraption. I don't know if I can classify it either as a spacecraft or as a spaceship. I am certainly in space, out and beyond in extraterrestrial land. I am riding in a flying object that's rather round and about one sixty-fourth the size of something bigger. It's something that's probably from the imagination of someone galactic, or an enthusiast of eccentric architecture. Or perhaps, even an offspring result that's crossed between the two.

When I look out the window, the view really isn't much except for comets, constellations, the sky, and from certain angles, the sun. It's quite a simple view, yet unquestionably beautiful and compelling. I focus my sight on a particular object that is thick in texture, and rocky in surface. It looks innocent, but quite dark, indeed.

In the midst of this simple and small environment, freedom and relief keep me at peace. I'm in a small contraption with not much but seating, but I am high above and far away from its main base. I am now somewhere in the galaxy, in between different worlds. I am beyond any visible horizon in a world where one sees no change.

I yawn and I close my eyes. Relaxation isn't mandatory. In fact, it's taken for granted to a point where the concept isn't something one becomes aware of—it's the norm. I stretch my arms and my legs. My breathing synchronizes with the gentle air entering the contraption, causing my eyelids to gently blink to the rhythm. I rub my hands through my hair, down the back of my neck, and voluptuously around my chest, until gradually reaching down to the seating of the chair's front, giving it a firm squeeze. My emotions and the atmosphere seem to share the same feeling of the black sky.

I stare up to the ceiling to find it solidly plain black, with small soft bumps. I wouldn't dare imagine counting every bump. It's probably an average of the same number of stars that are out there in the cosmos. One mustn't blame others' fascination of what lies beyond in this galaxy. In fact, there could be answers to questions that many may have been searching for throughout the millennia. As for me, I am completely uninterested in what's past this black sky. I am totally content with this contraption flying itself away from its base.

"She must have been on a different contraption," said Jeffery, hesitating. He closed the journal and put it back on the nightstand. He put on his boots then got up, went to the window, and stood to observe the stars again. Jeffery tried to see if he could catch sight of the sun that was mentioned in the journal but did not see it. He began gently speaking to the stars. "You all look so bright and so peaceful," he started. "If only I could be somewhere like that and far away from here. I don't understand this torment. It must be for some sort of reason, at least I hope so. No one likes to be tormented for nothing. And also, I really wish that I wouldn't return to the workforce. I don't even know why Alp sent me there in the first place, but I don't think that's where I will be in unity with destiny." Jeffery looked down and tried not to cry. He felt his emotions rise in his chest so he went back to the couch. He sat quietly until he heard some sound that he noticed was Caster's way of entering the room—right through and from the wall.

"You're up, I see," Jeffery heard her say from the other side of the divider.

"I am," he replied peacefully.

"You sure got your rest," she said as she glided over to him, smiling.

"I tried," admitted Jeffery.

"I told you the window at Dr. Peters's is huge," said Caster.

"You're right, it really is," responded Jeffery.

"Did you get a chance to read some of the journal?" asked Caster.

"I did," replied Jeffery. "And what do you have to tell me about it?" Caster glided closer to Jeffery then began to slow down.

"Her patient number was 514," Caster whispered. "You are patient number 451."

"Right," replied Jeffery, "really similar."

"She also saw the constellation of life," added Caster. "How much of the journal did you read?"

"Just her first piece," replied Jeffery, "the one about the contraption and the black leather seating."

"Ok," said Caster, "that's on another part of the contraption."

"And does it really disconnect from the main part?" questioned Jeffery.

"It does," replied Caster. "What really happened is she never actually flew away from the main part. She just gained access to there but didn't know that it could actually disconnect."

"Yeah?" asked Jeffery.

"She just pretended that it did. She went missing a couple of times then the guidemen detected her there and brought her back each time. She was warned not to do it a third time but she did anyway."

"And then what happened?" asked Jeffery. Caster frowned as some red lights glowed from her base.

"I'll tell you later," she said. "The guidemen are coming and you need to meet with Dr. Peters." Before long, the guidemen faded in.

"Hello, Jeffery," said Fred.

"Glad to see you," added Nate.

"Alright, boys, you know the drill," said Caster. Jeffery walked up and stood next to them as they held him, and looked at Caster. She seemed normal as if it were just an ordinary day, so Jeffery didn't fix his gaze on her. He watched the room fade out and the room with the escalators fade in.

"And now we wait for Dr. Peters?" he asked curiously, after the room completely faded in.

"Exactly," said Fred. Jeffery took a few paces ahead and observed. The escalators were moving a lot faster than the last time. Jeffery looked at the staircase by Dr. Peters's door and saw a gray crow standing on it. He looked at it closely and got a weary feeling in his gut. He turned towards the guidemen but they seemed very normal as they waited patiently. Jeffery looked back at the crow and the crow glanced at him then flew across the room, over one of the escalators. Jeffery wondered what was actually on the level directly above. He saw that the guidemen were walking towards him so he turned and saw that Dr. Peters had opened the door. Jeffery went up the stairs first, greeted Dr. Peters, then went straight back to the couch beside the large window. Dr. Peters and the guidemen entered and engaged in a short conversation. As they talked, Jeffery looked out the window and relaxed to the sight of the stars. The guidemen faded away, then Dr. Peters proceeded to the chair in front of Jeffery.

"Had a good rest, I hope?" he said casually.

"I tried," replied Jeffery.

"You seem a bit relaxed and less panicky," said Dr. Peters.

"I had a good sleep, I suppose," suggested Jeffery.

"Indeed, it seems like it. Did you read the journal?" asked Dr. Peters.

"Just the first piece she wrote," explained Jeffery, "the part about the contraption."

"I see," said Dr. Peters.

"What exactly is it that you wanted me to read about?" asked Jeffery.

"Well, you two are very similar," started Dr. Peters, "so I thought reading her journal would make you feel better."

"Interesting. Where is she now?" asked Jeffery.

"She went back to the workforce, and I heard that she is doing well," replied Dr. Peters.

"Is she really?" asked Jeffery. Dr. Peters nodded. "Was she a person?"

"She became one," replied Dr. Peters. "You didn't see her when you were there?" he asked.

"Not that I recall," answered Jeffery with hesitation. "They all looked the same."

"Well, I have some news for you, Jeffery," said Dr. Peters. "I do think that your stay here on *Contraption Hope* shouldn't be a long one. I think that you will be ready to return really soon," he explained with a smile.

"Is that so?" asked Jeffery. "And go back to the workforce?"

"Correct," replied Dr. Peters. "And you will do better the next time around."

"I *will?*" Jeffery asked incredulously. "That is not what Alp said. He said—"

"I told you before, Jeffery, what *do* these *gifted* readers really know?" interrupted Dr. Peters. "Now, would you please stay calm?"

"This isn't fair," said Jeffery sternly, glaring at him.

"Come, Jeffery, I have something to show you," instructed Dr. Peters as he got up. Jeffery watched him roll the chair to the center of the room and turned it to face the window. "Come on, sit there."

"Alright," said Jeffery. He did as he was told and looked out the large window at the galaxy as Dr. Peters prepared something. "What are you going to show me?"

"You'll see," answered Dr. Peters while organizing himself. Jeffery continued looking out the window and noticed that some of the stars seemed to form a constellation that looked a lot like the feather that Caster had lent him earlier. The stars that were closer looked a bit faint while the ones that were more distanced were very white and shiny.

"Alright, are you ready?" asked Dr. Peters as he got closer to Jeffery with a short, silver remote in his hand.

"I suppose so," responded Jeffery. Dr. Peters pressed a button and a large light-gray projector screen began automatically sliding down slowly, covering the window. He then went and turned off the lights and returned to his position, which was just to the right of Jeffery.

"What's this?" asked Jeffery.

"You shall see," replied Dr. Peters. "But please, watch carefully and don't say anything until the very end. Once it's done, we'll go back over there and talk, ok?"

"Alright," said Jeffery. "Did you do this with patient 514?"

"I did," answered Dr. Peters, "and, as I said, we'll talk some more later."

"Fine," said Jeffery. He looked at the screen while Dr. Peters pressed a button, turning it black. Jeffery then saw himself on the screen sitting in the room at the Fogbusts' before it transformed. He saw himself engaged in dialogue with George. "What is this?" Jeffery yelled.

"Relax," said Dr. Peters as he put his hand on Jeffery's shoulder, "I told you, just watch." Jeffery watched and listened to the dialogue. He saw the accidental killing of George, the arrival of the Fogbusts, and then, eventually, the meal they fed him and the staircase. Jeffery then saw scenes of himself with Lake Morgan, then scenes with Sabina, the lobsters and the unicorns. This was followed by his experience with Rick and Alp, and then eventually, his experience at the workforce with Ribs, including the tragic incident. After it got to the scene of the computer desk with Ribs, Dr. Peters pressed a button and turned it off. Jeffery sat in his chair, not moving a muscle. Dr. Peters switched the lights back on then came and stood in front of him. Jeffery looked at his hands and saw that the lines were darker and his fingers were oily due to his sweating.

"Would you like some water?" offered Dr. Peters. Jeffery slowly shook his head and looked down. "Well, let's go back over there." Jeffery stood and went to the couch while in shock and Dr. Peters followed with the chair.

"How did you get this?" asked Jeffery.

"We need to know as much as we can about our patients, here on *Contraption Hope*," answered Dr. Peters. "Now really, relax. The reason I showed it to you is so that you can get a closer look at your life and just see some of what you've experienced along the way."

"Well, the experience with Ribs was the worst," stated Jeffery.

"I saw that," said Dr. Peters. "Can you tell me more about Sabina?"

"What do you want to know?" asked Jeffery.

"Just about the two of you and how that went," replied Dr. Peters.

"Didn't you already see it all?" asked Jeffery.

"Now, don't be modest," said Dr. Peters, "if you want to go back to the workforce soon you'll need to talk about this."

"Did I say that I want to go back?" asked Jeffery sharply. "I do not wish to go back!"

"Sorry, I forgot," said Dr. Peters, "but, as I said, you will. You have no choice." Jeffery threw himself back in exasperation and put his hands on his face.

"Is there any way that I can avoid going back?" he asked after a short silence.

"No, there is not," said Dr. Peters with a sly smile.

"Do you think that if I go back, then maybe I might discover an exit and move on as Alp predicted?" asked Jeffery.

"I don't think so," replied Dr. Peters. "I have never seen that."

"Well, I do not think that I'll be ready anytime soon," said Jeffery. "Is that clear?"

"I am afraid that there aren't many options, as clear as that is," replied Dr. Peters. "I am the one who makes the decisions around here and I know what's best."

"And me going back to that torture is what you think is best?" questioned Jeffery.

"Not now," replied Dr. Peters after thinking for a moment. "This isn't your time. In fact, I think that it is time for you to go back and relax. The guidemen are on their way."

"Well, could you tell me more about patient 514?" asked Jeffery. "After all, I have not seen her, unlike yourself."

"Alright, just until they get here," replied Dr. Peters.

"What was her name?" asked Jeffery. After that, he saw the guidemen fading in, their sound indicating their arrival to Dr. Peters.

"Well, I will tell you all about it next time," said Dr. Peters after turning back to face Jeffery. "But for now, it is time for you to go and get some more rest. Come on." Jeffery got up and followed Dr. Peters to the guidemen.

"You need to take him straight to his room, right now," said Dr. Peters.

"Alright," replied Fred.

"He needs sleep?" asked Joseph.

"Yes, but Caster will take care of that," replied Dr. Peters. Jeffery went and stood by the guidemen, then looked towards the window.

"Rest lots," said Dr. Peters with a smile.

"Sure," said Jeffery quietly after glancing at him. He looked out the window until the room faded out. As soon as the other room faded in, Jeffery went straight to the couch and sat down with his hand on his forehead.

"He needs rest," Fred told Caster.

"I figured," replied Caster. "Alright, see you later." Caster glided to Jeffery as the guidemen faded out. Jeffery saw Caster wait until they were completely gone, then she looked at him gently. "I knew that that was going to be a difficult session for you."

"Boy, was it ever," said Jeffery. "I just, like, saw it as it all happened... "

"No need to explain," said Caster after gently hushing. "I know—I have been working here for years."

"I mean, you don't have to agree but at least understand," said Jeffery. "I shouldn't go back to the workforce. Can you see why?"

"I agree with you," said Caster. Jeffery looked at her and saw her looking back. "I absolutely agree."

182

"It was so violent and I didn't belong there," explained Jeffery.

"Yes, and you shouldn't go back," replied Caster.

"But he says that I have to!" protested Jeffery.

"I know—could you relax?" demanded Caster.

"I feel very uncomfortable," said Jeffery as he looked at her.

"Alright, will you just give me a chance to explain things?" asked Caster.

"Sure," answered Jeffery.

"Good," said Caster. "You see, everything here is a system," she began. "Has it ever occurred to you who actually owns this contraption?" Jeffery shook his head. "It's Ribs," announced Caster boldly.

"Ribs?" asked Jeffery, frowning.

"Yes, it's Ribs," assured Caster firmly and in utter disappointment. "He owns this contraption for when he runs into situations like yours, then he sends them here. And, believe me, there are lots." Jeffery kept looking at Caster, as he listened intently. "He pays us all. Do you think that Dr. Peters has any other choice but to send everyone back? No he doesn't. That is how this stupid system works. Ribs abuses everyone, sends them up here for treatment, and then has them sent back to keep his system going."

"This is unethical," said Jeffery.

"You really think that I think otherwise?" asked Caster with a frustrated glare. "He owns *Contraption Hope*—pays for it and everything. And by everything, I mean every*one*. That's right, Dr. Peters, the guidemen, myself and the whole crew."

"Revolting!" exclaimed Jeffery.

"Absolutely," agreed Caster.

"That explains why Dr. Peters thinks I am ready to go back," said Jeffery. "He knows that I'm not but he has to send me."

"That's right," said Caster, "and, like he really cares, anyways." Caster glided away towards the window as Jeffery looked out and saw that the stars were very bright. They were so bright that some of their light was shining into the room on its walls and floor. Jeffery looked at the floor and saw a small circle that was a few shades brighter than the rest of the reflected light. It glowed happily, which gave him a sense of hope and a little bit of happiness.

"And did you two talk about patient 514?" asked Caster.

"A little bit," replied Jeffery, "but not much." Reflected in the window he saw Caster sigh, so he questioned her curiosity.

"Perhaps I should tell you," she answered softly. She turned around and slowly glided back towards him.

"I do wonder why he gave me her journal," said Jeffery.

"Well, because he goes over her experience with some of the critical patients," said Caster. "All to make sure that they don't escape as well, except that he tells you lies at the end."

"Lies?" questioned Jeffery.

"Yes, she was sent here, but her condition wasn't critical," said Caster. "Therefore, she was kept in one of the standard rooms with doors, downstairs. The guidemen of course took her back and forth when Dr. Peters needed to see her, but in those rooms there isn't usually a lot of supervision."

"You're saying that she escaped?" asked Jeffery.

"Sort of," replied Caster. "Twice she gained access to one of the smaller contraptions that are attached and can fly away. She was, of course, caught, and she kept a journal, so she'd always write down her experiences."

"And then what happened?" asked Jeffery.

"Well, she didn't actually know that the second contraption could fly away so she always pretended that it could," explained Caster. "Until the third time she did it, she figured it out and set the timer. It starts at two hundred and counts backwards. Not long after she set it the guidemen caught her, so they locked it and managed to cancel it from flying. They took her down to Dr. Peters and… ”

“What?” questioned Jeffery, eager to know as he looked at Caster's sad face.

“And they killed her,” finished Caster. “She was a very sweet woman. Her name was Ayna. I monitored her a couple of times, and I had nice conversations with her, especially about the constellation of life. I was very angry when I found out that they had murdered her. I felt that there was no justice in this system.”

“That's horrible,” said Jeffery, his face bearing an expression of deep sadness.

“Yes,” agreed Caster. “She didn't recover fast enough, and she had broken the rules twice, so somehow, it made sense to them to murder her. But Dr. Peters of course does not share that part. He says that she ended up going back. He has this *happy* version of her not escaping and eventually getting rehabilitated back into the workforce and doing just fine.”

“That is so wrong,” said Jeffery.

“It is,” agreed Caster. “You know what sickens me, Jeffery?”

“What?” asked Jeffery.

“For some, to keep their own hope alive, they selfishly eliminate the hope of others,” replied Caster. Jeffery heard her words echo in his ears. He knew that this wasn't fair, but it was the truth. He had a flashback to the rock killing the people, all for Ribs's foolish entertainment.

“Well, I suppose I really have no other choice but to make my way back into the workforce,” said Jeffery hopelessly.

“Nope,” declared Caster. “I am going to help you get out of here.”

“How so?” asked Jeffery.

"Well, you are supposed to be resting, and Dr. Peters doesn't want to see you for a while, so I am going to fly you out to that contraption and get you to send it away."

"Ok," said Jeffery, puzzled, "but where to?"

"Oh, the galaxy is huge. You'll find somewhere to go," replied Caster.

"You don't think that they'll come searching for me?"

"No," answered Caster. "They will just be too worried about Ribs getting mad and having to pay for another contraption." Jeffery laughed but then realised something.

"And how exactly are you going to fly me there?" he asked.

"It's located at the very top. I know exactly where it is," said Caster.

"Well, yes, but how exactly are we going to fly up there?" repeated Jeffery.

"Watch," instructed Caster. Jeffery watched her closely, unsure of what to expect. First, she glided back a bit, and then raised her base into the air, which shrank the middle part of her. Soon, the middle part disappeared and her head and base came together in a clap. Finally, her form changed slightly as she got a lot wider and also higher from the top. Caster raised herself higher, sprayed Jeffery with a gray mist, and then leveled herself down to his eyes.

"What's this?" asked Jeffery.

"Just some mist to protect you from the atmosphere of the galaxy," replied Caster. "It can be a bit rocky and dusty." Jeffery watched her fly to the bottom right side of the window. Caster attached herself to it and applied some pressure. The window opened outwards and rose into the air while it remained connected at the top.

"Alright, get on," said Caster as she lowered herself to Jeffery's boots and turned sideways to provide a place for him to stand.

186

"Will this be safe?" asked Jeffery.

"Don't worry, you'll be fine," promised Caster. "I am not Ribs."

"Alright," said Jeffery. He took one last look at the crocksvenbulb before fully standing on top of Caster. He then looked at the nightstand and noticed the journal. "Wait!" he said hurriedly. He jumped off and went and grabbed the journal.

"Now, that, you're going to need to look after yourself, alright?" said Caster.

"For sure," replied Jeffery. He stood on top of her again, facing the wall as she faced the window. Jeffery then faced the window and tried balancing himself as best as possible. He looked out at the stars and smelled the air of the galaxy. Caster grew out two vertical lines that were made of her metal material. Jeffery looked down at them and saw them grow until they were at the level of his knees. Suddenly, they instantaneously wrapped around both his legs, forming a spiral.

"I told you that I'd hang on to you well," said Caster.

"Thank you," said Jeffery, "thank you so much!"

"Are you ready for me to take off?" asked Caster.

"I am," said Jeffery, his heart pounding while he clutched the journal.

"Be prepared," warned Caster.

Part II

On Contraption Ayna

Caster soared right out of the window and flew into the galaxy. Jeffery felt very off balance but didn't fall because of the tight binding around his legs. As Caster flew, she turned back in a curve, giving Jeffery a brilliant view of endless stars. He also saw a constellation of a big key that he couldn't help but wonder about. As Caster flew on, he saw a constellation of an empty glass bottle with no cork. Even though he was full of curiosity, Jeffery opened his arms expressing his gratitude for flying among the bright stars.

"Take a look," said Caster. Jeffery turned to look in her direction and saw that they were several yards above *Contraption Hope*. It looked exactly like in the picture in Dr. Peters's office, only much bigger.

"It's huge!" exclaimed Jeffery.

"Oh, yeah," said Caster. "I doubt that I have seen all of it myself."

"I can only imagine how Ribs got his people to build this," wondered Jeffery.

"That," began Caster after a pause, "is a very sad story with a tragic ending."

"What happened?" questioned Jeffery.

"Well, after completing it, Ribs claimed that about half the people who worked on it had died. And, according to records, they were all the ones who were promised double the payment of their currency."

"Oh, no," said Jeffery.

"It's horrible," said Caster with absolute disgust.

"I hate that man," said Jeffery. Caster plunged forward towards *Contraption Hope* then turned. As she did this, Jeffery caught sight of a small constellation of a snake. He wanted to get a closer look at it, but it was too far away and Caster had turned again. She flew towards the side near the top, where Jeffery saw what looked like the front of a small aircraft that was sticking out ready for takeoff.

"Is that it?" asked Jeffery.

"It is," replied Caster. "It is very well camouflaged. I actually forgot to tell you something."

"What?" asked Jeffery.

"It changes color after it blasts off," explained Caster. "It turns black so that it is camouflaged in the galaxy."

"Wow," said Jeffery. Caster flew to its side and went towards the window that was closer to the part buried in the main part of *Contraption Hope*. She went to the bottom left of the window and attached herself to it, applied pressure, and then moved away, allowing the window to slowly open outwards. After it was fully open, Caster flew in. She landed close to the floor and released Jeffery's legs. Jeffery began exploring the inside and noticed the black leather seats that were described in the journal. They were right up against the windows and were organized in four rows with five seats per row. The carpet was black and so were the walls. At the very front, Jeffery saw that there wasn't anything except for a black crocksvenbulb hanging on the wall. After looking at it, Jeffery walked into the third row from the crocksvenbulb and sat at the seat that was right by the window. He looked back and saw that Caster had closed the window which they had entered and was doing something to the ceiling. Jeffery looked to his left and saw that there was only a little bit of carpet, and by the wall on the other side was a black door that looked almost invisible.

"Alright, Jeffery," began Caster after flying down and into the row of seats where he sat, "I have just set the timer so you should be departing really soon."

"Ok," said Jeffery, "and how about yourself?"

"Oh, I wish I could come," said Caster as she softened her voice, "but I can't."

"Why?" gasped Jeffery.

"I wouldn't survive," answered Caster with a sigh. "I have to get recharged every so often, and if I leave with you, I will only have so much time left to survive."

"What do you mean?" asked Jeffery.

"It is how I was built," said Caster. "The guidemen are in charge of making sure that I stay charged, otherwise I will run out of function and can never have life charged back into me." Jeffery looked at her with his mouth open. He could feel his heart beat very fast as well as the pulses in his head and wrist.

"But you are such a good friend," he said with a shaky and quiet voice.

"Thank you, Jeffery, and so are you. You are wonderful and I am very glad that I managed to save you."

"You're sure that they'll never know?" asked Jeffery.

"Believe me, they won't," assured Caster. "They will be shocked at first but then they'll forget about it. And I am very glad that you're leaving. It killed me hearing about Ayna's death. I wish I had been able to save her this way. Alas, Jeffery, that is fate. You are destined to escape."

"Thank you," said Jeffery. "I wish there was something I could do for you."

"Just be careful and look out for yourself," replied Caster. Jeffery looked into her robotic eyes as she looked back at him. He felt their mutual sadness about saying goodbye echo throughout him, which only made him sadder. Caster quickly flew in closer, pecked him on his left cheek, then turned around and flew away. Jeffery watched her fly right into the door and disappear with a short sound. After she was gone, some gray and black powder splashed into the air then disappeared. Jeffery sat back and looked at the black crocksvenbulb as he held the journal tightly. He looked down at its hard gray cover and rubbed his hand on it. After holding it this way for some time, he felt the spacecraft depart from *Contraption Hope*, causing some turbulence. The spacecraft soared then turned away so that Jeffery did not get a last look at where he had been.

"Goodbye Caster," said Jeffery slowly, as he looked out the window. He looked around the black space that he was in, then back at the journal. He opened it and decided to read the next entry.

A while ago, I found this young lamb and I decided to keep him. He was very cute and very playful. Deep down inside, though, I have never felt that white was his real shade. I always thought that he deserved something more colorful. At least, that is what his personality indicated. He was never bland, bored or annoying. He jumped a lot, ate a lot, made very cute noises, and loved everyone and everything around him. Whenever I thought about his shade, somehow, he knew that it was on my mind, and would instantly become quiet and curl up somewhere. It was as if he knew that I knew that white wasn't his shade and he secretly agreed with me.

One night, I had him cuddled next to me in my room as I read to him. He enjoyed listening to me read. It always left a bright smile on his face and allowed him to have very sweet dreams. After he fell asleep, I rubbed my hands through him and watched him. He seemed to have been dreaming as I

191

felt a rush of positivity run through me. I felt like smiling and laughing like never before. Then, for whatever reason, as I rubbed my hands through his white curly hair, I remembered how this shade didn't suit him. Gently, in my head, I said, "I will change it for you and find you a color that you'll love." Right after I thought that, I saw in my head an image of myself at the store, purchasing dye. I thought that I should do that, and while I was looking at him, he opened his eyes and smiled at me, then right away closed them again and continued sleeping. I was so amazed at this that I knew that changing his color was the right choice.

The following day, I went to the market and looked at the different selections of dye. To my surprise, they had over eighty colors and shades to choose from. I looked through as many of them as I could and tried to decide carefully which one would actually suit him, not only because I liked it. After looking for a long time, I decided to choose a shade of blue. It was a rich cyan that I really liked and I knew it would make him look like a sweet candy. I considered navy blue, but realized that it would be too dark for his sweet personality. That evening, I dyed him, and I was stunned by his beautiful tone after I dried him. I watched him play and do his usual things in his new color and I felt thankful that I was able to do something.

That week, he developed a severe rash that left me worried about him. It started happening a little bit in the mornings or evenings of each day but then worsened drastically. I took him to a medicine shop to try and get him treatment, and I was told that I could treat him with a certain kind of ointment only if I shaved off his hair completely. I purchased the ointment then went home and shaved his hair. I gave him a warm bath then applied the ointment on him. I did that twice a week for about two months until his natural white hair grew back. After going through this with him, I realized just how brave he is, so I decided to name him Knight. As Knight grew, he got stronger, but he was just as sweet and playful as always. His hair got

192

fluffier and his legs grew longer. All along, though, I still knew that white was not his shade and he always seemed to agree.

One day, I went to the market again and decided to look for a dye that was more natural. I did find some but the color options were limited. While deciding, I remembered a dream I had had about Knight when he was a baby. In the dream, he was playing next to a lemon tree as I picked them for fresh, afternoon lemonade. I turned and looked at the yellow sun, which was bright, and I admired its light. After thinking about the dream for a while, I decided to choose yellow. That evening, I dyed him then blow-dried him after giving him a warm bath. I really liked him in yellow. I liked it more than the blue, in fact. Somehow, though, deep down inside, I knew that yellow wasn't his right color, either. Knight continued being his playful self until later that week. One morning, I woke up and saw that he had hives and was very itchy. I right away raced to the medicine shop to find more of the ointment. I managed to find some, and I returned home, shaved all of Knight's hair, and then began the treatment process again. While halfway through the treatment, I had a dream about my paternal grandfather, who died when I was born. I dreamt that I was sitting at a table across from him and we were engaged in a deep conversation. He told me that I should stop worrying about trying to change Knight's color, because eventually he would find the right one on his own. I thought about that dream for a long time, and especially after Knight completed his ointment treatment. I eventually decided that I should leave his color alone and that maybe, somehow, he actually would discover a shade of his own.

One day, not long after, I let him go outside to play as I cooked, and then I saw him come in, covered in mud. I was shocked at the sight. I had never seen him play in the mud before, so I quickly washed him. I felt strange about that situation. I thought about it for days and felt very uneasy about it. One night, before I got ready for bed, a man broke into my house and tried to steal from me. I quickly found the nearest weapon that I could, and chased him out of the house. After I chased him out, Knight evolved into a ball of black light and flew right into the intruder. The man shrank to about two inches tall, and disappeared in the grass. The ball of black light then evolved back into Knight, only now his shade was black. He came to me, speaking, and said that he loved me and appreciated all that I did for him, and he was now ready to watch over me. He kissed me goodbye, then ran outside and flew into the dark sky. Sometimes I see him flying at night. And when I do, I always remember to send him kisses.

Jeffery looked in front of him and saw a fascinating figure next to the crocksvenbulb. The figure was a lady in a black bridal dress that was very posh and accompanied by a matching black veil. What was fascinating about her was that she lacked a face. Jeffery took a closer look at her body and saw that it ended right after her neck. It seemed that she was lacking legs as she floated, and she did not stand. Around her central stomach area was a big brilliant-cut mirror, about the size of Jeffery's head, attached onto the dress. Jeffery froze and swallowed as he gazed at this deformed female figure. He glanced out the window and saw the constellation of life with its stars brighter than ever.

"Oh, Allie," Jeffery whispered under his breath. The female figure flew slowly towards him and caused him to feel extremely uneasy. Jeffery stared at her closely and watched as she got closer.

"I thought that you'd come," she said gently, "Jeffery."

"Who're you?" asked Jeffery, startled.

"This is *Contraption Ayna*," she replied. "I named it after myself."

"Ayna?" questioned Jeffery.

"Yes," Ayna replied.

"Patient 514?" asked Jeffery. Ayna paused. "I have your journal." Ayna remained still while facing in Jeffery's direction. Jeffery closed the book and held it out to her. A second later, the journal flew out of his hand and straight to her. Ayna seized it with her hands that were covered in long, black fashion gloves, and stared at it.

"I thought that I'd never see this again," she murmured softly after another pause.

"It was given to me by Dr. Peters," said Jeffery. "I read some of it. Forgive me, was I not supposed to?"

"It's alright," replied Ayna. "I know that many have read it." Jeffery watched her put it inside a pocket-like thing on the inside of her dress.

"Caster told me about this place, and she also told me a lot of other things. You know, about your death and all."

"It was atrocious," said Ayna. "Those guidemen are really cruel. They tied me down, beat me very hard with their fists and whips until I was soaked in my own blood. Fred took out a pocketknife and stabbed it into me."

"That's horrible," said Jeffery.

"But that's in the past," said Ayna. "How did you get here?" she questioned curiously.

"Caster helped me escape," explained Jeffery. "I just couldn't go back to the workforce so she helped me escape. She told me about this place and I read about it in your journal."

"Yes, that's why I named it after myself. I always wished to have it and fly away."

"And thanks to Caster we both are, now," smiled Jeffery.

"Indeed, we are," agreed Ayna.

"And that's the constellation of life," pointed out Jeffery.

"I see that," replied Ayna. "Caster must have shown it to you, eh?"

"She did," said Jeffery. "And she did mention showing it to you as well."

"And what was your struggle?" asked Ayna after a pause. Jeffery looked at her straight, as if she had a face. He smiled gently then ran his eyes up, down, and across her.

"Well, that's a really long one," he began softly. "Everything— others always seem to hold me to standards that they themselves can't live up to."

"Oh, pressuring isn't it?" comforted Ayna.

"Yes, so you can relate?" asked Jeffery.

"For sure," replied Ayna.

"I wonder," started Jeffery, "if you ever found out how it all really worked on *Contraption Hope*?" Jeffery stared at her brilliant-cut mirror and saw his reflection. He looked tired and worn out.

"I don't think so," answered Ayna. "Do you care to share?"

"Sure," said Jeffery, "Caster revealed it all." As he looked at the mirror, he saw it get a bit shinier as Ayna adjusted her posture. "And I wouldn't say it was my favorite revelation," he added as he glanced at her veil. Jeffery looked again straight into her mirror and waited for a reply.

"Well, I am curious," said Ayna.

"You see, Ribs actually owns *Contraption Hope*. The whole idea of it is to rehabilitate those he damages so that they can return to work for him. It is all part of a vicious system, you see?" said Jeffery. "In fact, Caster said that all the people who were promised more currency while building *Contraption Hope* actually died."

"That's savage," said Ayna.

"It is, it's unbelievable," agreed Jeffery. "And that's why he has Dr. Peters, to convince others that they're ready to go back. I was supposed to go back! I am just lucky that Caster saved me. She is a very kind friend."

196

"Yes, Dr. Peters is the worst," said Ayna softly. "He watched as they put me to death. In fact, he had a smile on his face." Jeffery looked right up at Ayna and felt tears in his eyes. "It was a really awful last minute."

"I am sorry," said Jeffery. "Want to know something strange? He, somehow, had footage that contained many events from my life."

"That doesn't surprise me," said Ayna, "he had one of mine as well. They sure know how to get hold of whatever they want."

"I wonder how?" asked Jeffery.

"I always questioned that myself," responded Ayna.

"It's pretty selfish and invasive," stated Jeffery. "I did not at all feel comfortable watching certain memories that I wanted to keep away from."

"I know," agreed Ayna, "I felt the same way when I knew much less. What hurt me was, after I passed on, I found out about all the lies they kept."

"Are you saying there is even more that I am not aware of?" asked Jeffery.

"Well, not that it matters, but yes," replied Ayna. Jeffery looked again at her mirror then ran his eyes down her fluffy black dress. He imagined how many revelations of truths she kept under it after discovering each one. "But don't be sad, we are not there anymore. We are now on my spacecraft, *Contraption Ayna*, and, thanks to Caster, we have flown away."

"I suppose so," said Jeffery as he felt his head begin to throb.

"I remember, before I was killed, I had met a really wise man. Alp was his name," explained Ayna.

"You met Alp as well?" asked Jeffery.

"Yes," replied Ayna. "He is very wise. He had the ability to connect with deceased ones. Once he told me that he found out that a man had lied to him so he told him: *As the living, you tell me all the lies you can, but the dead tell me all your truths*."

"That sounds like something he'd say," said Jeffery.

197

"Yes," said Ayna, "and my point is, one can only tell lies for so long." Jeffery felt comforted by Ayna's words. She offered him a sense of healing without even realizing it. Jeffery sat back and got a broader view of Ayna as she floated in front of him in her big dress. He glanced a few times at her mirror and at the crocksvenbulb, and then smiled at her gently. "Only for so long," she reassured. "Only time decides when it's ready for a revelation."

"And, I assume it is all just a matter of waiting," suggested Jeffery. Ayna did not say anything nor did she move, but somehow, he felt her smiling and agreeing. As he stared at her, a flash of pink light began to shine inside through the windows. Jeffery turned to look out the window next to him and saw that the light was getting brighter.

"It's not what you think it is," said Ayna.

"You really don't think that they have found us?" asked Jeffery worriedly, and in shock.

"They never will," replied Ayna. "Caster is correct." Jeffery was amazed at the fact that Ayna knew so much, including the thoughts in his own head. He felt her contraption turn right, which allowed the pink light to get brighter. Jeffery looked again and saw a large, pink gas planet that was very shiny and radiant.

"What is that?" he asked excitedly.

"I am glad you're feeling it," said Ayna. "This is planet Ice Mallow."

"Ice Mallow?" asked Jeffery.

"Well, it's about time you have something sweet," replied Ayna. "You might want to fasten your seatbelt." Jeffery quickly sat back and put on the seatbelt. He glanced out the window then looked at his reflection in Ayna's mirror. He noticed her contraption getting closer to Ice Mallow, so her mirror was reflecting all of its pink light. Ayna stayed in her place and balanced herself perfectly, floating in the air. Jeffery saw the pink light get brighter and felt a vast amount of healing energy flood the spacecraft. Before long, *Contraption Ayna* quickly dived into the planet and Jeffery nearly bounced out of his seat as the light got brighter.

Chapter Seven

Ice Mallow

After bouncing continuously on his seat and feeling as if the whole contraption was about to be blown away, Jeffery hit his head back against the seat, shaking up his internals. As *Contraption Ayna* traveled deep between the clouds of Ice Mallow, the entire interior began reflecting bright pink lights. Ayna's dress did so as well, lighting up her whole figure. Jeffery looked out the window and saw that all the clouds were glistening in several shades of pink. He took a look into Ayna's mirror and saw his reflection as if it were appearing under a hot pink filter.

Jeffery continued feeling off balance as the spacecraft continued soaring through the clouds. It plunged downwards sharply, creating even more turbulence. Jeffery turned his head towards Ayna again and was amazed by the fact that she was still in her place, unmoved. She floated with all her dignity, looking down, as if being held up on an invisible chariot. Her dress continued reflecting the planet's flashy, pink lights, which allowed her to shine with glamor. Jeffery secretly admired her appearance that resembled both her perseverance and her physical appeal—an inspiring sight that diluted the belligerent impact of the turbulence.

Shortly after, Jeffery heard a sound as if it were coming from the engine. He also noticed that the spacecraft had started traveling a lot faster. He turned to face Ayna, in an attempt to question what was going on, but he saw that she was merely floating and didn't change her position. Right away, Jeffery sat back and understood that remaining calm was his only option. He looked out the window and felt a sharper plunge forward, which created pressure on his stomach and caused him to gag. Then, *Contraption Ayna* started flying steadily and much slower. Jeffery looked out the window and saw that they had exited the clouds. He unbuckled his seatbelt then turned sideways to get a better look at the view.

The sky was a light shade of pink with some magenta sparkles. All around in the atmosphere, Jeffery saw so many different kinds of candy and sweets floating. They varied in size ranging from tiny to giant. He saw an ice cream cone floating that was bigger than *Contraption Ayna* and contained a large scoop of raspberry ice cream. Around it were some pink and magenta sprinkles in the sky. He also saw a chunk of milk chocolate floating and not far from it was a magenta ice cream bar that was filled with strawberry-flavored pink cream on a popsicle-stick that camouflaged well in the sky. He also saw many random jellybeans floating, ranging in various sizes and shades of pink. As *Contraption Ayna* turned and continued flying, Jeffery saw many more different kinds of candies and sweets floating about. He looked down and saw that there wasn't any land, but only more sweets floating at a lower altitude.

"Isn't this planet amazing?" said Ayna as the contraption lowered itself.

"It looks very *sweet*," replied Jeffery.

"One can eat all they want," said Ayna with a happy tone.

"You've been here before?" questioned Jeffery.

"In a sense," replied Ayna. "But that doesn't matter. Why don't you float around for a while and try some of the sweets?"

"That would be good," said Jeffery. He saw a gentle breeze of air from Ayna's dress travel towards the window causing it to open outwards, seemingly on its own. Right away, Jeffery smelled the sweet scent of fresh shortcake.

"You like it already, I see," said Ayna, taking notice of his contentment with the smell.

"I do," said Jeffery excitedly as he crawled out of his seat and exited through the window. He gently floated around and made his way to a fuchsia jelly cube that was floating by. He grabbed it with both his hands and quickly ate it. It was very soft and tasted like fresh berries and lemon—every tangy-sweet bite exploding in richness. After he finished it, Jeffery noticed that his hands were not sticky or greasy. It was like he hadn't eaten it at all! After that, a new jelly formed in the air and gently floated, exactly replacing the one Jeffery had eaten, as if it had never been consumed.

"Did you see that?" asked Jeffery excitedly, after turning around.

"I know, the sweet stuff here is eternal," answered Ayna. Jeffery saw that he was a few yards away from her, which gave him a clear view of her contraption. It was quite round, and rather small for a spacecraft. Nonetheless, it was very metallic and futuristic looking. Jeffery also noticed that Caster had been correct, it did turn black after breaking away and leaving *Contraption Hope*. Jeffery continued watching it as it floated peacefully in the sky with Ayna at the threshold of the open window facing him, above where he had been sitting.

Several kinds of sweets began floating towards the spacecraft. Jeffery saw a big marshmallow fly across that covered Ayna for a few seconds as it gradually floated away. He heard Ayna laughing out of pure happiness, which created a loving sense of comfort for him. Without noticing himself, Jeffery floated around and licked some ice creams as he kept glancing at Ayna, who watched him frolic happily. He floated towards Ayna and asked her if she'd like to join him in tasting the various kinds of desserts. That was when he noticed a small chocolate donut with pink glaze and lots of sparkles floating his way. Jeffery grabbed it and ate it in a few seconds.

"Man, that was delicious," he said with uttermost enjoyment.

"I would love to," replied Ayna happily, while closely observing.

"What would you like to try first?" asked Jeffery.

"I would taste them all at once if I could," replied Ayna, after another pause. "I am afraid, though, that my time has come to leave." Jeffery looked up at her with wide-open eyes.

"What do you mean?" he questioned.

"I… " started Ayna, then paused. She continued, "I shouldn't be in your way. I feel that you should get off here and continue your journey that you started before being sent to *Contraption Hope*."

"What do you mean?" repeated Jeffery.

"Everybody has a journey, Jeffery," said Ayna. "I went through mine and you're going through yours. It is time for you to carry on and finish it."

"Well, I don't think that I would have been able to carry on if Caster didn't get me out of there," stated Jeffery.

"That's correct," confirmed Ayna. "I couldn't agree more. But it isn't destined for you to stay with me for all of time. You still have a journey to complete, Jeffery. And, as Alp said, you still need to come face to face with the divine. In fact, the best you can find is often what you don't intend to seek." Jeffery floated upwards and quietly looked in her mirror. He took a final look at the big brilliant-cut glass that rested on her stomach, then looked at her veil.

"I see," he said softly.

"Well, you can't stop," insisted Ayna. "You don't want them to leave you faceless the way they left me." Jeffery took another close look at her and admired her innocence.

"That's a shame what they've done to you," he stated with deep sympathy.

"There is not much that can be done about that now," said Ayna. "But whatever, there is plenty of time for you."

203

"So, what's the plan?" asked Jeffery, ending his hesitation.

"Well," started Ayna, "I am going to leave." Jeffery looked at her with tears in his eyes.

"Where'll you go?" he asked.

"I will be somewhere in the constellation of life," replied Ayna. "If you ever see it, think of me."

"I certainly will," said Jeffery.

"Good. Thank you," said Ayna. Jeffery saw the same gentle, windy current come out of her dress and veil as it made its way around her contraption. "Goodbye, Jeffery."

"Goodbye… " said Jeffery, "Ayna," he added as the window gradually closed. After it was completely shut, Ayna stepped away from the window and her contraption flew away. Jeffery watched it shrink and finally disappear in the distance. "I'll see you in the constellation," Jeffery added quietly. He turned around and began looking at all the different candies.

While floating, Jeffery saw a cone float by with a scoop of chocolate mint ice cream on top. He floated towards it, grabbed it, and started licking the ice cream. He enjoyed it while floating and slowly turning in three-sixties, getting different angles of the view. After he finished it, he flew over to one of the giant sponge cakes and began eating parts of it, savoring the soft and well-scented cake and cream. Jeffery appreciated every bite then floated back a bit and watched all the parts he had eaten grow back on the cake.

He flew around with his arms spread open and explored as much of the planet as he could. As he flew, he plunged downwards and soared fast. He turned, flew forward, and then paused, floating, to observe. Jeffery saw lots of various kinds and sizes of candy afloat. A stick that contained six thick marshmallows dipped in white chocolate and drizzled with strawberry syrup floated a few feet away from him. Jeffery soared towards it and grabbed it. As he ate it, he valued every bite and even stopped looking around so that he could give it his full attention. After he had finished his exotic dessert, another one appeared next to him, but this one was drizzled with peach syrup instead of strawberry. Jeffery looked at the treat and felt a strong craving for it. Without hesitating, he reached for it, not ashamed of consuming more calories. The feeling of his sole existence afloat with all the delicious candies, on one giant planet, was enough pleasure and fortune for him, and eating the sweets was the perfect way to celebrate.

After Jeffery finished his second chocolate-coated marshmallow stick, he gently floated astray until he encountered a big chunk of chocolate. It was about the same size as *Contraption Ayna* and was magenta-colored. Jeffery got on top of it, then bent over and started eating it. It tasted like velvet cupcakes that were stuffed with chocolate and strawberry sauce but with the hard and milky texture of real chocolate. Jeffery was astonished at this and he continued eating. After he felt that he had eaten enough of it, he floated back and watched the chocolate re-form itself.

"Just incredible," said Jeffery. He turned around and saw another huge cone that contained two scoops of ice cream. The first scoop at the bottom was turquoise with indigo dots and the one on top was pink, very similar to the color of Ice Mallow itself. Jeffery flew to it and started licking the pink scoop. It tasted like bubble gum and was very sweet. After that, he tried the turquoise one and noticed that it tasted like a blend of blueberries, vanilla and fresh coconut milk. Jeffery took a few more licks then floated away backwards. After that, he opened his arms wide and spun around a few times as if he were dancing in the air. He flexed both arms and exposed his bare chest, which reflected some of the planet's pink light. He noticed that there were a few magenta sparkles around his chest and nipples that probably got stuck on him like debris. Jeffery laughed subtly, throwing his head back. While frolicking, he saw a small cube of chocolate cake float by with two big strawberries on top of it. One was halfway dipped in milk chocolate and the other in white chocolate. Jeffery grabbed it and ate it, starting with the strawberries, and eventually devouring the rest of the cake.

"In all my life, I never thought that I'd come to a place like this," Jeffery spoke sensually as he floated on his back in the sky. He rubbed his hand down his chest then between his thighs, and stared at a giant white jellybean with light pink spots. He considered floating to it but instead, he decided to continue lying there, enjoying the sensation. He closed his eyes and had a short nap, and, as he slept, he felt that he was held in two loving and firm hands of someone charming and caring. He felt sprinkling water being poured down on his bare chest as though it were coming from a watering can. This caused him to giggle in a flirtatious manner so he rubbed his hands on himself again as if he were washing.

"You are protected," said a male voice. Jeffery immediately knew that this was the same voice he'd heard while walking up the pyramid. He quickly opened his eyes and realized that this was just a dream. He looked around and saw the same candies and sweets that he had seen before falling asleep.

"I thought that I got in touch with my inner self for a second there," he muttered to himself. "I guess I got carried away." He giggled, then started flying as fast and as far as he could. As he flew, he encountered a lot more floating candy and sweets. Jeffery plunged forward and flew in search of something new. After flying for some time, he came to a halt and realized that there wasn't much on planet Ice Mallow other than its floating sweets. Feeling content with his happy realization, Jeffery floated on his back again and smiled at a giant, ball-shaped donut that was covered in powdered sugar. "I have never been at peace like this before," he said calmly. "Now I know what makes me feel happy and fulfilled: just being alone and away from things that worsen my wounds." Jeffery folded his arms behind his head and relaxed. After a while, a candy cane that was striped white, pink and red, came floating close to him. He realized that it was actually quite small, about the size of his index finger. Jeffery grabbed the candy cane then smiled at it. "In life, there's a lot of sweetness, you've just got to find it," he said before he began sucking the candy cane. After sucking about half of it, Jeffery let it go and it drifted away in the air. As it drifted, it re-formed itself and grew bigger than it originally was. Jeffery watched with amazement, and, before long, the candy cane turned entirely pink and floated upwards.

Jeffery stretched, then happily flew southwards, enjoying the breezy feel of cool air running through his hair and gently caressing his shoulders. He flew until he caught sight of something really interesting. He turned towards it then floated above on an angle to get a proper view. It was an extremely large cookie that was in the shape of a bowl that was filled with melted, dark chocolate. It was hot and looked very inviting. Jeffery pulled in closer and sniffed the comforting, warm and simmering smell of it. He felt as if he was waiting for something to come, something that was rather nurturing and forgiving. Looking closely at the chocolate, he saw that it was bubbling gently. The bubbles were small, and popped just before they got to be the size of a pearl. They contained pink and light-purple lights, which seemed as if they felt very happy being boiled.

Jeffery looked up in the sky and saw the rays of pink light shining down upon everything. He kept shifting his focus between the rays and the chocolate, feeling entirely at peace—on one end, below, the glowing rays that seemed to be filled with hope, and on the other end, above, the simmering chocolate that smelled like the rebirth of joy.

From above, a large green grape came floating. Jeffery quickly took it then dived down towards the chocolate. He dipped the grape in it then threw it in his mouth. He chewed its thick texture and appreciated the warm chocolate, swallowing the delightful sensation of the fruity treat. He looked to his right and saw a giant, flat and circular lollipop floating on a chocolate stick. It was patterned with pink and white stripes, swirling around. Right at the center of the lollipop, he saw a giant cranberry resting inside. It was vermillion and looked really juicy. Jeffery turned towards the lollipop and continued gazing at it. It looked very comforting.

"Now, that looks really good," he said after gazing at it a moment longer. He flew towards it, but he couldn't fly fast enough. He felt restrained and so he pushed harder, but found that he was only able to travel at a certain speed. "What's happening?" he questioned furiously. After a couple more attempts, he managed to fly a little bit closer to the lollipop, but then he saw it drifting away, slowly. The more he plunged forward the more it drifted away. Nonetheless, Jeffery continued attempting to get closer to it, but the closer he got, the farther away it floated. "Now, that's strange," he thought out loud. After a few more attempts, the lollipop began traveling faster. Jeffery paused then just watched it drift. It gently floated away with perfect balance. The farther away it drifted, the smaller it began to look in the sky, and the more pink it became, reflecting the planet's light. After watching for a while, Jeffery felt a sense of loss. He really wanted to lick it and eat some of its chocolate stick and the cranberry that rested at its center. He imagined how delicious they'd taste and how fulfilling it'd feel after enjoying them.

At the same time, Jeffery smiled with courage. He continued looking in the direction the lollipop had gone, knowing that it wasn't actually meant for him after all. "Certain things I am not really meant to have, I suppose," he said as the lollipop disappeared in the sky. "There are plenty of other sweets that I can have here."

Jeffery turned around and saw nine small, gelatin candies float by him that were about the size of his fingertips. They were puce-colored and round, as if trying to mimic some kind of berry, and looked very soft and chewy. As they floated together, they somewhat formed the shape of a diamond. After spotting them, Jeffery saw that they were floating towards him. "Those look good," he said curiously. They floated even closer towards him, captivating his sense of smell with their aroma. From his right, he saw a slice of peach float towards him that was topped with fresh whipped cream. Jeffery grabbed it and ate it in two bites.

Feeling fulfilled by the delicious slice of peach and the sugary sensation of whipped cream, he looked at the nine candies and saw that they had drifted even closer to him. Jeffery even felt, for a split second, as if they were calling upon him. He reached out his right hand and took one, holding it close to his eyes. He gave it a gentle squeeze and felt some strong vibrations come out of it. Its delectable smell grew stronger, then instantly, the candy tripled in size and turned scarlet, like a blooming poppy. Jeffery was so amazed by this that he popped it in his mouth and chewed it until it was consumed. It tasted like raspberries that were very high in quality. He then looked at the other eight candies and felt something different about himself.

"What could this be?" he asked. He saw a red light form a single, swirling pattern around his waist, which gave him a slight tilt. All of a sudden, Jeffery felt very balanced and stable, physically. He looked across at all the floating candies and sweets and noticed that his thinking had become clearer. He felt grounded, and that things around him were much more abundant than before. Looking down, he picked a second candy and felt it vibrating in the same way as the first one had.

Within seconds, it turned orange, and right away, Jeffery could smell apricot. He threw the candy into his mouth and ate it fast. Then, bright-orange light began to flicker by his groin, conjuring a strong rush of testosterone-driven lust, which dispersed internally throughout his entire body. His body vibrated strongly, which made him feel as if he wanted to kiss someone's lips very passionately, and paint a portrait of their remarkable lips. Jeffery picked another candy and looked at it closely. It also vibrated then grew to be triple its size, like the preceding two, but this one turned yellow. It filled the air with the rich smell of pineapple, and Jeffery didn't hesitate to eat it as well. After doing so, Jeffery saw a bolt of yellow lightning shoot out from under his belly button, leaving him with an indestructible amount of confidence within. He felt a strong sense of reassurance and he could hear voices telling him that he was able to do anything. He felt as if he owned everything, every candy, every cloud, and even all of Ice Mallow itself.

Jeffery picked out a fourth candy and watched it grow, turning light green, like an emerald. It smelled like kiwi, which lingered around Jeffery. Without hesitation he ate it, and saw a beam of green light surround his chest and upper back, causing his heart to echo across the planet. He felt that he was full of love and wanted to share it all around. Spreading his arms, he sent out that feeling, causing the green beam to release rays far away and beyond his sight. He felt his love extend out as if there were nothing greater than it. Jeffery also felt a strong need to forgive everyone and everything—even himself.

As he floated, Jeffery took notice of a very big cream puff that floated past. It looked really fresh, and seemed like it contained a lot of filling. He wanted to try some of it but it continued drifting. He looked back at the puce candies and picked up another one. This one turned light blue after vibrating. Jeffery right away threw it in his mouth. As he chewed, he tried to identify its flavor, but couldn't. It was a berry for sure, but some unknown berry that he hadn't seen or heard of before. He felt that his throat was clearing and he had an urge to speak.

"What is this?" he asked. Jeffery felt that his voice delivered his sentence so clearly and so smoothly that he wanted to sing. He stared at the big cream puff and struck a very high note, singing proudly with his operatic tenor voice. He felt the sound come from his diaphragm so smoothly that he continued singing, holding onto his note, without the need to breathe. After that, the cream puff popped in a giant burst and splattered cream and fruit juice everywhere. He kept staring in its direction and continued singing as all the smithereens of the cream puff fell away and vanished.

Jeffery paused, then looked back at the remaining candies. He picked up another one and felt it vibrate intensely. This one took a little while longer to grow, so Jeffery waited patiently, not looking away. Then, after a little while, it grew and turned indigo, filling the air with the smell of passion fruit. Jeffery ate it and swallowed it fast. "Of all of them, I'd say this one's my favorite," he said happily.

A circle formed around the center of his forehead, revealing a glowing, indigo light. Jeffery saw different colored auras around all the sweets that were floating and felt some energies traveling between them. Closing his eyes, he wished healing upon himself and everything around him. When he opened his eyes and looked around in the air, everything felt so loving. He picked another candy and stared at it. Its vibrations were even stronger than the preceding one but it instantly grew, turning violet. Jeffery smelled it passionately, and deeply inhaled the air that smelled of blueberries, taro roots and cream. He tossed it in his mouth, ate it, and felt the top of his head get lighter. He felt that his mind was clear and all his stress was relieved. A violet light emerged at the top of his head and formed a crown that came to rest gently on his head. Jeffery felt a nearby movement of something very divine and angelic around him and that he wasn't alone. He was able to sense the existence of many others, all of them invisible and meandering among the floating sweets. Jeffery could even hear their laughter and feel their happiness and love all around him, and in the sky.

He then looked at the remaining two candies. One of them floated closer to him so he picked it after a short hesitation. Its vibrations were very gentle and quite melodic. For a second, Jeffery heard what sounded like a symphony playing in the background. He looked around then back at the

211

candy. It grew slowly then eventually turned white. Jeffery held it close to his nose. Its fragrance was of dragon fruit and Jeffery could tell that its flavor would be much richer than the rest. Suddenly, after eating it, he lost his vision and all that he was able to see was a sheet of white light. His feet got very warm as a lot of energy formed around them. Even though Jeffery was blinded, he felt calm and at peace. He did not move a muscle, but floated gently, meditating.

"Relax, Jeffery," said the male voice from earlier. "I am watching you every step of the way. I need you to keep strong. You are doing well and my love to you is eternal."

"Who is this?" asked Jeffery in a calm manner, and with a gentle voice.

"You will know soon enough," replied the male voice. "Now, you must have the last one."

"Ok," said Jeffery. His vision returned, and he turned to look at the last candy as it floated nearer. He picked it up and waited for it to vibrate. It took a moment, but after it did, it eventually grew, turning fuchsia. Jeffery ate it right away and noticed that it tasted like a juicy watermelon. As he relaxed, pink light formed at the top of his head and circulated around his body, going downwards in a spiral. Jeffery felt a sense of himself and a very strong sense of clarity. He was relaxed and at peace, and far from harm's way. After noticing that all the lights and energies were gone, Jeffery felt something land gently on his head. He picked it up and saw that it was a candy cane, about the size of his palm. It was a bit thick and had stripes of all the colors of the candies he had eaten. He began to suck it and discovered that it tasted like all of the candies. Jeffery fell back and floated as he enjoyed and relaxed in the peaceful air. He looked at all the floating ice creams, donuts, chocolates and marshmallows and admired the whole planet deeply.

"The past influences the present to create the future," said the male voice. Jeffery closed his eyes and silently sent out gratitude. He then opened his eyes and finished the candy cane while floating about. Reflecting upon his miraculous experience, he felt much lighter in weight and balanced in his head. He noticed that he was able to smell the air better, which actually smelled very sweet. There was a fragrance of a flowery essence amongst all the candies and sweets, as if they were guarded with all of divinity.

When he turned around, he saw a small ice cream cone floating several feet away. Jeffery flew to it and grabbed it, causing a bit of liquid to splash. He drank the liquid that was contained in it, and discovered that it was fresh rosewater. After drinking it, he ate the ice cream cone, noticing that it was vanilla-flavored. Jeffery felt full but very light and happy. He flew around and did flips and other sorts of tricks, all with a big grin across his face. His vision was now much clearer and everything around him was in much better focus and color. He flew faster and passed a giant sundae, so he turned back and took a big cold bite out of it, then flew westwards.

As he flew, he saw some cupcakes that were floating, in various sizes; some were chocolate and some were vanilla—all topped with different colored icings and sprinkles. Jeffery flew at a big vanilla one that was topped with magenta icing, and started eating it. After taking a few generous bites, he watched the cupcake re-form itself.

"Can't go wrong with that," he stated happily. He flew northwards, then lifted himself higher in the sky. Among all the floating candy, Jeffery took notice of a big almond cake that was topped with a pile of grated, rich green pistachios. Jeffery paused and stared at the delicious-looking cake, then flew to it. He saw that it was shaped almost like a diamond so he started eating it from the edge. It was very sweet and tasted a little bit like honey. He enjoyed its rich texture and decided that he couldn't leave it without trying some of the pistachios. He flew to the top of the cake and nibbled on them.

Jeffery found it to be powdery and crunchy at the same time. He liked the mixture of honey-like cake and the saltiness of the pistachios.

Floating upwards to get a better sense of things, he noticed two small treats. One was a chocolate cookie that was about the size of his palm and contained white chocolate chip chunks. Next to it was pink jelly that was in the shape of an egg and slightly bigger than the cookie. It was also light in weight and almost camouflaged in the sky. Jeffery reached out for the cookie and started eating it. As he ate, he watched the jelly egg orbit around him peacefully at a slow speed. It gleamed as it slowly floated around him, showing off just how much berry juice it contained. Jeffery didn't take long to finish the cookie, and, after he did, he waited for the jelly egg to get closer. When it floated close enough, he reached out and took it, then bit off half of it. It tasted like cranberry, raspberry and cream, but was quite light in content. Jeffery liked that and really enjoyed its juice; he finished it, then flew downwards.

As he flew, Jeffery encountered a giant slice of lemon pie that was made of crust and layered with lemon jelly at the bottom, and with lots of coconut and whipped cream on top. He flew closer to it and landed on it gently. He started eating from the top then floated downwards, eating different parts of its thick layers. To his delight, it tasted really nice. The jelly was sweet and sour, and the cream was very soft and fluffy. After deciding that he'd had enough, Jeffery floated next to the pie and watched it re-form the parts he'd eaten. The sight of a sweet re-forming, each bite slowly patching itself and then leaving behind a shiny and untouched dessert was rather wondrous. After taking one last look at the giant pie, Jeffery lifted himself and flew upwards again. As he flew, he let his body twirl in the shape of a spiral. This made him a little dizzy, but the enjoyment of it left a huge smile across his face, expressing his strong sense of liberation.

After reaching a very high point up in the cool air, Jeffery saw a gentle, pink light shining around and felt a soft touch of air run down his upper arm. It felt welcoming and loving, but also indicative, which caused him to look around carefully. He heard some jingling that was very slow and yet harmonic. From above, he felt a small figure lower itself close to him. It floated a bit back, positioning itself right across from him. Jeffery turned around and saw that it was a very young boy. He was not even three feet tall, had very dark skin, and floated innocently, blinking his angelic eyelashes that fanned his gleaming, pink eyes. He had dark auburn-brown curly hair and wore a dress-like garment that exposed all of his arms and shoulders. It was pink, similar to his eyes, and its soft material reached his feet with a cut of a zigzag, that looked like reversed triangles pointing downwards. Around the boys neck was a necklace of seashells. Each shell was soft-pink and white, and thick in texture. Jeffery stared at the peaceful boy and the pink light that was around him. The boy quietly looked at Jeffery and gently floated as he held a pink cotton candy in his left hand that was about half his size.

"Who are you?" asked Jeffery curiously.

"I am Hal," replied the boy. "I am a bringer of destiny. I show up when needed, and advise."

"Well, that's unexpected," said Jeffery. "My name is Jeffery."

"It's great to see you," said Hal.

"Great to see you, too," replied Jeffery with a smile. "I like your outfit."

"Thanks," nodded Hal. "I see there's a bit of ice cream floating your way." Jeffery looked behind him and saw an ice cream cone floating closely that was double his size with three scoops of ice cream on top.

"You're right," said Jeffery. The bottom scoop was turquoise, the one in the middle was magenta, and the one on top was a very light pink and white, similar to the seashells on Hal's necklace. Jeffery took a lick from the

215

top part of the magenta ice cream along with a bit of the light-pink one, then the ice cream cone floated downwards and eventually away below him.

"Close enough," whispered Hal.

"Pardon me?" asked Jeffery.

"I said, you're close enough," repeated Hal. "You have had quite a relaxing time here on planet Ice Mallow."

"Well, I did," answered Jeffery, "it's been quite a journey."

"Yes, it's nice to get more in touch with yourself, now, isn't it?" said Hal. Jeffery looked at the child with a deep sense of curiosity.

"You seem to know a lot for someone so young," replied Jeffery.

"Well, it is part of my task," explained Hal.

"And what destiny do you bring me today?" asked Jeffery.

"Firstly, you're nearing completion," answered Hal. "You did lick the middle and top ice cream."

"That's good," said Jeffery.

"Indeed," agreed Hal, "and I see that you are stronger now, you've opened up many parts of yourself."

"You really think so?" asked Jeffery.

"Oh, for sure," answered Hal. "I can see it clearly. You have a much broader perspective now. There is definitely a lot of inner growth." Jeffery sighed gently then looked around him. He did feel much lighter and indeed felt like he had a stronger sense of clarity about things. He then looked at Hal and decided to pick his question carefully.

"Do you mind if I ask," Jeffery began, "would you be able to tell me what's coming next?"

"Certainly," said Hal. He reached out his cotton candy to Jeffery and instructed him to breathe on it. "Just lightly blow it—your breath will reveal what is there to see."

"Alright," said Jeffery. He leaned forward and gently blew on it, creating pink plumes that disappeared. A small pink cloud formed at the top, then came down and blended into the cotton candy.

"Well, there are a few small challenges coming up ahead," explained Hal.

"As if I need any more," joked Jeffery.

"Well, life is never a smooth road," enlightened Hal, "there'll always be clouds bringing light showers." Jeffery watched Hal hold back the cotton candy as he pulled out a small bit. Hal held up the piece and let it float into the air as Jeffery watched it carefully. The piece formed into the shape of two sharks that were positioned in a circle, turning slightly and facing one another's tails.

"What's that?" asked Jeffery.

"Sharks," started Hal, "are competitors, Jeffery. What I am seeing here is two figures that have always been in competition with one another, and their vicious cycle is continuing."

"And who are they?" asked Jeffery.

"I don't know," answered Hal. "I am feeling female energy from the two." Jeffery looked at the figure of the two sharks and watched it fade away into the air. Hal pulled out another piece of cotton candy and let it form into another image. Jeffery watched the pulled piece of fluff as it formed into the head of a ram that faced him angrily.

"And what's this about?" he asked worriedly.

"The ram symbolizes someone who is really going to butt heads with you," replied Hal, "like, big time. She seems to cause a lot of problems. This is definitely in your future." Jeffery looked at the ram very carefully and felt a little bit intimidated. As he watched it, it turned into an image of a shield. "That tells me that you will need to protect yourself from her," added Hal. Jeffery took another close look at the shield, then it gradually faded away.

"This is interesting," remarked Jeffery. Hal smiled gently, then pulled out another bit of the cotton candy. This time, the fluff turned into a vortex that swirled for a few seconds then spontaneously turned into a spade.

"As I said earlier, there is more conflict coming," explained Hal, "but you will be defeating it, and pretty well, actually."

"Well, I suppose that's good," said Jeffery.

"Indeed," agreed Hal. After the spade faded away, Hal pulled out another bit of fluff and let it float. Jeffery watched it closely and felt anxious while it was forming. Eventually, it formed into a heart with the letter S in the middle.

"This is from your past," explained Hal as he looked at Jeffery directly. "Someone fell in love with you but couldn't have you. There is an S in their name or in the name of a relative."

Jeffery thought for a moment. "Who could that be?" he wondered.

"I don't know, it's in your past," replied Hal. Jeffery thought deeply, then right away remembered Sabina.

"Oh, yes!" he exclaimed. "I know who this is."

"That person really loved you, but was not able to have you," said Hal.

"Unfortunately, that's true. She was very kind and beautiful," confirmed Jeffery.

"I see," started Hal. "Love is not easy."

"No, it's not," agreed Jeffery. After the image of the heart faded away, Hal pulled out another bit of the cotton candy. Jeffery watched with great interest. This time, the fluff just tore apart and formed several dots in the air.

"A lot of messages," stated Hal.

"Messages?" asked Jeffery.

"News," replied Hal. "You are going to hear a lot of things about others regarding several things."

"I see," said Jeffery.

"Yeah, you're going to know about a lot of things," Hal added. Jeffery looked at the several dots that were floating and decided not to count them because there were so many.

"I can tell there are a lot," laughed Jeffery. He watched the dots fade away, and then Hal pulled out another bit of the cotton candy.

"Are you ready for this one?" asked Hal as he pulled.

"Yes," replied Jeffery, watching the bit of cotton candy form after being released.

"I feel a positive vibe from this one," added Hal. The two watched closely until the bit of cotton candy turned into a loon floating on water, and a swan looking towards it.

"This looks beautiful," said Jeffery.

"It does," agreed Hal. "This is very interesting. I see here, that in the future you will be receiving a gift that is meant for you. And it seems that this gift is involved with a marriage."

"A marriage?" asked Jeffery.

"Yes, a marriage," stated Hal. Jeffery laughed then watched the image fade away.

"I wonder who I will be marrying?" asked Jeffery.

"You will know in time," replied Hal. "I just want to add one more thing."

"What's that?" asked Jeffery.

"I am seeing a really loving prayer being sent out to you. It is from a very good friend. I sense a strong female energy within this friend and I keep seeing the letters *C*, *R*, and *A*," answered Hal.

"Ok," said Jeffery, thinking.

"Yes, somebody who helped you in escaping something quite bad, actually," added Hal.

"Oh, yes," replied Jeffery. "She really did a great job."

"She wishes you well," said Hal. "Her message is to keep strong and keep carrying on." Jeffery got a nostalgic memory of Caster revealing all the information to him about *Contraption Hope*. He remembered how she had helped him escape and how she asked him to look after himself.

"I appreciate that," said Jeffery. "I pray for the best for her as well. It is horrible that they have her life depending on a charger."

"That sounds bad," said Hal softly.

"Will I ever get to see her again?" asked Jeffery. "Somehow, that is."

"She is not alive," answered Hal. "This is her soul returning."

"You mean she's dead?" questioned Jeffery as he looked down.

"Yes," replied Hal. "Her death involved a lot of smashing, I am actually seeing hammers. She's also showing me some men. I can't seem to count how many, but a few of them. It looks like she was bludgeoned to death."

"No way… " said Jeffery, crying.

"Stay optimistic, Jeffery," instructed Hal, "it's very important. In fact, peace comes to those who seek it!" Jeffery looked at the cotton candy and then looked around him. The view of everything seemed shinier than ever before. Jeffery looked at Hal and observed the innocent pink light around him. "I am sorry. Just remember that she is always around and never gone. And before I leave, make sure that you make the most out of your stay here on Ice Mallow, because your time here isn't lasting much longer."

"Really?" asked Jeffery.

"Yes," answered Hal.

"But I love it here," stated Jeffery.

"I do, too," agreed Hal, "but you ought to finish your journey."

"You're right," said Jeffery, "we all must."

"Yes," said Hal. "So, I'd better be on my way. It was nice meeting you."

"Nice meeting you too, Hal," said Jeffery. "And thanks for telling me about all of this."

"You're welcome, it's what I am here for," said Hal.

"Can I ask one last thing?" asked Jeffery.

"Sure," replied Hal.

"Is there one more piece of advice that you think I should have?" asked Jeffery.

"Actually, I do," answered Hal.

"What is it?" asked Jeffery.

"It's to think more about yourself," started Hal. "That's coming from your friend, actually. If you give too much of yourself to others, how much of yourself will be left for you?"

"That makes sense," said Jeffery with a sigh. He thought and reflected upon that for a moment. He thought about how much of himself he actually did give up for others and especially for their benefit. "Got it," he said confidently.

"Well," said Hal, "I need to go now. Good luck and keep strong."

"Will do," replied Jeffery. A bright pink light seared out from the front of Hal, around his chest area, and then wrapped itself around him, like a capsule. It then blasted, releasing a vibrating energy and disappeared, leaving behind lots of pink and white sprinkles splattering across the sky. Jeffery flew downwards, with the messages he had received in mind. As he flew, he saw a floating pancake topped with whipped cream and strawberry syrup that was about the size of his head. Jeffery flew to it and ate it. It tasted very sweet which helped him relax—just what he had needed.

He lay back and floated with his hands behind his head, breathed deeply and released as much energy as he could. Closing his eyes, he prayed that his stay on Ice Mallow would last a bit longer. Jeffery knew that this decision wasn't his to make, so he hoped and remained calm. He thought about the flavor of the delicious pancake and imagined that he was eating it again. In fact, Jeffery questioned if he'd ever again find a place full of delicious ever-growing treats like he'd found on Ice Mallow. He thought about the jellies, cakes, chocolates, fruits, and everything that he had tried. The thought gave him a sense of warmth and brought him closer to his inner self.

He opened his eyes and felt a strong need to fly westwards, though he was unsure why. He spread his arms, turned aside, and began to fly westwards and upwards at the same time. He flew until his body came to a halt on its own. Jeffery felt as if he had suddenly hit a wall, causing his head to shake a little. He tried to move, but felt that he was somehow limited. He was no longer able to fly and he felt that gravity was trying to pull him down, but something else was holding him up. Feeling slightly frustrated, Jeffery frowned and tried to move, then looked around and saw that all the candies and desserts were somehow still in place and unaffected. Looking ahead, he saw that many feet away and a bit above, some pink sparks were flashing. Jeffery stared at them and saw them get thicker and louder. A gust of wind began to blow, which calmed down the scene and created a slight shift in the movement. Jeffery tried to get closer but wasn't able to. He just stared with great curiosity as a beam of pink-white light flashed and startled him.

When the beam disappeared, a glittering silver line appeared then moved around and created a large circle. After it completed the circle, another beam appeared and transformed it into a giant light-pink crocksvenbulb. Jeffery widened his eyes in shock and stared at it. It floated just like the candies, with elegance, and shone lustrously. From beneath it,

222

wide magenta stairs formed and continued forming their way down. Jeffery watched the staircase that looked like it was tumbling as it formed. It began floating upwards, getting closer but still facing away. Once it reached him, it formed a step, which he landed on, and then it continued forming until there were about sixty more steps diagonally downwards. Jeffery took a closer look at the stairs and saw that they were covered in fine carpet and at both ends of each step was a small knit-design of light-pink and fuchsia tulips on a lime-green vine. He also realized that he had lost his ability to float. As he stood, he looked straight at the crocksvenbulb, greeting it with a proud nod.

"Whenever you're ready, you may go on," said the male voice from earlier. Jeffery looked around, and just like in the past, saw no sign of any man. He didn't respond but went down the stairs. "Not that way," said the voice. Jeffery, feeling confused, went back up to the top. The staircase pulled in closer to the crocksvenbulb, allowing him to touch it. It was ceramic, just like the ones he'd seen before, but this one smelled like fruit. Jeffery stood back up and looked out from its center. "Go on," repeated the voice.

"Fine," said Jeffery. The soles of his feet were sweaty and became very numb, which echoed in his head and worried him.

"You can't stop now," said the voice. "There's still more that's waiting for you." Jeffery's heart pounded faster, so he glanced around then looked right back out the center of the crocksvenbulb. He jumped up then dived right into it, head-on. As he fell, he continued facing forward until a puddle of thick, glowing, magenta jelly rose up and allowed his body to penetrate through it. Jeffery felt very moist and was momentarily blinded by the texture. As he fell, he saw many beams of white and pink lights flashing, creating images of flowers, birds and fruit. He continued falling downwards then felt his body turn and land with a thud, making him close his eyes.

"In every land there's treason, but in every land there is love," spoke a female voice. Jeffery opened his eyes and saw nothing but a sheet of many pink lights, so he closed his eyes again, feeling extremely light-headed yet eager to know whose voice that was.

Chapter Eight

And So We Meet

"In the land where there is treason, there is greed and blinding desire. It is the land where all pompousness resides; everyone seems to sell themselves to get the cheapest of products. Even worse, they sell one another for their own benefits. What I do not understand, is how they could consider their lifestyle to be a *standard* of some sort? And for what? Everything they do is discriminating to others... "

As the female voice spoke, Jeffery opened his eyes slowly and caught sight of a large golden vase that stood on the linoleum floor across from him. The floor was checkered orange and white and was very shiny. Jeffery skimmed his eyes across the tall, bright-orange wall above, and saw a large golden sword hanging horizontally, pointing towards the window to his left. On the handle of the sword was a sharply etched image of a deer that had a piece of orange amber at its center. Jeffery looked down at the vase and saw the same image of the deer etched on it, but bigger. It, too, had a piece of orange amber at its center. Jeffery saw that he was sitting on a burnt orange wooden chair that wasn't very strong. Even though it lacked sturdiness, Jeffery felt comfortable sitting on it and he didn't feel as lightheaded anymore.

"But, in the land where there is love, only *love* and its light guide the way. There is no need for any sort of standards—all we need is *love*. Only love can guide, and only love can teach; only love can move us along, and only love can provide us with precision and give us the strength to accept one another. Love is an endless cycle that brings no other than liberation. It brings us liberation from our evil deeds and our selfish needs. But, in the land where there is treason, they cannot accept this. Not that they can't, it is just that they fear the power of love."

Jeffery looked to his right and saw another orange wall that had two glass doors in the middle with wooden framing and heavy, golden hinges. To its left, Jeffery saw a sconce mounted that was made of a dark metal with glass on each of its four sides. Inside, it contained a ball of orange light that floated above a small platform in the center. Jeffery stood up, turned around and then faced right. That wall was also orange and had another sword hanging that looked exactly as the other one and also pointed left. He looked at the wall in front of him, which seemed quite far away, and saw a bed covered in an orange bedspread positioned to its far right, almost against the other wall. To its right, was a tall, thick, orange lamp that had a pattern of white hearts going around it in a spiral. At the center of the wall stood a small, burnt orange wooden table and a chair that matched the one that Jeffery was sitting on. And on the chair sat a lady, facing the wall.

"But I believe in destiny, and I believe that I will put an end to this misery. No one deserves to be judged and to suffer for things they can't control. We must all live together as one in unity and harmony," she cried as she continued looking at the wall. "And that is why I firmly believe that in every land there is treason, but in every land there is love. *Love*." Jeffery stood and looked at her and wondered if he could ask her anything without startling her. She buried her face in her palms, rested her elbows on the table and sighed. Jeffery looked to her left and saw an oval-shaped mirror standing on the table next to her. It was about the size of his head, with an orange rim. At its base was that same etching of the deer that held an orange amber at its center. Jeffery took another look around the room then looked back at the lady, who had become quiet and still. Suddenly, the whole room felt very quiet, as if every thought had ceased to exist.

"Hi," whispered Jeffery, cautiously. The lady remained frozen and the room felt quieter than ever. She pushed her chair back and stood up, still facing the wall. Jeffery saw that her dress had a corset on the back and was royal orange, with a white trim near the bottom. Her straight hair was brown, the color of milk chocolate, and rested perfectly on her rib cage. She had a few orange braids in her hair that were much shinier than her dress. Jeffery was also able to see that she was really slender. She turned around and faced him, revealing her skin that was light, like his, and her rather *sweet* face and sharp features. Around her neck was a golden necklace with an orange crocksvenbulb pendant, and close to her heart was a bold tattoo of the deer etching. Around the leg area of her dress was a zipper that was almost invisible. She bent over and unzipped it, then took out a small and smooth orange ball that was made of stone. She held it tight while staring at Jeffery.

"Hello," greeted Jeffery confidently.

"And so we meet," she replied. "Tell me, Jeffery, were you sent here directly, or were you at Sarm's?"

"Who's Sarm?" questioned Jeffery. The lady looked at him with a pause then focused on the ball in her hand.

"I see," she said after a moment of pausing. "Well, I know of you, Jeffery."

"You do?" asked Jeffery.

"Yes," she replied. "I am Senuv. I am the mother of this kingdom."

"And who is Sarm?" asked Jeffery.

"Sarm is my sister," replied Senuv, "and she is the mother of the other kingdom."

"Well, what's wrong?" asked Jeffery. Senuv put the ball back into her pocket then walked towards and around Jeffery as she spoke.

"You see, Jeffery, you have heard of God, Allie, right?" Jeffery nodded. "I believe in him, and so do all the other citizens in my kingdom. But we also believe in liberty and harmony. Some male citizens marry males, some marry females. Some citizens take on certain tasks that they prefer. It is just the way it is. In the end, in my kingdom, we all live together, with *love*." Jeffery listened carefully as she spoke, comprehending every word. "Which is probably why you were sent here rather than to Sarm's," continued Senuv. "We see each other almost every day and we try to negotiate how we can bring peace to resolve our conflict, but our citizens are too caught up in their philosophies, so that we have done nothing but fought wars forever."

"That's sad," said Jeffery, feeling moved by her words.

"It's horrible," cried Senuv as she continued wandering around him. "We need to live in peace, it's the only way. Sarm has very strict rules for her citizens that are making them backwards-minded. And, not to mention all the chaos that has been caused in the past due to her rules." Senuv sat down on the chair where Jeffery had been sitting and buried her face between her palms again. Jeffery could feel her anxiety and how she was devastated by everything she'd explained. As he walked closer to her she sat up, tossing her hair back.

"I don't know what to say," started Jeffery.

"As if it's your fault and there is anything to be said?" replied Senuv, sounding upset. "I just can't understand how so many others can live with this sort of thinking."

"Throughout my time," started Jeffery, "I have seen all sorts of ways that others think. I have seen one kill for his own benefits."

"One?" exclaimed Senuv. "I have seen that hundreds of thousands of times."

"Well, that's terrible," replied Jeffery, "but there must be a solution."

"Try telling that to thousands of citizens," answered Senuv, with her arms folded. "I am sick of the bigotry of those in her kingdom."

"Would I be able to see where she lives?" questioned Jeffery.

"Follow me," replied Senuv. She guided him out the door then turned right. As Jeffery followed, he noticed that they were on one level of a castle, and to his left, there was a balcony that followed along the rim of the walkway. He walked closer to it and looked down. There were many other round floors beneath, all with orange carpet and golden rims along their balconies. He saw that each level had several doors and decorations on all the walls and that all the doors were orange with either a white or golden frame.

Jeffery looked ahead and saw Senuv go down a staircase that was to the right. He followed her, noticing that the stairs were very wide and had the same orange carpet, and gold banisters that had jeweled peonies made of orange garnet patterned on them. Jeffery followed Senuv down the stairs and around the level below, then finally down another set of stairs. Senuv turned and went straight to one of the doors, allowing Jeffery to follow her in. She turned on the light, revealing all the details in the room. The walls and the floor looked the same as those in the previous room, but, at the center, there was a wide and bright orange rug that had beige patterns of flowers and vines. On it was a large wooden table made of red oak, with six matching chairs, and across from it was an orange electric piano with a framed picture of a map above it. At the piano was a matching leather seat, of a slightly lighter orange. The map looked old but the frame seemed new. It was the same color as the piano and had wide, pointy edges. To the top right of it hung an orange crocksvenbulb.

Jeffery looked at the chairs around the table. They were high and predominantly the same color, with burnt-orange upholstery. The tops were curved and the wood was cut into a pattern of flowers. In the center of each chair's head, Jeffery saw that there was a gem of a tangerine quartz at the center surrounded by white diamonds that formed the shape of a reversed triangle. All the stones were baguette cut and of a size that could have easily rested on his palm. He walked around the table and up to the piano, accompanying Senuv, who was looking at the map.

Down its center, horizontally, was a curved line that served as a divider on the map. To the left and close to the upper corner was a large, white and orange castle that slightly curved as it stood. It had several towers with various symbols that seemed as if they were summoning heavenly contact. Behind the castle, to the left, was an image of the sun. The rest of that side was painted with yellow-orange strokes depicting grass, and, to the bottom left of the castle, was a drawing of a brown compass, with the letter N at the very top of its center. In the other three corners were sharp arrows that pointed outside the compass's circle, indicating their direction.

On the other side of the curved line, was a white and ruby-red castle located on the mirror-opposite side of the other one. Other than their dominant colors, the castles looked identical in architecture and size. This side of the map had burgundy and vermilion strokes depicting grass. There were no symbols on this side, but something caught Jeffery's attention: on the bottom right side was an image of a gravelly looking cave that was very dark and painted in black, maroon and medium brown. From far off, it looked like part of the map was torn off. Jeffery looked at the cave and wondered what was so significant about it—its entrance was a huge gap that seemed to invite one to the pit of their morbid imagination. As he looked more carefully, he saw a faint line that was just a little lighter than the vermilion strokes run across the map between the castles. As it transitioned onto the other side of the map, it turned slightly darker than the yellow-orange strokes. Jeffery could hardly keep his focus on it as it was so faint. He looked carefully at the map, then glanced at the crocksvenbulb.

"And where exactly is this?" asked Jeffery.

"We are here," replied Senuv as she pointed at the orange and white castle. "We used to be united, but the kingdom got divided many years ago."

"I see. That must have been difficult," expressed Jeffery.

"It really was," replied Senuv. "It was very long ago, but it still bothers me. It hurts me especially to know that only one side of the kingdom truly understands love."

"I take it that there will never be a reunion if the other side will never understand love," suggested Jeffery.

"Exactly," said Senuv. She then stepped aside, pulled out the piano seat and sat down. "Would you like me to play something?" she asked lovingly.

"That would be nice," said Jeffery.

"Well, have a seat," said Senuv after indicating the table and chair with her palm up as if she were offering something. Jeffery walked around and pulled out one of the chairs and positioned it to give him a full view of Senuv and the piano. He sat down and faced her, and with a gentle nod that indicated he was ready to listen. Senuv played a couple of happy-sounding notes then looked at him.

"This song is called, "Happy That My Heart Can See," she announced. She then began to play and Jeffery listened carefully as he watched her. Senuv bounced with the tune and her fingers played fast, like children running in sheer excitement. Jeffery felt a sense of happiness echo through him, and he nodded to the harmony. Senuv ended the song with a few repeated notes, then turned to face Jeffery with a smile.

"I like it," said Jeffery. "It felt really fuzzy."

"I can tell that your heart was able to see that," said Senuv.

"Could you play another one?" asked Jeffery.

"Sure," replied Senuv. "Actually," she started, "I have a similar one that's called, "The Sun Isn't Far, My Friend.""

"*Oooo*, I like the title of that," said Jeffery. Senuv faced the keys again, then began to play. She played some slow, melancholic notes at the beginning then went into a harmonic melody that sounded similar to the first song but with more repetition. As Jeffery listened, he felt as if the song was telling him in a melodic fashion that he needed to appreciate something. After Senuv ended the song with a *boom* with the combination of a few notes at once, she turned and looked at Jeffery with her eyebrows raised. "Very good," said Jeffery.

"The sun isn't far, my friend," reassured Senuv as she grinned at him. Jeffery looked at the map and focused on the sun.

"No, it's not," he agreed.

"Would you like to hear another one?" offered Senuv.

"Certainly," answered Jeffery.

"This one is a little bit different," explained Senuv. "It is called, "We Used To Be One, My Sister." Jeffery glanced at the red and white castle on the map then looked back at Senuv and the piano. Looking down, she paused for a moment, and then breathed slowly.

"This one sounds intense," said Jeffery. Senuv didn't respond and kept looking down. Jeffery waited patiently until she played a note that echoed. She then played four more similar notes that echoed as well and then continued playing slow notes with sad-sounding vibrations. Jeffery took notice of Senuv's breathing as she sweated a little. As he listened, he closed his eyes and felt a deep kind of loss, the kind that happens without choice. He felt as if the song was saying that there was no control over the past and things are just the way they're meant to be. Jeffery kept his eyes closed until Senuv finished playing, then he gently opened them, and saw her looking down at the piano. "I am sorry," expressed Jeffery.

"It's not your fault," replied Senuv. As she lapsed again into silence, Jeffery glanced at the crocksvenbulb.

"I think," started Jeffery, as he looked directly at Senuv, "the wound is not as deep as it feels." Senuv turned to face him, unsmiling and her body almost fragile.

"You really think so?" she asked.

"I do," asserted Jeffery. "And you shouldn't lose hope."

"Interesting," answered Senuv, "if only you could see what we've gone through all this time."

"Tables can turn," insisted Jeffery. "I really want to meet Sarm, actually."

"You will," replied Senuv. "The reason I brought you here, before getting carried away with my songs, is that I wanted to show you the map."

"Right," started Jeffery, "I am curious to know what that dark place at the bottom part is."

"No one really knows for sure," answered Senuv. "But it's not a very nice thing, I can tell you that."

"I thought so," said Jeffery. "How did all this even start?"

"Well, centuries ago," replied Senuv, as she looked down for a moment. She then looked up at Jeffery and continued, "Our parents ran the kingdom. This was the only castle that had ever existed. Everyone lived together perfectly well. After we, Sarm and I, became women, our father built the second castle for us to have. We always had everything in orange with white, it's our family color. But a long time after, Allie decided that it was time for our parents to cross over and that Sarm and I needed to rule the kingdom as its two mothers. Things were fine at first. Not too long after, Sarm began to show a whole new side of herself. She changed the color of the other castle and claimed it as hers, also changing all the philosophies that we grew up with. The kingdom became divided because of the propaganda that she spread. Eventually, battles and wars took place, and a lot of other horrendous things. And then, she claimed that part of the kingdom as hers

233

and invited all those who followed her to relocate there, and they murdered all the ones who followed our traditional values who had lived there initially. They didn't even get a chance to relocate."

"That's horrible," said Jeffery.

"That's what happened," breathed Senuv.

"What turned her that way?" asked Jeffery.

"I remember that when we were growing up she tended to have alone time more often," explained Senuv. "Especially during the daytime, she always wandered off by herself. We noticed that she always questioned things and always had doubts. It was as if she had a need to explore something else, and something darker. Of course, that would never have worked when our parents were still alive, so, as soon as she had some distance and a whole castle to herself, she just grasped the opportunity. She painted the castle, altered things, and gradually gained control of it. Also, she was very skeptical of things."

"In a sense, have you always known that this would happen?" asked Jeffery.

"Yes," replied Senuv instantly, "and so did our parents. I remember, a long time ago, I talked about it with our mother, and we both always felt it. We just never did anything about it, and then they passed away, and... " Jeffery watched Senuv fall silent.

"And?" he questioned.

"And all this happened—we are divided," replied Senuv.

"I see," said Jeffery.

"Tell me more about you," inquired Senuv. "I am curious about where your journey started."

"Well, how did you know that I'd be coming?" asked Jeffery.

"After living for a few centuries, I have been around enough to know," laughed Senuv.

"Before coming here, I was on planet Ice Mallow," explained Jeffery. "Have you heard of it?" Senuv shook her head. "Well it's a very sweet place. Before that, I was on *Contraption Hope*, and a good friend helped me escape and I ended up on Ice Mallow. After some time, I arrived here, and I don't know why."

"I see," said Senuv. "God works in mysterious ways."

"I can't disagree," said Jeffery.

"He really does," reassured Senuv. "Not that I am trying to change the subject, but would you like to play a game?"

"A game?" asked Jeffery.

"Yes, you and I," replied Senuv. "We can play it on the top terrace."

"Sounds intriguing," answered Jeffery.

"Ok, follow me," said Senuv, smiling. She stood up and headed out the door, so Jeffery followed her.

"The top terrace, you said?" he asked curiously.

"Yes, I think you'll like it up there," answered Senuv. "The view is relaxing and the air usually has a gentle breeze."

"That does sound really relaxing," said Jeffery.

"Which is just what we need for the game," agreed Senuv.

As Jeffery was going up the stairs, he noticed a tiny hole in the carpet on one of the steps that looked like the head of a skull. He took a second look and thought that it looked more like a volcano instead. Rather than paying more attention to it, Jeffery walked until he and Senuv had reached the upper level and continued walking.

"Strange," he whispered to himself.

"I beg your pardon?" inquired Senuv.

"Oh, nothing," said Jeffery, shaking his head.

"Is everything alright?" asked Senuv.

"Yes, I was just catching my breath," replied Jeffery as he panted slowly. He felt his torso shake, making him uncomfortable.

"There are plenty of stairs in this castle," smiled Senuv lovingly.

"Indeed," agreed Jeffery, trying to smile back. He turned his head away and thought about that hole he had seen on the stairs, and wondered.

"We just have to go up a few more," warned Senuv. "The top terrace is near the highest tower of this castle."

"That explains why it's breezy up there," suggested Jeffery.

"Yes," agreed Senuv, "otherwise there wouldn't be a point for a top terrace, or so my father once said."

"I take it that he suggested on having one?" asked Jeffery.

"Well, there are a few," replied Senuv, "but this particular one he had designed for this game. The castle used to be smaller but after he and Mom became father and mother of the kingdom, he expanded it. He always believed that augmenting space allows for new things to come in. He just never guessed that that would include my sister turning away from our values when he built the second castle."

"Yes, that is ruthless," stated Jeffery. He thought again about the volcano and the skull and felt a shiver run down his spine. He looked at the wall to his side and saw a silhouette of a big ring with the letter *G* in the middle that suddenly disappeared. After that, Jeffery saw another silhouette, but this one was of a fox's head that looked very proud and also very intelligent.

"Most certainly," agreed Senuv without noticing what Jeffery had seen. "But you see, Jeffery, your farthest enemy is usually the one closest in blood."

After going up another floor, Senuv pushed open a big door that led to the top terrace, where they were greeted by a cool breeze. As Jeffery walked out onto the terrace, he looked in all directions, taking notice of just how huge it actually was. The floor was made of marble in various shades of orange and white. The front of the terrace was wide and semi-circular with tall white pillars that connected to the ceiling and to each other through low, burnt-orange stone walls, which served as a gate around the terrace. Jeffery walked right to the front to see the view of the rich, orange grass and trees. The sky was slightly lighter, and birds perched in the swaying trees chirped their melodies that sounded like hymns. Jeffery inhaled deeply and exhaled as he admired the view. It seemed to him like an elaborately painted illustration, creating a mood of admiration and nostalgia.

"Beautiful, isn't it?" asked Senuv as she walked closer to Jeffery.

"It really is," replied Jeffery, passionately raising his voice. "It has a certain feel that is really special."

"I know what you mean," said Senuv with a smile and a sigh. "Mom and I used to talk about it all the time. We used to have tea here sometimes."

"The sky looks very soft," added Jeffery. "You know, Senuv, I have seen the sky in so many colors but I think this one is actually my favorite."

"What other colors?" asked Senuv.

"Purple, yellow, black... " answered Jeffery then paused, "but orange is my favorite."

"I am glad," said Senuv. "The entire kingdom used to have it."

"And somehow, Sarm changed it?" asked Jeffery.

"Yes," replied Senuv. "Though I don't know how she did that."

"Is her castle designed similarly on the inside as this one?" asked Jeffery.

"For the most part," answered Senuv. "Father did want to have some alterations so that it looked more modern at the time, but generally, very similar. She did a few more renovations herself, but mostly it's the same. The color is what's most noticeable."

"So why red?" asked Jeffery.

"It has to do with a dream that she had a long time ago," replied Senuv. "She once had this dream—it was after our parents died—that she was watching the kingdom and it darkened a few shades. She felt the land get heavier, and she also saw her prosperity doubling. She said something specific about the numerology of it that I can't seem to remember now."

"She sounds avaricious," expressed Jeffery.

"That's Sarm," answered Senuv casually. "If only things would return to being the way they were... "

"Maybe there is a chance," said Jeffery. "I mean it, maybe there is."

"Well, that would be a miracle," replied Senuv. "Now let's play the game." She turned around and walked to the other side of the terrace, indicating to Jeffery to follow. After getting nearer to the wall, Jeffery saw that there was a door that wasn't visible from far away. It was short, and seemed more like a cupboard. Senuv opened the small door and took out two medium-sized containers that were metallic orange and held things that were pulling them down with their weight. She opened one of them and Jeffery saw that it contained some sliced, fresh cantaloupes. Senuv handed him a slice, then took one for herself.

"Juicy," said Jeffery after he bit off half of it.

"It's a good fruit," explained Senuv. "We always have some stored here and we eat it especially before playing this game." Senuv closed the container then put it back in the small door.

"So what exactly is this game?" questioned Jeffery. Senuv opened the second container, took out an object, and unrolled it. It looked not quite like a fishing rod and not quite like a gun.

"Here," she instructed as she handed it to Jeffery. It was burnt orange and made of hard plastic with thick rubber coating that felt soft but also very sturdy. It had a trigger that was coated with the rubber, and at the top, there was a small, soft, orange ball that covered the front hole. Senuv took out a second one then closed the container and put it back in the cupboard. "So what we're supposed to do," she started as she got up and walked back to the front of the terrace, "is pull the trigger and listen carefully for vibrations in the grass. Wherever you feel the vibrations are really strong, just hold it over your shoulder then toss it forward while still pulling the trigger. The ball will shoot and land on the spot and release some worms. After that, the birds will come by and eat it. Whoever feeds the most birds, wins."

"Interesting," said Jeffery with a short laugh. "I like this idea."

"I do, too," said Senuv. "Here, watch me." She pulled the trigger then started moving her aim while looking downwards from the terrace, searching for a spot. Senuv then held the object over her shoulder and quickly tossed it forward while holding it firmly. The ball bounced out, revealing that it was connected on a copper chain, and hit the ground after a few seconds. As it did, Jeffery saw that it camouflaged then turned into a pile of orange and beige worms that were quite thick. It bounced backwards, its chain rolling back into the gun-like object. "Now watch," instructed Senuv. Jeffery looked at the worms and, within seconds, a flock of seven round and chubby neon-orange songbirds, with short, thick beige beaks, landed, and started eating the worms in a huddle. Jeffery gazed at their cute characteristics and watched how they ate the worms. They tilted as they jumped from spot to spot, and some even split a worm in half, sharing it amongst the others.

"So cute!" he yelled excitedly.

"I know, eh?" replied Senuv. "And this doesn't really have a name. Father just called it a *thrower*."

"I see," replied Jeffery, shifting his gaze to it.

"The worms taste like cantaloupe, actually," informed Senuv. "And some of the beige ones taste like sweetened banana. They're artificially made for the birds."

"Wow... " said Jeffery, sounding astounded.

"Now you try," suggested Senuv.

"Alright," replied Jeffery. He pulled the trigger on his *thrower* and listened to the grass carefully. He aimed at a certain spot that was not far from the birds and felt his hand vibrating a little, allowing him to hear some sort of movement. Jeffery held the *thrower* behind his shoulder, then quickly tossed it forward and watched the ball fly out. As it plunged, he was able to feel the vibration of the chain rolling out. "That feels intense," he said with a small laugh.

"I know it does," agreed Senuv. The ball hit the grass and rested for a few seconds. Jeffery saw a pile of worms appear seemingly out of the air, and then the ball quickly wound itself back in. Before long, a flock of birds that was about triple the number as the preceding one appeared in the sky, landed and started eating the worms.

"Impressive," cheered Jeffery, giggling, "just look at that!"

"That's a big flock!" said Senuv, laughing along.

"Just look at them," said Jeffery.

"Now, what we do, usually, is just watch them eat until they finish," explained Senuv. "After that we shoot out another round and keep feeding them. Usually whoever feeds more wins, but I never really competed. I am just happy feeding the little birds."

"I sort of prefer it that way, too," said Jeffery. He watched the two flocks as they finished their meals and then flew off into the orange sky.

"Another round?" asked Senuv.

"Sure," replied Jeffery. Senuv pulled the trigger on her *thrower* and began searching. Jeffery noticed that she was taking her time, and figured that she was looking for a spot where the vibrations were most intense. Once she had located a particular spot, she threw the *thrower* forward and its ball plunged ahead. After the pile of worms appeared and the ball wound itself back in, a flock of ten birds showed up and began to eat.

"Not bad," said Senuv. "Your flock was the biggest."

"Well, it's not a competition," said Jeffery, after counting the birds.

"That's right," agreed Senuv. "I just get excited when I feed so many at once."

"I can relate," laughed Jeffery as he watched the birds eat. He then pulled his trigger and began locating a spot. Not far from where the birds were eating, he felt an intense vibration, so he right away threw towards it. After the ball landed, created the pile of worms, and wound itself back in, a flock of eleven birds arrived and began eating.

"Still more than me," laughed Senuv after counting them.

"I see," replied Jeffery.

"So, you'd have forty points or so, right now," added Senuv.

"I really love the way they eat," said Jeffery in admiration.

"Yes, they're very plump," agreed Senuv. As the two of them watched, the birds began eating from one another's pile. "Now, isn't that adorable?"

"Oh, yes," agreed Jeffery. "Do they do that sometimes?"

"Yes," answered Senuv. "Mother and Father used to enjoy it a lot."

"I must say, you're a very sweet mother. I am sure your citizens must really love you," Jeffery said kindly.

"They do, and thank you," agreed Senuv with a little bit of sadness. "You know, Jeffery, my dream is that the kingdoms reunite and that Sarm and I can be mothers of one kingdom again, just as our parents always wished."

"Don't lose that hope," answered Jeffery.

"You really are the man of hope, aren't you?" said Senuv. Jeffery turned and noticed that both flocks had eaten the worms and flown off.

"Another round!" Senuv focused on the grass then sent out another round of worms with her *thrower*. This time, a slightly larger flock of birds showed up and started eating.

"Sixteen," announced Jeffery after counting them.

"Let's hope you can feed more again," suggested Senuv.

"Sure," said Jeffery. He looked at the grass and pulled his trigger. As he shifted, he felt the vibration levels vary across the grass. After finally deciding on a spot, he threw his *thrower* forward and sent the ball plunging out.

"I think this one is going to be a lot," said Senuv.

"You think so?" asked Jeffery.

"I feel it," insisted Senuv. After another flock of birds flew down towards the fresh worms, Jeffery and Senuv counted at the same time.

"Fourteen," said Jeffery.

"Nope, you got sixteen," corrected Senuv. Jeffery counted again and saw that he had missed two birds that were a little smaller and huddled in between a few other birds.

"Oh, right!" he said. "I missed those two. They're so far down, that's why."

"And also, they're so young," laughed Senuv.

"And adorable," agreed Jeffery. He silently watched both flocks eat until they finished and flew away.

"You really like this game," said Senuv.

"I do," said Jeffery. "I like it especially because we don't have to compete. We can both just enjoy feeding different flocks."

"Exactly," said Senuv, "and, in the end, birds are fed, so we all win."

"And how about another round?" asked Jeffery.

"Sure," answered Senuv. "Why don't you go again?"

"Ok," laughed Jeffery. Then, within seconds, he threw forward.

"I think this one might be smaller," said Senuv, "the vibrations weren't that high in that area." After the ball wound back into his *thrower*, three birds showed up and began eating the worms. They were a bit bigger and seemed older than the previous birds. "I guess the older generation prefers the lower vibes," laughed Senuv.

"I suppose so," replied Jeffery with a short giggle. Senuv then aimed close to their right.

"We'll see about this next flock," she said after her ball hit the ground. After the worms were created a large flock of over forty birds showed up.

"Holy!" yelled Jeffery.

"That's a big one!" exclaimed Senuv. The two of them laughed as they watched the birds eat.

"I didn't think that I would live to see that," announced Jeffery.

"It's happened before," explained Senuv. "I've just never seen it happen next to three old ones!" Jeffery continued laughing with Senuv until the birds finished their meals and flew away.

"That was priceless," said Jeffery. "Thank you."

"You're welcome," replied Senuv. "Well, let's put the *thrower*s away."

"Alright," said Jeffery as he handed his *thrower* to Senuv. She walked back to put them away and he turned to face the view. He took one last look at the orange grass, trees and sky and tried to take it all in. He thought it was too huge to capture in one panoramic memory. Nonetheless, he admired it warmly and thought about the birds that he and Senuv had fed. He felt a slight breeze run down his shoulder, as if he were being touched by someone unseen. He looked down at his shoulder and saw nothing, yet felt that someone was sending a blessing of appreciation to him.

"Well," started Senuv, "ready to go and meet Sarm?"

"It'll be interesting meeting the other mother," replied Jeffery after turning to look at her.

"Ok," replied Senuv, "follow me." Senuv turned around and Jeffery followed her back inside the castle. She guided him up two staircases and around the third floor until they were greeted by another big door that was distinct—wide, wooden and with several tangerine quartz gems horizontally mounted across its center, all varying in cuts. The door frame was painted white and its hinges had wings on them that were made of brass and seemed very old. Jeffery looked down at the carpet and felt a strange movement beneath it. He looked back at the door and realized that it was actually two doors and that there were winged hinges on each side.

"Before we go, there is something that I should tell you," warned Senuv.

"What's that?" asked Jeffery, forgetting about the movement.

"The two castles are connected," she answered.

"How?" asked Jeffery.

"You'll see," replied Senuv. "I know it doesn't really show it on the map but I will explain. When Father and Mother built the second castle, they wanted Sarm and me to still be close in a way that no one could know about. So they built an invisible bridge that only we are able to see and it goes straight to the other castle. Needless to say, it's the same on the way back."

"That's quite eccentric," stated Jeffery with all honesty.

"I know," agreed Senuv. She reached into her pocket and took out her ball again. "Now allow me to warn you, Sarm is really feisty."

"I can imagine," replied Jeffery.

"Really," said Senuv assertively, "she can be quite difficult. I think you can handle her though. Just try not to disagree with her. That really makes her angry."

"Ok. Anything else I should be aware of?" asked Jeffery. Senuv hesitated, then looked down, her hand under her chin.

"Well," she started, "stick by me the whole way, and don't wander off on your own."

"And?" inquired Jeffery.

"I know, that's just common sense," Senuv scoffed. She put her hand down on her hip then looked at the door. "Really, just be aware, stay next to me the whole time, don't get on her nerves, and also, I strongly recommend you save any questions for later."

"And why is that?" asked Jeffery, keeping calm despite Senuv's uneasiness.

"Just because we need to keep aware of our surroundings, she has some creepy things in that castle," explained Senuv.

"Well, alright," said Jeffery.

"And, there is a chance that she may want to keep you, but I am going to hope not," said Senuv.

"Keep me?" asked Jeffery.

"To convert you to her philosophies," replied Senuv. "She is really twisted. She isn't humble and loving as I am."

"Now that's... " said Jeffery, then paused, "creepy."

"Yes, I agree, it's wicked," responded Senuv. "I think it's completely terrible how presumptuous she turned out to be."

"And if that happens, will you be able to rescue me?" asked Jeffery.

"I am afraid not," said Senuv. "Let's not dwell too much on that, though. I am sure everything will be fine."

"Alright," said Jeffery.

"Now, shall we?" asked Senuv as she gestured towards the doors. Jeffery nodded his head and watched her as she stepped forward and pushed them. After the doors flung open, Jeffery saw a big beam of orange and white light enter. "And, before I forget, the doors always open outwardly," she warned.

"That's interesting," said Jeffery.

"It's as if Father somehow knew," murmured Senuv. Jeffery stepped closer to see what the doors had opened to.

"Oh my!" he exclaimed.

"I know, it is gorgeous," agreed Senuv.

"Look at the design!" said Jeffery as he looked ahead of him. The bridge was made of slate tiles and painted light orange. Each tile had its own spectacular design but Jeffery wasn't able to perceive their details. He stepped outside and carefully observed as he walked, with Senuv following behind him. The sky had become brighter as did the grassy hills in view at both ends of the bridge. "And it is actually invisible?" questioned Jeffery.

"It is," replied Senuv as she walked slowly. Jeffery kept observing the bridge as he walked and found that every few seconds or so, it turned white for a brief moment then back to its original color.

"This is impressive," said Jeffery.

"It's unique," agreed Senuv. Jeffery noticed that along the walls on each side of the bridge, large eggs that were much taller than him appeared whenever it turned white. They were metallic, burnt orange in color, and sparkled lustrously under the sunlight. There was a ribbon tied around each egg and a large teardrop-cut piece of orange amber in the middle. Adding to their elegance, small, red garnet stones were scattered across each egg in no particular pattern. Seconds before they disappeared, parts of each egg spontaneously cracked, flashing yellow-orange light, like a radiant shock. Jeffery waited until the next time they appeared and curiously questioned Senuv about what they represented.

Senuv replied, explaining, "Eggs are a sign of youthfulness," she began after the eggs had disappeared. "At least that is what my Mother believed. Also, each egg comes from a parent. Her wish was that as Sarm and I lived youthfully in our own castle, we would still be linked to her."

"I see," said Jeffery. He turned to his left and saw that one of the hills ahead suddenly seemed higher and a bit nearer. He thought that it was some sort of illusion so he blinked then scratched his eyes and noticed that the hill was, in fact, closer. "Why does that hill suddenly seem closer?" he questioned.

"I don't know," replied Senuv as she looked down. Jeffery glanced around and continued observing the stupendous sight. Senuv tossed her hair back and fluffed out her dress, expressing her absolute comfort.

"Walking here is always relaxing even though it is a bit of a long walk," she said.

"How long?" asked Jeffery.

"Long enough, you'll see," answered Senuv.

"I wonder if it would hurt a lot if someone jumped off the bridge?" said Jeffery.

"Oh, Sarm and I did that a lot when we were children," remembered Senuv. "It doesn't hurt, it's just a long fall and seconds after we landed we'd float right back up."

"Really?" asked Jeffery.

"Well, only Sarm and I. Father designed it that way in case we were ever in danger and escaped through here."

"And now, what seems to be the only danger is her," stated Jeffery after thinking for a moment.

"Indeed," sighed Senuv. As Jeffery walked, he noticed the slate suddenly felt a bit heavier and less hollow. He looked back and saw that Senuv's castle was no longer in view. "Feeling the difference?" she asked.

"Something does feel different," replied Jeffery with a frown. "I feel that I am not even able to walk as quickly." He turned and looked to Senuv and saw that she was also walking slower.

"Just keep watching," she instructed. As Jeffery walked, he felt something come forward that wasn't quite a vibration but not exactly a swirl either. Everything in his presence seemed to move strangely and then suddenly he felt something large, flat and invisible penetrate right through all of him. He turned and looked at Senuv and saw that she was experiencing the same thing but with a much more relaxed facial expression. Jeffery also saw that everything around him had turned red, including the sky, the hills, the bridge itself, and not long after, Jeffery saw that the eggs were different also. They were burgundy and their stones had turned really dark, and around each egg, orbited a ring of crimson-red plumes. Jeffery glared at the change, and turned around in three-sixties.

"We are now at the red part of the kingdom," he indicated, "just as shown on the map."

"That's right," said Senuv. Jeffery looked ahead of him and saw a distant castle that was red and white. "We're almost there," she added.

"I am a bit nervous," admitted Jeffery. "But I am also anticipating this. I really think that I can make things work and reunite the kingdom."

"I hope so," said Senuv. "I have full faith in you. And like I said, it is very important to keep near me."

Chapter Nine

The Battle for Unity

"And, do we just go in?" asked Jeffery as they approached the door after walking a while longer.

"Whenever you're ready," answered Senuv. Jeffery looked at the door and realized that it was actually two doors, like the ones he and Senuv had exited from earlier, but these doors were red. Jeffery thought for a moment then turned and faced Senuv.

"Ready," he nodded, showing his courage. Senuv stepped ahead and pushed the doors open with full force.

"This way," she pointed before they entered. As Jeffery followed her, he noticed that the interior of the castle was the same as Senuv's, but the carpets were red instead of orange.

"So many rooms in these castles," he observed.

"Well, it's good to have storage for centuries-worth of things," said Senuv. Jeffery looked out to the balcony and saw that they were four floors up from the main level. He saw that Senuv was going down the stairs, so he followed her.

"How will Sarm know that we are here?" he asked.

"You'll see," answered Senuv. "She will know." At the bottom of the stairs, Jeffery noticed that against the red wall stood a tall statue of a muscular and strong-looking man with a sharp jawline and chest-length hair. His arms were folded and his legs were slightly apart. Senuv stopped walking, then paused to look at the statue.

"Is this your father?" asked Jeffery, after seeing the look of reminiscence on her face.

"It is," she replied quietly. She stepped up to the statue and put her head on its shoulder. "I miss him so much."

"I am sorry," comforted Jeffery.

"Come on," said Senuv as she stormed forward, trying to hide her emotions. "We can't stop now. Maybe there is hope." Jeffery followed her then glanced back at the statue. Soon after, they arrived at the stairs near the main level of the castle, greeted by the shiny red floor. At the end was a platform covered in scarlet carpet with two large matching drapes tied to the side, giving the place a strange feel. At the other end, he saw a matching door with fantastically etched patterns of sharks and falcons with a look in their eyes that seemed to define all of anger. Across the top of the walls, there was a row of metal, half-ovals elegantly placed with their bottom loops parallel, that emphasized exquisite expectations.

Feeling shocked at the sight, Jeffery noticed the presence of numerous large and metallic bug-like objects casually loitering. The bugs had two main connected parts that were somewhat egg-shaped, with one being the head, and the other being the base, both of them red. They were connected by a thick, black object that was about ten inches long. At the base, there were three dark-gray legs on each side that arched before coming down and connecting into the feet. Some of the bugs had black legs patterning variously with the gray ones. Finally, Jeffery observed their red antennas and small maroon eyes that gave them a heated look along with their sharp, metallic beak-like mouths.

"What are those?" yelled Jeffery, as he stood on the stairs.

"I know, I was freaked out, too, when I first saw them," replied Senuv, looking back. "They're called trinmpts and they are harmless. They just like to sniff around your toes a bit. Sarm got them because she thinks that they look grotesque and can scare away intruders—which they obviously do."

"They're disgusting!" exclaimed Jeffery.

"They are," agreed Senuv. "Now, this way... " She turned around and continued down the stairs. At the bottom, she stormed across to the center as Jeffery watched some of the trinmpts follow her and sniff under her dress. He followed her, and watched the trinmpts as they sniffed around his boots as well. After reaching the center of the main floor, Jeffery stood and looked around him at the castle. He saw countless balconies above and realized just how huge the castle actually was.

"I don't think I saw the main floor of your castle," he stated.

"It's pretty much the same except it's orange," replied Senuv, "and, of course, without the trinmpts or anything as ugly as that." Jeffery looked down to the floor and saw three of them sniffing around his feet.

"Please don't ever have those," he joked.

"Rest assured, I won't," answered Senuv.

Jeffery continued to look around him at the main level of the castle and glanced a few times at the trinmpts. He saw one standing several paces away from him that was casually staring at his face. As Jeffery stared back, he heard Senuv raise her voice and call Sarm's name. Jeffery glanced at her then back at the trinmpt and saw that it seemed undisturbed by Senuv's calling and was rather curious about his presence.

"Sarm!" repeated Senuv a little louder. She turned to Jeffery and winked at him.

"She likes to take her time, I assume," remarked Jeffery.

"Not really," said Senuv. "She is usually the first to storm out—oh, there she is." Senuv pointed at a balcony that was several floors up. "I knew she'd hear me, now she just needs time to get down here." Jeffery saw a female figure walk around the balcony then disappear. He looked at the balcony beneath it and kept staring at it from left to right as Sarm made her way down.

"As you may have noticed, the staircase doesn't go through one part of each floor," explained Senuv. "Sometimes they're at the center, sometimes near the end, and that's why at some levels they are wider and bigger."

"Ah," said Jeffery with interest. "It's going to take her a while to get down here," he added as he glanced at a trinmpt that was poking at the floor.

"It will," replied Senuv, "just treat her with love." Jeffery kept watching Sarm as she made her way down from one floor to the other. "Your hopes are high," she added as she leaned in closer as though she were listening to somebody.

"I think I can unite the kingdoms," Jeffery said to her. "Besides, Sarm is your sister, so in a sense, you share a heart." Jeffery looked Senuv right in the eyes and asked, "How did you know?" while he admired her innocence and ability.

"Cruelty can invade a heart, Jeffery, but a heart's love is always more powerful," she replied, looking back at him. Jeffery looked up while trying to keep her words in mind, and saw that Sarm was only a couple of balconies up, and just a few moments away from arrival. Then, he looked at the floor and saw that the number of the trinmpts had multiplied.

"Is it me or does it suddenly seem like there are more trinmpts?" he questioned.

"Nope, I think there *are* more all of a sudden," she replied, after looking down. She tried counting the trinmpts, and before long, Sarm arrived, entering from a staircase that was just a bit ahead of where he and Senuv were standing. She carried a smooth crystal ball in her hand that was burgundy and the same size as Senuv's. She walked right through the trinmpts with complete disregard and stood facing Jeffery, then turned to Senuv.

252

"And so we meet," greeted Sarm, glaring at Senuv.

Jeffery continued to observe her closely, taking notice of her vermilion dress that was very different from Senuv's. It was long and covered her ankles as well as her arms and had puffy padded shoulders and a low-cut neckline. Her skin, height and facial features were very similar to Senuv's and her voluminous hair fell just above her chest, with a few curls near the ends that were freshly put in place with a hot iron. Her red-brown lipstick, matched her dark-auburn hair, reflecting her unpredictable personality. Jeffery shifted his gaze back and forth between the two mothers who were stood facing each other on the same floor, breathing the same air.

"And so we meet," replied Senuv, gently smiling in return. Sarm gripped her crystal ball tightly then glanced at Jeffery.

"And who's he?" she questioned, deepening the tone of her voice.

"He's Jeffery, he was sent by Allie," replied Senuv. Both of them looked at him.

"Jeffery?" Sarm questioned him directly.

"Yes," answered Jeffery. "And you are Sarm."

"I am," she confirmed before turning to face Senuv. She held her crystal ball close to her chest as she sensibly observed.

"I think that it is time for the two kingdoms to unite," proposed Jeffery.

"You think so?" asked Sarm after shifting her gaze back towards him. Her voice was a little raspy but at the same time very feminine. Jeffery imagined her to be a mistress of thirteen men and knew exactly how to secretly get her needs met by all of them.

"I really do," he asserted. "Enough bloodshed and enough dividing. I think that everyone should live together as one, equally, regardless of their differences." Sarm glanced at Senuv again without moving her head. Jeffery felt a little bit of pain in his left arm but remained focused. He stood tall and stared directly at Sarm. As he stared at her, he felt as if everything around him glowed and had become redder, reflecting her internal fury.

"I've told you this for centuries, Sarm, your path really isn't doing anybody any good," added Senuv. "You are my sister, you have always been very sweet and—"

"Well, I was always sweet because I am the younger one," replied Sarm, interrupting her. "But lest you forget, Senuv, I am the most intelligent in the family. I know when something is wrong and needs to be fixed. Your way, like Mother's and Father's, just doesn't click with me and it clearly doesn't click with any of my citizens. How else do you think I managed to split the kingdom?"

"I disagree," stated Jeffery with a blunt tone. "I think you did all this for your personal gain and nothing more."

"Pardon me?" answered Sarm, sounding more serious. "Who do you think you are talking to?"

"Sarm, please," begged Senuv.

"No, you shush," scolded Sarm in response. She turned to face Jeffery and walked closer to him. "You don't know me," she told him clearly. "You have not been alive this entire time. You really think that listening to my sister's side of the story alone will give you the full picture of our situation?"

"And can I ask what does your side have other than segregation, attacks and uprising against your own family?" argued Jeffery as he took a step closer to her.

"You two, stop!" demanded Senuv as she stepped between them and distanced them by holding their shoulders. Sarm turned around and wandered away a few paces, revealing a red crocksvenbulb that was sewn onto the back of her dress a bit below where her hair rested. "I mean, he's sent by Allie, and he clearly believes this is all wrong. Don't you think that says something?"

"It only says one thing," replied Sarm as she turned around. "He was sent to you first, that's why."

"Now, don't be ridiculous," said Senuv. "Think about it."

"I think that Jeffery should spend some time with me and hear the rest of the story," argued Sarm.

"Fine," agreed Jeffery.

"What?" asked Senuv, sounding utterly surprised.

"I will stay," insisted Jeffery. "I will do whatever it takes to get you two to be mothers of one kingdom again."

"What? What are you talking about?" shuddered Senuv.

"I'm staying," answered Jeffery. Senuv turned her eyes towards Sarm who then smiled back slyly then looked at Jeffery.

"I can't believe—" started Senuv.

"Quiet!" interrupted Sarm. "Your touchiness gets on my nerves."

"As if your bigotry doesn't?" said Jeffery, sweat trickling down the back of his legs. Sarm glared at him, then instantly gave out a loud yell and plunged towards him.

"Sarm, no!" yelled Senuv. Jeffery stood still until Sarm got closer. Right before she laid her hands on him, he forcefully pushed her and caused her to fall backwards, sliding across the floor and scaring away some of the trinmpts. Senuv's face turned red as she covered her mouth with her hand and stared at her sister lying across the floor.

"This is going to be one bloody challenge," said Jeffery sarcastically. The two mothers looked at him and paused.

"You're awfully strong," hissed Sarm after sitting up.

"Thank you," replied Jeffery.

"What just happened?" questioned Senuv. "Jeffery, have you forgotten what I said to you?" she whispered.

Sarm stood up and fixed herself. She held her crystal ball close to her mouth and blew on it. "Senuv, get out of here," she ordered. "Come back in the morning and we'll see which one of us he will be fighting for."

"You're saying that a battle is on in the morning?" asked Senuv.

"There is," confirmed Sarm.

"A battle?" questioned Jeffery.

"Yes," insisted Sarm. "Now, Senuv, get out!" she yelled. Senuv quickly walked close to Jeffery and rested her hand on his shoulder.

"You take care and be careful," she whispered. "I am very surprised."

"You take care as well," replied Jeffery. He wanted to apologize for breaking his promise but he decided to stand strong. He faced Sarm and watched her malevolent eyes look straight into his. Senuv reached into her pocket and pulled out a necklace and fastened it around Jeffery's neck. Then, she walked to the staircase that they had entered from earlier and made her way back. Jeffery felt the necklace then looked at it and saw that it was an orange crocksvenbulb. As he held it, he felt Senuv's loving energy float around him.

"What were you thinking, charging at me like such an animal?" asked Jeffery in disgust.

"I'll admit," started Sarm, "you are very strong. But remember that this is my castle and only my rules apply here, do you understand?"

"I negate your rules," answered Jeffery. "I am here to talk sense into you."

"First, talk sense into yourself," scolded Sarm. "*You* came here. You need to listen to *me*. You need to hear me out entirely before you dismiss me, is that clear?" Jeffery didn't say anything. He noticed that she glanced at his necklace then looked back at him. "Is that clear?" she repeated.

"Fine," said Jeffery as he shook his head and looked down.

"Good," said Sarm. "Then follow me." Jeffery followed Sarm to the staircase that she had entered from.

"Where are we going now?" he questioned.

"You'll see, just keep quiet," replied Sarm bluntly. Jeffery gave her a very cross look that she didn't notice as she was walking ahead of him. They made their way up several staircases and, as they did so, Jeffery took a closer look and saw that the staircase was a bit different from the ones he and Senuv had entered from. The carpet was maroon with thin, black threads going through it, making it appear three-dimensional and captivating to the eye. The banisters were black with big, metallic red skulls on each end. After reaching the walkway, Jeffery followed Sarm, as she turned right and went around. He looked over the balcony and saw that the trinmpts seemed smaller due to him being much higher up. Jeffery frowned at them and turned away.

As he walked, he noticed a big portrait of Sarm hanging on the wall. The frame was oval, thick and made of rose gold. It had a swirling design around its rim that looked like stacked bangles. At the top, in the center of the swirls, there was a cat forming the letter S with its tail positioned near its head, while facing left and slightly looking up. In the picture, she stood on a cliff facing a panoramic view of the sun, sky, hills and a river that were all in different shades of red. Her face was not visible, only her back from head to foot, which revealed the crocksvenbulb that was sewn on. The view that she stared at looked very calming and reminded Jeffery of the top terrace at Senuv's. After walking past it, Jeffery looked back and took one more look at the portrait.

"Don't dwell on it," he whispered to himself. "It's probably a deception of who she thinks she is." Sarm came to a door, opened it and stormed through leaving it open for Jeffery. The walls and floor inside were made of mahogany and there were red carpets in various designs and patterns hung on the walls. In the center of the room was a black rug with an image of a red lotus at its center that did not match the hanging oriental carpets. At the far end of the room, there was a small wooden desk and a matching chair, and above was a picture of the same map that Jeffery had seen at Senuv's, except that the frame was scarlet. Sarm turned the chair sideways and sat on it, resting her elbow on the desk with her chin on her hand. Jeffery stood several paces away and looked at her while taking notice that the room had a small window that barely let any sunlight in, creating a rather gloomy atmosphere.

Jeffery observed Sarm and saw that she was sitting with one leg over the other, unashamed of expressing her disappointment through her crossed eyes. He stood tall, ready to hear what she had to say. She opened her mouth slightly and exhaled causing her hair to blow over her cleavage like a slight chill over dry land. As Jeffery stood and stared at her, the room grew dim, indicating that the sun was setting. He glanced out the small window that was high up and covered with black bars.

"So, what's your side of this story?" he questioned, facing her. Sarm didn't move but Jeffery knew that his words and voice echoed in her ears. "Aren't you going to speak?" he asked, raising his tone after waiting a moment. Again, Sarm didn't move, but she looked down and her mouth gently closed. "That's it," scolded Jeffery, "if you're not going to talk I am going back to Senuv's." He turned around and stormed towards the door. Just before he reached for the knob, Sarm called his name softly. He paused in silence.

"Please, come here," she said with an even softer tone. Jeffery turned around and saw that Sarm was looking at him with a look of desire in her eyes.

"I suppose that you are ready to speak?" he questioned as he slowly walked back.

"Sure," replied Sarm. She glared at him suddenly and sharpened her voice stating, "Under one condition, though."

"What?" asked Jeffery.

"You will never talk to me with that tone again, is that clear?" she stated as she quickly sat up and pointed her finger, startling him. Then, she stood up, walked right to him and gave him a quick slap on his cheek and ended her instruction with her mouth curved in frustration.

"Some mother *you* are," said Jeffery. "Now, do you want to talk or are you just going to argue with me?" Sarm went back to her seat and tossed her hair back, sweating as her chest turned red.

"Fine," she said miserably. "This all started a few centuries ago," she began. "Not long after Senuv and I became mothers of the kingdom, I felt differently about things. Well, not really, I always felt this way, but I couldn't speak of it because I did not want problems with our parents."

"What sort of things?" questioned Jeffery.

"Let me finish!" shouted Sarm sharply with widened eyes. "I felt that nothing was really making sense. It seemed to me that everyone living in harmony just wasn't balancing me out well enough. Everyone was the same and I was the only one opposed to everything and everyone. I was forced to wear their color and I was also forced to ensure that things were always happy and pristine." Sarm looked down and put both her hands on her head.

"Can you, seriously, speak?" insisted Jeffery. "None of that made any sense to me and you keep pausing for some reason. Speak!" Sarm kept her silence and then turned to face the other way. Her silence caused Jeffery's anger to rise internally, but he kept his mouth closed and his look fixed on her.

"You won't understand, Jeffery," said Sarm. "Things just can't be all the same, there needs to be some opposition to keep things balanced. And, years later, after I decided to split the kingdom and create new protocols, clearly, a lot of the citizens followed me. Not because I forced them to, but because they were feeling the same way I felt. And now we have our own kingdom. And, yes, sometimes wars and conflicts do happen, but I think we are better off on our own. It is those from Senuv's side that want this happy-united-we-be thing and are always trying to get us to live together regardless of our differences. But, no! In my kingdom, we have traditions and they have clearly survived throughout all this time. These traditions have kept us grounded. We can't reunite, Jeffery. I ask you, what about that do you not understand?"

"Senuv says that your kingdom's way of life is very unjust," started Jeffery.

"Yes, I've heard that said millions of times," replied Senuv. "We don't allow marriages between those who are not male and female, certain animals are not to be eaten, certain books need to be kept in every household, newborns go through a sacred ritual—Jeffery, this is our way of life. Also, we do not solely rely on faith as they do at Senuv's. We encourage perspectives from certain fields. I also encourage my citizens to be skeptical. I give them the right to vote for local representatives. They are happy—they are not doing anything against their will."

"It wasn't always that way," argued Jeffery.

"I know it wasn't, but it so happens that many citizens want this way of life and it has clearly survived for centuries before you suddenly appeared at Senuv's," responded Sarm, raising her voice a notch. "Senuv is pathetic. If she likes to live the way Mother and Father did, well, that's fine, but that doesn't flourish in everyone's gardens, Jeffery. I am not reuniting and surrendering after surviving and keeping this kingdom strong and alive for centuries, can you understand that?" Jeffery stood silently as he evaluated both perspectives.

"Is there absolutely no way your citizens and hers can coexist in harmony?" he asked. "It sounds like all they really need is some understanding between one another."

"Again, that's exactly what Senuv says," scoffed Sarm. "No! We are two separate kingdoms with two separate philosophies. We have the right to exist on our own."

"And what about the wars and conflict?" questioned Jeffery. "You can't at least find a solution for that? Do you have any idea what that does to Senuv?"

"She can think what she wants," insisted Sarm. "She is my sister and I am used to her ranting. She has always been seen as *that very sweet one*, and I don't value that."

"I adamantly don't support you," stated Jeffery.

"But thousands of citizens do," replied Sarm, "and that's the way it is."

"But Senuv feels that isn't the way your parents intended it to be," argued Jeffery. "Can you at least value that?"

"Well, our parents are dead, and things change. As I just said, I don't value my sister's thoughts and opinions. If she can't learn to see that for herself, she can just keep on living in that misery."

"Is it really that simple for you?" questioned Jeffery.

"Instead of antagonizing me," insisted Sarm after a brief pause, "why don't you try to understand our kingdom's way of life? I see you have kept Senuv's crocksvenbulb around you and that's fine. But just try to learn about my kingdom the way you learned about hers. What do you say?"

"What more is there to learn?" asked Jeffery.

"Why don't you follow me underground?" asked Sarm.

261

"Underground?" asked Jeffery.

"There are some underground floors in this castle," replied Sarm. "Follow me." She stood up and walked out the door and Jeffery followed her.

"So, what is underground?" he asked, walking faster and trying to keep up with her.

"Exactly as there are several floors here," replied Sarm. "It's the same idea, but underground. There is one room where I like to go to play music."

"You're going to play me some songs?" asked Jeffery.

"Yes," replied Sarm as she turned and walked down the staircase.

"On a piano?" asked Jeffery.

"Nope," answered Sarm, "I am sick of the keys. Before the kingdom split, all songs were played on the keys and I never really enjoyed that."

"Could you tell me one fond memory you have from back then?" asked Jeffery.

"Don't have one," answered Sarm instantly.

"There needs to be one," insisted Jeffery, making the argument worse. "Perhaps during the presence of your parents?"

"Not even that," replied Sarm stubbornly. "I was always more in the background and I was never truly understood."

"You should have tried to communicate your thoughts to somebody," said Jeffery.

"I used to write them in journals," explained Sarm. "When Senuv found them, a while after our parents died, she burned them. She claimed that they weren't filled with love."

"So you don't actually believe in love?" asked Jeffery.

"It's not the most important factor in this kingdom," replied Sarm, showing her confidence by maintaining her tone. "And what are you doing here?" she questioned while looking down at the floor. Jeffery noticed that there was a trinmpt standing there, looking about. He was momentarily startled but quickly closed his mouth so that Sarm wouldn't notice. "You must have gotten lost, idiot," she said to it as she picked it up.

"Why did you get these things?" asked Jeffery. "They look horrendous."

"I like them," replied Sarm. "They reflect a lot of what I believe in and they are here, in this castle, to resemble that. Plus, they scare away intruders." Sarm stepped ahead and threw it over the balcony. "Come on," she instructed. Jeffery continued following her.

"I could imagine you writing a song about them," he said sarcastically yet in a serious tone of voice.

"And, maybe I will," suggested Sarm. "My citizens will learn to play it." After that, Jeffery remained silent and continued following. Once they had made their way down to the first level below the main one, he saw that the corridors were different. They had burgundy walls and royal red carpets were placed over the narrow walkways that lacked balconies. Each floor existed on its own without the view of another one, and its scarlet doors were big with copper frames; between each of them was a framed picture of a shark, each picture capturing it in a different position.

"I don't think Senuv's castle has any underground floors," observed Jeffery.

"It does not," confirmed Sarm. "This was my idea. I needed more space so I built these underground floors. It's easier, and not out in the open."

"I have to say it's a bit harder breathing down here," said Jeffery.

"It is, but you will get used to it," replied Sarm. "Senuv's complained about it before and I always tell her to just shut up and deal with it. I tend to like really warm temperatures, anyway."

After descending to the next floor, Jeffery noticed that the wooden banister on the staircase had a fire lit on it, its flames burning but not

263

spreading anywhere. Jeffery felt shocked looking at them. Sarm ignored his reaction and proceeded forward into the corridor. As he followed her, Jeffery saw that there were several red crocksvenbulbs hanging on the wall. The feeling of weariness grew within him, but he didn't speak. He followed Sarm one more floor down and saw a door at the end of the hallway that was bigger than the other ones around. The lighting was even dimmer, and on both the walls and between all the doors were paintings of dark and mystical creatures, flaunting their claws and their faces not bearing a single smile.

Sarm proceeded towards the big door and Jeffery followed her as the energies around him made him feel uncomfortable. He took a closer look at the bigger door—it was burgundy and had a handle shaped like the head of an ugly figure with big black tusks.

Sarm opened the door that was to the left of it and entered, surprising Jeffery, as he was expecting her to open the bigger door. He followed her and saw that the room was large and the walls were painted vermilion. A bright-red leather chaise was set against one of the walls, and the floor was covered with a large rug with patterns of roses in various shades of red. The walls were covered with crocksvenbulbs and many portraits and ornaments of various sizes and designs. Atop a black shelf was an ornament of a shiny red skull with two long horns that looked like they had been burned. Next to the skull was a framed picture of a heart with an intricate pattern of flowers around its edge.

Jeffery walked further into the room then looked back. He saw a dining table with chairs that looked exactly like Senuv's in the room where she had played the piano for him, but with red upholstery instead of orange. Feeling intrigued by the semi-duplicate copy, Jeffery walked directly to the table and chairs and noticed that there was a difference in the pattern of the diamonds that formed the triangle on the head of the chairs. They were placed so that the triangles were upright and the gems in the center were rubies.

"I know," started Sarm, "my sister has one like it." Jeffery ignored her and kept looking at everything on the walls. There were so many things he couldn't seem to absorb all of them. Located very close to the dining table was a puce oval-shaped frame with a painting of Sarm as a mermaid. She had a bright-red fish tail and a matching bra shaped liked apples. She was posed like a backward letter *S* with her arms gently hanging behind her and her chin up, and seated on burgundy-colored sand with various treasures scattered around her. Jeffery admired the beautifully painted picture but then reminded himself to not be deceived by it. Close to the picture was a hanging ornament of a black cat's head with bright red eyes. Its pupils consisted of two lines, red and black, swirling like a vortex that caused discomfort to the vision. The initials *LM* were carved next to the cat's nose, but were tiny and almost hidden in its fur.

"And, where have I seen this before?" Jeffery asked himself as he looked away from the nausea-inducing pupils. He hesitated for a moment then continued observing everything else. He walked along the wall and noticed a medium-sized sword. Right under it was a mounted, red crystal ornament of a small phoenix; its wings were spread and its head was pointing upward. Jeffery felt drawn to it but did not dare to touch it. He examined it closely and saw a tiny butterfly on its neck.

"It must have taken a very long time to create all this," he said to himself. As he continued browsing, and moved away from the dining table, he came closer to Sarm. Near there, Jeffery saw a hanging ornament of a golden star that looked like a *welcome* sight compared with some of the other things that felt heavier and darker. Right next to it was a hanging crystal ornament of a book that was crimson with clear sides and about half the size of a finger. Jeffery continued skimming across the wall until he got even closer to Sarm and saw her sitting on the chaise.

"I take it that you like the décor in here," she said calmly without smiling.

"It's nice," agreed Jeffery. "It reminds me of a place I have been before." He looked at Sarm and saw that she was relaxing and holding her crystal ball. After a moment, she put it back into her dress and turned to face the wall behind the chaise where, among all the other ornaments, crocksvenbulbs and pictures, was a sparkling metallic-red guitar. Sarm stood up and took it down then walked around to where Jeffery was standing.

"Take a seat," she said as she adjusted the guitar strap over her shoulder.

"Ok," said Jeffery. He sat on the chaise and faced her. She quickly played a note and let it echo. After it faded out, she struck it again, warming herself up.

"Are you ready?" she asked.

"Yep," replied Jeffery.

"This song is popularly played amongst my citizens," she explained. "It is called, "Forever Live, My Kingdom." She echoed a few more notes and then played a tune that was electric and fast-paced. Jeffery watched Sarm and admired her fingers as they quickly played the instrument. The song ended with three echoes of the same note. "This song is very commonly played," repeated Sarm. "It is very patriotic and it reflects upon why this kingdom deserves to exist."

"It sounded good," said Jeffery. He took a closer look at the guitar and saw that on its bottom corner was a picture of a reversed wand with the number nine on it. Something about it sent a sudden chill down his spine. "What inspired you to write it?" he asked.

"A lot of things," answered Sarm, "a whole lot of things." She looked down at her guitar and ran her eyes across it as she slowly opened her lips and tilted her head forward, expressing a seductive side of herself.

"Like?" asked Jeffery.

"Well, I felt alone," replied Sarm. "I felt very alone. I knew that I couldn't allow myself to feel that way, though. I had a whole kingdom to run and I had to bring over more people from the old one, so I had to be strong. And at the same time, I felt very faithful."

"I must say, that is quite inspiring," admitted Jeffery, trying to sound understanding. "I can see why that was difficult for you." Sarm just glanced at the crocksvenbulb he was wearing and then shifted her gaze back to her instrument.

"And I know that I have many more centuries to lead," said Sarm. "So, I wrote this song to serve that purpose." She suddenly looked up and searched around the room as if she had heard something enter.

"Is something wrong?" asked Jeffery. Sarm stood in her place and kept looking around. She then looked back down at her instrument and smiled slyly. She began to play some melodic notes in a harmonic fashion.

"This one's called, "Entering through the Glass," announced Sarm as she continued playing her melody. As he listened, Jeffery felt some airy movement in the atmosphere. He glanced around then turned back to Sarm and saw that she was smiling as she played the song. "*Ho-ohhhhhhhh-ohhh,*" she sung, striking a low note. She slowly increased the rhythm of the song while gradually singing higher.

"*I'm entering through the glass, to get a sight of you in fright,*" sang a male voice that startled Jeffery. "*I can only weep this night, if I don't get a shock of you in fright...* " As the voice continued singing the verse, glittering red and maroon plumes entered through the wall. "*And I am entering through the glass...* " Lake Morgan entered the room and struck a high note after

267

singing the last word. The notes of his voice were synchronized perfectly with the harmonic rhythm that Sarm was playing.

Jeffery looked at Lake Morgan in shock. He was no longer blue, but maroon with a lot of glittering red sparkles. Sarm sang along with him as she continued playing. After that, she stood with her legs apart, lifted up the guitar to her left, leaned back towards her right while allowing her hair to fall back, and played a fast and catchy guitar solo with a big smile on her face. Jeffery watched again how fast her fingers moved as she played. When the song had finished, she tossed her hair forward and bent over, ending the song with a slight nod.

"How's it going?" asked Sarm as she turned towards Lake Morgan and walked over to him.

"Good," he replied. "I see you've got a guest."

"What brings you here?" asked Jeffery as he stood up.

"What brings *you* here?" Lake Morgan asked back.

"I know you two have met before," said Sarm.

"You are quite pitiable," said Lake Morgan to Jeffery.

"Hey!" yelled Jeffery. "I am here trying to reunite the two kingdoms and the two sisters. I asked *you*, what brings you here?"

"You weren't even man enough to love Sabina or survive Ribs's workforce," replied Lake Morgan in a degrading tone. "So, how do you think you'll accomplish that?"

"Because I believe that I can," said Jeffery, stomping his foot. "And how do you know—"

"Just relax, you're killing my mood," interrupted Sarm. "Really, Jeffery, just have a seat." Jeffery gave Lake Morgan a dirty look then sat back down, shaking his head. Lake Morgan burst out laughing in mockery and disrespect.

"I have never seen such a despicable figure as you," said Jeffery. "You preach about how a man is supposed to be but you're just pathetic scum and no kind of a man yourself." He turned his head to look at Sarm and saw that she had taken off her dress and stood now in an orangey red leotard made of plastic. She was bending slightly and showing off her shiny, light-red high heels.

"Play another song?" Lake Morgan suggested to her.

"Of course," replied Sarm with a sensual smile and tone of voice. "This next one is called, "The Feeling of a Great Man's Touch." Jeffery continued watching them, with a raised eyebrow.

"Ah!" said Lake Morgan with a tone of delighted approval. Sarm walked close to him and began playing a low note repeatedly. It was somewhat bouncy and reminiscent of a drum beat. Jeffery could see by the way she swayed her body and halfway-closed her eyes that she found it arousing. He watched the two curiously, careful not to miss a single movement.

"Can I ask what that song is about?" he questioned, trying not to show his nervousness.

"Just listen," answered Sarm as she continued playing the note. She nodded her head along gently and started playing a new tune. This music was jazzy and Lake Morgan floated comfortably as if he was patiently waiting for an erotic treat. Jeffery frowned and stuck his lower lip out. Sarm continued playing as she gently nodded while exchanging looks with Lake Morgan.

Jeffery glanced around the room and noticed a small picture that was hanging on the wall across from him. It was of a lady sitting on a carpet inside a tent, surrounded by comfy cushions. She had very dark skin, like chocolate, and curly black hair. She wore a burgundy belly-dancing outfit that consisted of a small piece of cloth that covered her mouth like a bandanna, with silver chains dangling from it that highlighted a heron tattoo on her shoulder. Next to her was a cherry-red hookah and some light smoke behind her.

"*La la la-la*," sang Lake Morgan as Sarm played. Jeffery looked at her and saw that she was looking at him while slowly licking her top lip. As Jeffery continued watching her, he noticed that whenever she looked at Lake Morgan, she almost never looked at his mask-face but at his plumes. After she finished playing the song she ended with a bow to Lake Morgan and a tossing back of her hair. "Just brilliant," said Lake Morgan.

"I have to say, that one bored me," stated Jeffery.

"I kind of figured," replied Sarm with a sharp tone as she glanced at him.

"A real man always appreciates what a woman offers," suggested Lake Morgan to Jeffery.

"I am curious, what man changes his color for the pleasure of a woman?" replied Jeffery in rebuttal.

"You have become a bigmouth since I last saw you," sneered Lake Morgan.

"And you—" started Jeffery.

"Ok, you two," interrupted Sarm, "I have had enough of your bickering."

"He's only become a bigger—" scolded Jeffery.

"That's enough!" yelled Sarm. "Jeffery, it's getting late, and I want to spend time alone with Lake Morgan. Why don't you go to sleep?"

"Where?" asked Jeffery.

"Just make your way to the very top floor," instructed Sarm, "and turn left. There are a few furnished rooms there and there is also one on the first door to the right, a floor below. Just pick any one of them and I will come to you in the morning. And, sleep well, because there's a battle tomorrow."

270

"The battle," repeated Jeffery.

"Yes, now go, you're wasting your time," ordered Sarm. Jeffery turned and looked at Lake Morgan and saw that he was merely floating in the air.

"Go on Jeffery, you must not upset Mother Sarm," he added.

"Gladly," replied Jeffery, biting his lip and narrowing his eyes. He glanced at Sarm then stormed out of the room. "Disgusting," he whispered to himself. He made his way to the top of the castle as instructed, which took him a long time.

Upon arriving, he saw that the top floor looked very different from the others. The walls were painted with white dots and the doors were much larger than the ones on the other floors. Jeffery turned left and walked past a few of them and looked down from the balcony. He could barely see the trinmpts, as he stared down for a moment. He felt some aches in his spine, shoulder and calves. He reflected upon the battle that was to take place the following day, then realized that he really did need to sleep. His aches worsened so he walked slower, his face expressing the sadness he felt. Jeffery imagined the two castles floating then coming together and forming one big castle.

Holding onto that thought, he walked towards one of the doors and, next to it, he saw a lamp shaped like a cylinder mounted on to a couple of bars, one at its top, and the other at its bottom. Its light was scarlet and somewhat dim. Jeffery looked at the bottom bar and read the initials *LM*. He looked at the top bar and saw an image of an octopus etched on its side. Scoffing, he walked to the door next to it, and realized that it was the fourth door from the staircase. He turned the knob and entered muttering, "He sure does get in peoples' faces."

The room was large, painted burgundy, and there were candles in white and silver sconces shaped like seahorses in various places upon the walls. To his left, Jeffery saw a large glass window with a magnificent view of the setting red sun and hills. Just next to it, to the right, was an outsized bed with a thick comforter that matched the walls and the view. Upon all the walls and between the sconces, were several crocksvenbulbs in various sizes and shades of red. In the middle of the ceiling, hung a huge crimson crocksvenbulb with candles in it, like a chandelier.

Jeffery walked in and continued to browse. He went straight to the bed and lay down on his back. His aches triggered tears in his eyes and numbness all over him. He got up, took off his jeans and boots, tossed them on the floor, and snuggled inside the bed, enjoying the soft pillows. As the sun continued setting he lay on his side, yawned a few times and felt his body weight pull him down as if it were guiding him away. Even though it was not dark yet, he fell asleep, with thoughts of the forthcoming battle.

The following morning, Jeffery woke up feeling cold and his eyes felt heavy due to dreaming all night. He adjusted himself under the covers and tried to keep warm. He moved his head and glanced at the big, hanging crocksvenbulb, then closed his eyes again. Suddenly, Jeffery remembered that he had been dreaming as he slept but he couldn't remember the dream. He got up and looked out the window, greeting the sunrise and listening to the sound of the birds singing. Jeffery felt that someone was approaching so he quickly went back and put on his jeans and boots, then walked back to the window and looked at the sky.

Jeffery noticed the burgundy drapes that were tied to the side and walked over to one of them. He felt its rough edge that had a thread sewn in a circular pattern down the length of the drape. Before allowing his mind to question his thoughts, the door opened.

"I see you are already awake," said Sarm. Jeffery glanced at her then continued looking out the window. "Well, come on, let's feed you something before the battle." Jeffery focused on the word *battle* and reflected upon it.

"Come on," Sarm repeated sharply. Jeffery turned around and followed her out of the room and a couple of floors down. After they walked further into the corridor, Sarm halted beside a door and asked him to wait. After she stepped in, Jeffery walked towards the balcony and looked down to see the trinmpts. He tried to remember his dream again and wondered if there were any connections to the castle. His thoughts were once again interrupted when Sarm came out and closed the door behind her.

"What's that?" he asked, while looking at what she held in her hands.

"A sandwich," replied Sarm, handing it to him. The bread was flat and somewhat burned. He took a bite and saw that the sandwich contained some herbs that varied in different shades of red and were quite tasty.

"What are these?" he asked as he continued eating.

"It's called floktrenatis," explained Sarm. "It grows wild in this kingdom and is favored by my citizens. I discovered it centuries ago."

"Interesting," said Jeffery.

"You are going to need your energy," said Sarm. "The battle will be intense."

"How intense?" asked Jeffery.

"You'll see," replied Sarm. She took her crystal ball out of her dress and held it tightly. "Ok, follow me," she said after Jeffery had finished eating. He followed her down the stairs and around several more floors, which tired his legs.

"Where are we going exactly?" asked Jeffery.

"Just speed up," replied Sarm. Jeffery attempted to walk faster but this made his legs hurt even more. After going down a few more floors, Sarm turned right and made her way down to the seventh door. Jeffery followed her as she entered, then closed the door behind him. He saw that within that room, the ground was made of many layers of cement and a small, red light bulb hung in the center of the ceiling. Right in front of him was a massive slide that looked like a tongue and curved downwards into an unfathomable abyss.

"Come on," instructed Sarm before she sat on it and slid away. Jeffery felt nervous but copied her after she had disappeared. As he slid, he felt somewhat safe because the slide was very wide.

"Jeffery?" called Sarm.

"Are you there?" he called back.

"I'm waiting for you," she replied. Jeffery continued sliding until he arrived at the bottom where Sarm stood waiting.

"Ok," started Sarm as Jeffery stood up. "Now, you need to keep up the pace. I am going to bring you to the battle. Fight hard, it will be one on one, and if you win, we will discuss how to annex the kingdom to Senuv's, alright?"

"And if I lose?" asked Jeffery.

"We'll discuss it further, fair enough?" answered Sarm.

"And didn't you say that you were adamant about not uniting the two kingdoms?"

"I am," replied Sarm. "But, if Allie sent you to Senuv's then that's a bit of a sign for me to do some reconsidering. Now, shall we proceed?"

"Fine," agreed Jeffery. Sarm looked at the cement wall and focused on it then closed her eyes and breathed in. A big part of the wall faded out and allowed the bright sunlight in, showing a glimpse of the outdoors.

"Come on," instructed Sarm, walking outside. Jeffery followed her and saw that they were walking on fresh red grass on a gentle hill. The view of the area was plain but calming and similar to the view from the window and in the maps. Across from them, Jeffery saw a structure that looked small in the distance and was overshadowed by surrounding hills.

"What's that?" asked Jeffery, pointing at the structure.

"The coliseum," replied Sarm, "that's where all battles take place."

"It looks small," stated Jeffery.

"Wait until you get closer and you'll see," replied Sarm, "it's huge."

"Was it also built after the kingdom was split?" asked Jeffery.

"It was," replied Sarm.

"I see," said Jeffery. "Is Lake Morgan going to be there?"

"Nope," answered Sarm.

"Good," said Jeffery.

"He's got other things to do," stated Sarm while trying to sound modest. "Now, walk faster." Jeffery picked up his pace and stormed straight to the coliseum. As he got close to it, Jeffery discovered that it indeed was huge and made of red stone that gleamed, expressing danger and wrath. From behind its walls, Jeffery heard a lot of shouting, so he knew that there were many others inside, waiting. After hearing this, his stomach began to ache, and then his head ached as well. Sarm stopped walking then went behind him and took off his crocksvenbulb necklace and put it in her dress.

"This would make you look very bad," she told him.

"Fine," said Jeffery, "Senuv already knows that I am on her side."

"And that she does," agreed Sarm with a scoff. "Now, this way." She led him around the coliseum, exposing him to more shouting. He began to sweat, and struggled to keep calm.

"Are we actually going to enter?" he asked, shuddering a little.

"Yep," answered Sarm. She walked several more paces then came to a halt.

"How do we enter?" questioned Jeffery.

"There are various ways for us, but for the public, there is a door on the other side," answered Sarm. "Now listen to me carefully, Jeffery. You are going to enter here in the same way we exited the castle. Keep walking forward then exit the door when you feel ready. Once you enter the battlefield, do your best, and remember, no one wins until one of you is dead, and that is how it works. So you must kill your opponent if you insist that Senuv and I unite our kingdoms."

"Hold on a minute," protested Jeffery, "this is way too intense! And nobody said anything about killing!"

"It's the only choice you've got," said Sarm.

"How did this get arranged so suddenly?" asked Jeffery.

"Jeffery!" scolded Sarm, "there is no time for your arguments! You are going to go in, kill your opponent, or let him kill you. Is that clear?" Jeffery looked straight into her mad eyes. "Do I have your word?"

"You do," answered Jeffery, exhaling. His body shook at the thought of what was to come. Sweat ran down his forehead and his aches worsened. "As long as the two kingdoms unite... " he started, his body shaking even more. Sarm continued looking him in the eye, and nodded once.

"Good," she added.

"And where is Senuv?" asked Jeffery.

"That's none of your concern. Are you ready to go in or not?" replied Sarm. Jeffery looked her right in the face seeing her eyes looking back at him sharper than ever. He glanced at the sky and felt tears come to his eyes. His pulse racing, he thought of turning around and running away.

"I'm ready," he replied with exhaustion.

"Good," said Sarm firmly. She stepped closer to the wall of the coliseum and closed her eyes as she breathed gently. A part of the wall faded out and she stepped in and turned back, giving Jeffery a fierce look. Jeffery stepped in with her and the wall faded back in, blocking out the sunlight and completely dimming everything around. Jeffery noticed that in front of him the sand created a long aisle that led to an exit. To the left of the exit, was a short staircase made of the same stone as the coliseum.

"Do we go up there?" he asked.

"Nope, you will be going out this way," corrected Sarm. "I'll be going up the stairs so that I can make my way to the stage. You'll see me from the battlefield."

"And when do I go out?" questioned Jeffery.

"When you feel ready," replied Sarm. "Just don't be too long." After that, she stormed off and went up the staircase, leaving Jeffery alone. He glanced around for a few seconds then walked close to the open door and looked outside, cautious of being seen. He saw that the light-colored sand extended outwards and made up the entire battlefield. Above it, were many rows of noisy citizens, all wearing scarlet robes with big hoods that hid their faces. Jeffery turned around and walked back a few steps, then bent down and leaned his back against the wall. He sighed and relaxed as he thought about what to expect.

"So I actually have to kill to unite the kingdoms?" he thought out loud. "Is it even worth it? Is it something that I must do?" Jeffery felt the urge to kick the wall but instead, he looked towards the exit. He saw that the citizens were growing more excited and that their anticipation was escalating. "You're not the ones who have to kill or risk getting killed," Jeffery said with a scoff. He couldn't make sense of why such a battle would excite so many. After resting for another moment, he stood up and walked close to the door. He saw that some citizens took notice of him and began pointing in his direction. He took a step closer to the threshold and stood up straight. After silently saying a short prayer, he stepped out.

Flexing his muscular body, Jeffery strode straight to the center of the colossal battlefield. He saw thousands of citizens watching who were becoming more excited by the second. Looking to his right, he saw the stage high above some of the rows, and sectioned off on its own and there was Sarm, standing at its center between two knights in metallic red and golden armor. Jeffery faced her and saw that she ignored him as she browsed the view.

"You must be enjoying that," said Jeffery, huffing in disgust but knowing that no one was able to hear him. He looked around and saw several exits located around the coliseum. Then, he looked back in Sarm's direction as he wondered what to do. As he waited, Jeffery saw a man come out from one of the exits that was close to the stage. The man stomped towards him with all his might and his head pointing down, as if he was preparing for a vicious attack. As he got closer, the more of his appearance Jeffery was able to see. The man was tall, olive-skinned and very slender. He was also topless and wore jeans and black boots, but was less muscular than Jeffery. His straight, black hair was combed from the sides and bounced above his head as he stomped, carrying a knife in his hand. He glanced at Sarm and saw that she was watching and the crowd shouted even louder, indicating that the battle had begun.

Jeffery watched his opponent get closer as he prepared himself for the attack. The man came towards him with his fist raised so he quickly ducked and jumped to the side. The man let out a growl then attempted a second attack but Jeffery dodged him again. He threw himself back on the floor and landed on his hands, then kicked hard at the man's ankle and quickly stood up. The opponent lifted up his leg and screamed in pain then ran fast towards Jeffery. Jeffery pushed him down to the floor and landed on top of him. The man dropped the knife and tried to strangle Jeffery, turning him over. With the sand burning his back, Jeffery struggled to get the man off him and then managed to roll over and get on top again. He punched him hard in the nose and jumped back, catching his breath. The man covered his nose with his hands, sat up, got to his knees, and bent forward. Jeffery walked back and noticed that the crowd was cursing and stomping, expressing their rage and disapproval.

He turned to face Sarm again and saw that Senuv was standing right next to her. He smiled at her then turned back to face his opponent who had stood up and was planning his next move. Then, the man ran towards him and dodged forward. Jeffery kicked him hard in the stomach, pushed him down to the floor, and then kicked him in the temple. The man screamed in agony and the crowd got angrier. Jeffery turned to look at the two mothers and saw that they both had frowns on their faces, confusing him. Realizing that the man was still alive, Jeffery quickly looked at him and saw that he was struggling on the floor, immobilized by pain. Jeffery kicked him a few more times then threw sand in his eyes.

Jeffery quickly searched for the knife and, once he had found it, he picked it up and ran towards his opponent. As the man struggled, Jeffery grabbed his head, lifted up his chin and yelled, "This is for you, Senuv!" The crowd screamed as he stabbed the knife right into the man's throat which caused his blood to splash and gush rapidly. At that moment the crowd exploded in anger. Jeffery stood up proudly and walked away facing the stage, completely ignoring the crowd's cursing and yelling. He saw that both the mothers were in shock, and were shaking their heads. Still feeling confused by Senuv, Jeffery jogged closer to the stage and saw that she was talking to Sarm. He watched them closely then saw Sarm step forward. "I killed him!" he called.

After a brief pause, Sarm looked up and sang an opera that echoed loudly, causing some of the citizens to plug their ears. Jeffery watched and saw that, as she sang, the sand in front of him moved in peculiar ways—a little to the left then a little to the right and closer to his feet. Not long after, a figure emerged from the ground and started extending upwards. It went fast, revealing itself to be a gigantic blood-red beast that stood over sixty feet and had giant black tusks and muscular hands. His eyes were glowing red, and all his veins were throbbing in outrage. He growled, echoing his guttural and monstrous voice while holding up his enormous arms, revealing his burgundy body hair. At his center, there was a giant red crocksvenbulb which he flaunted proudly. Jeffery stepped back and got a clearer view of his round head that revealed his humongous teeth that were sharp like swords and grew down to his muscular legs and elevated back up like a vertical accordion. The beast then let out an even louder scream that hurt Jeffery's ears.

"What's going on here?" shouted Jeffery. The crowd got excited again and began to cheer. He quickly ran to the side to get a view of the stage again, and saw that the mothers were giggling as the beast turned and faced him. Jeffery's heart raced causing him to panic. The beast jumped up high in the sky then landed right back down, causing a slight earthquake. Jeffery fell to his side and felt a burn across his right shoulder, which caused him to scream. Before being able to decide on what to do, Jeffery found himself being picked up by the beast and raised over sixty feet into the air. The beast squeezed Jeffery tightly in his hand so that he wasn't able to move anything but his head. Feeling intimidated and crushed, Jeffery screamed as he had never before. He screamed so loud that he couldn't hear anything but himself and his ears popping painfully.

The crowd cheered harder causing him to feel absolutely humiliated. Jeffery turned his head to face the mothers and saw that they stood right next to each other, each with her hand by her heart, laughing at the sight of his ordeal. Jeffery yelled and cursed at them while screaming at the top of his lungs. He suddenly noticed that the sun had shifted in shape. It turned into a giant, red crocksvenbulb with a slightly smaller, orange one at its center, totally reinforcing the mothers' deception. Right then, Sarm struck another high note with her arms open.

Jeffery's eyes were full of tears and his whole body felt like it was in a sauna as the beast squeezed him. Jeffery looked down and watched Sarm. After she ended her singing, she grinned and the beast swung Jeffery forward and aggressively slashed him with one of his tusks, decapitating him then tossing his head high in a circular motion. Jeffery's head spun around the entire coliseum and then landed on the stage, right between the two mothers' feet, as they both laughed hard and the crowd cheered.

Chapter Ten

Seeking Forgiveness

Jeffery opened his eyes slowly, and saw a large beam of bright, white light shining as if it were blasting through infinity. He closed his eyes again, but he could still see the light through his eyelids. Once he had become slightly accustomed to it, he looked around and saw that he was in a familiar realm that contained nothing other than the light itself. It was like a white galaxy with no planets, stars or meteors. Jeffery tried to move his hand, but then realized that he didn't have hands. He tried to shake a leg, but realized that he lacked legs as well. Feeling confused, he looked down and saw that his body was gone—he was merely an invisible ball of energy that was shaped like a cloud, about the size of an apple, and he still retained many of his memories. Feeling wobbly, he floated and practiced moving in this new form.

Before long, Jeffery saw a cream-toned light appear that was shaped like an oval. He watched it as it grew and evolved into a bigger and brighter beam. It was warm, calming and safe.

"And a lifetime just ended," spoke a familiar male voice.

"Yes," replied Jeffery, feeling at ease.

"I've been watching since before I communicated with you at the pyramid," answered the male voice.

"You sound very familiar," admitted Jeffery.

"Your spiritual awakening on planet Ice Mallow... Also, I gave you a premonition in your dream at Lake Morgan's... "

"Yes, I remember very clearly," stated Jeffery. "I'm curious about who you actually are."

"I'm Allie," replied the male voice. "Some know me as *God*."

"Oh, yes," said Jeffery, "I've heard of you by many throughout my journey. I don't believe that I've ever seen you before."

"I know," answered Allie, "you are a really young soul. I guided you myself to ensure your protection. My, you are so brave to have gone through that lifetime learning all those lessons."

"Thank you, Allie," said Jeffery. "Is this what you actually look like?"

"I can disguise myself," answered Allie. "Old souls know my real form though."

"What is your real form?" asked Jeffery. He instantly received a message of the image of a mirror in his mind. "You're willing to reveal that to me?"

"Yes," replied Allie. Jeffery watched closely as the light intertwined in very special ways and created unexplainable forms, leaving him in awe. As the beautiful light formed a figure, it revealed a face of a woman with very relaxed features, large dark-brown eyes and straight, platinum blonde hair that Jeffery knew was much longer than he could see. The woman smiled at him, and all he could hear was the word *love* repeating slowly.

"Allie?" asked Jeffery sounding surprised. The woman nodded, still smiling. Jeffery also smiled and stared at her with absolute amazement. "I am astonished!" he exclaimed. "You look incredible! I never would have imagined!"

"Thank you," said Allie.

"Why—how is it that everyone thinks you're male?"

"I assume that my voice is that of a man's," replied Allie. "I think it's really for their own powers and benefits. They all need rounded ideologies to fit inside those crocksvenbulbs of theirs."

"Those things always made me uncomfortable," stated Jeffery. "Well, maybe Senuv's and Sabina's were ok, but I never really liked any of the other ones."

"I know," answered Allie, "and what has that taught you? What lesson do you take from this?"

"It shows me that... " started Jeffery, "others need morals and principles to live by and pass on, even if they aren't entirely true or just," he finished.

"I can take that," said Allie.

"I feel that some have even imprisoned themselves in them," suggested Jeffery.

"And how did you do otherwise?" asked Allie.

Jeffery thought for a moment then replied saying, "I can't say that I did much better." He looked down for a moment then back up at Allie. "I feel that I was actually fooled by them to some extent."

"That's fine," replied Allie. "What many have in their minds is that I judge others for their actions. I don't. I never have, nor will I ever. My role is to guide every soul to where it needs to be. I never judge. I always love eternally. Even those who've lost faith in me, Spirit continues to guide them until they eventually learn the truth for themselves."

"That is beautiful," said Jeffery.

"It is," agreed Allie, "everything is a continuous realm filled with love, transitions, learning and sometimes even... glory." As Allie continued to smile, Jeffery felt more loving energy float around him like a ring, giving him the urge to cry. "The secret of life, Jeffery," she started, "is what you learn, discover about yourself, and what you create and give back." Allie's

284

words echoed across with light rays causing minor vibrations. They sent a strong feeling of positivity and graciousness throughout Jeffery's soul that left him feeling deeply touched.

Jeffery thought about the battle that had occurred and how angry it had made him learning about Senuv's deception. He also thought about how the beast had killed him in front of thousands.

"I get the sense that you are reflecting upon your final moments," proposed Allie.

"In all honesty, I am," answered Jeffery.

"And what can be learned from that situation?" asked Allie.

"One must be aware of deception," replied Jeffery. "And also betrayal. It hurts to be fooled and deceived by someone."

"Yes," agreed Allie. "I think it is a savage thing to do."

"And devious," added Jeffery. "I thought that Senuv was a really sweet woman. I thought that she was legitimately hurt by the situation. Little did I know that it was all a façade." Allie nodded. "I really wanted to see the two kingdoms unite. I thought that that was my purpose for being sent there."

"They knew you were coming," explained Allie, "Spirit told them so and that this was a lesson planned for you. That is a lesson that many need to learn: authorities who hold higher power are always in bed together. They portray an image of being moralistic, conservative, or sympathetic, but really, it is all a charade for their own benefit. The only thing that guides you out of free will and love for your own protection and good is Spirit. And that is why you saw so many signs along your path and felt things as you went along." Allie's nurturing words flowed within Jeffery's soul. As he listened, he saw a vision of a light bulb flashing.

"That's very enlightening," he replied. "If only I had known."

"That's totally ok," assured Allie. "No being will ever know all the information in the universe. That's the way it is. Everything someone thinks he *knows* is not even a speck of dust compared to what is really out there." Jeffery felt a strong sense of relief hearing this.

"Why do so many do such evil things?" he questioned. "For instance, Ribs, he murdered a lot of people."

"Some do the most evil of deeds for their own selfish benefit," replied Allie. "That especially happens when they lose faith. A sole man sometimes may feel that he has the capacity to become a god or own the universe, which shuts him down from learning about everything that exists around him in various time dimensions."

"It's horrible," added Jeffery.

"It is, no doubt," agreed Allie. "Unfortunately though, it happens. Lest you forget, many beings oftentimes think that they know everything about something. They might know a lot, but still, there's never an *everything* for anything. It is always an incomplete puzzle without edges. That is what many need to realize and accept, thus they are sent into many lifetimes to learn so."

"I agree," replied Jeffery.

"And facts are sometimes based on an opinion," Allie went on to explain. "Sometimes some facts are untrue as well, all depending on the wording of things and how they are expressed, especially for what purpose. Think back to Senuv's philosophy, before learning who she really was, and compare it to that of Lake Morgan's."

"Yep," agreed Jeffery, "most certainly."

"Now, the trick is, not to fall into such. And, if you do, you just learn from it and Spirit will guide you in the correct direction," explained Allie.

"I'd like to speak to the mothers if that is somehow possible," said Jeffery.

"It is," replied Allie. "As a spirit, you can approach that side as an animal." Allie moved to the side and created an oval with many rays of white light and then revealed Sarm and Senuv, astonishing Jeffery. They were sitting in a room that was furnished in red carpets and couches, drinking tea by a window.

"Quite the battle I must say," expressed Sarm, "especially that I was dealing with two journeys at the same time, Jeffery's and Marco's."

"Yes, indeed," agreed Senuv. "I'll admit, I really did not like deceiving Jeffery. He was a really kind soul. I am aware that this was planned for him, but I wish that he'd forgive me and understand that I never really had a choice." Jeffery turned to Allie then looked down, feeling guilt.

"You can go to them," suggested Allie. "In fact, I think you should."

"Very well," replied Jeffery. He faced the oval lighting and projected himself into it. He felt as if he was actually next to them, then saw a red dragonfly enter through the window and land on Senuv's arm.

"Oh," she said.

"We've got a visitor," observed Sarm. Senuv put down her tea and took out her crystal ball. Jeffery leveled down his energy and frowned at her.

"I am feeling that this is Jeffery's spirit," started Senuv, "and he is quite unhappy."

"Your betrayal led to my death," projected Jeffery.

"I am getting a vision of an orange cat, and I am seeing a skull as well," explained Senuv. "I just heard the word *betrayal*, he is saying that my betrayal is the reason he died."

"I learned so many truths about others," Jeffery projected.

"He is now showing me masks dropping which tells me that a lot of things have been unveiled to him in the afterlife," explained Senuv, looking at her crystal ball.

"But, I still forgive you and I wish you both happiness," projected Jeffery.

"I am seeing two large flowers," said Senuv, "and I am hearing the word *forgive*. He forgives us and is wishing us happiness." The two mothers looked at the dragonfly in admiration.

"I feel that he has more to say," insisted Sarm.

"It is me, Jeffery," projected Jeffery.

"He is showing me the letters *E, F* and *Y*," explained Senuv, looking up.

"Yes, that is definitely Jeffery's spirit," confirmed Sarm.

"Down your path, you will learn a lot more," projected Jeffery.

"He is showing me a path," said Senuv, "and I am feeling a future vibe from it. I feel that he is saying that we will learn something down the road."

"Interesting," said Sarm.

"And, I will have a story to tell," projected Jeffery.

"I am seeing an image of a fishing rod," added Senuv. "I feel that he is a storyteller." Jeffery breathed out and set himself back a bit. The dragonfly then flew off as Sarm and Senuv watched it exit. Allie shut down the oval lighting, making them vanish out of sight.

"How did that feel?" asked Allie.

"Good," replied Jeffery, "really good."

"As a spirit, you can always go and deliver messages," said Allie. "That's what it is like in what they call in their time dimension, the *afterlife* or *the other side*."

"Incredible," said Jeffery.

"Why don't you go off and wander about?" suggested Allie. "Maybe other beings will channel you, too."

"Ok," agreed Jeffery. Allie looked up and closed her eyes. As she meditated, another beam of silvery-white light came shining down upon Jeffery. As he watched her, she faded out along with all the light, leaving behind a view of white trees, white hills, and clear water that reflected its surrounding foliage like a photograph. Jeffery flew off into the woods and danced as he enjoyed the magical sight of the place. He flew very high in the cloudy sky then came back down and relaxed over a tree branch. Below him was a walkway made of cream-colored stone that was covered in white petals. Across it was a park bench that had its back carved into various vines of flowers. Jeffery flew over and floated above it as if he were sitting down. He observed the view while breathing in and appreciating the fresh air, expressing his gratitude and noticed that around the corner by some of the trees was a small flower bush. The flowers had little faces and they all exhaled sparkling mist that dissipated over neighboring shrubs. Jeffery smiled again with contentment and gratitude.

As he relaxed, two men approached from the walkway; one of them, who was a few inches taller, had his arm around the other man's shoulder. They both wore white tuxedos with black and silver accents and pointy dress shoes. They both had brown hair and eyes, and well-kept beards. The taller one stopped, causing his partner to do the same, and faced him.

"Look at me," he started, "we're not really alone anymore, we now have each other."

"We do," agreed the shorter man, "it just would have been really nice if all of our families were here to celebrate our love for each other."

"Maybe in time," said the taller man. They continued staring at one another and then he pulled him in and the two kissed.

"You two look very gorgeous," said Jeffery with great admiration. "Whoever isn't with you is surely missing out by not having you in their lives." The men paused, and the taller one looked in Jeffery's direction.

"Is everything ok?" his partner asked.

"I felt something by that bench," he replied.

"You've been feeling things like that recently, what could it be?" said the shorter man. The taller man rubbed his hands down his partner's shoulder and looked at him.

"Maybe Spirit is just satisfied with the fact that I love you," he answered. He leaned in and the two men kissed again.

"That's incredible," said Jeffery, "you two deserve the best." The taller man grabbed his partner firmly and they continued kissing for a long moment. They looked at each other again and continued walking with their arms around one another. "I send you both lots of love and a lifetime of happiness and joy together. May your marriage be blessed for all of eternity," prayed Jeffery. As the two men walked away, Allie arrived, walking from the woods behind the bench and took a seat next to Jeffery. He saw that she was just a few inches over five feet tall, wore a sparkling, silver dress, a white fur coat and matching high heels.

"Aren't they beautiful?" she asked with her deep male voice.

"Very beautiful!" replied Jeffery.

"Love is a very important thing," taught Allie. "It does not matter the sex or the age of the two beings, what matters is the love between them."

"I concur," agreed Jeffery.

"Did you love anybody?" asked Allie.

"I did not, unfortunately," replied Jeffery.

"And, do you think that no one was in love with you?" inquired Allie.

"I think there *was* someone, actually," replied Jeffery.

"And what was her name?" asked Allie.

"Sabina," answered Jeffery.

"Right," said Allie, "and are you sure there was no one else that was perhaps disguised?"

"Not that I can think of," replied Jeffery, "life was a long journey for me."

"Yes," said Allie. She opened one side of her fur coat and let out a beam of white light. Inside it formed an oval shape which revealed Sabina. She was lying on the beach with a sad expression on her face, as all the lobsters played around her and unicorns flew back and forth. Jeffery focused on her and, before long, found himself as a purple dragonfly flying close to her. He landed on her lap and looked her right in the face.

"Oh! Hello there," greeted Sabina.

"Hey," said Jeffery happily, even though he knew she couldn't hear him. He then flew and circulated around her head then went back to her leg. Sabina reached out her hand so Jeffery flew and landed on it. "I miss you," he called. Sabina smiled, pulled him in closer, and petted him with her other hand.

"You are very beautiful," she said "and you feel very loving."

"Thank you," said Jeffery. "I am sending you lots of love and healing." He flew forward, gave her a kiss on the lips then flew away up into the clouds, and after they turned white, he flew downwards and searched for the bench where Allie sat. After finding her, he flew straight down and sat next to her, realizing he wasn't in his dragonfly form any longer.

"That was beautiful," said Allie. "She really misses you."

"I miss her, too," said Jeffery. "I never thought that I'd see her again."

"She is a sweet soul," added Allie. "She is thinking about you right now."

"I felt that," agreed Jeffery. He sighed, then looked at the trees. He saw that some of them were curved and some were standing straight. Some stood close to one another and some were farther apart.

"Is there a reason you never pursued her?" asked Allie.

"Oh, Allie," started Jeffery, "I am sure you know exactly why."

"Well, that's something we need to talk about," stated Allie. "Life is never complete without love." Jeffery sighed.

"Sabina wasn't the one for me," he explained calmly.

"I know," confirmed Allie with certainty. "She did teach you some valuable lessons."

"That's true," said Jeffery with a nod. "Unlike Lake Morgan."

"Until he's around Sarm," laughed Allie. "But he will learn, just keep sending him love and healing."

"Well," started Jeffery, floating, "it is much deeper than just emotional concerns."

"How do you mean?" questioned Allie. Jeffery sighed.

"I really couldn't love Sabina," he went on to explain. "She's a great woman. She taught me a lot of things. I just didn't feel that way towards her. For one, I couldn't love women that way, and not only so, but I also didn't feel like I was put in the right body."

"Well, you see, Jeffery, you chose to enter that body," replied Allie. "When a soul chooses a body, it chooses to go where it can create and manifest the most. As a very young soul, you probably weren't aware of this and chose the body nearest to you."

"That was definitely a mistake," said Jeffery.

"That's ok," insisted Allie, "I love it when a mistake is made because it is an opportunity to learn."

"That's believable," said Jeffery, "I just think that I could have done more in that lifetime had I been a woman."

"I know," admitted Allie. She glanced around and then looked back at him. "But there is a point that you are missing," she stated.

"What would that be?" questioned Jeffery.

292

"You see," she started, "in that lifetime, you dwelled too much on materialistic aspects such as your body and your surroundings. I understand it was confusing for you, but lest you forget, you are a soul, more than you are anything."

"True," agreed Jeffery, "but I never knew that."

"I know you didn't," reassured Allie. "That isn't the point."

"What's your point?" asked Jeffery.

"My point is, so many on that time dimension are put into boxes and labels over silly and aesthetic things like gender, political ideologies and whatnot. What everyone needs to know, is that they are not part of these categories and boxes, really," Allie explained passionately. She turned and faced Jeffery. "You are a spiritual being. And, on that time dimension, you were in the body of a human with an aura. You needed to love, to create, to learn and live as part of the continuum. Also, Jeffery, being a man or a woman is not about masculinity and femininity as you were taught—it is about how much individuals contribute to the world and the universe as members of these sexes, nothing more." Jeffery allowed Allie's words to echo in his ears as he gazed at her in amazement, feeling the rise of an epiphany in his small soul. Allie stood up and walked to the center of the path. She opened out her arms and danced in a circle. "Look at me!" she called.

"You look beautiful!" cheered Jeffery, watching her.

"As God, I see nothing about men or women, I just see all the souls that have been created and I love them all unconditionally. I do not judge, I do not hate and I never have wrath. I am the being of eternal love and infinity," preached Allie. "I am the most loving energy that watches over our universe." She then stopped dancing and stood facing Jeffery with her arms open. "Come here, Jeffery, you are beautiful inside and out. I love you." Jeffery flew towards Allie, but after flying halfway he realized that he could

293

no longer move. His sight was fixed on her as she smiled and blew gently at him. Jeffery felt an extreme and unexplainably beautiful warmth around him. He felt as if he were being hugged by something gigantic that all the planets couldn't hold. This brought tears to his eyes as he stared at Allie and felt her glorious love. It was the biggest thing he had ever felt. White light flashed everywhere and covered the view of the forest and the walkway.

"There is nothing like the love of God," he thought.

"Thank you," said Allie, "and there is nothing like an individual soul." After a moment, Jeffery was able to move again. He saw that he and Allie were back at the original place where they had met.

"That was amazing!" he exclaimed.

"Everything can be amazing if you open your mind to all possibilities," answered Allie. "I mean it, everything is possible." Jeffery looked at her in admiration, noticing light feathers circulating around him. He couldn't perceive how such a force as Allie could exist. She looked at him gently as he felt her sending him healing energy and hope that felt much stronger than his divine experience on planet Ice Mallow. Jeffery thought about something and wondered if Allie was able to hear it. He then looked at her and found her smiling directly at him.

"Well, I never specifically said that that lifetime was over, now did I?" she replied. Jeffery just looked at her and thought. He sent her a prayer of gratitude as he continued to float. "Yes, that's close to what I already have in mind." Allie closed her eyes and breathed in carefully. Jeffery watched her and admired her beauty. She opened her eyes and looked straight at him again while closing her hands and fingers together in the shape of a ball. She released her thumbs and turned them around each other seven times, keeping her focus on him as he watched carefully. Then, she brought up both of her hands in the shape of a prayer close to her lips and blew at him again as gently as she could. Jeffery saw more feathers fly in his direction and felt

294

more love go right through him, creating a magical essence that he could not fathom. It felt overwhelming but also wonderfully positive, filling his soul with happy tears. All of a sudden, Allie seemed ever so beautiful with her hair around her face that bore her gentle and angelic smile. Jeffery fell back at the strength and size of her energy. His breathing became heavier but his vision remained clear.

"I felt it!" he gasped. "I have never felt anything so beautiful and so loving! This is very special." Allie kept looking at him and continued to smile. As Jeffery gasped and panted, he felt as though he had turned into rubber, but then felt himself begin to augment. Before long, skin grew on him and hair grew out of his head. He saw a new nose appear and a chin. His whole body shook and grew out different parts as a bright, white light flashed and covered him in a peach gown with a white, angelic trim near the bottom. His hair grew beige blonde and dark brown, like black coffee, and was fashioned into a braid that landed at his waist in front of his shoulder. His hazel eyes grew back and were almost the same size as Allie's. Jeffery looked down as the white light surrounded him and closely observed his transformation. Allie worked her hands and created an oval-shaped light which turned into a tall mirror. Jeffery looked at the reflection and saw a beautiful, young lady looking back. He looked down and felt himself and noticed that she was actually him.

"What just happened?" he questioned in surprise, while noticing that his voice had also changed. "I'm a woman!"

"Yes," agreed Allie with uttermost happiness, "and you can pick your name, too." Jeffery looked at her and at the mirror then turned around in a circle.

"Call me... Catherine," she said happily.

"Catherine you are," replied Allie.

"Oh, my God!" expressed Catherine happily. She ran straight to Allie and gave her a big hug. "Thank you so much."

"You are most welcome, darling," replied Allie. Catherine then stepped back and observed herself again. "There is one more thing."

"What is it?" asked Catherine. Allie stepped closer to her and handed her a necklace. Catherine looked at it and saw that it was a white gold chain that had a matching pendant of a cross. At its center, there was the letter A engraved. "It's beautiful!"

"Keep it on you at all times," said Allie. "I am glad you like it."

"I will certainly do so," answered Catherine. She put on the necklace and proudly centered the pendant by her heart.

"Do you feel better now that you are a woman?" questioned Allie.

"I couldn't be happier," replied Catherine.

"Good," said Allie. "Just remember, it's not your body that makes you who you are, it is your own soul. And remember that every time you hold that cross."

"I shall," answered Catherine as tears ran down her face. Allie stepped forward and gave her another hug expressing her warmth and love. Allie turned away while wrapped in thought. "What's the matter?" asked Catherine. Allie turned around and faced her.

"Are you ready to go back and complete your task?" she asked with a serious tone.

"I am," replied Catherine with a nod. "I hope that I will see you, though."

"I am everywhere," replied Allie. "I am the eternal love of the universe and all galaxies. And Spirit and I will be watching over you."

"Thank you," said Catherine.

"I love you," said Allie.

"I love you, too, Allie," replied Catherine. Allie moved her hands again and created some white light with silver outlines. In her head, Catherine saw lightning that felt rather negative. She kept quiet though, and watched Allie sift the light. Allie turned it into a large rectangle, vertically placed it beside her and pushed it from the side. It opened inwards, like a door, and a view of a rich, green and comforting forest was revealed.

"Whenever you are ready," instructed Allie, facing Catherine.

"Alright," Catherine replied. She thought for a moment, then walked towards the forest. Allie looked up, shone some more light, and Catherine stepped in.

Chapter Eleven

A Being with an Aura

Catherine felt various leaves rubbing against her arms as she meandered through the forest and smelled its fresh essence. She inhaled it all, sensing that she was receiving greetings from afar. The sun shone brightly over her, causing the peach sky to brighten as if it were mirroring her happiness. After noticing some of the shiny, peach streaks in some parts of the grass and the absence of bright beams, she turned around and realized that she had completely stepped out of Allie's realm. Still reflecting upon her encounter with Allie, Catherine looked up at the sky and searched for traces of her. She didn't see anything in particular, but she did feel a very warm energy around her that grew warmer as she focused on it, and brought tears to her eyes.

"Love," Catherine told herself, "it is the answer to the universe." She stepped forward, then knelt down on the ground to observe a light-peach rose. She smelled it, as if she were absorbing all of its fundamental nature, and was reminded of lust, love, passion, hope and reassurance. Leaving the rose in its place, she stood up and walked away, remembering the duty that awaited her. She put her hand on her cross and contemplated what she would do next. After clearing her mind, she sat down again and decided to see what was around her. The forest had a jungle-like feel and it seemed very familiar.

The wind gently blew through the leaves, their dancing movement catching her attention.

After appreciating that magical moment, Catherine stood and exited the forest and found herself upon a hill that was slightly above some flat land. She took a deep breath and inhaled the fresh air again, then continued strolling until she reached a calm moor. Surrounding her was thick, green foliage and the grass beneath her was the same—reminiscent of a silky blanket. She continued walking while admiring the serenity of her surroundings and the peach sunlight that touched her skin with a gentle glow.

Ahead of her, Catherine saw a large rocky cliff that was made of very hard, gray stone. It looked small because of its distance, but Catherine knew that this was a deception. On top of the cliff stood a castle that looked different from the twin castles of Senuv and Sarm. It was wider, a little bit shorter, and predominantly peach colored with some white accents. Its windows reflected the sunlight, bouncing back a luminous, golden-nectar glow that created an optimistic atmosphere.

Suddenly, Catherine's heart sank. She walked a bit to her right but noticed that the castle couldn't be seen entirely from an angle. She walked a little bit towards it as the sunlight got brighter. As she glanced at the cliff, she saw a silhouette of a skeletal fish that quickly disappeared when she shifted her focus. Catherine looked back at the spot but saw nothing. She tried to read the cliff, looking for more signs, but in her mind, all she received was a vision of gates closing causing her body to pull back as she saw this. She turned her head away, and in her heart, she sent out gratitude as she clasped her cross in her hand.

"Whatever is meant to be, will prevail," she said aloud. "I am grateful for it and will accept whatever learning is meant to come of it." Then, Catherine saw small, white circles appear that were about half the size of her iris, floating in the air around her. Her body felt lighter as the number of circles multiplied. "Oh," she murmured. The energy of the phenomenon was of a very high vibration and very loving, making her feel lightheaded and also causing a slight shake in the lithosphere. Feeling as if she were floating, she looked up and saw more of the little circles populating the air. Soon she began to see small lights flashing and flickering rapidly, like fireworks—some were green, some were blue and some were magenta. As she watched them, Catherine felt touched, loved, and protected by many angelic forces. The flashing lights kept flickering as the tiny white circles danced around them, celebrating. Catherine could not believe her eyes. She reached out her arms and wept with joy, and as she watched she felt her soul being illuminated with a wondrous awakening.

"Thank you!" she called out. The circles danced as the flickers bounced for a while longer, and then they slowly faded away. Catherine fell to her knees and looked down as some of the small white circles lowered themselves over her, dissolving in the atmosphere. She pulled her braid close and allowed her mind to readjust as if she were re-entering a former time zone. Her breathing slowed, tiring her, but she felt hopeful and envisaged a candle burning out, signifying that a long transition was about to end.

After Catherine opened her eyes and looked around her, she saw that everything seemed brighter than ever. The grass beneath her danced with the blowing of the wind and the cliff glistened as if it were smiling. The sun looked larger, seemingly refueled with unfathomable years of youthfulness. She glanced at the cliff and again saw a flash of the skeletal fish silhouette near the horizon. Its energy felt heavier, but not enough to distract her from her angelic surrounding. As she looked around, more of the tiny circles floated in every direction. Catherine heard tiny footsteps nearby but didn't catch sight of anything. She focused again, and not long after, a small deer emerged from the forest and came to her, rubbing its apricot-color coat against her and putting its head under her shoulder.

"You add delight to the serene environment," said Catherine as she touched the innocent animal. The deer ambled off and she watched it disappear into the forest. She looked behind her and saw two wolves appear at the top of the hill. They were a bit bigger than the deer, fluffier, and with the same apricot tone. They focused on the castle for a moment then ran towards it. As they did so, many more wolves appeared and followed. Catherine quickly stood up and asked, "And where are all of you headed?" She looked at the cliff after the wolves passed her and then looked back, only to see that many more had appeared and were running in the same direction. She looked more closely at them and saw that their eyes were in many different shades and colors.

Catherine turned around again and walked towards the castle as the number of wolves continued to multiply. She held her head up and fluffed out her dress, knowing that her divine wisdom and knowledge was with her. She enjoyed the stir of the wind that was caused by the stampede of the wolves. One wolf accidently rubbed its fur on her as it ran past. Catherine glanced at it then shifted her gaze towards the castle. After a little while, she came close to the top of another hill so she stopped to observe. The hill was steep and led to a flat, grassy surface, and right in front of it was the base of the high cliff that stood many feet above. Catherine looked to the castle on top and saw that it was indeed quite broad.

The wolves rushed down the hill and past the cliff into the surrounding forests. Catherine looked back at the cliff and saw an illusion of a big sunflower that disappeared a second after it had appeared. Expecting that a sense of joy awaited her, Catherine ran down the hill as fast as she could along with the wolves, enjoying her agility as she raced through the serene environment. As she ran, she couldn't help but think of previously learned knowledge and wisdom that inspired her to run faster and closer to the cliff. Feeling impeccably free, she looked behind as she tossed her braid in the air and saw that many more wolves were running behind her, their lustrous coats like bouncing lights on the contrasting green hill. Once Catherine came within a few paces of the cliff, she stopped, panting, and watched the wolves run off into the distance. By the time she had caught her breath, the wolves had disappeared from view, leaving her alone before the cliff and unable to see the castle above. She stepped closer, placed her right hand on the cliff face, silently said another prayer, and then climbed with full force.

The sun shone over her as she climbed, and before long, Catherine reached the top, feeling fatigued but ever so ambitious. She hopped over the edge, stood tall, and smiled at the castle as she opened her arms, celebrating. She fluffed up her dress and walked around the castle, observing all of its fine details. As she walked, she took notice of the view of the forests below and stared in exhilaration. Naturally, the forests seemed smaller, but yet, very magical. She looked for wolves but didn't see any. She continued staring at the panoramic scene as she walked around the cliff's edge and thought about how far she had come.

Catherine walked over to the castle entrance that consisted of two wide, peach-colored doors and two tall, white pillars that stood on each side. The pillars seemed identical until she got close to them. She saw a statue of an anteater popping out from behind the left one and onto a separate base. Catherine walked over to the second one and saw a statue of a fruit basket structured in the same way. After feeling the one to her right and its attached statue, she went and knocked on one of the doors. She waited a few seconds then knocked again. The doors remained closed and not a footstep was to be heard. Catherine entered, closing the door behind her. She fluffed out her dress once again, brought her braid around her shoulder and close to her heart, then proceeded forward.

The main level of the castle was smaller than the main floor at Sarm's and Senuv's. The floor was covered with a huge, light peach-colored rug that had many drawings of peach and white caterpillars, cocoons, butterflies and monarchs. The walls were slightly lighter and had white, ceramic sculptures of men's heads affixed in various spots. In front was a large and wide staircase with silver banisters that slightly curved in the middle, giving it a voluptuous aesthetic. Above it was one balcony and next to it was a large arch. The floor over there was bare and had a pattern of small hourglasses painted on it.

Catherine turned to her left and saw a rectangular side table that was pushed against the wall. On it was a collection of white and peach candles of shapes and sizes. Close to the center was a chessboard checkered in peach and black with a gilded outline. The chess pieces looked like small dolls of men and women, and on one side of the board they were all dressed in peach-colored robes, except for the pawns, which were each dressed in chain mail and a helmet. The King and Queen had bald eagle heads standing out from the center of both their crowns. The opposing side wore black robes and the pawns wore golden gear. Catherine looked closely and saw that each piece wore a peach crocksvenbulb somewhere on it.

"Are you lost, there?" kindly asked a voice. Catherine looked to her right and saw a woman descending the staircase. "The castle is a little tricky sometimes," the woman added.

"I don't think so," answered Catherine. "I feel that I have found my place."

"Really?" asked the woman. She walked across the floor and approached Catherine. "I am Mary," she said as she reached out her hand.

"I am Catherine," replied Catherine as she shook Mary's hand. "You seem very gentle."

"Why, thank you," replied Mary, turning pink. She wore a peach suit jacket with matching blouse and skirt, peach leather boots, and had a solid-peach headscarf tied around her that revealed only her eyes, mouth and nose. There were three golden pins horizontally placed on her suit jacket: a Star of David, a cross, and the word *Allah* in script shaped like the letter *W*. Around her neck was a necklace with a pendant of a peach crocksvenbulb. "Are you here for the banquet?" she asked.

"The banquet?" questioned Catherine. "What banquet?" Mary looked at her and said nothing. "What banquet, Mary?" she repeated.

"Well, I've been expecting you for quite some time," explained Mary. "This way." She pointed towards the side table and walked to it.

"That doesn't tell me much," said Catherine, following.

"Just a minute," insisted Mary. She reached into her pocket and took out a deck of tarot cards then shuffled them in her hands. She put the deck face down on the table then turned to face Catherine. "Pick three then place them facing down." Catherine put her hand on the deck and felt vibrant energy run up her arm. She picked up the deck, drew three cards as instructed, and then returned the deck to Mary. Mary moved her hand over the three drawn cards as she kept her eyes closed. "I've never felt anything like this before," she stated. Catherine smiled gently as she waited patiently. Mary opened her turquoise-blue eyes, feeling touched by a graceful mist.

"I feel it also," said Catherine. Mary paused as she looked at her then turned to the cards and flipped one. Catherine took a close look at it and saw a picture of a beautiful woman standing with peach and white ribbons around her and the number *three* written near the top. Her dress had a pattern of triangles on it and below her bare feet, the card read *Empress*.

"You're very nurturing and very secure. You are like a natural mother," told Mary. She flipped the second card then gasped. Catherine looked at it and saw an image of another beautiful woman in a similar,

304

pristine setting except that she floated in the air in front of several stars and a crescent. The card read *High Priestess* near the bottom and the number *two* near the top, above the woman's blonde bun. "Prosperity! You're aiming for your purpose. I also feel that you are well guided on your path," finished Mary.

"Thank you," said Catherine. "I am glad to know that."

"The High Priestess always ensures this," explained Mary. She turned the final card and gasped again. "Look at that!" she exclaimed, expressing her excitement with a bounce.

"She is beautiful," agreed Catherine, looking down at the card. There was another woman on it floating in the peach-tinted sky and tilting to her side. Her long, black hair was blown sideways as two crystal chalices floated, one on each side of her. The one to the left had a teardrop above it and the one to the right had an ignited arrow pointing away. Near the top, the card read the number *fourteen* and near the bottom, *Temperance*.

"Very strong sense of moderation in your material word," explained Mary, "and lots more divine guidance, keeping your emotions stabilized. You are not the type who can be fooled any longer. In fact, you are here to guide." Catherine put a hand on her heart and looked at Mary directly. "And look, they are all upright," indicated Mary. "You pulled three cards from the higher arcana and none of them reversed!"

"I am blessed," breathed Catherine gratefully.

"My faith has changed a lot over the years," began Mary, "and I can tell that you have gone through similar changes. And now, you have come to release yourself." An image of a peach-colored monarch butterfly, with a pattern of a fish on each wing, flashed before Catherine's eyes. She shook slightly then clasped her cross.

"I have," she confirmed. "Faith in yourself is very important and cannot be taught by passing it down. It is learned, and only through a life journey."

"I couldn't agree more," answered Mary.

"We've lived it," said Catherine.

"Indeed, we have," agreed Mary. "And about this banquet," she continued, "it's for you."

"For me?" asked Catherine.

"It is," replied Mary, "allow me to show you."

"Please do," said Catherine.

"This way," indicated Mary as she pointed in the direction past the staircase. The two of them walked towards the stairs as they discussed their philosophies.

When they got to the top, Catherine followed Mary to a separate part of the castle that felt a lot higher in elevation. She saw that the walls ranged in patterns and texture, even thought they were dominantly the same color with more white sculptures of male heads and vases decorating various corners. There were also a few glass peach and white ornaments of angels that reflected the abundance of sunlight that entered the castle.

"I really love birds, I feel that they bring good luck and are also very gorgeous to look at," spoke Mary.

"Yes, me too," answered Catherine. "I once met a really wise man who had birds—he was definitely blessed to have his skills."

"I can imagine," stated Mary.

"Why do I feel a lot higher all of a sudden?" asked Catherine.

"It is part of the infrastructure," explained Mary. "This castle has a really unique design to it that is supposed to make you feel various ground elevations. I am not sure how exactly, but I know that when it was built it was meant to be a place for feeling grounded—which explains why you had the Empress card earlier."

"Interesting," agreed Catherine as they approached an oval-shaped door.

Mary stepped ahead and led them into an extremely dim walkway. "Do watch your step," she cautioned. Upon entering, Catherine heard voices of people chattering away as if they were located in another room.

"Thanks, it would be easy to trip in here," she said, feeling virtually blinded.

"We are backstage," explained Mary. "In fact, we are behind the curtain—follow me." Catherine walked a few steps ahead until Mary came to a halt and faced her, seemingly wrapped in thought. Catherine was able to see Mary's outline, like a silhouette, but couldn't see where she was facing. "Now, wait here. I am going to go out where that light is, give an introduction to everyone and then you may enter as soon as I call your name. They will most likely applaud as you enter."

"Ok," said Catherine.

"Any questions before I go on?" asked Mary.

"No, I think that's clear," replied Catherine.

"Good," said Mary. "Now, remember, just tell it from the bridge. There is no need for you to be shy and not explain everything that needs to be told. After all, they are expecting you and you do have a lot to clear up."

"Thank you, I will," said Catherine.

"Good luck," wished Mary. Catherine watched her walk away and enter into the light. She stepped closer and leaned her ear in. The chattering ceased, and the moment that it did, she remembered the flash of the skeletal fish that she had seen earlier on the cliff.

"Welcome, everyone," started Mary, softly. "I am very glad that you are all joining us. I have a very special speaker for you. I have spoken to her

307

earlier myself, and she is phenomenal. She is a very gentle soul with so many things to share. I hope that you will all learn a lot from her today."

To Catherine, the silence of the crowd felt like the lowering of a casket. As she listened, she felt a gentle rub of air run down her arm but saw nothing other than the darkness. She looked up and felt that something was floating above her, but before she could give it any attention, Mary spoke again.

"As I am sure you will take a lot from her, ladies and gentlemen, allow me to introduce to you, and welcome, Catherine," finished Mary as the crowd clapped, the sound of their stinging palms echoing in the darkness. Catherine composed herself and walked out onto the stage with her head high and a glorious smile on her face. She did not take notice of the crowd but walked straight to Mary who was standing behind a peach-colored microphone with a crystal dragonfly placed at the center of its stand. Mary greeted her, kissed her on both cheeks, and walked away. Catherine fluffed out her dress and turned towards the crowd.

"Good day, and welcome," she began as she observed the hall that was furnished with long banquet tables, and guarded by the marble walls that varied in different shades of peach and golden. Right behind the tables and towards the top was an arched window that allowed natural light into the hall. Beneath it was a giant portrait of the cliff and the castle itself surrounded by a view of the forest. And by the edge of the cliff, there was a tall woman who wore the exact same dress as Catherine but looked much older and had light-brown hair that was tied up around her head with a braid going around it. In the sky above her, Catherine noticed a few stars that were patterned forming the constellation of life.

Catherine turned her gaze to the crowd and immediately saw the Fogbusts sitting at one table. Apple had a frown on his face while Fruit smiled. Close to them was Sabina with her elbows on the table and her chin in both her hands. Next to her was a woman with dark, curly hair that swirled around her jawline and was much older than Sabina, yet resembled her very well. Her purple dress was similar to Sabina's and was accompanied by a shawl around her shoulders. At another table, Catherine saw Alp sitting in his younger form next to Rick in his merman form. They were accompanied by several mermen who all had jugs of beer beside each one of them. At the end of that table there was Ribs, along with several people, looking disinterested. At another table, there were many more people, and close to the center sat Dr. Peters and the guidemen, also staring at the stage while totally expressionless. And finally, at the last table, there were more people, and close to the window, sat Senuv and Sarm as Lake Morgan closely floated above and nearer to Sarm, flaunting his glitter. Catherine saw Hal sitting quietly at the end of that table while holding onto his cotton candy, facing her with his curious, shiny-pink eyes. She skimmed across them one more time and realized that each one of them carried their crocksvenbulb somewhere close.

"I really wasn't expecting to see you all," she continued. "As I am looking, some of you might recognize me and some of you might not. I can promise all of you, though, that you-all have seen me in another form. If I announce the name Jeffery, can you remember a man with this name?" Most of them nodded with expressions that varied. "Well, good, I was Jeffery, but now I am Catherine. Life has been a nonsensical journey for me, thanks to all of you. Some of you have taught me to love, and were great examples. And some of you were treacherous and left me in agony." Catherine finished her last sentence by focusing her gaze on Ribs. "Some of you were loyal and went out of your way to help me," she added while looking down. "And some of you were deceiving and selfish," she finished as she looked at Dr. Peters. "Also, some of you may have tried to be comforting and loving, but unfortunately, you failed to keep your integrity," stated Catherine as she looked at the two mothers and Lake Morgan.

"It is not my job to judge any of you for your behavior. For those who were kind, I am eternally grateful to you and I send you love and gratitude. And for those who weren't, I forgive you and I send you all the healing that you need. What I need all of you to know is that I am not someone that anyone can control or manipulate to their satisfaction." Catherine paused and looked around the crowd. She remembered some painful moments that brought tears to her eyes but she stood strong, allowing every memory to greet her with a vicious flashback. "One thing that I want you-all to learn today is that we are all equal, regardless of the forms that we come in. Life is like a theater, and we are all the actors on its stage. We each have different roles to play and when we cross paths, it is always for a reason. Nothing in life is coincidental, everything is preordained and determined by fate, cosmic calculations, Spirit, and of course, God—whom some of you refer to as Allie." Catherine looked at everyone's facial expressions and saw that some were in tears, some frowned, and some sat completely still.

"And more importantly, I wish to give you-all a better understanding of myself, and what I have learned on my journey," Catherine went on to explain. "I am a spiritual being. I am in the body of a human with an aura. I am a soul. I love... I create... I learn... and I live in a continuum. When everyone looks into my eyes, and listens to my voice, I want them to feel the spirit within me. I want them to see past aesthetics and labels of their societies. If one can learn to feel the energy of another being upon many other things, only then can they understand life at its very core." Sabina put her hand over her heart and Fruit cried. Senuv and Sarm looked down as their eyes sparkled and Hal smiled brightly. The rest sat there as the guidemen

310

exchanged looks with one another. Catherine looked at the doorway close to the stage and saw Mary standing there looking down.

After turning to face the crowd again, Catherine felt some anger rising from the banquet hall. She stood in place and looked at everyone, bearing in mind what she'd noticed. She then looked at Ribs who had his fist clenched and then looked at Apple who had a small, mellow smile on his face. Catherine, thinking of what else to say, browsed around and then focused on the portrait under the window. She looked at the lady closely and got a flashing vision of a knight putting his sword back in his scabbard, which to her, felt very strong and comforting.

"And, I conclude this speech by sending you-all the love and blessings from Spirit. Amen," finished Catherine with a short nod. The crowd clapped as Catherine gently smiled and watched. She took a few steps back and felt that some of them truly absorbed everything she had said, and sent her love in return, as others did not. Catherine also felt anger and resentment rise from some of the tables along with other negatives energies. She remained tranquil and watched them until they finished clapping, as Mary entered the stage with tears in her eyes.

"You did great!" complimented Mary as she hugged her.

"Thank you very much," answered Catherine, "it was very soothing."

"Oh, I felt it," said Mary. She held Catherine's hand and then walked closer to the microphone.

"Isn't she full of wisdom?" called Mary to the crowd.

"Rubbish!" shouted Ribs before anyone could say anything as he clenched his copper crocksvenbulb, his veins seeming about to burst.

"What do you mean?" questioned the older lady next to Sabina.

"He was a fool!" yelled Ribs as he banged the table. "He did not have a clue about how to work nor how to keep his mouth shut. Because of him, I could have lost my entire workforce!"

"I agree," added Apple, "but maybe it wasn't his path."

"*Her* path," emphasized Sabina, "she's a woman and you must respect her. Besides, who really cares about your workforce?"

"Shut up!" replied Ribs.

"Well, he wasn't able to defeat the beast," stated Lake Morgan.

"Oh, come on, that was planned!" replied Sarm with a scoff and sounding annoyed.

"I don't care," yelled Ribs, standing up. "You really think all this *love* speech can generate any profit?" Catherine looked at Fruit and received a wink from her.

"What's he mad about?" whispered Mary.

"He's a horrible being," replied Catherine quietly, "he murdered some of his own people, believe it or not."

"He wasted my time!" continued Ribs. "And his behavior in my office was extremely offensive!"

"Maybe because she needed to save herself from you murdering her the way you murdered some of your people," replied Mary calmly through the microphone, causing the entire hall to look straight at him, gasping, or with their jaws dropped.

"That wasn't necessary," whispered Catherine.

"How does it feel being on the spot," asked Mary, while ignoring Catherine's remark.

"Please, Mary," begged Catherine.

"A man should always claim responsibility for his actions," Lake Morgan said calmly.

"So you're saying that all those people who died were not by accident? You deceived us all?" asked one of the female people. "So my brother didn't return after working on that contraption not because of their spacecraft being hit by a meteor, but because you murdered them?" scrutinized the male person next to her.

"That's disgusting!" cried the older woman.

"You should be ashamed of yourself, punk!" cried Fruit. Apple quickly shushed her and whispered in her ears. The people started crying and Catherine felt the stage slowly move.

"Did you feel that?" she questioned Mary.

"What?" asked Mary. The stage moved again only a little faster.

"That," replied Catherine.

"Oh," said Mary. "I hope that nabob isn't causing it."

"Don't be surprised," answered Catherine as the arguing and hollering continued throughout the banquet. Then suddenly, a giant flash of white light appeared above Catherine and several rays soared across the hall, startling everyone. Mary screamed, then quickly turned around and ran off the stage.

"What is that?" shouted Senuv.

"Look!" pointed Apple.

"Oh my God," cried Fruit. The light got bigger and brighter so that everyone had to cover their eyes. Catherine stood there with her hands open before her and closed her eyes. She felt high vibrational energy around her that was filled with love and divinity. The moment was so intense that Catherine felt something gently rubbing against her own soul. She greeted the familiar energy with a smile.

"I welcome you," she said kindly. "I welcome you." The light completely disappeared and there stood Allie right next to her, sans her fur coat. Her arms, shoulders, chest and back were bare, revealing her soft and smooth olive skin. "Allie," smiled Catherine with her hand over her heart.

"Hello, Catherine," responded Allie, smiling back.

Catherine reached out and gave her a tight hug, then went to the microphone and introduced her publicly, "And, this is Allie!" Catherine observed all of the facial expressions and saw that everyone's eyes seemed to have tripled in size.

"Allie?" questioned Apple.

"God?" asked Fruit.

"You actually exist?" questioned Lake Morgan.

"You're a woman," said Senuv. Allie strolled towards the crowd and then began walking in the air casually after leaving the stage, as if the force of gravity was subject to her own manipulation. She continued towards the center as everyone kept their eyes on her in utter surprise. She smiled gently at everyone and continued wandering through the air.

"I see that some of you have lost faith in me," began Allie. "I also see that some of you never have. Either–or, you all think that I am a man." Allie sighed. "Alas, does it matter?" she questioned. "What matters most isn't how you visualize me and what you choose to call me. What matters most, is that you realize and understand my significance as an energy force. I am the eternal love around you. Along with Spirit, I guide everyone, I do not judge. I never judge anybody. There is no purpose in doing so. I allow your spirit guides to guide you to wherever you need to go."

Catherine watched everyone carefully and noticed that many were confused between Allie's figure and her voice. She silently prayed that people would see past that and actually comprehend her powerful words. Then, she looked at Ribs and saw that he was standing on his chair with his mouth wide open. She sent him healing and wondered what was going through his mind.

"I don't expect to be worshipped," continued Allie as she wandered above them. "I just expect all of you to learn to love yourselves and those around you so that you can continue living in this continuum. What bothers me a lot is when beings take control of other beings and do horrible things." Everyone turned to face Ribs. "And no, I do not wish that anyone would point their fingers towards anybody," cautioned Allie. "I prefer that we all forgive and send healing to one another. I also expect that from this day henceforth, everyone treats everyone with love and respect. You are all blessed and forgiven."

"Amazing," whispered Catherine to herself.

"I see all of you with your crocksvenbulbs," continued Allie. "You think all your philosophies are encompassed within them, be it about me or other things. I am not one paradigm stuck in one circle that needs to continue living under certain expectations and rules, no." Allie watched everyone carefully and stood facing the window. "I am like the sun," she stated while opening her arms. "I like to be in the middle and have a good view of everything around me instead of choosing one object and limiting the horizon of my mind to its angle." Catherine held her cross tighter. "And so should you," finished Allie. She walked back onto the stage and stood close to Catherine.

"That was extraordinary," expressed Catherine. Allie stood facing her, reached out her soft hand, and caressed Catherine's cheek, sending a generous rush of loving energy throughout her being. Allie leaned her forehead onto Catherine's for a moment then took a step back.

"I have a gift for you," she said calmly.

"You do? More than everything that you've already done for me?" asked Catherine.

"Reach out your hand, Catherine," instructed Allie with a smile. Catherine held out a hand as she shook with curiosity. "Remember that I love you and I am always watching you, and so are your spirit guides."

"Thank you," replied Catherine. "I love you, too." Allie looked at Catherine's hand and blew some white smoke that then did a small twirl in the air and wrapped itself around Catherine's hand. It gradually faded out and formed a small present on her palm. It was wrapped in shiny, peach wrapping paper that had a pattern of silver hearts. It had a beige ribbon around it that was tied at the top with a tiny gift bow stickered beside it. "Oh," said Catherine.

"Open it," said Allie. Catherine opened the present, dropping all of its wrapping paper. She revealed a white jewelry box with a silver cross on it that had the letter *A* in peach at its center.

"I feel that it is moving," said Catherine, her heart racing as she heard movement from within the box.

Allie continued smiling gently and said, "It's for the start of your new journey."

"Oh my!" yelled Catherine after opening the box. "I can't believe it!"

"Hello," greeted George as he looked at her from the box. Allie laughed.

"I can't believe it!" repeated Catherine. She let the ladybug onto her hand and dropped the box. "I am so sorry!"

"It's alright, don't worry about it," answered George. "It's great to see you again." Catherine's tears ran down her cheeks like tiny creeks.

"I never ever thought that I would see you again," she cried.

"*Always* expect the unexpected," laughed George. Catherine put him on her shoulder then ran and hugged Allie tightly.

"Thank you so much," she sobbed.

"You are more than welcome," replied Allie. After standing back, Catherine put George back on her hand then held him close to her heart.

"I love you," she told him.

"I love you, too," answered George. Catherine looked up and noticed that the hall was empty. The tables were still there but everyone else had disappeared. Catherine glanced at the window and saw that it was still in place and so was the portrait hanging below it.

"That's strange," she said. "Where'd they go?" she asked while turning to Allie.

"They're gone," answered Allie.

"Where?" questioned Catherine.

"It doesn't matter," replied Allie. "That journey is over. It is time to begin your new one as a woman, as Catherine."

"Alright," said Catherine. "I am ready." George jumped down and ran to the middle between her and Allie. He turned and faced Catherine, his face lighting up with a suspicious grin. Allie blew some thick plumes at him out of her mouth and nose that gradually turned nectar in tone. George grew much bigger in size until he was almost half of Allie's height. He evolved into a man wearing a peach tuxedo.

"Oh my," said Catherine as he reached out his hand and walked closer to her.

"I think that you deserve a little extra," winked Allie.

"Thank you," said Catherine.

"Yes, thank you," said George to Allie.

"You are both welcome," responded Allie. "Love comes in many ways."

Catherine smelled George's fragrance that lingered around the two of them, making the moment feel enchanted. In her mind's eye, she saw a circle of alternating black and white swans swimming around his head. And before thinking any further, she remembered Hal's earlier reading.

"Come, it is time to begin your journey together," said Allie before looking up and closing her eyes. She gradually faded out and became another beam of bright, white light. The light formed a staircase, each of its steps a

317

white cake with peach accents, that extended outwards to the window as it opened and revealed the stone of the cliff.

"Shall we?" asked George.

"Yes," answered Catherine, wiping away her last tear. She put her arm in George's and allowed him to walk her up the cake staircase. She noticed that each time they stepped, the cake reformed itself just like the sweets on Ice Mallow. "Amazing," she laughed.

"Allie creates beautiful things," reassured George.

"Oh, absolutely," agreed Catherine.

After they exited through the window, George walked Catherine around the cliff and close to the entrance of the castle. As they walked, several trees sprang out of the ground, then grew to several feet in height, and instantly blossomed. Their blossoms were peach, wide and abundant on each tree as they danced to the tempo of the gentle breeze. George guided Catherine close to the edge then held her in as they both admired the view of the magnificent, darkening peach sky and the surrounding forests. As Catherine watched, she noticed that in the distance, there were some shiny stars that formed the constellation of life. Within them, she saw *Contraption Ayna* flying. Catherine sent out love to her and watched the contraption fly until it disappeared. She closed her eyes and whispered a prayer.

"Dear God, dear universe, dear holy spirit world, and dear spirit guides. Thank you for all of your blessings and for watching over me during the most difficult times of my life. I am grateful to be healthy and to be who I am today, and I look forward to the wonderful things that are yet to come. I am thankful and fortunate to be me. Amen." Catherine received a vision of flowers that transformed into a gorgeous beam of blissful white light. She opened her eyes and turned to face George. His brown eyes turned to her hazel ones as his chestnut hair reflected all the lights of the surrounding tones. She leaned in and, kissing his lips, she couldn't feel more grateful for having him.

Made in the USA
Middletown, DE
03 April 2017